SAVAGE DUKE

USA Today Bestselling Author
ALEXANDRA SILVA

Cover Design: Raven Designs
Editor: One Love Editing
Formatting: Alexandra Silva

Copyright © 2022 by Alexandra Silva
All rights reserved.

This book is a work of fiction, Any references to real events, real people, and real places are used fictitiously. Other names, characters, places, and incidents are products of the author's imagination and any resemblance to persons, living or dead, actual events, organisations or places is entirely coincidental. All rights reserved. This book is intended for the purchaser ONLY. No part of this book may be reproduced in any form or by any electronic or mechanical means, including information storage and retrieval systems, without written permission from the author, except for the use of brief quotations in a book review. All songs, song titles, and lyrics contained in this book are property of the respective songwriters and copyright holders.

No AI training: Without in any way limiting the author's [and publisher's] exclusive rights under copyright, any use of this publication to "train" generative artificial intelligence (AI) technologies to generate text is expressly prohibited. The author reserves all rights to license uses of this work for generative AI training and development of machine learning language models.

Disclaimer: The material in this book contains graphic language, violence, and sexual content intended for mature audiences, ages 18 and over.

Author's Note

Dear reader,

I'm so grateful that you picked up Savage Duke. I hope you love this reimagination of the Jack the Ripper legend as much as I adore these characters. If you are familiar with this urban legend, you know that it is bloody and violent. Although this story is set in contemporary London, it is every bit as dark as the original with some triggering content such as, and not limited to; serial killers; murder; stalking; torture; manipulation and narcissistic behaviour; dubious consent; mental health issues; graphic violence; death of parent/sibling; serious health condition (blood disorder).

Thank you for taking a chance on Henry and Eve.

All my love,
Alex

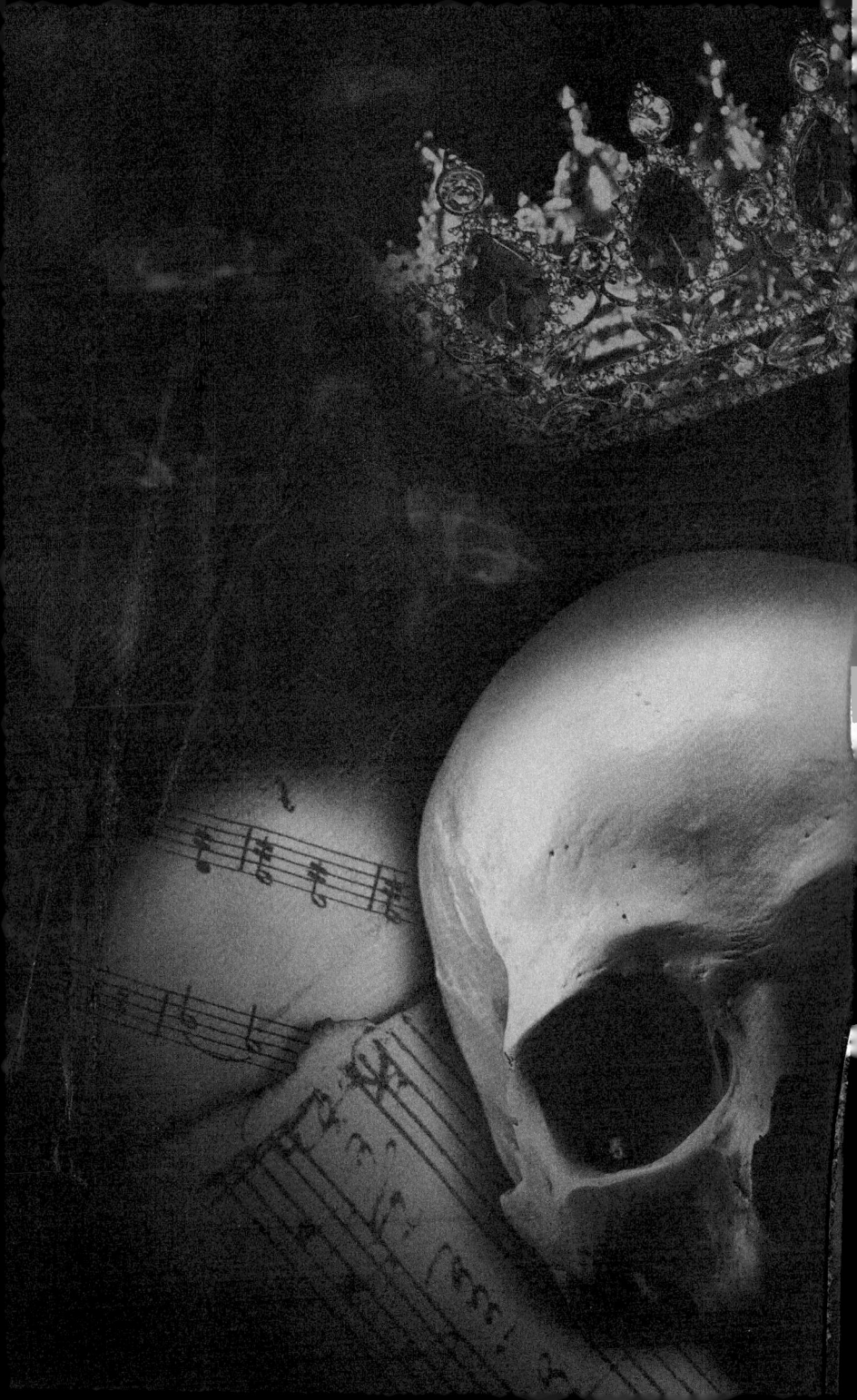

"we were both created in chaos,

we were both born to destroy.

you were like death,

and i was like war.

and where we collided,

darling, i loved you."

—born disasters, k.a.

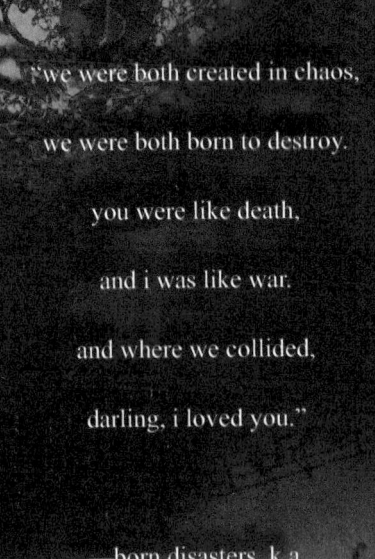

PROLOGUE

Henry

It starts with a single drop of blood. An oath. An allegiance that spans centuries, encompassing history and lasting lifetimes. It's a pact that you live and die by from the moment you're marked. A wolf that's part of a pack doing what it takes to protect the crown and all its fallen jewels.

"Henry?"

I look up to find Percival standing in front of the secret door, his livery unruffled even though his chest is rising and falling with his rush to deliver the message—a simple nod that tells me what I must do now.

Taking one last deep puff of my cigarette, I throw it into the fire as the clock chimes two in the morning. Perfectly in time with the itinerary I planned.

I'm not sure if he hates me or fears me, but I am certain that my presence makes him uncomfortable. Percival never hangs around—like the grim reaper. He leads death to the girls he's procured and quickly turns his back before the scythe has reaped another soul.

Today, however, he balks as I stand. The Persian rug beneath my feet cushions the quiet thud of my boots as I meander to the sideboard beside him and glance down at the instruments on it.

Gloves. Syringe. Switchblade.

The gloves go on first. I suck in a deep breath, then blow

them open, making it easier to pull them on with a snap.

"You're still here," I point out as I check the pistol over and slip it into the back of my dark jeans. "It's too late to grow a conscience."

Percival lured these innocent girls into the devil's den, handpicked and vetted each one to serve wolves, but somewhere along the way, he grew careless, and now I must take care of the problem.

He continues watching me intently while I make sure the switchblade is in working order. Closing the knife one last time, I fist the steel instrument in my hand before picking up the syringe in the other and pocketing each. One in the left, the other in the right pocket of my hoodie.

"Don't forget your promise."

"Henry."

"A man is only as good as his word."

At my remark, he shrugs. "She's just a girl."

Yes. Just a girl. A loose end I must cut off with my blade. A danger to the integrity of the crown. A reason my father's corpse is rotting in our family vault.

Tightening my grip around the switchblade, I observe the guilt darkening his steely eyes. It doesn't matter how many throats I slit or bodies I maim, the guilt never touches me. This is who I am. It's what I do. I'm a protector of the crown. A killer. Death. I don't feel. I strike, and I'm done. And in the dark, there's nothing beyond me. A monster that I've made my peace with.

Something Percy should do instead of grabbing my arm as I turn for the door.

"Just a girl," he tells me as though he's begging for the life of the lamb I'll slaughter tonight.

Just a girl. There's no "just" in our world. A sharp scoff pushes past my lips at his tormented frown before I correct him. "A whore like all the others."

"Pawns," he states with an empathetic tilt of his head that causes my anger to flare. "They're nothing but pawns."

"They are whores." He's been the keeper of this place long enough to know this.

Letting myself out of the room, I wait to hear him leave through the panel door. It won't take him long to make it downstairs, in time to see today's sacrifice out.

The hallways of the old building are pitch-dark. The scent of spirits still lingers in the walls, sweetening the bitter edge of tobacco and dulling the sinful air still warm with sex, debauchery, and depravity.

There's nothing but the apt hush that fills the place. The stillness in the air is heavy with my mission to kill. Every step is punctuated with the steady beat of my heart. Taking each carpeted stair down. One by one. Eating up the distance between me and my prey. Killing time between me and my target.

The front door opens, and I halt, watching and listening.

"Need a ride home?" Percival's muted question causes her to frown while she casts a questioning glance around her.

"No. No." The girl shakes her head when she looks up at him again. "I-I'm meeting a friend."

A friend. That's what she's calling him—the enemy. My enemy. The blood of my father's killer.

"I see." Percival nods, the dull light from the ancient chandeliers doing very little to shadow the pity lining his face. He gives her shoulder a firm squeeze, inspecting her from head to toe.

Soon, her skin will be mottled with death. Young, supple flesh will decay around her delicate bones.

What a waste. I bite silently to myself while he continues prinning her.

Tugging the front of her coat closed, Percival tells her, "You get home safe now. Won't you?"

I can sense her smile through the muted hum of her exhale, and a snarl growls deep in my chest.

How dare she fucking smile. I trusted her beguiling smiles and innocent laughter, and she betrayed me. After I gave her my confidence, and after everything, she would do to me what her friend and his antimonarchist organisation did to my father.

"Don't look back," Percival says as she stands in the doorway, the faded glint of golden hair making my hands ball in the pockets of my trousers.

The girl is beautiful. A delicate flower ready to be plucked by greed and gluttony. Swallowed up by those that want more than the fortune they already have. It's blasphemous, but it's the way of the world. We always want what we shouldn't have, and those of us who can have it don't think twice about discarding it when we're done. And I am done with her.

The syringe in my right fist threatens to crack, the blade in the left heavy and eager to spill blood as she looks back, eyes searching the surrounding shadows before she pulls up the hood of her long coat and steps out into the rain.

"Don't look back," Percival reminds her as I take the last several steps down and she disappears into the hazy sheet.

He's trying to raise her awareness. There isn't a person on this earth that won't look back when told not to. It's human nature.

"There's no way you can save her, Percival. She was dead the moment she walked through these doors with ill intentions."

"Make it quick," he tells me with a grimace.

I always do. Quick and painless, something my expert hands have perfected over the years—clean, precise cuts for those that deserve it. But her, my pretty little whore, I don't know what she deserves. Not yet.

With a scoff at him, I walk into the downpour, pulling the hood of my sweater over my head before I grip the syringe and blade in my hands again.

I know these streets like the back of my hand. Even in the torrential rain, I can navigate them with ease.

It's two o'clock in the morning. London is quiet under the cover of darkness and rain, and before the devil's hour, the real monster stalks his prey. Quick, steady steps drowned out by the roar of the sky. The flash of light highlights her small figure as she tries to run through the deluge in her heels. Meanwhile, my stride eats up the distance between us, the syringe in my hand at the ready.

A few more steps and my presence looms.

The girl pauses.

The hood on her head is blown back by the gust of wind as she spins to look up at me. "Your Grace."

I strike.

Looking into deep brown, panicked eyes, I whisper, "Darling."

It starts with a single drop of blood. A prick that dulls the senses, leaving the prey defenceless, loosely hanging between life and death.

ONE
Henry
five months earlier

"People that drink tea should be shot." I hate the smell, the scent, and most of all, the memories it stirs. My grandfather, the late Duke of Gloucester, used to have a pot on the go at all times. He was my favourite person, and then he died. It was a most unfortunate and anticlimactic death.

One morning, we all woke up, and he did not. As with every morning that I visited his room, there was a tray with his pot of English Breakfast tea, Butter Puffs, and smooth strawberry jam at the foot of his bed. That morning, it went cold. And on that day, the sweet scent of tea became one I hated.

"It's you that should be fucking shot for being a coffee whore," Simon laughs. We've grown up together, much like our mothers. He's my mother's favourite godson. She loves him like my grandfather loved tea. I suppose he's lucky I don't hate him. And I have a lot to hate him for, the same way he has so much to feel guilty about.

With a teasing grin, he picks up his bone china cup by its dainty arm and makes a show of drinking the rest of his tea like a fucking girl.

Fuck, I've missed him. I don't say that about many people, but out of every fucker I'm surrounded by, Simon is the easiest to people with. I hate him, and he knows I do, but we also know that before I felt this way about him, I loved him. I loved him as a brother. And somewhere beneath all the history between us, I still do.

"How long are you back for?"

Simon shrugs, diverting his eyes to the toast rack. "Too long," he eventually says with a dry chuckle.

A couple of years ago, his family was struck by tragedy. Since then, he's barely stepped foot in the country. The last two years have seen him negotiate deals between the wealthiest and most unsavoury in the world. In turn, they've made the earl of Rochester wealthier than he already was. Some would say he's filthy rich, and they wouldn't be wrong, given where a lot of the money he's made has come from.

"Do they know you're home?"

"This isn't home." His eyes scan the newspapers in front of us. "And no, no one knows I'm in the country. There's something I need to see to, and once it's done, I'm heading back to New York."

His phone rings, and he stands to take the call outside the room, cutting our conversation short. Someday, he might actually confront the shitshow he left behind and that he's trying to ignore by staying away.

"My mother will be upset that her golden boy hasn't visited," I call after him as Percival, the Wolfsden Society secretary, walks through the double doors of the Hush Lounge.

It's early morning and quiet. The girls normally parading themselves are out of sight, just as the men that normally use them are home with their wives. The den of depravity is a front for the Wolfsden Society, a ghost society made up of twelve dukes, earls, and lords and headed by the king. We're knights of the crown, doing what needs to be done to protect and honour it from those that would see it disgraced and forgotten.

"What do you have for me?" I ask Percival, stirring a teaspoon of sugar into my coffee.

He's stopped just inside the doors, and he's staring at me as though wondering how to approach an unruly beast. I can't blame him. There have been times when we have butted heads, especially when my father was passing his duty to me. At times, it seemed like he was trying to test my patience more so than my resilience and loyalty.

Simon pauses in his tracks, watching as Percival comes to stand in front of me, dragging in breath after breath. His eyes meet mine, and instantly, the heaviness of the recurring nightmare I awoke from earlier assaults me. The weight drops to the pit of my stomach like lead ripping through the air.

I'm on autopilot as I push to my feet, ready to act, even though my feet are glued to the Persian rug beneath them. I know what's coming as Percival shakes himself off from his trepidation and draws in yet another deep breath. The air freezes as my chest strangles my lungs, squeezing the exerted thrum of my heart into a deafening hammer that makes it impossible to hear the words he speaks when his mouth opens and his lips move.

No words are needed because I feel death chill my veins now as it did the morning I walked into my grandfather's bedroom to find him permanently asleep with his tea beside him. Darkness blusters inside me as his lips continue to move, but no words cut through the thundering in my ears. The storm is spinning in as it does in my dreams, threatening to rip me apart from east to west, but in reality, it's snapping my head from my neck and cutting my knees from beneath me. North and south pulling apart, quaking and shattering the world. A catastrophic seismic break.

"Henry?" Simon slaps my shoulder. The pity in his touch pulls me out of my head as he breathes out a long sigh. "Fuck, mate...I—"

"When?" The question rolls from my tongue, suffocated by the lump in my throat. "How?"

My eyes are burning with an anger that scorches and grates down the back of my throat as I swallow the urge to thwart the man standing in front of me. Again and again, while I listen to Percival answer my question.

"We don't know when exactly. Your mother found him in the

car this morning as she was leaving for the airport."

"What do you mean 'she found him'?" Simon asks while I'm trying to work past the fog, a storm of questions hurtling at me from every side.

If it really was my mother who found my father, he would've been within the palace gates. He would've been home. Secure.

"His car was parked outside their apartment."

Our stares meet, pity and sorrow glaze over his eyes while mine are blurred with unsurmountable rage and grief.

The Severn Bridge is down.

The Duke of Gloucester is gone.

My father is dead.

The last time I cried, I was seven years old. It was the day I discovered my hate for tea.

"His driver?" I ask, ignoring the lurch of my stomach when I glance down at the teapot on the table.

"We're trying to locate him, but—" Percival pauses when I step forward, his eyes dropping to my fisted hands. They're aching for destruction. The violence within me is screaming, rattling at the cage holding it back, saving the world from my chaos.

"But?" I take another step. "But what, Percival?"

"Henry," Simon murmurs as he steps between me and Percival. "First things first," he reminds me to push through my vicious instinct. He's always been the mild-tempered one of the two of us, the mediator of the pack. "Your mother."

"My mother," I growl, inhaling the leafy scent that overwhelms my surroundings.

Anger, grief, and all these unsurmountable feelings that I cannot contain. And that goddamn smell. Tea. I hate tea. I loathe it so fucking much that—

My hand swipes over the table, hurtling the teapot to the floor.

"Your mother," Simon states, clearing his throat.

"Where is she now?"

Percival sighs with his downcast gaze fixed on my feet. "At his side."

"Security?"

"The Duchess is safe, Henry," Percival tells me with a solemn nod. "Margaret won't leave your father's side. She's refusing to let the coroner take his body until you get there."

"Good," I spit down at the floor through my grinding teeth. "No one touches him."

Pushing past him and Simon, I don't give Percival time to warn me of the danger surrounding us. I've lived with it all my life, the same way my father, his father before him, and every other Sloane heir has lived with it. As long as there's a threat to the crown, we will always be in danger. I'm past caring if they come for me; in fact, I would welcome it. I would relish painting my hands with their blood.

Treasonous blood for royal blood—the life force that blazes in my veins.

"I'm coming with you," Simon tells me, following me out to the front of the club. The early June morning is cool, and the air is quiet. Eerily so. It seems that I might hear ghosts whisper through the green branches of the wolf tree in front of Hush if I listen past my roaring pulse.

I could waste time arguing with him, but the only thing I need right now is to get back to Kensington Palace to check on my mother and see my father's corpse with my own eyes.

"Get your head straight," Simon says when we're in the back of the chauffeur-driven sedan.

Two unmarked police motorbikes overtake us as we leave the gated mews behind St. James's Palace. They race ahead to clear the way while another sedan follows behind. The procession hits home, slamming into my burning lungs with a force that causes me to sputter, but I pull it back with a clench of my teeth.

The drive to Kensington Palace from the club feels too long. With every second that ticks past, it gets harder to contain my fury. The Palace Avenue gates are open, with police guarding the long road leading to the residency gates that are opening in the distance. There are no police, and the guards seeing us through these gates hold their composure. It's all quiet and still as always, with the faint hum of London traffic in the distance muffled by the tall trees protecting our privacy.

When we round the corner of my parents' apartment, my heart stops. The pounding in my ears falls silent at the sight of my father's Aston Martin.

"Fucking Seychelles blue," Simon chuckles dryly. "Every fucking motor ruined by that god-awful paint job."

A laugh erupts from deep down in my gut. Shock. Realisation. I don't know what it is, but it's choking me. I can't fucking breathe as we come to a slow stop behind my father's black Maybach, and the driver's door opens.

"You're going to take my mother inside and keep her there until I'm done."

"If you think she's going to let me drag her away—"

Before he can finish, I jump out of the car, telling him, "She doesn't get a choice."

Simon may be faint-hearted with his poetic view of the world, but I'm not. Not even the sadness in my mother's eyes as she looks up at me when I pull her from the car gives me pause. My only concern is how this happened. With all the guards and security in this place, how did anyone get to him, and how could they get away?

"Don't make me leave him," she hiccups breathlessly, blood-crusted hands grappling at my forearms. "Don't make me walk away."

A hand grips mine to steady herself as she coughs through her relentless sobs. The dishevelled state of her is fucking tragic. Black tracks run down her cheeks, bleeding through the lines of her face. I pity her and the pain she feels. I wish that I could rip it from her. The sight of her falling apart like this, so broken, is wrong for a princess and a Royal Lady of the Order of the Garter. She's better than this. Made of strong stock.

"Get inside, Mother," I order as softly as I'm able. Emotions may not be something I tolerate, but I feel our loss too. I feel it twist my bones as it shrieks, crying for justice. "Clean yourself up."

"Henry…"

"Go!"

At my gritted remark, she pulls back with a shudder. "How can you be so—"

"I'm everything he made me."

"Jac—"

"Stop wasting time," I snap.

It causes her to sob harder when I pass her to Simon just as Percival finds us. He's out of breath and barely able to relay that Arthur has been escorted back to Buckingham Palace. While Simon is distracted, my mother slips back inside the car.

"Get out," I bark at her through my clenched teeth. This isn't like her. Heartbroken and mourning or not, she knows better than to be difficult. Wasting time will only make it more difficult to figure out what happened to my father. "Don't make it harder for yourself."

Hopeless dismay trembles in her regal countenance.

"There's something you need to know," she whispers up at me, grasping my hand and tugging at me until I crouch.

The scent of cloyed blood fills my lungs, the metallic tinge chilling me to the marrow of my bones. I'm unbalanced when she pulls me closer, her arms wrapping around my shoulders so that her sobs wrack into me as I am met with my father's corpse. I refuse to let any of it sink in. To accept the sight in front of me.

After a few steadying breaths, she murmurs into my ear, "His briefcase is gone. It's all gone, Henry." Deep blue eyes flash to mine as I glance down at her. "It was all in there."

"What was in there?"

"Everything. If anyone finds out…" A stuttering breath wracks through her. "It will destroy us."

"What's in the briefcase, mother?"

With a shake of her head, she twists to face the windscreen, leaving my father in open view again. This time, it hits. Reality slams into me with a force of a sucker punch.

He's drained blue. A corpse. His grey hair is flecked with red spit where he choked on his own blood. While I follow the trail of spatters, she squeezes my hand the same way I remember her doing on my first day of school. The grip of her trembling limb tightens more and more the longer I peruse my father's limp body to the centre of the stain on his side.

"It was always going to come to this."

Ignoring her statement, I lean across her to examine my father's wound. A single stab between his ribs. The sixth and seventh, I guess from simply looking.

"His lung." I pause at the almost quiver in my voice. Taking a deep breath of the heavy air, I carry on. "It was punctured."

"It's just one." A manic laugh escapes her. "One wound. Just one," she repeats over and over again as I reach forward and trace the tear of his claret-stained shirt. "One-one deep cut."

"It's all it takes," I retort, rubbing my thumb over my index and middle fingers. The sticky blood gloops and crumbles, almost instantly turning to dust that I rub into my palms as I pull back to crouch in front of my mother once more.

The anger that I've been pushing down roars in my chest, echoing above my raging pulse, drowning out the furious thoughts in my mind with only one promise. The only one I can give her while I wipe the fresh tears from her bloodshot eyes.

"Their days are numbered."

She nods. "Here."

Glancing down at her lap, I watch as she pulls out a flick knife from the pocket of her loose trousers and holds it out to me. It looks out of place in her dainty, manicured hand. As bloody as it is, it's as gentle as ever when she places the knife in my hand.

"It doesn't matter what he taught you," she tells me, closing my hand tightly around the weapon used to murder her beloved. "There is no mercy in justice. Be your worst. Do your worst." Sagging back into the seat, she rests her head awkwardly on my father's shoulder. "Bleed them dry, Henry."

With a nod, I stand and pocket the knife. There won't be any fingerprints on it, and if there had been, she would have contaminated them enough that it doesn't matter anymore. The only important thing is the justice that it will serve as I hunt down my father's murderer.

A man that lives by the sword dies by the sword. And I plan on making good on the promise I made today—I will hunt. I will find. I will kill.

TWO

Henry

"From dust we came, and to dust we must all return," I repeat the last line of the eulogy I gave earlier at the church as I raise my glass to toast my father—the Duke of Gloucester, a wolf like every man sat around the table.

"But from ashes we rise," Arthur states, touching his glass of Penderyn whisky to my Blue Label Johnny Walker. Although I prefer cognac, this is the only way to toast my father—with his drink of choice.

Backing the single dram, I cast a glance about me. Having gone over the security footage from the palace and Hush the night my father was murdered, there's only one conclusion: it was an inside job. And while there's nothing for me to go on yet, given my father's driver still hasn't been found, I find myself scrutinising every set of eyes watching me. The instant Arthur smashes his glass into the Victorian hearth, the howls start, a tradition of the Wolfsden Society when we lose one of our own.

It's what wolves do when one of their pack is lost. They howl to guide them home, physically or spiritually. The howls have barely quieted when the music starts. The steady chords of the piano in the corner fill the panelled walls, closing them in with the flicker of the fire. It's not until the violin joins in that it all becomes stifling.

Memories of countless parties and quiet mornings where my

father would have Fauré on repeat. It's as though I can hear him humming along now. His desk could be in the corner of the room while he makes notes in his journals that will eventually become texts for future doctors. My father, the doctor, was a pioneer. My father, the Duke of Gloucester, was a hard man. He was Jekyll and Hyde.

While I'm in my reverie, the men disperse, leaving our round table empty, barring the two seats to either side of me.

Arthur calls one of the girls over with a wave of his hand. As she comes our way, he gestures to our empty glasses.

"A toast," he announces as the almost naked girl puts a fresh glass down for him after he smashed the last and pours our drinks. Lifting his Welsh whisky, he levels me with steely eyes while he flattens his other hand on the table in front of me. "To His Grace, the Duke of Gloucester," he says, revealing my father's signet ring beneath his palm.

Again, I back my drink instead of dressing my finger with my family's heirloom. The air is growing hotter and turgid. It's getting harder to breathe as the music echoes around me.

Two weeks, and I'm still searching for a needle in a fucking haystack, any fucking clue as to what happened the night my father walked out of this place with his briefcase in his hand, and got into his car, to be found in the morning by my mother. Sans briefcase and most of his blood. The irony isn't lost on me—the man that dedicated his life to studying blood died soaked in red.

"Henry would want you to wear it now," Percival tells me in a hushed tone when I flip my empty glass over the ring like a cloche.

I don't want it, and I don't want anyone else to have it. Much like my duty.

Even though I'm not a sentimental man, it seems wrong to step into my father's shoes so quickly. He was laid to rest only hours ago, locked away in our family's vault to rot.

"It's just jewellery," Simon murmurs on my other side, and when I look up at him, I find him twisting the ring that used to belong to his father before he burnt to cinders along with their country manor.

Just.

"What if I *just* don't want to?"

"Put it on, Henry," Arthur coaxes.

I glance at the ring again, trying to ignore the wail of Fauré's Opus as it grows to a deafening crescendo. The pitch of the strings rakes through me. I can feel the weight of the gold ghosted around my finger. The weight of the promise I made my mother when my father's blood stained my hands. The only *just* left is to give her the justice she wants.

"Put it on," he presses, punctuating his words with the slam of his solid crystal tumbler on the mahogany tabletop.

His insistence throws the last of my patience and control. Today needs to be over fast. My sensibilities are on edge, and every nightmare I've had every fucking night of my father's drained body assaults me.

I can't think. I can't breathe. And their fucking eyes on me, eagerly waiting for me to fill in the hole my father left, make me feel sick.

The music.

The expectations.

Every fucking memory that's ghosted around this fucking place. The fucking drone of the never-ending song.

"Quiet," I snap at the duo in the corner as the whirlwind in my head overwhelms my control.

It's the shrill rip of the violin that causes me to glance their way, pulling me from the storm inside.

I hate tea, and I hate that fucking sound. But the instant the echoes of it disappear, the hole in my chest screams louder until I'm searching for it.

The girl is the first thing I see clearly in days. Percival arranged for her to play tonight. Apparently, she was one of my father's favourite gems from the Royal Conservatory, which he and my mother are patrons of. I'm not sure why Percival was so adamant about having her here, and I don't care either. For all I know, he's trying to recruit another girl onto Hush's books.

"You're being absurd." Arthur blows out an irate breath.

He's annoying the fuck out of me. If he could disappear, I'd be grateful. In fact, right now, what I need is a distraction. Pushing my chair from the table, I focus back on the corner of the room. The girl is watching me intently without a shudder or quiver when I glower her way. She's a small thing, not like the other girls in the club. Her long blonde hair is styled in loose waves that hang down past her waist, covering up pale golden skin that her skimpy dress has left exposed.

A faint, pitying smile tugs at the corner of her full, deep-caramel-painted lips. There's not enough beauty in the world that could tame the loathing that blazes inside me. Pity is for the weak, and I am not weak.

I could wrap my hands around that delicate neck of hers and snap it like a twig. Dark eyes narrow on mine as though she can read my thoughts, even from a distance.

Yes, I could tear you to pieces, I tell her silently when the slight quirk of her lips wavers. She knows. The girl knows I could rip her apart limb from limb—and this is the most exciting thought I've had in weeks. I could. I should. And maybe, maybe I will. Perhaps it will be the highlight of my father's wake.

"Come here, girl," I order, sitting back in my chair while she continues gawping with wide eyes.

The white-knuckled grip on her violin and bow shakes while she debates her move. She's fresh within these walls. Innocence glimmers in her eyes as she glances at Percival for approval.

"Don't look at him for permission." My bark brings her eyes back to me. "He's here to serve and please, just as you are."

"Go easy." Simon stands, a hand squeezing my shoulder in silent caution before he leaves.

He knows me better than anyone in this room. Simon knows how far I can go beyond any conscionable limits. And he knows when to walk away for his own good. Our loyalties may be tied to one another by the Wolfsden oath, but nothing will hold me back when I snap.

The pianist starts playing another of the classics that my father used to love. Clearly he didn't get the memo before, but he gets it instantly when the almost empty decanter of scotch shatters beside his fingers. The sound of the crystal smashing cuts through the dark haze clouding my senses, slowly eating away at my sanity. Finally, he stops.

God, I don't know what's worse. The wailing of the music or the stark silence that's followed it. Now, there are more eyes on me. Fear and curiosity mix together. The smell of the first would've been sweeter from the girl, but she's watching me as though she can see the chaos inside me, and it doesn't faze her. Meanwhile, her grown piano companion looks set to shit himself.

"Leave," I instruct him, focusing back on the girl.

She's holding on to the violin tightly, like a shield of sorts. Although she's not affected by what she sees in me, she's got enough sense to know that she's not safe. But to think that anything or anyone could protect her from me shows just how novel she is here.

"Now, girl, put the violin down and come here."

Percival levels me with a silent warning. When I ignore his unspoken caution, he stands and leans across the table to ensure I acknowledge him. "Henry..."

"I'm not my father," I retort. They were thick as thieves, to the point that Percival was his eyes and ears. "Warn me again and I'll cut out your tongue." Pulling the flick knife from the pocket of my suit trousers, I drop it on the table beside the ring.

"She doesn't belong to the club, Henry," he continues through gritted teeth when the girl finally comes close.

Pushing back in my seat, I coax her closer with a crook of my finger, gesturing for her to present herself in front of me. When she's standing between me and the table, I ask, "What's your name, girl?"

In the golden glow of the chandelier above us, the lustre of her skin is hypnotic. The only thoughts in my mind are of what I could do with such supple flesh. How it would feel beneath my hands and how easily it would marl with my rough touch.

Taking a deep breath, she replies, "Eve, your grace."

Eve. Such a worldly name for such a seemingly innocent thing.

Honeyed eyes hold my stare as I watch her brush her hair over her slender shoulder.

"Tell me something, Eve."

"Yes," she murmurs, her voice breathy but steady.

"Did you sign the nondisclosure?"

"Yes, Your Grace."

Percival stands abruptly, his mouth gaping, about to intervene, when I silence him with the raise of my hand. Looking around her, straight at him, I say, "Well then, it doesn't matter who you belong to. Does it? This pretty little mouth has no choice but to stay silent."

Eve's audible swallow draws my attention to her throat. The hollow is sucked in with her first noticeable shudder, the first murmur of her fear calling to the monster inside me. Every one of my muscles is clenching, burning and aching to let loose.

"You can fuck off now." I tell him while I observe the way her body tenses at my perusal. The discomfort she feels awakens an intense thrill deep inside me—predator and prey breathing the same air. "Your job's done here, old man."

Arthur flips my glass over, bringing my attention back to him as Percival walks out. "A man is only as good as his word."

The gold wolf's head glitters in the light, with its ruby eye glinting at me when he holds my father's ring back out to me.

"It was always going to come to this," he reminds me, sounding like my mother. "There's no use trying to put it off or overthinking it. Our fates were long written before we were ever imagined or conceived. You know that as well as I know that one day the fucking crown will be on my head."

"He's not even cold yet."

"Yes. Yes, he is. Your father was cold before he took his last breath." A scoff pushes from me at his statement. The truth is a vicious bitch, even though I know it so well.

Maybe if I'd done more to keep my father safe, we wouldn't be here right now. Destiny wouldn't be staring me in the eyes, waiting for me to grab it with both hands. It doesn't matter how long I hold out; so long as I breathe, my duty will always be hanging over me. A dark cloud of impending doom.

I am my father's son. Just as he was his father's and his father was heir to this seat around this table with our family crest carved into it.

"This is the only way you can make it right."

"And we will make it right," Percival assures from the open doorway. "I swear it."

"Put it on, Henry. Put the ring on and be done with it."

Snatching the ring from him, I thread it onto the small finger of my left hand so that the beast's head covers the crowned wolf tattoo we all share. A mark of who we are. A symbol of our pack. The Wolfsden Society.

"Happy?" I hold my hand up.

The weight of my future has never felt so astounding. While I have much to do, the distraction beside me is far more appealing right now. Needed, even. And it's calling to me from the depths of her big brown eyes.

My lungs burn with the choke of my chest around them, the same unrelenting force causing my hands to fist with the need to squeeze every inch of her. I want her breaths to rasp for mercy and her hands to claw for dear life as I rip her apart.

"Don't you have a whore to fuck?" I snap at Arthur. He's still watching me as though there's more he wants from me. Like a hungry man taunted by another's feast. But I'm not sharing this one. Not today, at least.

With a top-to-toe glance at Eve, he laughs and walks away. The friction of the air around us instils itself in the silence he leaves behind. It's a buzz that heats the blood pumping through my veins while Eve stares at me in apprehension. Uncertainty begins to drag her breaths the longer I sit, admiring the rise and fall of her ample chest. Every little hitch threatens to spill her plump tits from the bustier of her dress, the seam of the lace holding the deep V together straining.

"Drinks." With a snap of my fingers, I call to the girl standing in the corner of the room.

"Your Grace." She acknowledges my request quickly as she brings the decanter of cognac over with two glasses. When they're filled, she slinks back to her shadowed corner with barely a shuffle of her bare feet on the Persian rug.

Eve and I are alone again. She's on edge as I reach around her to my drink, ghosting the curve of her hips with my arm. Leaning over my thighs, I brace my elbows on my knees so that my face is level with her stomach as I take a leisurely mouthful of my drink. The proximity makes her squirm, causing the warm, sweet scent of almond oil and rose to fill my lungs when I pull in a deep breath.

"Have you ever fucked royalty, Eve?"

Neat eyebrows scrunch as she glances over her shoulder at the girl in the corner. Pity softens her dainty features when she turns back to me, levelling me with an indignant glare. "I'm not one of them, Your Grace," she states bluntly as I trail my gaze up her chest.

"One of who?"

"Your girls."

"You mean the whores."

Swallowing audibly, she pulls back her shoulders defiantly. "No, I mean one of the-the…"

"Whores." I finish for her what she's incapable of saying through her politeness. "It's what they are. They're here to fuck and serve."

I relish in her obvious discomfort with another long sip of cognac. The rich, sweet fruit aroma mingles with her scent—a perfect match that makes my mouth water when her fidgeting brings her closer, close enough that I can feel the heat of her body seep through my skin.

"You know where you are, don't you?" The tip of my index finger cuts the air in front of her stomach, from one side to the other, while the others curl tighter around the tumbler in my hand.

A hiss preludes her sharp retort. "I'm not a whore."

"Good. I don't fuck whores." Disbelief narrows her light brown eyes with a scoff. Her features are expressive and bright, making her as easy to read as an open book right in front of me. "And I'm not fucking you."

"Oh." She lets out a relieved breath that relaxes her demeanour a tad.

"Sit."

"Why?"

"If you have any sense of self-preservation, you won't question me again." When I push to my feet, dropping my empty glass beside my seat, she traipses back into the table. "Now, sit."

"On the table." Although it's technically a question, the tone she uses makes it sound more like a statement.

Smart-arse.

A low chuckle rumbles in my chest, catching me off guard. Eve's head tilts in surprise before a small smirk tugs at her lips, and she hitches herself up on the table. For such a petite thing, she has long, shapely legs that would feel as good as they look wrapped around me. Just as her smart mouth would feel sublime with her choking on my cock. If I were to fuck her, which I won't. There's no way I'm touching her, even if my cock is throbbing in its regard for my thoughts.

Not going to happen, I assert to myself, rolling my shoulders back to stretch out the tense heat coiling in my muscles.

"I'm sitting," she tells me with a haughty cock of her brow.

"Would you like a medal?"

"Like yours?" Eve nods at my chest, where my military and dignitary decorations are pinned on my black dinner jacket. There's a bitter edge to her question that gives me pause as I turn to fetch her violin. "Come on, it's not like you actually went to war and earnt them, is it? You have people to fight your battles for you. Don't you? When was the last time any of you aristocrats and princes actually fought for your country?"

The remark twists at my insides. With the political climate we're in and the plots to abolish the monarchy by any means possible, it strikes a dissonant chord, reminding me that there's no such thing as safety, not even within these walls.

My hand grips her instrument tightly as I return to my seat, pulling it back a few feet to put enough distance between us so that I can see her fully. I want to take in her whole picture, to see through her as she seems to see through me.

"And what do you actually know about any of it? You're just a fucking child. A naïve one at that."

An acerbic snort twists her face. "My childhood ended when my dad was killed fighting for you lot. I stopped being a child when my brother died fighting your war."

"And here you are, serving us lot like they did." She scowls at me with her jaw clenched so tight that the lines of her soft features sharpen. When she makes to stand, I warn, "Walk away from me and you won't make it out of these walls."

"I'm not serving you."

"Why are you here, then?"

"A means to an end." Eve shrugs, shuffling back on the table until her legs are hanging over the edge. The stones on the straps of her shoes cast rainbows between us every time the light hits them. "It's part of my scholarship at the conservatory, and it looks good on my résumé. I'm not serving you; I'm serving myself."

The honesty burning in her eyes fills me with an intrigue that overshadows the need to break her indignation with my bare hands. Tears glitter heavily on her lashes like precious pendants begging to be plucked. Something about her grief warms me. It sings to my reverie. Like the patter of rain lulling the thunder in a storm, Eve's visible sorrow fuzzes my roaring rage. I'm not sure I like it, but the distraction silences the storm in my mind, making it possible to think past my hunger for revenge and my thirst for blood.

An eerie quiet engulfs us as she stares down at her lap, allowing her long hair to curtain her face. I watch as she picks at her short nails for a moment, observing the way her right index finger is always slightly bent away from her other fingers. Years of being on the bow would do that, but she still has childlike, small hands that show she is young, contrary to her buxom hips and tits.

"How old are you?" I ask, plucking the middle string of her violin with my thumbnail.

Eve tucks her thick, golden strands behind her ears while glancing up at me from beneath dark lashes. The spirit she possesses shines from the depths of her gaze. An unspoken challenge. There's a wildness in her that I don't know if I want to tame, spur, or break.

How far can she be pushed until it breaks? My thoughts meander with the flutter of her lashes, and my pulse stutters in time with the motion. How long would it take to break her?

All that relucent life within her taunts me the longer she stands strong. I've never wanted to touch something as much as I want to touch her. To feel the warmth of blood and the velvet of soft skin.

"Nineteen," she answers.

A bratty teenager. "Definitely not fucking you," I scoff out loud, even though I'm telling myself.

"I don't want you to fuck me."

"I'm not going to."

"Do you want another medal?" she growls with a roll of her eyes as she looks around her to allude to the nature of the place we're in.

Fuck! I want to punish that mouth of hers until all that sass she owns is streaming from her eyes, pleading for mercy. I've never felt this unrelenting, unshakeable need for anything like I do for her. And I know that if I give in, we're both fucked. I'll destroy her, and I'll ruin myself. But worst of all, I'll enjoy it more than I crave it.

Glancing at the mantel clock as it chimes midnight, she brushes her hair back into a high ponytail, holding it there for a beat. Her skin is flushed as warm as I feel, and when I extend her violin to her, she has a moment of pause before she takes it with a confused expression.

"My mother is the patron of your school." It's a pointless remark, and I don't know why I made it, except for the fact that it shows her to be even more at my mercy, in some way that I haven't quite figured out yet.

"Means to an end," Eve repeats. There's pride in the upturn of her nose and the tip of her chin. "We're not all born with a silver spoon in our mouths."

"No, some were born to bite the hand that feeds them." Anger blazes in her eyes, burning so fiercely that it has my pulse racing. As much as our tête-à-tête is distracting me, I cut off her smart retort before it leaves her lips. "Quiet now, Eve. The only sound I want to hear coming from your direction is your violin. You're going to play for me."

Silent astonishment tugs at her frowning face as she takes the bow I offer her. Confusion and debate war in her stare as she tucks the violin to her chin. The action is so familiar to her that the comfort it brings her is instant. The love she has for her instrument and music lights up her entire demeanour with the quick warm-up of her fingers and strings.

"Your father and your brother," I say when she stops. Maybe it's the sound that reminds me so much of my own father that prompts me. Or maybe it's the soured vestiges of our conversation. In truth, the longer I think on how to carry on, I realise that it's my disregard for their sacrifice that is nagging me. "They did an honourable thing…protecting their country. You, me…they fought for us all." Just like my father.

Eve nods. This might be the only thing we ever agree on, but I like that it thaws her to me. "What would you like to hear?" she asks me in a soft, wet whisper.

Those fucking breathtaking tears hang on her lashes again, threatening to fall if I don't pluck them for myself. And I want to, so much that my fingertips ache for it. I might have to sit on my hands to stop myself if we carry on like this.

"Your Grace?" she prompts.

"Anything." In truth, this wasn't what I had planned for her. And although my physical needs are disappointed that I'm holding back, the rest of me just wants to hold her here for as long as I can. I want to revel in the distraction that she's provided me with. "Everything…but what they asked you?"

A small smile tugs at the corners of her lips as she drags in a deep breath and stands. The instant she begins to play, I'm hooked, completely suckered into the lonely melody of Barber's Adagio. A pang of beauty hits me square in the chest, lighting every one of my senses. And if I didn't think she was beautiful before, she's the most wondrous thing I've ever laid eyes on. Lost to her music, Eve's magnificent. So breathtaking that I don't know if I'm ever going to let her walk out of here again.

THREE

Eve

The door opens, and the door closes. The monotony of my day to day becomes starker by the second, with every ding of the bell above the coffee shop door. The small independent cafe doesn't get half of the footfall it could, given its basic offerings, but it gives me time to catch up on my coursework while making enough money to rent a small flat and still have energy to work evenings at Heath House, a private members club where all the politicians go along with their richer-than-God acquaintances. It's part of the reason I ended up at Hush last night.

Hush.

Seems like my whole universe has suddenly fallen silent, with my thoughts blaring nonstop. All I can hear is his voice. It's always there in the background, even while I'm trying to focus on the pizzicato rhythm of the music playing around me. I've never met a man so forthright and surly. Every word that comes out of his mouth is cutting, and I hate that even after four years of looking after myself, he made me feel like a child. I hate that for a moment, when he was boiling over with grief, I felt sorry for him. Sympathy, empathy, and naïve stupidity had me thinking that there was some humanity in him.

How wrong was I?

Or I thought I was until he tried to make me feel better about Dad and Joe.

Or maybe he was buttering me up to make up for the arsehole, shithead behaviour.

One last attempt to get into my pants. The cynic in me jeers as I give up annotating the sheet music in front of me and start cleaning up.

Maybe I can close early, eat something before starting my shift at Heath Hou—the thought is gone before I've had the chance to finish it and the door dings open again.

"Hi, what can I get you?" I ask, spinning away from the fridge.

It takes a second too long for my brain to catch up with my eyes. But when it does, my chest constricts. People like him don't come to this coffee shop.

"Hello, Eve." He smiles warmly.

The softness of his greeting leaves me confused. Last night, he was as cool as the others, even if he tried to spare me from the Duke.

"Hi." He comes closer, perching himself on one of the counter stools. "What can I get you?"

He continues to smile while appraising me from top to toe. "What do you recommend? What's the house speciality?"

Okay…clearly he hasn't got the measure of this place. "Coffee. Tea. Ummm…"

"What tea do you have?" I point at the shelf by the coffee machine where the teas are lined up below the menu. "I'll take a pot of Earl Grey."

Resisting the urge to laugh at his request, I grab a mug and side plate and serve him his tea with an espresso cup of milk on the side. This is the fanciest drink I've served the whole time I've been working here.

"Do you happen to have a slice of lemon?"

"Listen…" I pause to allow him to fill in the blank with his name because the few times we've met, he hasn't said much to me; he's been in the background.

"My name is Percival Kent, and I—"

"Right, well, Mr. Kent, this isn't one of your posy caffs with all the fancy trappings. We serve coffee, tea, and muffins. If you're lucky, they're only a day old."

He laughs. "Sugar it is."

Watching him sweeten his tea, I wait for him to divulge what he's doing here. When he doesn't, I ask, "What do you want, Mr. Kent?"

"You're not as soft as you look." The deep timbre of his chuckle ebbs into awkward silence. "There's a space at Hush," he states.

"Right?"

"I'd like to invite you to fill it."

Is he serious? "No, thank you."

"I don't think you understand, Eve."

"But I do. I'm not your kind of girl." Last night's experience was more than enough for me to know that Hush isn't for me. All those women with their bodies on show for the men to ogle and touch as they like…the memory alone makes me cringe.

"It's not what you think," Percival says, pulling a dark envelope from inside his jacket. "There's more information in here—" He puts the envelope down on the counter. "—but the long and short of it is that we'd like you to play at the club a few nights a week."

"I don't have a few nights a week. I bartend at Heath House and—"

"Are you a bartender or a violinist?" he cuts me off. "This is a unique opportunity, Eve. It will open many doors for your future career. Think Royal Philharmonic, and you wouldn't need to work here or anywhere else with the pay cheque we would give you."

"Why does it sound like you're trying to buy me?"

"Because Hush has the best of everything. We cater to all

the whims and pleasures of our members, and your talent certainly holds the promise of the best that the Royal Conservatory has to offer." Taking a leisurely sip of his tea, he gives me time to think over his offer.

It sounds too good to be true. Paying placements are rarer than rocking horse shit. While I want to turn him down after last night, I don't want to cut my nose off to spite my face. It wasn't terrible, and in the end, it felt good playing for someone that was actually listening to me rather than being background noise. I can still remember the way the Duke's dark eyes held me. I can still feel the rush of his closeness. The volatility inside him was palpable and electrifying.

"There are other perks too," Percival hums, putting his tea back down.

"I'm not like the other girls. You can't buy my—"

"Your only job will be to look beautiful and play your violin. Nobody will touch you in any way you don't want them to." Standing, he nods at the envelope in my hand. "Even with both jobs, your study grants and scholarship, you won't make what we're offering you."

"You don't know what I make."

"It's my job to know everything about every person that walks through the club's doors, whether they're a member, an employee, or a guest. I know how many hours you work and how much income they bring you. I know all the family you have left." He levels me with a soft stare before continuing. "There's nothing I don't know about you, Eve."

It doesn't surprise me that he knows so much, which only makes me feel sheepish about my earlier remark. Still, I'm torn. Accepting his offer feels like I'm selling my soul to the devil.

"Tell me who else would offer you the opportunity to do what you love and pay you for it. Handsomely," he stresses. "Even if you don't like who we are or what we do behind closed doors, you know that giving this chance up because of your pride and sense of morality is foolish. You don't strike me as a foolish girl." His warm smile makes another appearance. "Maybe a little innocent and naïve, but not foolish."

No, I'm not stupid. Any other person at the conservatory would be chomping at the bit to accept his offer. I should be biting his hand off, but every time that he's almost convinced me, I remember how uncomfortable last night was. I liked it and I hated it, and when I left, I couldn't stop looking back. It felt as if I'd forgotten something behind. It still feels like something is missing.

Maybe it's my dignity because all I've been able to think about since I walked out of the door was how it felt when the Duke was watching me, the intensity in his dark eyes pulling me in with every glance.

Every breath of air we shared still burns in my lungs, like a ravenous pine for life. I don't understand it. I don't know if I like it either. But even with his surliness, I keep going back to the words he spoke of my dad and brother. For that small moment, there was warmth in him. It was palpable and disarming. For a fraction of a second, there was a glimpse of kindness.

I felt more in that room with him than I've allowed myself to feel in years. And while I look around me at the white walls and brown floors cluttered with cheap tables and chairs, I feel nothing again. The music in the background is lifeless—dead notes littering the air.

"I'll think about it," I tell Percival as he starts for the exit.

"Don't think on it for too long," he says, looking over his shoulder at me.

"You said no one would touch me."

"Not unless you want them to."

"Okay," I breathe out, ignoring the nagging feeling inside me.

Turning to face me, he grins. "Okay?"

Maybe I'll regret it. Perhaps I'll wish I'd never step inside those walls again, but for now, I just want to see the Duke again. I want to feel something other than alone or lost in my skin.

"When do you want me to start?"

FOUR
Eve

The mirror doesn't lie, and neither do the offerings of my budget wardrobe. The anxiety of starting at Hush tonight has made me question everything from what I'm wearing to what my hair is doing and how short my nails are—too short to be painted red. The only saving grace is my discounted designer heels that my sister-in-law bought me for my eighteenth birthday.

Tugging at the off-the-shoulder sleeves, I make sure that the cut-across neckline of my black dress sits just above the cups of my strapless bra.

"The joy of having tits bigger than your head," I grumble at myself, giving up on scrutinising and worrying over my outfit any longer.

Once I've applied another lick of my dark nude lipstick, I grab my violin and small backpack with my essentials for the evening. Eye drops, moisturiser, and other female essentials. Because sod's law says that my cramps are a sign aunt flow is on her way, and it would just be my luck that I come on tonight while at work.

With a quick spray of my rose body spritz, I head out of the door, locking all three locks to ensure I don't have any unwanted visitors tonight. Considering how affluent the surrounding areas are, Whitechapel isn't the safest. But I'm good at keeping my head down and my rape alarm at the ready when I'm out at night. Besides, it's what I can afford while paying bills and feeding myself. The textbooks and sheet music aren't exactly budget-friendly, even if I buy them mostly third/fourth-hand and well loved.

"Don't you look pretty," the downstairs neighbour hollers as I reach her landing. She's got her cuppa in one hand and cigarette in the other.

"Hey, Clara." I wave at her. Normally I'd stop to chat, but I don't want to get to the club smelling of smoke.

"Where you going dressed like that?"

"Work."

"Work? Like that?"

Pausing in front of the window protector, I check my reflection again. Maybe the dress is too short? This is one of the two decent dresses I own. The rest I got in charity shops or as hand-me-downs from my sister-in-law.

"You playing somewhere?" she asks, eyeing my violin case.

"I have my first proper gig at this fancy place…do you think I need to change into something a bit less leggy?"

"I think you oughtta watch yourself around these parts, sweetheart, dressed like that and with them shoes." Leaning back into her door, she peers inside as her little girl comes to join her on the doorstep. "Oi, Alfie," Clara yells for her son.

The seventeen-year-old takes a moment to show his face, but the minute he sees me, he smiles. "Need an escort to the bus stop again?"

"No, it's not dark out yet."

"Don't matter." Clara bats my reply away, throwing him the keys to her Corsa. "You take Evie to the bus and wait for her to get on it. Your dad will be here to take you by the time you get back. No fucking shady business when she's with you. You hear me, Alf?"

With a salute at his mum, he takes my violin case from me. "Come on, then, Cinders, your carriage awaits."

"I can walk."

"Nah, it's fine." He shrugs at me, his cocky grin getting broader when we reach the bottom step and he offers me his hand in a mock bow. "If I go back up there now, she'll knock my block off. I'd rather take my chances out there."

When we get in the car, Alfie gets us going quickly. The music is blaring loud enough that the bass rattles my eardrums with a string of expletives from the lyrics.

"You want Mum to pick you up later?"

"No, I'll be all right."

"You're a beautiful girl, Evie, and beautiful girls don't do good on their own. Not on these streets." Debate tugs at his brows before he reaches beneath the steering wheel and pulls a knife from a concealed tear where the carpet meets the side of the middle console. "Take this."

"Alfie…"

"Don't look at me like that. It's protection. Better safe than too late to be sorry." He shoves the knife into my hand. "I'll get it back off you when I return from my dad's."

"I have this." I dangle my rape alarm between us. "I don't need a knife. You shouldn't have it either. You could get into a lot of trouble."

"You really think that shitty little thing is going to keep you safe?" A cynical laugh rumbles from him. "Fuck, man, I thought you're meant to be smart?"

Only a few minutes late, my bus appears in the side mirror as he pulls up to the stop. While I grab my violin from the back seat, I give him back his knife before flinging my backpack over my shoulder.

"Be careful, Alfie."

"Watch your back, yeah, Cinders?" he calls at me before peeling off to catch the green light ahead, performing a highly illegal U-turn that has the traffic erupting into a chaotic cacophony of sirens and cursing.

The instant I'm on the bus and tucked away on the bench close to the driver, I take the thirty-minute ride to Zen myself. Barber's Adagio plays on repeat the entire journey while I clear my head.

I've never been so damn nervous in my life as I walk through the backstreets of Westminster to the private mews where Hush is located, by Whitehall Palace. The thought of starting a regular, well-paying music gig is as exciting as it is terrifying. Then there's the prospect of seeing the Duke again. It was stupid to google him after Percival left me. Doctor Google only made my curiosity worse with the limited information I found out.

Henry Albert James Dorchester-Sloane is the second cousin to the prince. His mother, Princess Margaret, is cousin to the King of England, and his father was one of the most revered haematologists in the world, aside from being the Duke of Gloucester.

"Evening, miss." The guard at the gated mews comes to greet me when I stop outside the gates, still debating whether I've made the right choice in coming back here. His stare rakes me from head to toe as I watch the black plume of his polished metal helmet lightly bluster in the evening breeze.

"Evening," I reply, flitting my attention to the assault rifle clutched to the side of his black-and-silver-cloaked garbs.

"ID?" he asks when I hand him the staff card that was in the envelope Percival left with me.

It takes me a moment to fish out my driver's licence, but once he's checked it over, the guard calls me through the side gate. While I pack away my ID and purse into my backpack, a chauffeured car comes through the wide double gates. It's dark and sleek, and when I make my way up the mews, it crawls slowly beside me.

The tall limestone buildings on either side of the street block out the city. It's like walking back in time. Gold-railed window boxes are blooming with blood-red and deep purple flowers. Meanwhile, the black streetlamps are all decorated with a gold crown on the top, with three wolves holding up the glass casing of the gaslights.

The wolves are everywhere, from the manholes on the cobbled road to the drain grates along the side of the pavement. They watch from the mouldings on the buildings, corbels, and gargoyle-like faces with sharp teeth, claws, and crowns. Together with the eerie quietness of the early evening, it gives the place a forbidding air that causes me to shudder when I go up the steps to the expansive building at the very end of the mews.

A small roundabout sits behind me with a tall, ancient-looking tree planted in the middle. The trunk is wide enough that it blocks the view of the gates at a distance when I look behind me. Clearly, it's meant to hide the entrance of the club from prying eyes.

The door opens before I knock. I feel like Belle walking into the Beast's castle, except it's a Palladian mansion house hidden in the midst of royal palaces and parliament buildings.

"Good evening, Miss Cameron," the butler greets me with a hunched bow. It's an odd welcome, and it only heightens the foreboding crackle in my chest when I look over my shoulder to find the sleek Mercedes paused at the bottom of the steps.

The dark tinted windows make it impossible to see inside, but I can see a shadow within. I feel it watching me as I stare at the glass as though somehow I'll be able to see through it eventually.

It's only when the butler clears his throat that I turn away, but that feeling remains. I can't shake it off, and ignoring it is impossible as I greet the man in front of me with a shaky smile.

"Back so soon." He beams far too brightly, given he couldn't get rid of me fast enough the last time I was here.

"You're telling me."

"I'll have these taken up for you," he informs me while taking my violin case and backpack from me.

Tugging on a thick gold rope hanging from the ceiling by his desk, he waits for a girl to appear from a concealed panel door on the wall behind him.

She's about average height, taller than me but a lot slimmer. The body chains draped over her body and the black gauzy robe over them do nothing to cover up her dignity.

"Take these up to the suite, Mary," he tells her, handing over my belongings.

Her gaze greets mine. It's then I notice the dark freckle at the top of her cheekbone. She's the girl that was serving drinks during the dinner.

"Hi." I smile at her, but all I get in return is a stoic blink.

"Off you go, Mary." The butler shoos her away with his hand.

The last time I was here, he practically kicked me out of the door when I left. I'm surprised it didn't leave my arse bruised. Today, however, he's all grace and niceties while he ushers me through the chequered hallway, along portrait-draped, panelled walls. I don't know what's going on, but it's got my insides knotting anxiously.

When I look back, Mary is watching us from the bottom of the stairs, holding my backpack in one hand and my violin in the other. A small smile tugs at the corners of her mouth before she starts up the imposing staircase.

"Mr. Kent asked to see you," the butler tells me when we reach what looks like the door to a study. After a brief knock, he opens and holds it for me to enter.

The rich scent of leather and cigars hits me instantly, followed by the warmth of burning pine. There's an indistinct murmur of music coming from the gramophone to the side of the doorway.

Weird place to put a record player, I think to myself, listening to the scratchy vintage sound. This place is a time warp. History engulfs every one of my senses as I walk deeper into the space of dark floor-to-ceiling panelled walls, brass fixtures, and rich, jewel-toned furnishings.

"Eve," Percival sings from behind a large mahogany desk.

Although the evening outside is balmy, a fire is crackling in the hearth below a group portrait of men. They're all in similar dinner suits to the ones the men were wearing when I was here last. On their faces, they carry stern expressions that make them look cold and auspicious.

"They're the founders of the club," Percival tells me as he comes to stand beside me. "That right there—" He points out the man in the bright red jacket. "That's King George the Fourth. He was one of the more extravagant and frivolous monarchs. He had a penchant for collecting precious things…beautiful things." With a side glance, he grins at me. "Something that hasn't been lost in his kin."

Percival's not a small man, but his presence now doesn't feel at all as imposing as it did the other night when the other men were present. Maybe it was the sombreness of their mourning. Perhaps it was the novelty and the curiosity of being in the same room as those powerful men. It doesn't matter how many maybes I think of, it's him that comes to the forefront of my mind every time. It's him I remember as clear as rain. Dark eyes, warm skin and a volatility that kept my heart chasing its own rhythm for dear life.

"I have your contract for you to sign." Percival extends the papers towards me. "You're going to see things that might make you uncomfortable. Hear things that might shock you. But what you must always remember is that what goes on in these walls stays within these walls."

"I understand." I take the papers from him, glancing over the page before I read through it.

"If you have a problem, you come to me first." When I nod, he offers me a gold pen. "If anyone comes to you with questions about the club, you come to me directly."

"I don't talk to many people, so…" With a shrug, I take the pen from him, weighing it in my grip as I read through the last clauses of the paperwork.

It's near on identical to the one I signed for my one-night stint, barring the clause that stops me from taking on any other jobs while I'm employed here and another that demands regular health checks by their appointed physician.

"People will approach you about the club, Eve, and you must maintain confidentiality at all times. In all things. If you fail to do so, there are consequences beyond the termination of your contract."

"I have my own doctor, and I get checked over regularly." I

change the conversation because I know what working at these places entails. During my time at Heath House, I learnt very quickly that the men who frequent these places guard are precious about their privacy. They guard themselves with everything they have.

"Yes." He smiles, moving on. "I'm aware of your medical history. I told you before, it's my job to know everything about everyone that walks through the door of the club."

"But…but you can't—"

"There is no I can't, won't, or shouldn't when it comes to protecting the club and its members. I know everything, Eve, as I need to protect and look after you. I'll provide you with the medication you need, and you won't say a word to anyone about it. Especially not the Duke."

I nod. It's obvious he knows more than he wants to vocalise, and if he's going to help me get the medication I need, I'm not going to argue with him. Even if I feel completely vulnerable.

My condition isn't something I share with many people. When I was little, it made teachers treat me differently to my classmates, and as I got older, having a nontransmissible blood disorder made people around me uncomfortable. So I stopped talking about it to anyone. Von Willebrand doesn't make me a leper; it just makes paper cuts sort of deadly.

"The men are going to like you, and it's important that you don't fight them. For your safety."

"You said no one would touch me," I snap back, peeling my eyes from the dotted line that I was about to sign.

I've already quit the coffee shop and my bartending gig at Heath House. I need this job if I'm going to pay my rent and afford to pay for my prescriptions as well as food.

But… "I don't want them to touch me. I-I'm not a—" I stop myself from finishing the sentence. I'm not in any place to judge anyone for doing what they have to in order to get by. It's simply that I'm not comfortable going to those lengths myself.

"Trust me, if everyone knows what's good for them, they

won't even look at you for too long."

"What do you mean?"

"There's an order to things in this world."

The Duke's remark from the other night rings in my thoughts. *He's here to serve and please, just as you are.*

"You mean rank."

"Something like that, but we'll call it rules of practice. And if rules of practice say no one touches you, then…?" Percival leaves the question hanging for me to answer.

"No one touches me." There's tantamount relief and curiosity as the study door opens abruptly, and one of the men from the other night stands in the open doorway, looking between the two of us.

"So you see, as long as you follow the rules too, you are quite safe and well taken care of." Percival gestures for him to come in. "This is our legal counsel, Julian Seymour."

The man is taller than Percival, with dark hair that makes the blue of his eyes appear icy even in the warm flicker of the fire. The top two buttons of his black shirt are open, and his deep green tie is wrapped around one of his hands. There's an inconvenienced look about him, as though maybe his plans to wind down have been scarpered.

"Are you ready to sign, Miss Cameron?" he asks me abruptly, his eyes pulling together with a boring stare that tells me it's not just his gaze that is cold. When I don't reply, he glances at Percival with a wide, expectant expression. "Have you taken her through it?"

"We've gone through it."

"Well then." He stands impossibly taller. "Are you signing or leaving?"

Whoa, the curtness of his question causes me to take a step back into Percival. He's older, maybe old enough to be his dad. Stupidly, that creates a false sense of safety in our closeness. At the same time, between the two of them, I feel like the child that they think I am. I'm so out of place that my comfort zone is a universe away. I've been suckered into a black hole, and I have no clue where I've landed.

"Miss Cameron." He grinds out my name with an authoritarian edge that makes my heart leap out of my chest.

The urge to run is overwhelming. But as I eye all my potential escapes, it becomes clear I don't have any. I'm sandwiched between these two men—one that has been seemingly nice and the other, a stranger that's got every anxiety I had over accepting this job screaming at me.

Why did I come back? I ask myself.

My vision is going hazy as my blood pounds colder and colder in my veins. Faintness tugs at my extremities. The instinct to fight or flight is kicking in, and I'm about to push the stranger away when another figure appears.

"Give her some fucking space, Julian." As blurred as he is, his voice is the most familiar thing in this room. And I cling on to it, using it as a grip out of my panic. "I told you to make sure she signed, not to scare her away."

"She shouldn't be here," Julian spits over his shoulder.

The Duke blows out a bored breath, coming closer until he's side by side with Julian. "It's not your decision."

He's taller than I remember. His eyes are darker than I recall. A dark, coffee liquorice—so intense when you're his sole focus and so moreish that when he diverts his attention away, you crave it desperately.

Without his jacket on, his shoulders look broader in his crisp white shirt. The strapping of his dark red braces that match his tie emphasises their thickness. He has a natural strength and power that's breathtaking and terrifying in equal parts. The longer I take him in, the more he reminds me of a sculpted god holding court in a museum or gallery. I reckon, like Atlas, this man could bear the weight of heaven on his shoulders for eternities without crumbling.

"Sign the contract, Eve," he instructs, plucking the papers in my hand and putting them on the side table beside the couch.

"Go on, sign your soul to the devil, little girl," Julian mutters with a low scoff when I move towards the table.

The slow spin of the Duke's body is corded with tension as he faces him. "Shut your fucking mouth, and do your goddamn job. I'm not in the mood for your sulking." Turning back to me, he gives me a top-to-toe once-over before telling me, "Nobody will touch you."

The dark rake of his stare over my body is as palpable as a physical touch. I feel it burn over me, causing my bones to tremble when he takes a half step closer so that we're only a breath apart.

"Do it, Eve."

I nod, keeping my eyes on his as I grip the pen in my hand tighter and lean over the table.

"Sign."

My hand shakes as I follow his command with my heart hammering in my throat and my breath cloying in my lungs while he moves to stand behind me. I feel him watching me, every whisper of the pen on the paper making my insides vibrate.

"Good girl."

Good girl. The words echo through me like a sudden heat wave. The lines of his jaw sharpen as I stand straight and turn back to him. I'm completely, utterly mesmerised. I've never seen or known a more beautiful man. Not on a magazine, certainly not in person.

Holy fucking crap.

They say the devil was heaven's most beautiful angel, and looking at him, it really is gospel. The Duke still has his eyes trained on me when he plucks the pen from my hand and throws it down on the table. Every move is so purposeful and graceful, even with its brusqueness, that it makes me very aware of myself, causing me to stand taller. I pull my shoulders back until it feels as if my dress might pop around my bust, the crisscross back straps cutting into my flesh.

"Eve?"

A gasp escapes me at the sudden sound of my name from his lips. It's promising, deep, and so gravelly that it vibrates through me in shivers I can't control.

Clearing my throat, I all but squeak, "Mmm?"

"Wait for me upstairs," he instructs with a lick of his lips. They look too perfect and sculpted to be human flesh. Maybe they're hard, chiselled stone and it's why he can't really smile.

In all the photos I found of him online, not a single one showed him smiling. The impassiveness he possesses is distanced and cold. However, I keep going back to the time we spent together last week, scrutinising the one smile he offered when he spoke of Dad and Joe and that sudden, short-lived laugh.

"Upstairs," he tells me again, causing my chest to squeeze tight at the deep timbre of his voice. The frantic rhythm of my pulse stutters for a few beats as I turn to leave.

I swear I feel him touch the small of my back, tracing the dandelion tattoo I got shortly after Joe died. However, when I look at him, his hands are balled at his sides while his stare is glued to the top of my arse.

From the expression on his face, I can't tell what he's thinking. But there's a glint in his eyes that makes my insides wrench. His lips pucker as his hands push inside the pockets of his suit trousers, so big and masculine that they don't fit properly, leaving his pinkie finger hanging out with the ruby-eyed wolf glaring at me. The urge to run is overruled by the pull deep inside of me, like a lasso knotted around my organs so that I feel every move he makes around me.

I take a step back, and he steps forward. We're toe-to-toe, and my pulse is racing. I wait for his next move as he holds me with his unwavering stare. Our surroundings fade. My blood hammers relentlessly in my ears. And still, I'm paralysed. Waiting.

Watching and waiting as my heart threatens to jump out of my chest.

Watching and waiting while the air in my lungs begins to burn.

Watching and waiting while he holds his narrowed gaze on me.

I might just pass out when he says, "Go."

The guttural growl sets me in motion. One foot in front of the other, with Percival following behind me. The music that had been a murmur in the background becomes louder. I can't hear a single thing going on inside the room when the door shuts behind me, leaving me out in the darkened hallway, questioning my sanity and every decision I've made since I was sent here.

FIVE

Henry

The door to the suite is wide open when I round the corner of the darkened corridor. With the golden light spilling into the hallway, it's impossible to hide in the shadows while I watch Eve pace the floor at the foot of the bed. Her slender legs look lithe in the tall heels strapped to her dainty ankles. Leaning over the high footboard, she drags in deep breaths as though steadying herself.

I can't help the thoughts that assault me at the sight of her bent over like that. The short skirt of her dress barely covers the curve of her arse cheeks, and the stretch of her calves…

Fuck, my hands tighten at the overwhelming need to take her. Just like that.

With her hair tangling around us and her supple tits heavy in my hands. Every time I set eyes on her, she appears more and more enticing, and it's becoming harder to resist the urge to touch her.

But she's just a child.

Julian's right—Eve's a pretty, untainted little girl. She has no idea where she really is. Who I am or what I do. Eve doesn't belong within these walls, let alone in our world. At some point, it will burn her, or worse, it will obliterate her. She's as delicate as the dandelion etched at the bottom of her spine. That right there, more than anything Julian warned me of, is a reminder of her fragility.

Maybe bringing her back here was a mistake, but it's one I can't regret, even if I don't want to corrupt her. There's a purity inside her that makes her different from any woman I've ever encountered.

If keeping her in my sight is the only way I can have her, then that's what I'll do. Because the serenity she possesses is everything I want right now—the silence to think and the distraction to feel something other than rage.

Revenge has been my constant companion since my father was murdered. I live it, breathe it, taste its bitterness every damn second of every godforsaken day. It's scorching my veins, fuelling the blood thirst and stoking my fury. It's a recipe for disaster that I need to shake myself from if I'm going to keep the promise I made to my mother and myself.

Blood for blood.

The large rug muffles my footsteps as I walk inside the room. It's not until I shut the door behind me that Eve realises she's not alone anymore. There's a panicked glaze to her stare when she spins to find me.

Fuck if I don't want to devour her right here and now. Fuck if I don't want to squeeze my hands around every inch of her soft flesh. Swallow her whole and tear her apart, all at once.

"Your Grace," she breathes out tremulously, hot breath seeping through the cotton of my shirt.

When did I get so close? I ask myself, taking yet another step forward so that she steps back into the bed.

"I want to fuck you, Eve." The growl rumbles from me as I brace my hands on the footboard on either side of her hips. A deep shiver rolls through her. Maybe it's fear.

Is it fear?

"Does that scare you?"

She doesn't reply, but her silence is telling. The flitting of her eyes over my chest and her short rasps of air. My grip on the footboard tightens as I resist the need to shake a response from her.

"Eve."

SAVAGE DUKE

Honey eyes flash up to mine, and with a deep inhale, she tells me, "You said no one would touch me."

"Nobody." Leaning over her, I suck in her sweet scent. Almond and rose. So fucking mouthwatering. A delicious promise of what's beneath her clothes. "I said nobody, not no one."

With her face tipped up to mine, there isn't a single tendril of her hair shadowing her confusion. There's a fleeting second where she looks as entranced by the pull between us as I am. This heat is all-consuming. I can't think past the hunger it stirs in me.

"Do I look like nobody to you?"

"No," she whispers with a shake of her head. "No, Your Grace."

"Henry." I'm not my father. Even if I am wearing his ring and sitting in his seat. "You can call me Henry."

"I was told to address you as Your Grace."

"Do you always do as you're told, Eve?"

Her silent, unwavering gaze is the only reply. It doesn't matter how long I wait for an audible response; she doesn't give it to me.

"I brought you back here," I say, pulling myself back.

This is something I haven't done in a really long time. Not just because it's more hassle than the fucking is worth when I have no intention of taking it further than that. But also because last time it ended badly. Besides, I've outgrown these games. The only reason I come here aside from official club meetings is to watch Arthur's back when he's too busy getting his cock sucked.

Eve watches intently while I remove my tie and wind it around my hand before throwing it behind her on the bed. Her nervousness grows by the second as I remove my cufflinks and pocket them, proceeding to unbutton the collar of my shirt.

"Why?" she asks tremulously.

"Didn't I tell you not to question me?"

A deep breath hollows out the bottom of her throat as her jaw clenches tight. Chagrin glints in her narrowed eyes as she pulls herself straight. Standing taller, she takes a step forward with her small ring-decorated hands on her hips. There it is. This is the fire that brought her back here, to me. I like it. More than I realised and definitely more than I care to admit. Eve may be young, but she's headstrong in her morals.

"You said you didn't want to fuck me."

"No," I chuckle at the indignant bite of her remark. "I said I wasn't going to fuck you."

"It's not what I'm here for."

"I'm your means to an end." I remind her of what she said this place was to her for that one night and what it will be from now on every time she walks through the door. "You're here to serve me. Only me."

Rolling up the sleeves of my shirt, I stand behind her. Our bodies aren't touching, but the heat of her body moulds perfectly to mine, just as I know her soft curves would, and that mental image is enough to get me hard. My cock aches in its straining confines while my blood blazes at the mere thought of all the things I want to do to her. And there is nothing but my fraying willpower stopping me. Nothing but the knowledge that she's too young for me. Too innocent. Too perfect. And definitely too good to be fucked like a whore in this place.

When I move to sit on the edge of the bed, she spins on the spot, following me with her steady gaze. I'm tempted to play with her a little. Tease her apprehension and stoke that fire of hers some more. But I want her to come back tomorrow and the night after that. I want her to come back to me every fucking night until I'm done with her.

"What do you want from me, Your Grace?" she asks when I lean back on the bed, bracing myself on my elbows.

"Right now?" The rake of my gaze over her body causes her to squirm. "Right now, Eve, I want you to play for me."

"What would you like to hear, Your Grace?" There's a victorious glint in her light brown eyes when she uses my formal address again.

"Anything."

"Anything," she echoes, picking up the case and setting it on the bedside table to take out her violin.

"Yes. Anything. Everything."

A soft sigh escapes her when she faces me again, her violin tucked to her chin and the bow at the ready.

"Except what they told me to play."

My chest fists tightly around my insides at the whisper of the words I told her the last time she played for me. I don't know what it means, but I do know that I need to guard myself against this feeling. Nothing good will come of it. Nothing but death.

The sudden pounding on wood jolts me out of my sleep. Before I've opened my eyes, something feels unusual. It's not just the jarring sound that gets louder as I rouse myself from the clutches of the deep slumber I was in; it's the musk in the air and the feel of the bedding.

"Henry?" Percival calls. "Henry!"

Fuck, what time is it? I open my eyes to nothing but stark darkness. No barking. No claws clicking around me. *Where the fuck am I?*

It takes me another second for the last moments of last night to dawn on me. Eve.

Sitting up on the bed, I turn the lamp on to find all the curtains drawn. My empty glass is sitting beside my cufflinks and tie on the bedside table, along with my phone and wallet. Yesterday was one of our evenings together. Last thing I remember, she was playing for me. But there's no sign of her now.

Eve's chair is neatly tucked into its usual corner beside the fireplace, and her belongings that are usually by the wardrobe are gone. However, my jacket is neatly hanging on the wardrobe door by a padded coat hanger, with my shoes sitting on the floor below it.

The door crashes open into the chest of drawers as I'm getting to my feet.

"We found him," Percival blusters directly at me. He's out of breath, and his words are slurred with urgency, but I understand him well enough that my pulse is thrilled. "We found the driver."

"About fucking time," I snap back at him, grabbing my belongings from the bedside table and stuffing them into the pockets of my suit trousers before I put on my shoes. "Take me to him." The order snaps from me as I throw on my jacket and check the inside pocket for the flick knife that took my father's life.

Fuck, I've waited far too long for this. It's been over a month since we laid my father to rest. Weeks and weeks of looking for the man that betrayed him. He didn't trust easily or keep many around him, aside from his footman and his driver. He used to call them his cogs because they kept his day to day ticking.

"He's dead, Henry."

"I told you I would deal with—"

"We found him swinging," he states from behind me as I charge out of the suite. "And he was marked."

"Marked." Turning, I focus on the iPad he's holding out to me with a black-and-white photograph glaring on the screen.

"Eyes, mouth, and heart." The grim tenor of his voice matches the image he's showing me of the driver.

His eyes are slashed. His tongue has been cut out. And there's an *R* half encircled by a *U* gouged over his heart.

United Republic.

"This was in his mouth." Percival holds out his open hand, showing me the bloody button resting in his palm.

"A button?"

"A mother-of-pearl button." He stresses his statement like it's got some kind of importance to us. "The calling card of the East End Coster Kings."

"Why would the United Republic be working with gangsters? It doesn't make sense."

"I'm looking into it, but this complicates things," he tells me, worry clouding his voice as I take the button from him and pocket it.

I ignore his questioning glance as I ask, "And the driver? Where did you find him?"

"Swinging from the tree." His eyes flit to the window on the far side of the room, overlooking the wolf tree outside the club's door.

That oak tree was planted when the Wolfsden Society was first created by King George IV in 1821, a year into his reign—a group of his closest allies that would swear to protect the throne from those that sought to destroy it for a united republic. That tree is over two hundred years old—a wolf tree, symbolising strength, honour, and protection.

"How?"

"I've got security looking into it, but the only time that would make sense is during changeover. Footage is being pulled right now."

"How is it we've been breached again?" First the palace, and now Hush.

A sombre expression blackens the weariness in his eyes. Whether we say it out loud or not, we both know this can only mean one thing— "There's a traitor in our midst."

I've known it from the very beginning, and now it's time I do something about it.

SIX

Eve

"So go on, tell me about this new job." Jess, my sister-in-law, smiles at me while we wait for the kettle to boil.

"There's not much to say," I reply, aware that there's not much I can tell her.

Although she wouldn't tell anyone my business, I signed the contract. There's also this nagging thought that I'd be betraying Henry, and despite his surliness, he's been nice to me. A part of me is always waiting for him to flip, but for now, Dr. Jekyll isn't around.

In fact, there are times when I find myself enjoying his attention. The way he watches me is intoxicating, to say the least. Sometimes, his eyes are so intent on me that it feels as though he's somehow touching me, even from the distance he puts between us.

"That's not what your eyes are saying or your silence," she chuckles teasingly.

"Well, it pays well, and it helps with the scholarship credits thing. I mean…"

"You mean?" Jess coaxes me to finish with a gentle bump of her shoulder to mine.

While I finish making our teas, I think about what to tell her that will satisfy her curiosity. There isn't anything, though. Jess will just keep going until I tell her everything, and I always do.

Or normally, I do.

"It's a means to an end." I shrug, grabbing both of our teas and heading outside so she can have her cigarette before we wash the dye from her hair.

"A means to an end, as in you hate it? If you do, I'm sure they'll give you your job back at Heath House. They still haven't found anyone to replace you." She sits on the wall in front of her place. It looks straight into the lounge, where George, my eight-year-old nephew, is working on the puzzle I brought for him today. When she lights her cigarette, I sit beside her. "I've picked up some of your shifts, but they won't let me do any more overtime. It's so stupid."

"Is it? You can't do overtime on your overtime, Jess. At some point, you need to rest."

"Cash is king, Eve, and it definitely trumps beauty sleep. I'm desperately trying to get George into a better school." She gives me a grimacing sigh with a long pull on her smoke. "Last week, he kicked his teacher because she accidentally touched his hand."

"She knows he doesn't like being touched."

"Yeah, she does, but it was an accident when she was helping him put his coat on."

"There isn't room for accidents with kids like him." Jess has had the same problem with every mainstream school George has attended. The teachers just aren't equipped to deal with the special needs of an autistic child.

"It took a lot of arguing with them to get his suspension retracted. At one point, I even considered flashing my tits at the headmaster," she jokes, but her grin doesn't reach her eyes.

"Jess…"

"It wouldn't have worked, anyway." A dry laugh pushes from her rolled lips. "I don't have the tits for it, and I'm not his type."

"You're an idiot."

"You didn't answer my question." God, she's like a bloody dog with a bone. "Do you like your new job?"

After a short debate while I check her hair, I tell her, "It's not that different from Heath House, except that instead of making drinks, I'm playing my violin."

"You're the entertainment," she sings with a wide, proud smile.

"And your hair is done."

"We should celebrate this. You're finally doing what you love and getting paid for it. Joe would be so proud." Her voice warbles with the remark. "He loved listening to you practice."

"He did…" Before he went off to war and came back a completely different person.

"How about I treat you to dinner? Say thank you for doing my hair and celebrate your new milestone."

"Why not?" It's Sunday afternoon, and for once, I've actually got time to myself. I'm caught up on coursework and my composition research. That in itself is a miracle, but with only one job to work three nights a week, things are looking kind of great.

For the first time since Joe died, there's a light somewhere along the darkness I found myself in. For so long, I've just pushed myself to keep going because that's what he would have wanted, and now, I'm actually enjoying life again. I want to play for myself rather than to make him proud. It feels like I'm living.

I want to get out of bed and do more than just get through the day. More than that, I'm finding myself counting down the days, hours, minutes, and second of every day until the door of the suite closes behind Henry, and he looks at me like I'm the light in his darkness.

Typical British summer—one minute, it's hotter than an inferno, and the next, it's raining cats and dogs. Pulling my hood over my head, I run down the steps of the Royal Albert Hall. I clutch my violin case to my chest tightly, hoping that I can make it to my bus stop on the Knightsbridge main road before I become a drowned rat.

I'm running as fast as I can when the first roar of thunder cracks through the sky, and I jump out of my skin. I've always hated thunderstorms. Since I can remember, I've had a senseless fear of being struck down by lightning. When it flashes around me, I freeze beneath the awning of one of many boutiques on the quaint parade.

"It's just a storm. Just a storm," I remind myself repeatedly while pacing in front of the window, hugging my violin for dear life.

For a moment, the weather settles down a tad, and I contemplate gunning it for the coffee shop, but I know that I'll just end up freaking out the second it picks up again. Instead, I try to distract myself with the pretty dresses in the window display.

It works for a while as I admire the expensive silks and lace of the designer pieces. I couldn't afford them even if I sold a kidney on the black market. But it doesn't stop me from imagining what it would feel like to wear something so beautiful. I bet even the ugliest person in the world would feel drop-dead gorgeous.

"Odd time to window-shop?" a familiar voice calls over the heavy patter of the rain.

Another crack of thunder rumbles around me as I spin to look behind me, followed by a blinding bolt that causes me to scream out loud just as my eyes meet his.

Shit! Fuck! *It's just a storm*, I yell at myself in my thoughts as Henry's stare narrows on me.

"That's probably the most reasonable reaction you've had to me," he says, getting out of his car to stand beneath the awning with me. "Took you a while."

"Lightning frightens me," I blurt down at his feet, embarrassed before the admission leaves my lips.

"You don't say," he retorts before adding, "It's just an imbalanced attraction of positive and negative. When they come together, there's a balancing discharge that creates lightning."

"Well, that balancing discharge kills on average two thousand people every year."

"Worldwide," he chuckles.

I'm glad that my stupid fear has humoured him. "What are you, the weather police?"

I glare up at him to find Henry grinning. Momentarily, I'm lost for words. My thoughts scramble at the sight. He's ridiculously handsome at the best of times, but smiling—gosh, he's breathtaking.

The darkness in his eyes is endless, an abyss that makes the grey skies appear brighter somehow. Even with amusement softening the sharp lines of his face, there's still an austere severity to his expressions, regal and menacing and yet so hypnotising that I feel it tug deep in my chest, a powerful magnet pulling me to him.

Not that it lasts long, but it's enough to distract me until the next flash hits, and I'm shaking in my soggy shoes again. The loud squelch earns me a top-to-toe inspection.

"You're soaked," he says in a matter-of-fact tone as he takes off his jacket and wraps it around my shoulders.

"It's pissing dow—" Catching myself too late, I go quiet.

It's only now that I realise he's as soaked as I am. We're standing on the edge of the canopy, in the middle of the pavement with the awning over me while he's getting completely drenched.

"You're wet," I rasp.

The sight of his dark hair slicked to his face makes my fingers itch to brush it back or tease the waved ends into the curls they're coiling into. Instead, I tighten my arms around my violin case, making sure they don't act of their own accord.

"Get in the car, Eve."

"What?"

"Pardon."

I glance over his shoulder at the fancy sedan behind him. Swallowing down my sheepish embarrassment at his correction, I echo, "Pardon?"

"I'm taking you home." Before I can protest, he's prying my violin from me, followed by the backpack hanging off my shoulder.

"No. No…i-it's fin—"

"You're going to catch a cold."

"No, it's fine. I-I'm fine."

All joviality falls from his face. The lines that had been soft a second ago are sharper than ever.

"Don't argue with me, Eve. I don't have the time or patience for your insubordination right now."

But he has time to take me home? I don't get the chance to voice my thought because he's walking towards his car. Henry places my violin and backpack in the front passenger seat with his driver before opening the back door for me to get inside.

I could protest, but I'm certain he'd trample over my effort to stand my ground. Besides, the cold is seeping into my bones.

"Get in," he orders with a purposeful glance from me to the open door.

Fuck it, it's just another means to an end. There's a lot of that at the minute, and it all revolves around him somehow. Carefully sliding inside, I stare up at him. Henry isn't smiling or glaring. He's watching, closely and maybe a little cautiously, as though I'm the one that's trampling over him.

"Good girl," he finally says when I've buckled my seat belt.

Good girl. The words echo in my head just as they did the first time he uttered them to me. Satisfaction warms my chest, along with a sense of pride I don't quite understand. But I like the way it makes me feel, as though I have really done something worth commending.

SEVEN
Eve

Grey clouds burst with warm golden rays that blur my vision in the awkward silence of the drive. I'm staring out of the window, trying to distract myself from the fact that this is the closest Henry and I have sat for a long period of time. Meanwhile, he's scrolling through his phone with a scowl that could make the devil shit his pants.

Something's wrong. I can feel it roiling in my gut with every grind of his jaw. The whole time, he keeps to his side of the car, like there's an invisible line he can't cross. But his stare flits to me once in a while, and it's gone as soon as it meets mine in the glass.

"You can drop me off here," I tell him when his driver turns into the estate I live on.

Suddenly, I'm very aware of how stark apart our worlds are. Especially when the horror in his eyes morphs into disgust. Henry doesn't even try to hide it as he instructs his man to take me to my door.

"It's really not necessary."

"Just tell him where you live, Eve," Henry insists.

In all my life, I've never been ashamed of who I am or where I come from. But right now, there's a lingering trepidation in my chest that makes it hard to breathe as I direct the driver to the door of my building, not that he seems to need the direction because I swear he's already taking the turns before I even say anything.

But it's impossible for him to know where to go, and it just goes to show how on edge I am about having Henry here.

The cars dotted around the courtyard car park aren't shiny and pretty. There's graffiti everywhere and decades of posters plastering the concrete walls. I'm watching Henry take it all in and waiting for the penny to drop. Everything he thought about me is wrong. There's nothing special or precious about me that's worth his time or money.

The truth is a scary thing. Scarier than being a fifteen-year-old orphan staring at the prospect of foster care. The car comes to a stop in front of my building, and before I can get out, Henry's already rounding the car.

He's still soaked through, with his white shirt stuck to his back, making it impossible to miss the tight muscles corded below it. The powerful lines bulge and coil with his every move. I'm mesmerised by the natural ebb and flow of his athletic body and caught red-faced when he opens my door for me to get out.

There's a tightness around his eyes and jaw that tells me there's a lot he wants to say right now, and that is enough to turn lusty thoughts into a sickening turn of my stomach.

"I'll take you up," he says, grabbing my belongings from the front of the car and walking me through the battered door of the building.

The overwhelming smell of pee makes me cringe as we walk up the first flight of stairs. I haven't noticed it this bad before. By the time we reach Clara's floor, the smell of urine has morphed into fresh laundry from all her air fresheners dotted on the landing and up the stairs leading to my floor.

"This is me," I tell him, pointing at my door with my thumb.

"I gathered." For the first time since I got in his car, the grim lines around his face soften. It's not quite a smile, but there is some humour in his expression.

"What's tickling your balls?" I blurt out.

"I beg your pardon?" His brow raises with a cock of his head to the side as he looks down at me.

Foot, meet mouth. If today could just crawl back to where it came from, I'd be grateful. I don't bother explaining it's just a thing Joe used to say; instead, I go about letting myself in.

"What amused you?" I ask again, turning to find him admiring the dinosaur planters on the ledge of the wall overlooking the courtyard of the flats.

"Your fondness of dinosaurs," he tells me, lifting my violin case as evidence.

"It's more of love by association."

I walk inside, and he pauses on the threshold. It feels odd having him in my space, and even though he seems to have made peace with his surroundings, there's still an air of distaste when he looks around.

"You can come in," I say when he leans forward and puts my backpack down by my shoe rack. "So long as you don't have a cat hidden somewhere that you intend on swinging around…"

"Am I making you nervous?" The question catches me off guard.

Let's be honest, there isn't much about him that wouldn't make a girl nervous. For one, his presence fills every space he enters. Then there's the fact that he's tall and broad and just huge, really. Without heels, I have to crane my neck to look at him properly. Then there's the surly attitude. He's a whole dark, brooding aesthetic on tall, muscular legs. So, yes, he makes me nervous. Henry makes me feel a lot of things.

"Eve?" he calls my name, coaxing me to answer his question.

"Why?

"Because you're rambling. I've never heard you ramble before."

Shit. "I'm sorry, Your Grace," I murmur, shucking off my wet trainers to the side before I stand in front of him again.

"Eve…"

"Why don't you like being called that?"

"Because." He shrugs in reply. The lightness in his face all but disappears, and my insides twist violently at the change in his demeanour.

"Just because?"

"Just. Because."

It's a shame since he suits that title more than any other Duke I've ever known of. Henry has that regal air down to a fine art. Actually, he could be the fine art with all his chiselled edges. But there's more to him and his dislike of his title than he lets on, and I'm curious enough to hope that one day, I might get it out of him. When he's not out of his comfort zone.

"My car will be waiting for you every morning," he states suddenly. "Andrew will take you wherever you need to go. Anywhere you want to go."

"What?"

"Pardon, Eve. You say pardon or excuse me."

I don't tell him that it's how he talks, not me or most people around here. We're straight talking in these parts. No frills. No fuss. You get what you see.

"Andrew will make sure you get around. Safely." He tags on the latter, punctuating the word with a glance at our surroundings.

"I am safe."

"Are you?"

"Yes, I am," I reply, sucking in a breath to steady my temper. It was obvious he felt some kind of way about this place, and while I can understand that it's a shock to his system, I've never once been embarrassed about my roots, and today won't be the day that changes. "I don't need a chauffeur. I can get myself around perfectly fine."

"Don't be difficult."

"Difficult? What are you smoking?" The humour that we shared moments ago is completely gone. If looks could kill, I'd be bleeding out from his cutting glare. But it doesn't stop me. I'm on a fucking roll, and my temper is going with it as I take step after step in his direction, telling him what for. "This is the real world. People don't live in palaces, drinking brandy that's thousands of pounds a bottle. We don't have drivers, or cooks, and people to sniff our arses and tell us how wonderful we are when our egos take a beating."

Like a beast unfurling, he stands taller than ever, watching me without any recognition of what I'm saying. Callousness paints his face with indifference, as though I am nothing. Shit on the bottom of his ridiculously expensive shoes would be more important to him.

"What is wrong with you?" I growl, pushing my hand into his chest when my toes touch the tips of his shoes. "I'm safer slumming it with real people than I'll ever be with your lot. If you don't feel safe here, then you get in your fucking car with your poxy driver and go. Go back to your whorehouse and—" I stop.

A cold hand flattens over mine, still pushing into his chest. It's the first time he's touched me, and the feel of his touch is nothing like I expected. Calluses roughen the pads of his fingers and palms.

Fuck, my train of thought falters at the contact. Slowly, his fingers curl around my hand. Their grasp gets tighter by the second. In a lightning move, he twists my arm, pinning it behind my back as he pushes inside my flat and presses me into the wall.

The sound of his grunting breaths claws through me. Hot and sticky, they coat the shell of my ear when he lowers himself to my level. When I try to shake him off, Henry grips me tighter, the sharp scream of pain from my straining shoulder causing my eyes to water.

"You silly girl," he spits, low and mean. He's going to bruise me. I can already feel my blood pooling beneath my skin. "Don't ever fucking touch me."

I'm going to be left with his mark on me. The rhythm of my angry heart stutters. The thought ebbs to a heated whisper, seeping deep into my bones.

And I still, with his front pressed to my back, hard, muscled flesh grinding me into the wall. His cruelty blankets me. It smothers my senses until I'm completely overwhelmed.

I don't know what possesses me, but I push back into him,

seeking the shuddering strength of his control as his lips ghost over my ear.

I can't breathe when he bites out a gravelled curse. "Fuck."

That low groan lances through me. Strong hips rut into my arse, grinding over me in warning and lurid promise. And I feel him. Big and hard. And wanting.

Suddenly, all the anger in my chest pools between my legs.

"Aaah..." The mangled sigh escapes me.

He's touching me, and I'm feeling him. All of him. His hunger. His need. His lust. Most of all, his rage. I feel it all pulse between us, and it sets me on fire.

Henry's lips trail down to my neck, their warmth tracing my skin in lieu of their physical touch. I'm not sure if he's going to bite me or kiss me. Maybe both?

All I can think is that I want it. I thirst for more. For it all— everything. To unravel him. Break him. Punish him. Torture him. I want to make him hurt. More than that, I want to make him want me until he can't breathe or see straight. All these things that he makes me feel and want, in spite of the way I loathe him. In fact, I want him to hate me to the point that it kills him to desire me.

The loud ringing of his phone cuts through the maddened haze of our closeness. Still, Henry doesn't release me. If anything, he twists my arm harder, using all his weight to push himself off me before he spins me to face him. It all happens so quickly that I can still feel his rough hold on my arm while his hand is already pinning my back to the wall by my throat.

"Talk like that to me again and you won't like what happens to you."

"What are you going to do?" I choke out the words. "Kill me?"

A sneering grin pulls at the corner of his mouth. "One way or another, I will be the death of you." Flexing his grip, his hand hitches up my throat while his thumb strokes along my jaw to my lips. "Your blood will be on my hands, darling."

"Is that a promise?" My sore rasp snaps with the squeeze of

his hand around my neck.

Tears burn my eyes as they drip hotly down my face, much to his pleasure. I can see it shining black and rotten along with my reflection in the depths of his eyes.

"It's a guarantee." With a shove into the wall, he releases me.

The deafening trill of his phone blares again. This time, he doesn't ignore it. Digging his phone from his pocket, Henry walks away as he answers it. Before he leaves, he picks up his fallen jacket in the doorway and looks back over his shoulder at me. "Until tomorrow, Eve."

"Don't count on it, *Your Grace*," I grouse at him through the pulsing burn in my throat.

A tawdry smirk is his only response as he disappears out of my door, and I rush to shut it as quickly as I can, locking the bolt at eye level and securing the safety chain below it.

This is it.

There's no way I'm going back to their cesspit.

I'm done.

EIGHT

Henry

The sound of the papers slapping the desk in front of me is barely audible over the "Ghost Song" playing on the gramophone behind me. The piano and violin entrance me, but all I can think about is Eve. How beautiful she looked with all her rage flushing her cheeks. How good she felt in my choking hold. I could kill her for her smart mouth. But the incessant need in me wants her.

My cock is still hard. My blood is still hot. But my rage is morphing into something I've never felt. Something magnificent. An uncontrollable disease. A sickness that craves her beyond all sense and reason. My darling Eve—she has no mind of the beast she's awoken or the devil she's baited. People like her don't survive monsters like me.

"Are you listening?" Julian asks, his voice crackling with an irate gravel.

"Who's going to tell him?"

All eyes flash to me. Percival. Julian. Simon. The prime minister, Benedict Gladstone—our ally, if not by want, then by necessity and loyalty to his youngest daughter. Georgina married Lord Emsworth, the king's first nephew by his outcast sister, the late Princess Alice. If we burn, he and his family burn with us.

"It's not our business to tell the Prince of Wales that his father is dying. It's for us to stop the press from leaking the information before we're ready for the country to know." Benedict is right, but the Wolfsden Society doesn't have secrets. "Do we know where they got the information from?"

"It's not the kind of information that's easily accessible," Percival tells him, topping up his water. "In fact, it's not accessible at all. All documents relating to the monarch's health are in writing only and kept by his physicians."

Fuck, my father's briefcase.

It makes sense now why my mother wouldn't tell me what was inside it to make the fact that it's missing a dire prospect.

"It will destroy us," she said. Pity, she didn't say why.

Percival glances at me. I know what he's thinking because it's his job to know everything that's happening in these walls and those within them.

"My father knew," I state. There's no point in beating around the bush or trying to pretend that the blame doesn't lie somewhere at his feet—now my feet because, like his title and everything else, I've inherited that too. "His briefcase is missing. I think it was taken when he was killed."

"You think?" Simon asks with a dubious cock of his brow.

"I know. It's not in his office at home or at the university."

"Hospital?" Julian chips in.

"He hasn't been to the hospital in a while, not that I'm aware of, and my mother would have told me if she thought it was there."

Simon laughs at the absurdity of my mother knowing something we don't. He might be her favourite godson, but her loyalty is to her cousin, the king. "What does your mother have to do with it?"

"Nothing, but she noticed the briefcase was gone first. I think she knows too, and she was told not to inform us."

"Right now, none of that matters." Benedict checks through his phone. "We need to address this problem." He gestures down at the draft printouts of the front-page headlines for tomorrow morning. "Priorities first, gentlemen."

"I could put an embargo together, but we'd need to move

quickly." Julian starts making notes in his Moleskine journal. "Once they start printing, we're fucked. Get press relations on the phone, and I'll handle it."

"They'll want a trade," Simon states.

"Well, the press relations people at the palace need to figure that one out. Or…" Julian releases a long hiss before he suggests, "Make it an embargo. Give them a date to print that gives us time to iron out what we want the public to know, and Arthur a chance to deal with it."

"If you think he's going to deal with it, you're living in la-la land." My own remark throws me back to Eve's outburst. She doesn't know shit about anything. All she knows is what she sees—the barest of minimums. "He's going to go off the fucking rails."

"Then it's up to us to stop that from happening or cover it up." Benedict stands, checking his watch at the same time as his phone rings. "I have to go, but keep me abreast of the situation, and for the love of God, make sure it doesn't get outed before we have a way of spinning this with some level of reassurance and sensitivity all round."

"We're on it," Percival reassures him. "But we can count on you to help navigate the situation?"

"I wouldn't be here otherwise. It's probably wise to line up a distraction for the prince."

"We have plenty of distractions here."

"Perhaps one with good press. Maybe something that will endear him to the public."

"What are you suggesting, Prime Minister?" I stand to see him out while Percival and Julian start to make calls.

"Distractions go both ways. The public already knows him as the playboy prince. With the king sick, they will want him to clean up his act. He needs to step up and act like a king or at least give the illusion of it. It's the only way to stop the country turning against us all." We pause in front of the door where the music is loudest. Annoyance paints his face as though he can't think through the noise.

"We like to make sure the walls don't have ears." The irony of my statement isn't lost on me, given the reason why he's here.

"Yes." He smiles, narrowing his eyes up at the chandelier before he takes a step closer and adds, "Don't forget about the fixtures. The replaceable parts are easy to overlook."

"Percival's looking into that too."

"Start with what you have. Don't procrastinate or wait for the next thing. The next incident is always worse than the last." There's a sombreness in his eyes that says his advice comes from firsthand experience. "If you need anything off the books, let me know."

"We are off the books, Prime Minister."

A low scoff rumbles to a short, dry laugh. "I mean *that* that never happened."

"Thank you for the offer, but I'm a firm believer in doing things for myself."

"Very well." He nods, giving the room a final sweep of his stare before he heads out.

"Give your daughter and Freddie my regards," I tell him as he heads down the hallway to meet his assistant at the front desk.

When I close the door, Simon calls me over to where he's standing in front of the fireplace, looking at the portrait of our ancestors. With barely a glance down at the bar cart, he pours us both a drink. Scotch for him and brandy for me.

"We've become soft," he says suddenly, holding out my drink to me. His voice is below a whisper, but the hard expression on his face speaks volumes. "This would've never happened in their day. Treason wouldn't be shrugged off."

Taking a sip of my drink, I mull over his words before I reply. "I'm not shrugging anything off."

"You're not?" He laughs bitterly.

"What the fuck do you want, Simon?"

He turns to me with an irked frown. "I want to be done with this shit so I can get the fuck out of here and get back to my life."

So whatever it is you're planning on doing, get it the fuck done."

The irony of the conversation makes me laugh, even though my insides are twisting in agreement with his ruthless sentiment. We might be above the law in most respects, but we still have to maintain the integrity of the Wolfsden Society. There are rules we abide by.

"The king is dying, Henry," he reminds me. "Our days of operating on the basis of 'What would King George want us to do?' are coming to an end. We know what Arthur would do right now, and as soon as this is out, he'll be the new king in all but the pomp." When I don't say anything, he adds, "Benedict Gladstone knows it, and we both know he agrees. Use what we have, and fuck the lot of them."

"Aren't you meant to be the one mediating our actions?"

"There comes a point where mediation and negotiation are useless, and action is the only way forward."

"And we're at that point?"

Simon looks at me with a glare. "They killed your father. Tortured his driver. I think that line has been well and truly crossed. What's next? Who's next? If it's true that the Republican is in bed with Charles Chapman..." He throws back the rest of his drink. "We need to be fucking them before they fuck us."

"Drain their blood before they drain ours." He nods. "The Chapman Syndicate has eyes everywhere, Simon."

"Maybe they're in here." Gesturing around us, he pulls back as Julian joins us with Percival beside him. "You said there's a traitor in our midst. What if it's not a traitor? What if it's a mole?"

"We do not want to start a war with Chapman's lot," Percival growls. "It's suicide. Charles is a fucking kingpin. He hired hitmen to assassinate the police investigating him. He's got more people in his pocket than—"

"So do we. What's the point of this fucking place if not for resources? Simon's right—we take him out before he helps the Republic eradicate us." I see Percival's point, but he's wrong. This is fight or flight, and we've been here too long to tuck our tails between our legs now. "We hit him where it hurts, and soon enough, the bastard will rethink his ties."

"You're starting a war," Percival sighs.

"But it's been a long time coming," Julian tells him before going back to the desk where we were earlier.

Pulling a leather file from his briefcase, he hands it to me. When I open the file, there are several small photos paper clipped around the edges.

"What's this?"

"The people that run his most lucrative business," he replies.

"Sex trafficking." Simon is practically rubbing his hands together.

"What's in this for you?"

"Well"—he grins—"I know a man who wants his turf back. There's a network of spas that were introduced to the East End soon after Chapman's Soho brothels were shut down by Scotland Yard. Frustratingly, they were run by a Thai madame that took the fall along with some of her muscle, leaving Chapman to edge his way out of town."

"What's in it for you, though?"

"Well, this man I know has lost his business to Chapman, and he's willing to pay well to get it back."

"Excuse me?" Simon might be happy to get involved in shady shit outside of what we do for the Wolfsden Society, but I'm not. As far as I'm concerned, Chapman and whatever pimp he's got on his books can rot in a ditch.

"What?" he bites back at me.

"Pardon. It's fucking pardon," I bark, throwing the file in my hands down on the couch. "What the fuck is wrong with people and their inability to talk properly?"

What. The word rips through me, reigniting my anger from earlier. I shouldn't have walked away. I never walk away. But Eve's messing with my head, and now more than ever, I shouldn't be thinking of her. Except that fucking word put her and her maddening eyes at the forefront of my mind.

What. Fucking. What.

"Mate, you might want to shit whatever's crawled up your arse. You're losing the fucking plot and—"

Before he can finish, I grab the open collar of his shirt, twisting it in my fist. "I'm not your fucking pawn. I'll do what needs to be fucking done to cover our arses, but when I'm done, I'll fucking gut your man too."

"At some fucking point, you'll have to jump off your high horse," he calls at me as I turn away.

"Every man in this world is out for themselves," my father always told me.

He was right.

"Even the ones bound by honour and duty."

He was right too.

Picking up the file from the couch, I head for the door.

James Sloane was always right, and I'm done thinking about honour, duty, and every other fucking thing in my way. I'm done toeing lines.

This is war. My fucking war.

NINE
Eve

Seven in the morning, my alarm goes off as always, except I'm wide-awake. I've been staring at the glow-in-the-dark stars on my ceiling for hours. The sound of squealing tyres from the street racers driving doughnuts around the car park made it too easy to think about Henry's reaction earlier. He didn't hold back his thoughts. Didn't even try to hide his distaste.

Getting up, I pull on the thick cardigan folded over the footboard of my bed. Before I head to the kitchen for my morning cuppa, I catch sight of the bruises around my throat. It's not surprising, but my insides lurch at the sight. I swear I can still feel his hand wrapped around me. So tight. So strong.

"Fuck," I groan, tracing the marks with my fingertips.

Just as he hitched his hand up my throat, I trace my neck up to my jaw. A shiver rolls through me as I swipe my thumb over my lip, raking my thumbnail over it like I've imagined Henry doing. And maybe…maybe I'd bite him.

Another shiver works its way through me when I suck my thumb into my mouth, watching my cheeks hollow as my body aches for something more. My lungs are burning as my breaths shallow. I'm so hot that my skin might shrink around me.

"God…" I sigh, sitting back on my bed, staring at the mirror hanging on the back of my door.

"You're an idiot," I keep telling myself as my thumb con

ues rubbing over my lip and my other hand strokes up my thigh. It's too soft and too small, but I can pretend. I can imagine Henry's large hand kneading its way up my thigh, leaving more marks like a souvenir. A token of where he's been, how he's touched me.

"No." The protest escapes me when my fingers graze my underwear. It's hot, damp, and... "Fuck!" The light touches feel so good. Too good. But it's not enough.

Not after having felt his body pressed to mine. Hard muscles and chiselled grooves. I don't know much about guys, but I know that he's all man. I know that he's big, and having him inside me...

"Mmm..." A moan escapes me as I dip my fingers under my knickers.

I'm wet. Wetter than I've ever been. Needier than I've ever felt. It doesn't matter how many times I stroke through my slick flesh or how hard I rub myself. None of it is enough. Because it's not him.

Even though I want to hate him, I can't. Even though I shouldn't want him to touch me again, I do. Although I swore I wouldn't go back tonight. That I was done with him and our weird meetings. I'm not.

Every waking thought I've had has led back to this. An overwhelming need that I've never felt. A want that coils deep inside me. So deep that it hurts the more I try to ignore it. I can't sate it even though I've tried and I'm still trying.

My fingers push inside me, stroking and stroking and stroking, harder and faster, as I close my eyes and picture him. My duke. Looking into my eyes. Wanting me. Needing me.

Come for me, darling.

"Yes," I whimper, falling back onto the bed. My legs are wide open, and my body is writhing for more of his rough touch.

The hammering force of my heart against my ribs makes it impossible to catch my breath or myself.

Come, my pretty little whore.

Yes, Your Grace. "Ahhh..."

ALEXANDRA SILVA

I'm getting hotter. My body is getting tighter. *Holy Christ*, I can't take it as my insides spark and my entire being implodes. My breath rips out of my lungs over and again.

Good girl. The words echo and echo, and satisfaction seeps deep. His voice roots itself in my bones, so good that I hate myself for needing him so much.

It's there. Just like he said it would be. Henry's car is parked outside the door to my flats. The black sedan comes to life the second I step outside. I stand there gaping at it in disbelief. Of course, I should've known he meant it and that nothing I said would sway his resolve. Henry isn't the kind of man that takes no for an answer, but I'm not giving him any answer right now.

Pulling my backpack over both shoulders, I walk past it. And I continue walking as my phone rings. The tone sounds angry compared to its usual trill. Maybe it's because I know it's him. Perhaps it's my guilty conscience. Last night, this morning, and every time in between that I touched myself to thoughts of the Duke of Gloucester. To the memory of his angry touch and hungry stare.

Looking over my shoulder as I make my way to my bus, I find the car following steadily behind me. The driver, Andrew, has his sunglasses on even though today's weather isn't much better than yesterday's.

At least there are no thunderstorms in the forecast. I breathe a sigh of relief that's cut short when my phone rings again. I could ignore it, but I know that he'll just keep ringing. In fact, he probably has someone on hand to redial my number for him until I pick up. He's that rich and that obnoxious. But somehow, the thought makes me smile.

I'm not the only one incapable of staying away.

Henry's thinking about me as much as I'm thinking about him. I hope that it's torturing him as much as it's aggravating the crap out of me.

"Oi, Cinders!" I pause as Alfie stops on the opposite side of the street. "Get in!"

Andrew stops his crawl as I debate whether to keep going or to take Alfie's offer of a lift. When my phone rings again, it makes the decision for me.

"No," I answer the call as I cross the street and get into the Corsa.

"Get in the car, Eve." The gritted edge to Henry's voice makes me shiver as I look over at Andrew and notice him taking a photo.

"I have a ride."

Alfie gives me a curious look, to which I reply with a smile. I feel it shake when Henry growls back down the phone. "Don't fuck with me."

There's something in the depths of his voice that gives me pause. Something's wrong; I feel it deep in my gut. Maybe this isn't the right time to give him the proverbial finger, but I've made my decision. Now, I'm committing to it.

"I wouldn't dare, Your Grace," I mutter into the phone before ending the call and buckling myself in.

"Your Grace?" Alfie laughs, pulling a U-turn that pushes my innards all up into my throat.

"Jesus! You're never going to get your actual licence if you drive like a bleeding maniac all the time. Not to mention that you're going to end up getting hurt." I'm hugging my backpack and squeezing my legs around my violin case to stop myself from jostling all over the place.

"Who was that on the phone?" he asks me with a half-cocked brow.

"No one." It couldn't be further from the truth, and he's already made me admit as much.

"No one, yeah? That must fucking kill his ego." Alfie bursts out into a wicked laugh, however, his words remind me that eventually, Henry will come find me. When he does, I might not live to regret this.

The pit of my stomach twists with the vibration of my phone. A text. I already know it's from him.

> **Unknown**
> 6pm Tomorrow

I stare at it. *Tomorrow?*

Disappointment sinks deep into my gut. Even imagining his angry fingers tapping out the curt message gives me no satisfaction.

Today is our day.

Why has he cancelled? That thought is overshadowed by the fact he's changed the time too. What if this is it? What if he's ending our time together?

I'm panicking when the phone vibrates again.

> **Unknown**
> You won't like what happens if I have to come get you.

A smile cuts my face at the sight of his bad-tempered words. Maybe I wouldn't like what he does, or maybe it's exactly what I want. After yesterday, there's a burning curiosity inside me about what would happen if Henry completely let go. If all that control holding him together were to unravel. And just as relief eased the knots in my gut, the apprehension of threat causes butterflies to flutter wildly.

6:00 p.m. tomorrow can't come soon enough.

Henry's thinking about me as much as I'm thinking about him. I hope that it's torturing him as much as it's aggravating the crap out of me.

"Oi, Cinders!" I pause as Alfie stops on the opposite side of the street. "Get in!"

Andrew stops his crawl as I debate whether to keep going or to take Alfie's offer of a lift. When my phone rings again, it makes the decision for me.

"No," I answer the call as I cross the street and get into the Corsa.

"Get in the car, Eve." The gritted edge to Henry's voice makes me shiver as I look over at Andrew and notice him taking a photo.

"I have a ride."

Alfie gives me a curious look, to which I reply with a smile. I feel it shake when Henry growls back down the phone. "Don't fuck with me."

There's something in the depths of his voice that gives me pause. Something's wrong; I feel it deep in my gut. Maybe this isn't the right time to give him the proverbial finger, but I've made my decision. Now, I'm committing to it.

"I wouldn't dare, Your Grace," I mutter into the phone before ending the call and buckling myself in.

"Your Grace?" Alfie laughs, pulling a U-turn that pushes my innards all up into my throat.

"Jesus! You're never going to get your actual licence if you drive like a bleeding maniac all the time. Not to mention that you're going to end up getting hurt." I'm hugging my backpack and squeezing my legs around my violin case to stop myself from jostling all over the place.

"Who was that on the phone?" he asks me with a half-cocked brow.

"No one." It couldn't be further from the truth, and he's already made me admit as much.

"No one, yeah? That must fucking kill his ego." Alfie bursts out into a wicked laugh, however, his words remind me that eventually, Henry will come find me. When he does, I might not live to regret this.

The pit of my stomach twists with the vibration of my phone. A text. I already know it's from him.

Unknown
6pm Tomorrow

I stare at it. *Tomorrow?*

Disappointment sinks deep into my gut. Even imagining his angry fingers tapping out the curt message gives me no satisfaction.

Today is our day.

Why has he cancelled? That thought is overshadowed by the fact he's changed the time too. What if this is it? What if he's ending our time together?

I'm panicking when the phone vibrates again.

Unknown
You won't like what happens if I have to come get you.

A smile cuts my face at the sight of his bad-tempered words. Maybe I wouldn't like what he does, or maybe it's exactly what I want. After yesterday, there's a burning curiosity inside me about what would happen if Henry completely let go. If all that control holding him together were to unravel. And just as relief eased the knots in my gut, the apprehension of threat causes butterflies to flutter wildly.

6:00 p.m. tomorrow can't come soon enough.

TEN

Henry

Dark clouds gather over the city as I drive from my loft in Execution Dock to Hush. My mother's voice fills the Defender as it starts to rain, a steady light drizzle that lightly soaks through the air. The summer that promised so much has nothing but disappointment in store.

"Your father gave the king his word. He agreed to carry the burden of his condition, and now it's your turn. You've inherited his burdens too."

"No kidding," I mutter, turning into the gates. "Might be the understatement of the year."

"Sharing your burdens is what will make them easier to bear. Sharing them with someone you trust. Someone that cares for you."

I know where she's leading with the conversation, and hoping to nip it in the bud, I chuckle, "Do you want me to share my burdens with you, Mother? Cry on your shoulder when things get hairy?"

"We both know you've never been a mummy's boy," she replies with a sad laugh that gives me pause as I'm about to get out of the car. "You always did run around after your father, constantly trying to please him."

"And right now, I'm hunting down the people responsible for his murder."

"You'll find them. I have every faith in you." The assurance in her words is all I need to know that she's been talking to Simon behind my back.

"What did he tell you?" I ask, sounding a notch sharper while I get out of the car and lock it behind me.

"He?"

"Don't play silly buggers with me, Your Highness. What did your golden boy tell you?"

"Nothing. Simon told me nothing except that you're handling it." The smile in her voice gives it away that she knows more than she's letting on.

"And?" I nod a silent greeting to the butler that greets me.

"What else did Simon tell you?" I press, taking the stairs up to the fourth floor one at a time, slower than I normally do, as I buy myself time for her to confess.

"You're sending one of your…"

"One of my…?"

"*Girls*," she growls, disgust coating her response. "You're sending one of them behind enemy lines. You're sending a whore to a whore house. Like sending a prisoner home."

"Yes, I am." Clutching the file that Julian gave me the other day, I grin at the anger in her words.

Margaret Dorchester-Sloane is the epitome of grinning and bearing it. You'd sooner bleed a stone than get any real emotion from her. But since her husband died, it seems her walls have cracked.

"Do you want to know why?"

"Because you're either extremely foolish or very certain of the outcome you desire."

"The best way to torture a man is to gut him of his entrails one by one. Take every organ that keeps him living and crush it in front of his eyes." The sound of her audible swallow makes me chuckle. "I'm going to gut the bastards, one organ at a time. Starting with the Republicans' kingpin friend Charles Chapman. I'm going to bleed that cunt dry just as he had my father bled dry."

TEN

Henry

Dark clouds gather over the city as I drive from my loft in Execution Dock to Hush. My mother's voice fills the Defender as it starts to rain, a steady light drizzle that lightly soaks through the air. The summer that promised so much has nothing but disappointment in store.

"Your father gave the king his word. He agreed to carry the burden of his condition, and now it's your turn. You've inherited his burdens too."

"No kidding," I mutter, turning into the gates. "Might be the understatement of the year."

"Sharing your burdens is what will make them easier to bear. Sharing them with someone you trust. Someone that cares for you."

I know where she's leading with the conversation, and hoping to nip it in the bud, I chuckle, "Do you want me to share my burdens with you, Mother? Cry on your shoulder when things get hairy?"

"We both know you've never been a mummy's boy," she replies with a sad laugh that gives me pause as I'm about to get out of the car. "You always did run around after your father, constantly trying to please him."

"And right now, I'm hunting down the people responsible for his murder."

"You'll find them. I have every faith in you." The assurance in her words is all I need to know that she's been talking to Simon behind my back.

"What did he tell you?" I ask, sounding a notch sharper while I get out of the car and lock it behind me.

"He?"

"Don't play silly buggers with me, Your Highness. What did your golden boy tell you?"

"Nothing. Simon told me nothing except that you're handling it." The smile in her voice gives it away that she knows more than she's letting on.

"And?" I nod a silent greeting to the butler that greets me.

"What else did Simon tell you?" I press, taking the stairs up to the fourth floor one at a time, slower than I normally do, as I buy myself time for her to confess.

"You're sending one of your…"

"One of my…?"

"*Girls*," she growls, disgust coating her response. "You're sending one of them behind enemy lines. You're sending a whore to a whore house. Like sending a prisoner home."

"Yes, I am." Clutching the file that Julian gave me the other day, I grin at the anger in her words.

Margaret Dorchester-Sloane is the epitome of grinning and bearing it. You'd sooner bleed a stone than get any real emotion from her. But since her husband died, it seems her walls have cracked.

"Do you want to know why?"

"Because you're either extremely foolish or very certain of the outcome you desire."

"The best way to torture a man is to gut him of his entrails one by one. Take every organ that keeps him living and crush it in front of his eyes." The sound of her audible swallow makes me chuckle. "I'm going to gut the bastards, one organ at a time. Starting with the Republicans' kingpin friend Charles Chapman. I'm going to bleed that cunt dry just as he had my father bled dry."

"Henry..." she sighs with trepidation.

"Isn't that what you want, Mother? Justice? Blood for blood? A life for a life? Isn't that what I promised you?"

"Yes."

"And it is what you want, isn't it?"

There's a stretch of silence as I walk inside the meeting room and put the file down at my seat. The ornately carved table has a large oak tree in the middle with nine branches leading to nine seats, each hand carved with the crest of its wolf. The three other seats are at the roots. They're the only seats that never change—the monarch, the Gloucester, and the Rochester. At one point or another, the others will change according to the ties the monarch chooses to keep closest.

"Answer my question, Mother."

She's taking her time answering me as though she's debating her reply. Or perhaps it's her conscience she's battling with. Either way, I don't have time for it.

"Yes," she finally whispers. "It's what I want. Justice."

"Good." *Because I'm painting this fucking town red.*

Ending the call, I focus on the file, opening it so that my notes stare up at me, along with the ones Julian had already made and the photos.

"Your Grace." A female voice calls my attention. "Mr. Kent said you wanted me to come up."

I glance up to find one of the prettier girls in the club standing in the open doorway. She's in her normal clothes, a floral dress and bright green heels that make her appear almost as tall as I am. Her hair is loosely braided down one shoulder with her long fringe tucked behind her ears while her make-up is very minimal. She looks better like this than when she's draped in gold body chains and her make-up is dark and dramatic.

"Close the door, Elizabeth." Her eyes widen, watching me carefully as I pull out a chair for her and gesture for her to sit once she closes the door. "I have a job for you."

Just as I slip Chapman's photo from the file, placing it in front of her, the door opens, and Simon walks in with Julian traipsing in behind him.

"You started without us," Simon observes, stating the obvious as a way of announcing his presence. Not that any could miss it. He's like a dark shadow looming in the room.

He's not happy with my plan or the fact that it involves him getting his hands dirty. It doesn't matter how well we pull this off, there's always going to be something that goes awry.

"I have other things to do today aside from hiding in my hotel."

"You don't have a hotel," he retorts, sitting in his seat like a king on a throne.

"Neither do you." Blowing out a deep breath, I continue addressing Elizabeth. "That man"—I point at the image in front of her—"is Charles Chapman. He's an East End gangster, the head of the Coster Kings syndicate."

Picking up the photo, she scans it carefully. I give her a moment before I go into the details of her assignment. The girls of the club are our eyes and ears. Lord Varys had his Little Birds, and the Wolfsden Society has Hush.

"You're going to seduce him," I tell her, taking the photo from her hand and putting it back in the file. "He likes a young mistress, and he enjoys parading her like a prized pup."

Elizabeth flashes a worried stare in my direction. "What do you need from me?"

"I need you to tell me his every move, particularly who he meets with. We have reason to believe he's working with the United Republic, so we need you to look out for any of these men." I place a few other photos in front of her. "And where they meet."

"Okay." She nods, examining the photos in front of her the same way she did with Chapman's. "But I don't want to die."

"You won't if you do your job properly. Fuck him, watch him, and report back to us."

"Every Tuesday, Chapman visits the White Hart," Simon tells her.

"His pub in Whitechapel," Julian explains.

"That's where you're going to meet him." Simon continues telling her the plan we have in place while I gauge Elizabeth's reaction.

Her almost white, wavy hair is swept off her face, but she keeps combing her fingers through the loose tendrils as though it's in her eyes. A nervous habit that becomes more apparent the longer she listens.

"Stop." I tell her, cutting off Simon. "If you don't get that habit under control, you're dead."

Slowly her hands drop to her lap, but as Simon continues, she does it again. I don't care if she has a death wish, but I do care about getting the information I need. And I need her for that part. Slipping a fencing sabre from one of the displays, I ignore Julian's questioning stare as I slash the flexible blade through the air.

"Carry on," I tell Simon when he pauses, as confused as Julian.

It's not long as he continues that Elizabeth makes to fuss with her hair again, and I whip her hand with the tip. The whistle of the blade cuts through her surprised scream.

"Carry on," I tell Simon again as Julian calls my name in protest.

"What are you doing?"

"Saving Lizzie's life," I retort, rounding to her other side when Simon continues.

It takes a little longer for her to forget the first whip. But surely, her unpunished hand eventually moves to fuss with her hair. Again, I whip this one with the sabre, harder this time so that there's no surprise and only pain in her garbled curse.

"Keep going," I tell Simon before he pauses.

"You're going to bruise her hands," Julian growls under his breath.

"Better to have bruised hands than a bullet to the head." It was the motto that got me through the intense Royal Marines training: *Better to suffer in preparation than to die in the field.*

91

When I was deployed on the secret missions where we were raiding heavily guarded compounds of terrorists and dictators, I was grateful for all the suffering during training. It saved my life and the lives of the other commandos. And it's why I don't stop or go easy on Elizabeth. If she doesn't want to die, she needs to break her habit.

"From the top," I tell Simon to repeat the plan he's just taken her through again.

I don't care that she's sobbing or that her hands are bruised a deep red; we keep going. Again and again, as many times as it takes for her to learn. Eventually, she stops herself from touching her hair. Eventually, she flattens her hands on the tabletop and takes every word in without any telltale nervous tick.

Elizabeth is listening intently, learning the plan, and although her face is blotchy from her pained tears, she knows as well as I do that she can pull this off. She can look the devil in the face and smile her pretty little lies without getting burnt.

"The tracker?" I ask Julian, putting the sabre back on its stand with the other fencing swords.

"Sterling's on his way up," he informs me as I pour Elizabeth a hard drink and set it in front of her, along with a small silver dish of ice.

"For your nerves and your hands."

"Thank you, Your Grace," she whimpers before drinking down the generous dram in one and then icing her hands.

"Give me Chapman," I say, pulling my handkerchief from the pocket of my jeans and creating a cold compress. Elizabeth takes it without pause. "I'll make it worth your while."

There's a low knock at the door as she nods at me. Elizabeth is a good-looking woman—I can see why the men liked her so much. However, there's nothing all that special about her aside from her Scandinavian looks.

She's just another woman that's walked these floors. I pity her and the fact that this is the best thing she'll ever do. But pity or not, I'm grateful that she's going to aid me in getting justice for my father.

Lord Sterling sets himself up on Elizabeth's other side. Lining up everything he needs on a silver tray, he waits until I'm done before he numbs the area behind her ear with local anaesthetic. Once he's given it time to take hold, he makes a small incision and inserts a tracking chip. His celebrated surgeon hands work swiftly, gluing the incision back together and applying some butterfly strips to reinforce the hold.

"We still have the mistress problem to think about," Julian tells me as I prepare to leave.

"I thought about it," I reply. "And I'm dealing with it."

I've gotten my hands dirty and bloody many times before. Enough that the resolution to our problem doesn't faze me. Chapman had his people murder my father and his driver. He took something I loved from me, and now, I'm going to take everything from him. Starting with Martha Tabram, his mistress.

The night is dark and long. With the muggy August air, there's no breeze to blow the stench of the gutters away. Everything is so stagnant here, including time.

"Come on," I mutter at my watch as the seconds tick past slower than erosion.

My grip on the flick knife tightens as I continue etching the tip along the pearlescent face of the button in my hand. *W.* For wolves and the war that we're about to wage on the Coster Kings and on the United Republic.

There's a rattle of shutters as the rollers of the Victorian warehouse entrance open. Pocketing the button and the flick knife into the front pocket of my hoodie, I take out my Glock and screw on the suppressor while watching for the mistress' guards. I've watched them patrol this place for the past few nights.

Dumb and fucking Dumber don't know the first thing about

protecting themselves, let alone a charge. They spend more time on their phones and smoking than they do looking out for danger.

Fucking imbeciles.

They're first to come out, cigarettes lit and making enough noise that when I follow the shadow of the commercial bins to the back of Chapman's pub, they can't hear the scuff of my rubber soles on the loose gravel.

"I need a piss," he tells his buddy, checking his watch like I've checked mine the past three hours while I waited for them to surface from their hole.

"Hurry up," the other groans. "I need to go too before the delivery gets here."

Fuck, I need to make this quick. I breathe out the adrenaline-spiked air filling my lungs with every deep hammer of my pulse. It's not my first rodeo. This is what I do. Still, there's always that last pull of morality before I make my move. The point of no return.

Elbowing the side of the large bin, I watch Chapman's goon approach to inspect the noise. As I'm about to pull the trigger on him, the alarm of their car suddenly blares, and he turns his back to me.

A cat. The scoff pushes out of me, propelling me forward as I slam the grip of my sidearm into the base of his skull. There's barely a sound as he collapses down on himself into the damp ground.

The night is quiet.

The dark is calm.

There's peace in the stillness around me. For a brief second, at least. That first hit is the most cathartic. It releases the pent-up tension, opening the cage doors for the monster to come out and play. It is freedom.

Stepping over his listless form, I slip the gun back into the holster beneath my hoodie and follow the shadowed path to the warehouse.

There she stands. The perfect prey. The first piece of my retribution. A harlot that sells innocent girls to the highest bidder.

Mercy, the voice in my head reminds me of the syringe in my pocket. I could numb her last moment on this earth. It would make it easier for me, but easy seems a cop-out. There's no reward in easy, and my father certainly didn't get it that way either. And neither will she.

Gripping the knife in my hand, I flick the blade out, wrapping my arm around her mouth so that her scream is muffled, and she falls back into me as I drive the blade into her side. The smothered screams gurgle as her lungs fill with blood, and I drag her back into the shadows.

Hot blood coats my hand before the metallic-tinged air fills my lungs. And I see him then—my father.

Mercy, the voice says again. *Mercy.*

It was the one thing he hammered into me. No matter how brutal his lesson was, mercy was somehow his form of redemption. I don't know about redemption, but retribution is the one thing I'm certain of as I drive the knife again and again into the strumpet's flesh. With one last slash, I slit her throat, allowing her body to hang long enough that its weight almost tears through to her spine.

There's only one thing left when she's limp. Pulling the button from my pocket, I shove it into her mouth. My pulse is roaring. My blood is boiling. My entire being is vibrating as I watch her body drop to the ground. Life is hanging on by a fraying thread as I walk away.

One down...

ELEVEN

Eve

The candlelight flickers in the darkened bathroom. I breathe in the warm almond-scented air and allow it to relax me deeper into the water. The rehearsal for the end-of-term showcase ran late, making me grateful that Henry moved our time together to tomorrow evening.

I miss him. I miss the short bursts of conversation he strikes up in between the music. Oddly, I even miss watching him work at the coffee table in his suite. Ridiculously, I miss our silences too. They're heavy, like a weighted blanket that envelops you. An overwhelming ache flutters in my heart.

Maybe he misses me too. The thought whispers softly, trying to soothe the longing inside me. That unrelenting yearning to feel his touch, his breath on my neck, his fingers squeezing my flesh. The savage bite of his words as he threatens to tear me apart. But mostly…*mostly*, I long to feel his weight over me again. The unforgiving hardness of his body pressed into mine.

God, I want him. I want him so damn much that my need for him suffocates me.

The ringing of my phone in my bedroom jolts me up in the water. Pulling a towel from the radiator next to the bath, I get myself out of the bath and wrap it around me as I race to my room, practically tripping over my own feet in the hopes that it's him and that he wants to see me.

"Unknown" flashes brightly on my screen, and before the call goes to voicemail, I answer. Excitement swells in my chest as apprehension squeezes it tight.

I can barely get words out as I whisper, "Hello?"

A deep breath rasps down the line. The sound of sirens in the background is jarring. They're too loud. Too close. And panic unfurls deep inside me, making it impossible to catch my breath or think past the sudden assault of fear.

"Hello?" I call into the phone. "Henry? Is that you?"

I know it's him. I feel it in my gut and in every fibre of my being, as though we're somehow connected. My body hurts, and my head throbs with an unrelenting scream.

There's another deep rasp that I hardly hear past the blood pounding in my ears before the call dies. My first instinct is to call back, but there's no number. I can't call or text.

What if something's wrong?

I'm not sure why Henry would call me if something's the matter. But the feeling doesn't go away. If anything, it grows the more I force myself to ignore it.

By the time I've dried myself and I'm about to put my pyjamas on, I'm a head case of nerves and dread. Before I can talk myself out of it, I put on an outfit that I know will be all right for the club—a black tube dress with a high neck that covers the marks on my neck and black chunky-heeled boots that are easier to walk in than the shoes I normally wear to the club. As I head for the door, I check my backpack to make sure everything I could need is inside.

The block is eerily quiet as I take the stairs down quickly. Clara's place is so quiet that it seems wrong. I put the feeling down to my already edgy nerves that have me chasing the stairs down faster when I go through the darker spots. As I run out the door, I notice the sedan parked right opposite me.

Since Andrew will take me anywhere, I get in, much to his surprise from the raise of his browns in the rearview mirror.

"Do you know where he is?" The question bursts from my

lips before I even think of greeting him. "Umm, sorry. Hi? Good evening?" I'm not really sure how to greet him now that I think about it.

"The Duke?" he asks me in return.

"Yes. Him."

"I don't keep His Grace's diary, miss." There's a terse edge to his reply that gives me pause. However, before I can say anything, he asks me, "Where would you like to go?"

"Can you take me to him?"

With a deep breath, Andrew starts the car. He starts crawling away from my building at a snail's pace. "Like I said, Miss Cameron, I don't keep the Duke's diary."

Okay. "Hush. Please take me to Hush."

Without a word, he speeds up. The drive is unnervingly quiet. He's watching me in the mirror, the same way I'm watching him—warily. I think he's mad at me from his cumbersome inhales and exhales every time our eyes meet. Or maybe he doesn't like me. I don't know, and right now, I don't care either.

The car has barely come to a stop when I jump out and run up the front steps to the club. I almost fall through the threshold as the door opens before I knock.

"Miss Eve." The butler smiles at me.

I wave at him as I start up the stairs, breathlessly taking up the second and third flight so that my head is fuzzy and my throat is ripping raw when I reach the top.

Holy shit! Either I'm unfit as hell, or that's a lot more stairs than usual. I'm a panting mess, folded over so that my hands are braced on my knees. Desperately, I try to catch my breath before I head to the suite.

A pair of brown leather brogues appear ahead of me before he speaks. "You shouldn't be here, Miss Cameron."

Flashing my eyes up, I catch the man's hard stare. Icy blue. So cold that I'm frozen to the spot even as he attempts to turn me around. It takes me a moment to remember his name from our encounter a little over a month ago in Percival's office.

"Go home."

"Where's Henry?"

His brows furrow, morphing his austere expression into an irate sneer before he tells me, "Not here."

He's lying. My dad always told me that not saying enough is as telling as saying too much. Aside from that, I know Henry's here. I feel the electricity of his presence in my bones.

"Go, Home, Eve. *Leave.*" Julian takes a commanding step towards me. He's so naturally frosty that I can't stop myself from backing away a couple of feet so that I'm on the edge of the top step.

"Turn around," he instructs through gritted teeth.

This is as far as I go, though. Steeling myself, I pull my shoulders back and stare him in the eyes. If I can deal with Henry's anger issues, I can definitely deal with this guy's authoritarian glower.

The agreeable part of me fleetingly considers doing as he's ordering me, but I've been here before with Julian. I have a feeling that if he gets too close, the outcome right now will be the same as last time. And so, I dig my heels in, curling my toes in my boots as if that will give me extra stay-put power. I hope it does because I'm precariously balancing on the edge of the tall flight of stairs with nothing to catch my fall and a gene fault that could make this game over for me.

"No." I shake my head, emphasising my reply as his chest almost touches mine.

Our wills battle it out between us in the silence. He's considering his options, and I'm hoping that this standoff goes my way.

"Do as you're told," the order booms from behind me, sending my heart into a frenzy.

I'm hot, I'm cold, I'm everything in between. Most of all, I'm elated that the feeling in my bones was right. Maybe I'm not so crazy for believing that there is something in me that is not just attuned to him but that recognises his existence.

Excitement makes it hard for me to breathe as I lean to the

side, slowly deviating my stare from Julian to where Henry is standing in the hallway leading to the room where I first laid eyes on him. Exactly like that night, there's a darkness in his eyes that twists my insides. A pull that I can't resist as I step around Julian and go to him.

Something's happened. I don't just feel it in my bones; I can sense it with every bit of my DNA. There's violence burning in his eyes when I stop in front of him.

Rough hands grip my hips, pulling me flush to him even as he tells me, "Get out of here."

"You called me," I murmur, hovering my hands over his chest while I shake my head at his command.

A shudder steels his entire body when my fingers brush over the loose cotton of his black T-shirt. He smells of soap, like he's just washed. As if our bodies aren't already touching, I step deeper into him, enough so that his hands grudgingly claw to my arse.

"Turn around and walk out, or I drag you out myself," he growls, leaning over me so that his lips are close enough that I can taste the vicious edge of his words as they cut through me.

This man might be the biggest arsehole in the world, but I know firsthand how these military men work. Their hard shell is impenetrable until it cracks. Then they're just like any other human—vulnerable.

"Go for it," I bite back, low enough that the words die a whisper over his jaw. The dark stubble makes my fingers burn with the urge to feel its scratch, the same consuming graze that I still feel ghosting the curve of my neck since yesterday.

Henry's hold on my arse tightens, and the squeeze of his hands sends a frisson of heat and pain through me that causes me to whimper. Before I can brace myself, he heaves me up the length of his body, throwing me over his shoulder as he starts towards the stairs. A muscled arm wraps around my thighs while his other hand fists my dress at my lower back.

Every step is punctuated with an angry breath. Every jolt threatens to crush my lungs. Still, I don't fight or argue. He called me. I know it was him. It could only be him. The devil called, and I came running. I came to him because it's what he wanted. It's the reason he called me.

My blurred surroundings come to a halt. Suddenly, Henry drops me to my feet with a shrug of his shoulder. There's a savage cruelty in the way he shakes me off him and spins me to face the wall of the alcove at the top of the first flight of stairs. The draped curtain keeps most of the light out as his front presses to my back, pinning me with his weight.

Little does he know that this is exactly what I was yearning for when he called. His body on mine. His weight over me. That in his stubborn spite, he's giving me what I want.

"Will you ever do as you are told?" he barks into my ear with a hard tug of my hair as my nails claw at the silk-lined wall.

Henry doesn't give me the chance to reply. Wrapping the length of my long hair around my throat, he pulls it taut so that I can barely pull a rasp of air into my lungs. My eyes blink up in a sidelong glance that catches a slither of his seething expression.

"Is this what you want, Eve? To be fucked like a common whore for everyone to see?"

I should shake my head. I should fight him. Scratch and claw at him until he releases me. Instead, I lift my face to his, twisting so that the rope of hair strangles me harder. I've never felt as alive as I do right now or as close to death as when he glares deep into my stare.

"Is it what you want, Your Grace?" I push the hoarse words from my mouth, barely squeezing the air through my constricted airway. "To fuck me?"

The dark rake of his gaze skims over my face as he spins me to face him. My hair loosens around my neck a fraction, allowing me to gulp down lungfuls of the hot air between us. If ever there was a beast in this world, I am looking at him. His hackles are up, and his teeth are bared in a dangerous glower that contorts his far-too-beautiful face with a furled brow.

Oh, my heart.

Oh, my stupid, idiotic, senseless heart.

I can't contain it as it batter-rams into my ribs, trying to burst from my chest to his. Maybe that's the only way he can have a heart—by stealing mine.

"Why are you here, Eve?" He blows out a frustrated, defeated breath.

His large, rough hands bracket my jaw, lifting me to the tips of my toes so that we're face to face when I reply, "You called." Denial flickers across his face, but before he can verbalise it, I tell him, "Maybe you're an entitled bastard, but you're not a liar. Are you?"

"You don't know what you're doing." Henry tightens his grasp on my jaw as he pulls in a long breath. "Tonight is not the night for you to be here. To be near me."

"I came…" I murmur over his lips as my hands flatten to his chiselled stomach. "I came because you called."

"And?" he asks, the indifference in his voice wavering.

"And I couldn't stay away. I-I just can't, and I don't really know why. It's just—"

"Just." Henry repeats the word as though it has some hidden meaning I'm not aware of.

"A part of me," I whisper, unsure if I should be admitting this to him. He'll probably think I'm some crazy, psychopath stalker he's got to cut loose, but it's the truth. I've never been a liar, and I'll never be a liar. So, with great trepidation, my hands clamber up his torso. "Something inside me recognises something in you, and I can't stay away."

Stroking my fingers lightly over his jaw, I relish the scratch and prickle of his thick stubble.

"My soul," I breathe as he comes closer. Perfectly moulded lips hover over mine. "Your soul. I don't know, Henry. I—"

I'm cut short when he trails his nose to my hair and his lips press to my cheek. Hard and unyielding, just as I imagined them to be. After this one chaste kiss, nothing will ever feel as good or as right. One kiss from him, and my heart beats like it's living a thousand lives all at once. I'm ruined and doomed, and there is nothing that could be enough. I will take whatever he gives me, how he gives it, without question or reservation. I'm greedy and gluttonous for him. I want all his kisses and his never-ending touch. I want him more than my yearning soul can bear.

"Fuck," Henry hisses over my burning skin. His lips trail to my ear as he tells me, "You don't belong here, darling."

Darling. Just like the first time he called me that, my heart stutters, skipping a beat or two before it trips and stumbles back to a fast-paced thrum that echoes at the back of my throat.

Every word in my vocabulary disappears, leaving me speechless, completely wordless as he continues to hum into my ear, "My sweet, darling Eve. You're too good…too pure." I shake my head, and he pulls back a tad so that our stares kiss while he nods affirmation of his statement and his thumbs stroke over my lips. "You're too young. Too fucking young for this."

For him. That's what he means because he's lived life like I never could. He's fought in war and seen the worst of humanity. I wish I'd known all of this that first day we met or that he had told me then instead of me reading it all online. If we could talk about more than my music or about my day, he would realise that I'm not too young or pure or whatever it is he thinks about me.

But if that's how he feels, then why… "Why did you call me?"

His face falls at my question. Pity, guilt, disgust, regret…so many knives to my foolish heart that I can't think past the pain to stop myself from welling up.

"Why?" I choke out as he braces himself over me, a hand pushing into the wall on either side of my head.

"Because I needed to hear your voice." An ugly, teary snort blusters from deep in my chest. "I had to hear your sweet voice at a distance because the possibility of crossing the line with you is too much, Eve." He breathes out my name like a curse. "And it can never happen."

Heavy tears drip angrily from my eyes, leaving bereft tracks down my face. It shouldn't matter. He shouldn't matter. This was always a means to an end. I do this job, and I get the credit and reference I need to help bolster my chances into a decent career. It was never meant to be this. I was never meant to care. And he was never meant to mean anything. Yet here I am. My heart is breaking into smithereens in front of his eyes. My heart, which had been bruising and battering itself to get to him moments ago, can't seem to find any kind of rhythm.

Pushing onto my tiptoes, I crane my face as close to his as I can, licking my lips as I inch them closer to his. He kissed me; why can't I kiss him? Maybe it's all he needs to see and feel that I can be what he needs no matter what my age says about me.

"No," he snaps, pushing off the wall and taking a couple of steps away from me. "No, Eve. You're a child," Henry states. It's a slap in the face that wakes my anger. "You shouldn't be here, and it's time you leave."

"Why?"

"Go home."

"Okay." The indignant hiss chokes from my lips as I stand tall and drag in an agonised breath.

If I can just stop my tears for a second so I can leave with at least some of my dignity, I'd be grateful. Stepping around him, I pause at his side, lifting my stare to his in a show of defiance.

"I'm not coming back," I tell him as I make to leave.

"Yes." His hand flattens to my stomach, stopping me from walking away. "Yes, you will. You'll return tomorrow like you were meant to."

"I won't."

"You will, and we will carry on. Three nights a week, you'll play for me. I'll listen and watch, and it's how it'll be. No touching. No—"

"Goodbye, Your Grace," I cut him off, pushing past his hand and walking away.

Everything is a blur. The surroundings that have grown so familiar become a treacherous road that I can't walk quick enough.

Although I know that he's right, I will come back tomorrow. I keep telling myself that it's not because of him. I'm not returning for him. It's for me. This is a means to an end, and that's all it will ever be.

And just like that, I lose another piece of myself to him. Henry Sloane. The Duke of Gloucester has made a liar of me.

TWELVE

Henry

The gates to St. James's Palace open slowly, allowing me another glimpse at the front-page headline of this morning's *Telegraph*.

WHITECHAPEL MURDER, AGAIN!

East London has seen another woman brutally murdered in its backstreets four months on from the fatal attack on Emma Elizabeth Smith. Miss Smith was a North London resident and mother of two. She died in hospital on April 4TH, two days after sustaining serious injuries as she left a known brothel in the late hours of the night. Although no suspects were named, it is believed that Miss Smith was set upon by vigilantes who have been protesting the presence of the establishments in the area.

Last night's attack heralds calls for police to take action. The unnamed female victim is said to have been leaving the White Hart pub late in the evening when she was savagely attacked to her death. Police are yet to release the identity and further details of...

The tentative knock on my window interrupts my reading. *Emma Smith*. The name is familiar enough that it gives me pause as I establish whether the connection to the mistress will complicate things for the Society. Last night was messier than it should have been, but maybe this vigilante issue will help cover up our involvement. Either way, with his mistress dead, Chapman will be on the lookout for a replacement, and Elizabeth is ready.

After I've parked, I grab the newspaper and the file underneath it before heading inside the Prince of Wales' residence. As a child, I remember spending a lot of time here with our parents. Before Arthur was the heir apparent, and our biggest concern was who would win whatever competition we thought of between us. As there was no body of water at this residence, fencing was the main sport here. After we tried bringing back jousting a few times, we were banned when we almost took each other out for good.

"Good afternoon, Your Grace," the footman greets me as I head up the stairs to Arthur's apartment.

Since my father was killed, security has been amped up around the Prince of Wales. Or maybe it's the fact his father is dying and wants to protect his heir. Either way, it feels odd having security inside the house as well as outside. Knowing Arthur, this will be driving him crazy.

"Afternoon." I nod down at him as I reach the landing for the first flight of stairs.

"His Highness has…*a visitor*," he tells me with a telling raise of his brows.

Of course he does. "Thank you for the warning," I say before I continue up to the top-floor apartment overlooking the gardens and St. James's Park across The Mall.

It's oddly quiet as I walk inside the private living quarters. Despite the light drizzle outside, the windows are open, allowing the cool air to circulate around the open-plan living space. While I wait for Arthur to appear, I make myself a strong coffee and sit in the window seat with my newspaper.

The article doesn't say much more on my crime. Percival made sure the chief of police silenced the investigation before it even started. But a part of me is disappointed that all that's said is speculation. I'm a man that owns his actions; I don't pass my blame on to others.

Taking a sip of my coffee, I try to push down the frustration of it. In the end, all that matters is that I'm closer to justice, and the Society is closer to getting a spy in the United Republic camp. Taking them down is the only way we're going to survive when Arthur finds out that the king is dying. The people's king. The only thing stopping the United Republic's poison from taking hold.

My phone rings as I'm about to go knock on Arthur's door. I can't wait around for him all afternoon. I have plans, and after last night, I have every intention of making sure Eve turns up. Even if I have to go get her myself.

Calling her was a mistake. It was wrong and reckless. But I was so out of touch that I needed something desperately to ground me. I needed something that would pull me out of my blind rage. And it was her. *Someone.* My beautiful Eve.

"Andrew?" I answer, getting up from the window seat and taking my empty cup to the kitchen. Everything is sparkling, almost new from lack of use.

"We need to talk. Urgently," he stresses.

"What about?"

"I think this would be better in person."

Andrew was one of my men. We've gone on countless missions together, blown up some impressive hideouts and executed terrible men. There's no one else that I would trust so implicitly with my life as I trust him. In a way, I'm glad he was too fucked up to pass the mental health assessment. There comes a point when you see so much with your eyes open that you can't unsee it when your eyes are closed.

"Tonight?" he asks.

The urgency in his voice sets me on edge. "Is Eve all right?"

A bitter laugh escapes him before he replies, "Yes."

"Did she get in the car?"

"No."

"You followed."

"I'm following your orders."

"What does that mean?"

"It means I'm following the girl and tracking down the briefcase," he snaps back at me. It's obvious something is wrong, and before I hang up, I agree to set up a meeting at Hush.

There's a stretch of silence that I try to fill with something other than concern for him. I stare out at the treetops, watching as the drizzle picks up. However, not thinking about the conversation with Andrew means there's only one other thing on my mind. Eve.

I picture Eve's small frame swamped by her wet clothes. Shivers wracking her body. A body that felt all too good pressed up to mine. The heat of it too fucking good to ignore. The suppleness of her curves too perfect to resist. And my cock remembers the feel of her plump arse rocking back into me all too well.

I could have fucked her then. Sated my cock with the heat of her wet cunt. I could have fucked the insolence right out of her, along with her screams for mercy. Fucked her hard until I was buried so deep inside her that she would bleed for me.

The thought sends a shudder through me. It's all I've thought about since I laid my eyes on her—every way I can fuck her. Every way I can break her. Every way I can make her bleed with words and cries and my nails clawed deep into her flesh.

The air in my lungs congeals at the thought. My blood is pounding white-hot through me, causing my cock to ache and strain in the confines of my jeans. The desperation of my body for her is unrelenting as it weeps and burns for her.

"What are you staring at?" Arthur's sudden question draws me back to reality.

I adjust myself, tugging the hem of my Henley as low as it will go. Not low enough to hide that like a pubescent boy, I'm hard as a rock at the thought of a girl.

Arthur gives me a questioning stare as I shrug. "Nothing."

"You made the front-page headlines again." He nods at my

newspaper on the kitchen counter while he finishes buttoning up his shirt and fixing his sex-rumpled hair.

"I'm only responsible for one," I say, grabbing the file beneath the newspaper and following him back to the lounge area.

"Are you all right?"

The question surprises me, catching me so off guard that I don't know how to answer. The truth is that for a brief moment, I wasn't. For a brief moment, I wanted to go back and cut the bitch to pieces. There's no doubt in my mind that I would have if Eve hadn't answered her phone.

With a nod, I shake the thought out of my mind as I focus on Arthur. Quietly, he meanders to the drinks cart in the corner of the white-painted room. He seems so out of place in the midst of the flowery decoration. It's hard to take him seriously sometimes when we're sitting on the emerald-green couches, surrounded by the matching drapings with purple, red, and gold weaved through them.

"You didn't say you were coming over today." Arthur holds out a drink for me, and as I take it, he adds, "The tailor's coming to fit my suit for the Heroes of Our Lifetime gala thing tomorrow evening."

Shit. "I'd forgotten about that."

"Too busy fucking the violinist." He grins knowingly. Except he doesn't know shit. And the longer I withhold the knowledge of his father's illness from him, the deeper my betrayal of my oath to him goes.

I swore on my life that I would always protect him, in front of God and the Wolves. I promised that I would go beyond what his state bodyguards are lawfully able to do in order to protect him. Withholding the truth from him is going to cause him more harm than good. Yet here I am, debating if I should hand him the file in my hand or not.

"Nice," he sings out. "Her pussy's that good that she's got you daydreaming."

"I'm not fucking Eve."

"Sure, I believe you. I mean, she's only in your suite every night."

"Three nights a week, and I don't touch her." It sounds odd when I hear myself say it, but I don't care.

"So what the hell do you do if you're not fucking her?"

I take a sip of my brandy and shrug. "I listen to her."

"You know," he smirks at me, "sometimes mouths are meant for fucking. And if I recall, she's got a lovely mouth with rather inviting lips."

"I listen to her play, you pillock."

That seems to be the best joke he's heard in a very long time with the way he bursts out laughing. The bastard even snorts and spits some of his whisky over me. "Dear God, what on this green earth is wrong with you? The girl is young, attractive...and I've heard violinists have strong hands."

Sucking in a deep breath, I ignore the lewd expression lighting up his face. It's really hard to keep to my oath when every fibre of my being is twisting with the need to smack him one in the teeth.

"If you don't want her—"

"Finish that sentence and you won't ever have to worry about the weight of the crown on your gormless head. I'll make *you* the front-page headline of every national newspaper."

The room darkens suddenly as a deluge pours from the heavens, and just as I'm about to check the weather app on my phone, a crack of lightning fills the room, followed by the rumble of thunder.

No doubt Eve won't have an umbrella with her. At some point, she probably read somewhere that someone died after lightning struck theirs, and that would be it. No more umbrellas. The girl is naïve and unreasonable enough that she'd rather get doused instead of take precautions. Just as she'd rather risk my anger instead of getting in the fucking car I sent for her.

"What's going on, Henry?" Arthur asks, topping up my drink before he sits on the other side of the sofa. "You got that thunderous, I'm-about-to-slit-a-throat look on your face."

"Surprise, surprise. Another shit joke comes out of your mouth."

He grins. "I'm nothing if not full of surprises."

"You're full of shit."

"You're full of psycho tendencies," he retorts, so quickly that it hits me out of nowhere. "But…each to their own and all that nonsense."

"Everything I do is to keep you and the future of the monarchy safe."

"I was teasing you," he tells me. But we both know he wasn't. That was an off-the-cuff, unfiltered thought. Arthur said what everyone else thinks. "Seriously, why are you here?"

The folder in my hand is heavy, the information inside the country's most guarded secret. One that he needs to know for his own good. But there's a sliver of pity in his eyes when he waits for me to speak that reminds me of the hollow bleakness inside me. It makes me wonder what it would've been like to live with my father's impending death on my shoulders. It occurs to me that maybe bearing the weight of this secret for him is the best way to protect him from himself.

"I'm not going to stay the duration of the gala tomorrow."

Arthur gives me a pointed look. "Why?"

"There's somewhere else I need to be."

"And who's going to babysit me?"

"Julian."

"Great. You're going off to not fuck the violinist, and I'm stuck with the eternal widower." His laugh is peeved and exasperated at the same time.

"I'm not seeing Eve tomorrow." I take another sip of my drink, stopping short of his refill. There's enough going on without me getting caught driving under the influence. "It's Wolfsden business."

"Then why don't I know about it?" The cock of his brow tells me he's going to keep pushing for the answer he's looking for.

"Sometimes, you don't need to know everything." The double meaning of my statement isn't lost on me, but he nods.

"Why Julian, though?"

"Because Simon is still avoiding his family."

"At least it's not one of the old guys. Last time you couldn't go to a function with me, I had the Right Honourable and Gallant Samson Roves hitched to my arse the whole night. Do you know what that did to me?"

"I dread to think." Roves is a staunch military man. He was lieutenant general of the Royal Marines when I first served under him, before I was appointed captain general. Fun isn't in his vocabulary, or at least not Arthur's kind of fun. "When I was under his command, his idea of a good time was cling filming the toilets beneath the seats."

"He was not that jestful when I was landed with him." He groans, just as another flash of lightning fills the room and thunder rolls through with it.

"The poor guy had just found out his wife was fucking his deputy." Checking my watch, I realise that it's almost four thirty. Eve will be leaving the conservatory soon, and she should be heading straight to Hush. I know she's likely to be cursing me for moving the time, but she has no need to go home and get changed today. Not with what I have planned.

"I need to head off, but I'll meet you here tomorrow, and we can convoy to the event."

"Why did you actually come here?" Arthur gets up as I do, following me to the door of his apartment. "You barely touched your drink, and you had nothing to tell me besides that you aren't doing your job."

Clutching the folder tighter in my hand, I roll my eyes at his remark. "You can be such a little bitch. Do you want to cry about it too?"

"Maybe I do. You've just wasted some fucking great brandy."

"I'm driving myself today."

"Yes, I heard you've had Andrew stalk the girl for you." The impish grin on his face has me fisting my hand, ready to shut him up at his next quip. "It sounds to me like you should fuck her and get her out of your system or…"

"Or?"

"Or accept that you *like her* like her."

"That's not how it is. I enjoy her music."

"Her music," he chuckles with a shake of his head.

"Yes, Eve's really rather good."

"Maybe I'll make her a spot in my father's birthday concert lineup."

"It worries me when you offer to do something nice for a stranger," I tell him as I walk out of the door.

When I'm a few feet away, he calls after me, "She might be my next cousin."

Refusing to let that thought settle, I flip him the bird as I keep walking away.

It's not like that. I might find Eve fascinating and fuckable, but aside from that…she's still just a young girl. A beautiful, talented young girl.

One that I will not touch.

THIRTEEN

Eve

I shouldn't be here, I tell myself for the hundredth time since I walked through the club doors. Starting with the way I look right now—a sodden mess—to what Henry said yesterday. I don't know how we're meant to sit in a room all alone, just carrying on like yesterday didn't happen. At some point, it'll be too much, and what happens then?

The twist of my insides answers my own question. I know what will happen. More than that, I want it to. I just don't know if I can bear waiting for it. Waiting for him to lose control again or for him to accept that there are only two ways this ends. Whatever this is.

One, we walk away for good. Two, we accept the inevitable. It's really black and white, and better than anyone else, I think he'd be the one to understand that.

"Evening, Eve," Percival says with a small smile as he walks down the stairs. He pauses a moment to take me with an amused chuckle. "Did you walk again?"

"No, I got the bus."

"It just decided to pour when you got off."

"Something like that." Not really. I had every intention of walking here from the conservatory. It's not all that far, but halfway here, the heavens opened, and I had no choice but to get on a bus.

Andrew wasn't following me today. After I walked past him outside my flat, I didn't see him again.

"We might have to find you a raincoat before you send him crazy." The smirk on his face makes me laugh. He likes the prospect that my stubbornness gets to Henry.

In truth, it makes two of us. I enjoy getting under his skin. Poking the bear has become the most exciting thing in my life. I just wish that he'd poke back. The thought causes me to blush at my unintended innuendo.

"I'll send up a hot chocolate to warm you up," he tells me as he continues down the stairs, looking back over his shoulder when he reaches the bottom with a beaming expression.

Today, Hush is busier than I've ever seen it. There are suited, important-looking men everywhere and barely dressed girls around them. The sight isn't all that shocking compared to some of the scenes I've seen walking down the street where I live. However, the sounds wafting over the music from the communal room are enough to get my pulse racing. Laugher, moans, and casual conversation bubble around me as I carry on walking up the stairs.

"Here to join us, milady?" A girl stops to look me up and down.

There's an angry twist to her red-painted lips when I smile instead of replying. From her tone and the way she addressed me, I can tell that she doesn't like me. I'm not sure why since I haven't spent any time with the staff at Hush. I come in and go up to the red suite, and when my time is done, I leave. Just like Henry instructed me to.

"I'm sorry." The apology rolls from my lips as she steps in front of me, stopping me from going up the last step.

I'm still on edge from the thunderstorm outside, and a part of me resents my stubbornness for not giving up the ghost and getting in the car with Andrew this morning. I'm wet, cold, and pissed off at myself and the ridiculous British weather.

Today has been a mess of unrelenting thoughts and replays of last night. I've never felt so torn within myself. For hours, I debated not coming today, no matter the consequences. But the truth of the matter is that I can't afford to be jobless. I have rent to pay that barely gets covered by my study grants, along with everything else that I need to keep my head above water.

"You just think you're so much better, don't you?" the girl asks, squaring up to me when I try to go around her.

Tucking myself into the wall, I shake my head in reply as she looks down on me. Close up, the woman looks older. There are age lines around her dark eyes that her eyeliner has run into, making them look deeper.

"I-I'm sorry, I—" I try to step back down one step to give myself room to get away.

Given how Henry and I left things yesterday, causing a scene in the middle of the club is not what I want to be doing right now. People are milling around, flitting from room to room. As though we're invisible, no one looks our way. It's odd how even in the open view of everyone, we feel so hidden away right now.

"The Duke of Gloucester has himself a lady," she sings in a mocking tone while taking a deep curtsey. Her stare flashes to mine, as quick as a snake's bite and just as poisonous. "But you won't be a lady when he's done with you. You'll be like the rest of us."

"Oh, fuck off, Cat," a familiar voice groans before the girl that was serving at the memorial dinner appears. "Leave her alone. Go on!"

"You got yourself a new pet, Mary? A pretty little bitch to train?" A disdainful leer paints the woman's face so that she looks every bit as catty as she sounds. When she steps back, she gives me another top-to-toe scowl before turning to Mary and doing the same. "Suppose you got to keep yourself in their good books. They might drop you otherwise."

Mary doesn't respond. Instead, she watches as Cat saunters away with an exaggerated sway of her hips. From behind, her body is completely on show through the translucent fabric of her red robe.

"Don't worry about that one," Mary tells me when Cat's out of sight. "At some point, her pity stay will run out. Maybe that's why she's got it in for her. The late Duke kept her here as his little spy. He's gone now, and you've taken her place."

"I haven—"

"Like I said, don't worry about Catherine. She's got something to say to everyone."

I smile, not sure what to reply. But I can't help the feeling like I'm on dangerous ground.

"Let me walk you up." Mary threads her arm with mine. Her perfume is so strong that it burns my lungs, but every time I think I have a chance to put a bit of space between us, she squeezes her arm tighter. "You should come for drinks with us one of these days."

"I don't drink."

A deep laugh bubbles out of her. "Oh God, you better start. It makes all of this a lot easier." Mary side-glances at me with a wry face. "It can get very touchy on days like today. It's why Cat's fretting. They always send off those memos out when they're about to get new blood in."

"Memo?" I ask, following her up the second flight of stairs.

"You know, the reminder that we're to keep our mouths shut or else?" She looks over her shoulder with her brows hitched up high, alluding to the *or else*. "If information don't stop being leaked, soon enough, they'll get the bridles out for a lot more than just play, and if that don't work, then they'll turf us out one by one."

A confused chuckle rumbles in my chest at her exaggerated mannerisms and remark. "A bridle?"

"Oh Lordy," she laughs, tugging me up the top step before we head up the next flight of stairs side by side. "It's a popular… *toy* around here."

Although I don't know what she's talking about, I continue chuckling along with her and nodding as if I know exactly what she's saying.

"He'll get it out for you soon enough. Henry Sloane is as dark as his father. At one point, girls started disappearing after they saw to the late Duke, and there was a rumour that he'd fucked them dead."

"Oh," I choke out. All my humour is completely gone because the few times that I met Henry's dad, he was kind to me. It's why I felt compelled to play at the memorial dinner they held for him. It's why I can't bring myself to be scared of his son's mercurial temperament. Still, my heart is pounding in my chest as my mind takes me back to the way he's touched me. The spoken warning and unspoken threat of what he could and would do to me. It's not until now, this conversation, that I really feel as though he would follow through on both.

"The new Duke never fucked here. Not until you. He watches, though. He likes to watch in the dark corners. Especially the prince. He watches the prince like…" She pauses when we reach the Red Suite. The red tassel key is in the lock, and when I open the door, she peers inside.

"What's he like?" Mary asks, staring at the bed as though she's never seen anything like it before.

"I-I d—"

"That's enough gossiping. Don't you think?" The deep voice comes from behind me.

When I spin to look at him, a shiver rakes all the way through me, chilling me past my rain-soaked clothes and pruning skin. His stare bores into mine with a fierceness that has the marks he left on my body pulsating.

"Apologies, Your Grace," she whispers with a deep curtsey.

"Off you go, Mary." He waits for her to be gone before he moves towards me. "No one goes in my room. No one looks inside my room unless I say so. Do you understand?"

It's not like I invited Mary inside or asked her to have a look. Besides, this wasn't something mentioned before. "I didn't know. I—"

"Now you do. Don't let it happen again." Any of the warmth

he had in him yesterday is gone. I'm not even sure he wants me here with the curled-lip glower he's levelling me with.

I nod, watching as he steps forward again while I step backwards. Henry is wearing a dark, long-sleeved top with dark jeans. He looks taller than ever. Oddly, the casual attire makes him look more dangerous with his sleeves rolled up to his elbows, showing thick, corded forearms that taper to strong wrists and large hands.

Henry doesn't stop until I'm in his suite. It smells as good as home, a mixture of him and beeswax polish, along with history. Regal, well-kept history that pulls you back in time the second you're engulfed by it.

The scent fills my lungs, warming my blood and calming my hammering pulse so that I can hear him as clear as the pouring rain outside.

"There's a robe in the bathroom. Get washed," he orders in a plain voice, with his stare roving down my body all the while. "Warm yourself. I'll be back soon."

There's no room to argue as he turns and goes back down the hallway towards the room where his father's memorial was held. Meanwhile, I close the door and go about my usual ritual, where I put everything in its place.

The violin case by the coatrack where I hang my jacket and where my shoes are parked. Moving the chair in the corner close to the bed, I place my backpack next to it. It's important that I know where it is and that I can get access to it at all times. My Desmopressin is in there, and if I get a bad nosebleed or pluck a string hard enough that it causes a bleed, I need to be able to get to it fast.

A nervous energy overwhelms me as I stand by my chair and stare at the door. I'm waiting and waiting and waiting for him. There's a low knock on the door before a maid walks in with a tray in her hand.

"Your hot chocolate, miss," she tells me as she brings me the drink.

As soon as I take it from her, she leaves with a glance at

the bed. Nothing else is said, and I'm left in the silence of the suite with only my thoughts for company. I pace around in circles, holding the sickly sweet drink in my trembling hands as Mary's words keep echoing in my head.

"The new Duke never fucked here. Not until you."

For the first time, it occurs to me that every person in this place thinks I'm in here sleeping with Henry.

Not sleeping.

They believe he's doing to me what the other men do to them. My eyes fall to the bed. It's the first time I truly notice its size and how imposing it is. It's all dark wood and rich red bedding. Silks, satins, and mahogany. Hand-carved scrolls upon hand-carved scrolls.

"I'm not a child," I whisper, trailing my fingers over the carved beast in the centre of the footboard.

A gold ring dangles from its mouth with a scarlet rope wound around it in a three-way knot.

"I wish he'd do more than touch me." I breathe out some of the building disappointment, tracing the elaborate strands of the knot.

He wants to. Henry as much as admitted it yesterday. Besides that, I feel it deep in my gut, in the marrow of my bones. And I want him to. I want him to do things to me that I've never done with a man.

"What part of *get washed* didn't you understand?" I jump out of my skin, almost spilling my drink everywhere, at the sound of Henry's stern voice.

When I spin to look at him, there's a grim sharpness to the lines of his face that causes my heart to collapse into my stomach. A man shouldn't be this beautiful and beastly all at once. It's not natural. It's not human. But it's him. Simultaneously alluring and intimidating.

"You are not washed." Walking towards the bathroom, he scowls down at my soggy ballet pumps with a shake of his head. "Do I have to wash you myself?"

"I'm not dirty." The remark blusters out, taking all the air from my lungs when he faces me again.

Bloody hell, he's a beast.

The fitted black top leaves little to the imagination. There isn't a single muscle on him that isn't cut and sculpted to perfection. If this is apparent with his clothes on, I can only conclude that every naked line is etched deep, and each slab is roped.

Henry's got the airs of a prince, the body of a soldier, and the attitude of a god. A volatile and commanding god that betrays very little mercy or softness, if he actually has any.

"Do you want to catch a cold?" I shake my head in response, earning myself an exasperated growl from him as he disappears into the bathroom.

It's a moment before the sound of running water fills the room and Henry reappears. A heated thrill rushes through me at the sight of him ready to take matters into his own hands. However, it's followed by fear as he toes his chelsea boots off and places them by my shoes.

An inexplicable dread makes me question my appearance. Both Mary and Catherine have toned, nipped, and tucked bodies. Nothing jiggles when they move. Their boobs are perfectly high and just the right size so that they don't need constant support. I'm not like them.

I hate exercise, and my diet revolves around what I can afford and what I have time to cook. Not that I can actually cook. I can't. I'm not fat, but I'm not skinny. My tits aren't itty-bitty perky pear drops, and my hips are generous to match.

"Well?" he asks, standing a few feet in front of me.

"I'm fine. I don't—"

"When you're here, you do as I want." The remark cuts through my words. "You're here to serve me. To please me." Henry comes closer. My eyes are glued to his broad chest as he tells me, "I want you to get in there. Wash the rain off your body and warm yourself up. Not a single part of this is a request or an option. It's a command, and I'm paying you to obey."

Glancing up at him, I swallow down the niggling feeling balling in the back of my throat.

I'm not a whore. I tell myself over and again. *I'm not a whore.*

But the basis of our relationship is money. He pays me for my time by the hour. Until now, he hasn't touched me. Yesterday and the day before were blips on his promise to never touch me or fuck me. However, today, something's shifted in him. As much as I'm curious, I'm also nervous.

"Off you go," he instructs me, taking the drink from my hand and placing it on top of the chest drawers closest. "Get in there and do as you are told. For once."

Drawing a deep breath, I nod and slowly trudge to the bathroom. He's following behind me. The immensity of his presence looms in the open doorway as I get inside the bathroom and freeze at the sight of the large tub and the overhanging shower still spraying into it.

"Shower…bath…" he murmurs from behind me as I pull my turtleneck over my head and look over my shoulder to find him watching me intently.

Again, I recall Mary's words. He likes to watch. Is that what he intends to do?

Is he going to watch me?

Dark eyes follow the trajectory of my top when I discard it on the floor beside me. My heart is thumping into my ribs, making it hard to catch my breath when he leans into the doorframe. Every single one of my pores is buzzing with a staggering heat that only grows the longer we watch each other.

I'm unnerved and on the verge of imploding. Meanwhile, he looks as cool as a cucumber. Right in his comfort zone. Settled in for the show.

Unbuttoning my chinos becomes the most clumsy act of my life. With my hands trembling, I fumble with the button, the hook, and the zip. Sweat begins to form on my skin, even though I'm shivering as goosebumps pimple all over my body.

God.

Fuck.

Shit. Shit, shit…shit.

I tug the trousers over my hips, dragging in breath after breath to try settling myself. But he's watching me. I feel his stare rake over me, and slowly my dread booms into a bellyaching knot of anticipation when I bend over to peel my chinos off my legs, and he groans. The rumble cuts through the spray of the water, a low curse that echoes silently around the room, growing to a deafening gong inside me.

What's he going to do while he watches me? I glance back at him as I straighten.

The sight of him all pent up and coiled tight sets me ablaze. Henry's so highly strung that he might snap like an over-taut string plucked by a sharp nail. My eyes rove down from his clenched jaw, slowly taking in the effect my body has on him. The bulge of his crotch is unmissable, and I can't help staring at it and remembering the way it felt pressed up to the top of my arse. I wonder what it would feel like to let him inside me. How would he take me?

"You don't know what you're asking for," he states, his voice dry and gritty.

In truth and actuality, I don't. But in a bone-deep, gut-wrenching, and body-aching kind of way, I do. I know exactly what my entire being is asking for, and it goes against every single one of the morals my father and brother instilled in me. It goes against every promise I ever made myself. Still, I crave it more than anything I've ever wanted.

"Stop, Eve," he growls when I turn to face him and take a step forward, mirroring his.

Every inch of me is alive. My skin has a life of its own as it tightens around my bones. The pores on it blister and burn. God, my boobs feel so heavy, so sensitive, that the friction of my bra over my hard nipples hurts. Every move that causes the material to skim over my skin lances a sharp bolt of electricity into my belly.

"Eve...stop."

I pause in front of him. "Why?"

Rough fingertips ghost over my hands at my sides as he draws in a deep breath, as though he's bolting his resolve and strengthening his willpower.

"Fuck." He spits out the curse between gritted teeth, taking another step forward so that my body is skimming his.

My breasts rub on his torso with my shallow breaths. It feels good. Too good. Like if I do it enough, I'll come from the friction alone.

"You're tempting the devil, Darling." The rasp of his voice causes me to shudder as a current of excitement rolls from the top of my head to the soles of my feet.

"Is he going to bite?"

Bleak, angry pools widen, sucking me right in, deeper and deeper with every shallow breath. "Trust me, Eve—"

"I do." More than I know I should. More than he believes I should, too, from the wry twist of his lips. "I do, Your Grace."

A low chuckle rumbles from deep in his chest. "You don't want me to sink my teeth into you. They come with claws..." Leaning down, he whispers into my ear as his nails scratch over the back of my hands. "And violence, and..."

An arm wraps around my waist with unrelenting and unforgiving force so that my body bows into his, and the heat of his erection seeps through my underwear. I'm hot. I'm wet. I'm wanting. All for him. Only him.

"And?" I pant.

"I'll destroy you," he sighs heavily, mournfully, while his eyes narrow on the marks he left on me. "I'll fucking destroy every inch of you. Body—" He hitches me off the ground, carrying me to the bath. "—mind," Henry states, lifting me over the edge to deposit me on my feet in the warm water, "and soul."

Taking a step back, he watches intently as the water soaks through my white underwear. Moulding his palm to my jaw while his stare traces my exposed curves, he tells me, "I'll destroy all there is of you before you have a hope in hell of stopping me."

"Henry…" I part call and part cry out his name on a murmur when he pulls back and retreats out of the bathroom.

It seems as though he's memorising the sight of me when he grips the doorknob and pauses in the doorway again. As he walks backwards, he closes the door, telling me, "Take your time."

The instant he's out of sight, I'm bereft. My insides tug at themselves to go to him. I can't, though. Some warnings are meant to be heeded, and this warning—*his warning*—is one I need to.

FOURTEEN

Henry

The sound of the running water is maddening. My mind loops the conversation we just had along with the image of her almost naked, wet body. I don't know what I'm doing anymore.

Why do I keep her coming here? Eve with her sass and defiance, she's proving to be impossible to resist. Last night was proof of it, and yet, here I am—incapable of staying away or keeping her away. Because it's true. A part of me has found a part of her that is liberating. Eve's honesty is refreshing.

Maybe Arthur was right. Perhaps I should fuck her out of my system. Get the itch scratched and move on. I should, but I won't. Because having her here—*having her near*—offers me a reprieve from duty and the person I need to be now. She's the breath of fresh air I never imagined I could get ever again.

There's a knock on the door at the same time as my phone vibrates in my pocket. While I answer the call, I open the door to let the maid in with the service cart.

"Set up over there," I tell her, pointing towards the fireplace, where the large couch and coffee table are situated. While I watch her do her job, I listen to Simon relaying the outcome of his trip to the East End.

"I dropped Lizzie off down the road from the White Hart," he says.

Just the name of the pub stirs the animal in me. I can smell blood, feel it warm my hands and seep into my clothes. I feel it now as I felt it yesterday. A thrill sparks inside me, needing more. Blood. Violence. Death. *Revenge.* Justice isn't enough anymore.

"The beer here is…not bad." That's the sign that he's got eyes on our bait.

"How did she seem?" Percival asks.

Our plan of action didn't quite get his approval, but if Chapman is going to work with the United Republic to take us down, we need to incapacitate him. Fast.

"Fine," Simon replies as I check my phone to make sure the tracker we put on her is doing its job.

"Tracker is working."

"Good. Net's out; let's see what we catch."

"Simon?" Percival calls as he's about to hang up.

"Percy."

"Don't leave until you're certain Chapman's taken the bait," Percival sighs. "If he doesn't, bring her back."

"No." That's not going to happen. Lizzie isn't coming back until she has the intel I need. She's going to tell me every fucking move Chapman makes. "I don't care if you have to spread her legs in front of his face—make sure he laps her up."

"Fuck off and get fucked, twazzock," Simon grunts down the phone. "This isn't my first fucking rodeo. It's what I do, and I do it really fucking good."

"Get it done, then," I tell him, ending the call as the maid finishes setting up dinner.

Before she leaves, I hand her Eve's sodden jacket from the coatrack and point down at the shoes. It's almost seven in the evening, and shops are beginning to close, but somewhere, something will be open. If not, I'm sure there'll be something in this place that will do.

"I need clothes in that size." I nod at the coat in her hand while pointing down at the trainers on the floor. "And shoes in the size of those."

The maid lets out a sigh before she nods. "Yes, Your Grace."

Anything else?"

Actually, yes. "An umbrella." This storm is going to continue for the next few days at least, or so the Met Office has warned. "Make sure the clothes are warm."

"Your Grace," she sighs again, looking like there's a tonne of pressure on her shoulders.

She doesn't know what pressure is. If there's one thing Percival has made certain of for the staff, it's that they are well paid and looked after. There was a big upheaval when my father named him the new secretary, and it only got worse when he started changing things. But Percy is a good man, or at least he has good intentions for those under his care, and he believes that keeping the staff happy is a means to keeping them loyal. I'm not sure that's true anymore, given where we've found ourselves, but I admire him for the sentiment and wherewithal to make change to the archaic working order of things.

The suite door closes, leaving me to check on the maid's set-up. It's all very last minute, but everything I asked for is here. While I wait for Eve to join me again, I put the ancient television on. It looks like it could be older than me—it's so bulky, and the picture is grainy—but it works and serves the purpose of distraction as I flick through the channels.

Five minutes feel like hours. The slow drag of time makes it seem an eternity before Eve appears out of the bathroom. The gold strands framing her face are flicking wildly in all kinds of directions while the rest is tucked into the collar of the robe. It's huge on her, swamping her tiny figure all the way to her toes. It makes her appear smaller.

"I'm washed," she states quietly with a shrug. There's an obvious discomfort in the way she's rocking on her toes. The flush of her cheeks is brighter than I recall it ever being. But the one thing I notice the most is the way she's staring at the ground, as if she's too embarrassed to look at me. Or maybe she can't bear to. Regardless, I don't like it, and I won't stand for it.

"I can see," I tell her, hoping that she'll look up at me. When she doesn't, I add, "I can smell it too."

That addictive sweetness of almond echoes around the room, and I wish that I could breathe it all in, gulp it all down into my lungs and steal it all for myself. I wish that it was enough to satiate the hunger clawing deep inside me to have her. Especially when her eyes flicker to mine.

Fuck. My muscles tense at the needy haze in her stare, making it overwhelmingly clear that I'm in trouble. I shouldn't be here. At least not with her. But all the woulds, coulds, shoulds, mights, and all their fucking relatives don't mean shit compared to the way it feels to be in the same room as Eve. To share the same air and feel the warmth of her soul light up this fucking black-and-white world.

I miss colour and freedom. I miss the burn in my lungs and the spark of electricity in my blood. She brings it all back. Her presence is like a drug, except I'm not addicted. My life is dependent on it. On her. I need her to feel something other than the demand to wreck and ruin.

"Come." I beckon her towards me with a wave of my hand. "Sit."

Eve looks down at the coffee table. Confusion pinches her face as she takes in the dishes. She's impossibly quiet as she sits on the other end of the sofa, as far as she can from me.

"Are you cold?" I ask.

Eve shakes her head in reply, but she burrows deeper into the bathrobe until she's practically buried by it. Her skin is so pale that she looks ghostly. Then there are the bruises I left on her neck. As much as I like my marks on her, they look severe. A lot more than they should. I may have grasped her roughly, but not enough to mark her so that in contrast to her ashen complexion, they appear so savage.

Although she's told me she's not cold, I stand and put the fire on. It takes quickly enough that I can get back to feeding her.

"There's dinner." I gesture down at the coffee table. "I know that you didn't have time to eat before you came tonight."

Her stare widens on me as I take the dome off the food. She's regarding me with uncertainty as I crouch down, pulling a cushion from the couch, and sit on the floor opposite her.

"I don't know anyone that doesn't like shepherd's pie."

"Sheep," she whispers with a faint smile that disappears as quickly as it appeared.

"No. No, I suppose they don't." I chuckle at her remark, and her smile appears again. Not for long, but it's enough to lighten the air somewhat.

While I serve our plates, she sits on the floor like me. Her eyes are glued to the television behind me as she asks, "How do you know I haven't eaten?"

"Because you came straight here from the conservatory."

"Yes, but how do you know I didn't eat while I was there? Or maybe I got something on the way here…"

"Did you eat at the conservatory?"

"No." She shakes her head, taking the plate of food I hold out to her. "This is a lot of food."

"When was the last time you ate?"

She shrugs. "I won't be able to eat it all."

"Then eat what you can."

"You shouldn't be so wasteful." Eve's whispered words ebb away as she stares down at the plate.

"Feeding you isn't wasteful, and if it bothers you so much to leave food on your plate, I suggest you eat it all." I fork a mouthful of the pie into my mouth and watch as she continues staring down at the plate, raking her fork through the food. "You don't like it?"

"It's been a while since I ate this." There's a hitch to her words that makes it sound like she's holding back tears through the faint quirk of her lips.

Slowly she takes a small bite and then another, and another, and I didn't realise I was so invested in her enjoyment of the dinner I asked the kitchen to prepare. But the more she eats, the better I'm able to enjoy my food.

"When I was little, my dad made this for dinner every Tuesday. Lamb's expensive, and he wasn't the frivolous kind. Thing is, he saw so much poverty when he was deployed that he made a point of teaching us to make the most of what we had."

It explains a lot about her and the way she carries herself. The clothes she wears and where she lives. More than that, I can understand why she is so defensive about it. Enough so that she would go toe-to-toe with me.

"Lamb was always more expensive from Friday to Sunday because everyone would be having roast dinners on the weekend. On Monday, it would still be good enough to keep on display, but by Tuesday, if it wasn't sold, it would be thrown out, so the butchers used to cut down on the price."

Eve looks up at me with the softest expression she's ever graced me with. No smile. No scowl or glare. It's just her beautiful face and her fluttering gaze. If I could hold on to this image for life, I would.

"This is really nice," she sighs before clearing her throat.

"Do you want a drink?" I show her the bottle of pinot noir that's been left to breathe.

"I don't—I-I don't drink wine," she tells me nervously. A pensive frown draws her face, as though she expects me to know that already. "I don't actually drink alcohol. It doesn't agree with me."

"How so?"

"It goes straight to my head." She shrugs, but the tension in her smile tells me there's more to it.

Maybe something she doesn't want me to know or that she's uncomfortable sharing with me. But I make note of it. One way or another, I'll discover it for myself.

"Water is fine," she tells me, going back to her food.

I pour her a glass of water and myself some wine, watching to see if me drinking it in front of her makes her uncomfortable. Normally, if a person has a bad experience with alcohol or has history with it, they aren't comfortable with others drinking around them, but Eve doesn't bat an eyelid. It's odd, and it only makes me more curious about her reason.

We're almost finished with dinner when she asks, "You didn't answer my question. How do you know I didn't eat?"

After a short debate on how to answer, I settle for the obvious. "Andrew."

"Your driver?"

"He's whatever I need him to be."

"What does that mean?" She glances up at me with her brows pulled tightly together and her lips puckered into a curious pout. "He's whatever you need him to be?"

"I don't sound like that," I point out first, and before I can continue, she tells me, "Yes, you do. You sound like you have your mouth so stuffed with plums that you can't open your lips to get your words out like a normal person. Maybe you should get your man to take them out for you instead of stalking me."

"Why do you make a habit of picking fights?"

A wry grin tugs at the side of her face before she tells me, "I'm not picking a fight, Your Grace."

Could've fooled me. Eve's like a jawbreaker. Just as I think I'm getting past the standoffishness, she hardens herself to me again, constantly pushing and butting her head with mine as though I'm her sworn enemy.

"Then what are you doing?" I reach across the table to refill her glass of water.

Before I pull back, Eve grasps my wrist. Taking the bottle from me and placing it on the floor beside her, she leans forward. It doesn't matter how hard I try to resist the urge, I can't stop myself from glancing down past the gaping collar of the bathrobe, straight at her full tits.

Fuck, I don't know if she's doing this on purpose or whether it's pure coincidence. All I know is that my cock is instantly aware of her nakedness. My heart is jackhammering into my ribs as her eyes glance from me to her chest.

"I'm not picking a fight, Henry," she whispers, looking back to me. "I'm pushing your buttons."

Her grip tightens when I try to pull back, asking, "Why?"

"Because," she breathes out as I stand, and she stands with me, rounding the table to stand in front of me before she continues. "Because the only time you allow me to see past what you want me to see is when you're pushed to your limit."

Eve steps closer, and her hand trails up my arm. It hovers over my chest, waiting for me to chase its warmth.

"I told you not to touch me."

She flattens her hand to my chest. "What are you going to do about it?"

If it's my limit she wants to find, maybe it's time I showed her that I have none.

I'm a killer.

A monster.

Her worst fucking nightmare.

FIFTEEN

Eve

*O*h, my God!

My back hits the wall, expelling all the breath from my lungs in one go.

Jesus!

The force of the impact rattles my bones as Henry's body presses to mine. His hands cuff my wrists, lifting my arms over my head until I'm on my tiptoes and my body is arched into his.

"I told you not to fucking touch me," he repeats, gritting the words out between his teeth as he peers down at me with a scowl.

My insides twist violently when he nudges my legs apart with his knee. When he straightens, Henry's thigh slots between my legs, pressing and grinding until my heart is leaping up into my throat. His eyes are on mine, and I can feel his breath lick over my lips. The heat blooms over my face, seeping deep into my skin and bones, coursing through my veins until I'm ablaze.

"I told you, Eve," he groans into my gaping mouth. "I warned you…"

My chest… God, my chest is so tight that every bruising gong of my heart aches and aches. And he's so close that I can taste the bittersweet tang of wine in the air between us. I want him to kiss me. I need his lips on me and his mouth to devour me. Desperately. Endlessly. Unlike I've ever wanted or needed anything.

Please. Please, please…please! I silently beg as one hand

encapsulates both of my wrists while the other traces down the length of my arms. Henry strokes down my face with the back of his fingers. Slowly. Too reverently. It's so torturously good that a moan escapes me. And as he gulps it down greedily, his mouth crushes to mine.

"Mmm," he rumbles into me.

It's heaven and hell and every bloody ring of purgatory there is in between. The sensation of his teeth raking along the bottom of my lip causes me to squirm over his thigh. I'm dying a thousand deaths as his hand trails down my neck, skimming over my breasts as he opens the robe.

Hot, hard, and punishingly, his lips roll over mine. A hunger has woken up deep inside, and I can't get enough as his tongue licks into my mouth, stroking mine while he sucks the breath right out of my lungs. The taste of him is bitter at first. The residue of the wine lingers on his tongue with a dark cherry whisper that makes it impossible to resist the urge to drink him down, to lick and bite back as he releases my wrists and tunnels his fingers into my hair, tugging and pulling before he licks a hot trail over my jaw.

"I've imagined this," he rasps roughly into my ear. "What you taste like. Sweet and innocent, but you taste too ripe and too wanting. Too good to resist."

Henry nips my ear as he pulls back, the sharp slice of pain causing me to mewl.

"You want to push me past my limit, Eve?" The way he says my name sounds like he's trying to smother me with it. "I don't have a limit," Henry growls, pulling away just enough that he can unbuckle his belt with one hand and hitch my thigh onto his hip. "I was preserving you, silly girl."

The buttons of his fly pop open as soon as the top one is undone. The sound of it turns over my insides. Fear chokes me at the sight of his erection tenting his underwear. I want this. I do.

I do.

I want him. To feel him. To have him. Most of all, for him

to take me with all that volatile strength he possesses. I imagined this too. I've imagined it more times than is right.

"I like you pure and whole," he tells me, freeing himself from his underwear. The length of him fills me with a panic that pounds in my chest, screaming in my ears as my blood comes to a boil. "Do you think you'll be whole after I fuck you?"

Shaking my head, I flatten my hands to the wall behind me. I've never been so scared and excited in my life. It doesn't matter how deep my need for him goes; I'm afraid of what he'll do to me. Afraid and anticipating. Because my fear only feeds my need.

"You'll feel me so deep…" He strokes his dick. Once, twice, and as he does it again, he traces the glistening head over the bottom of my stomach, leaving a hot, wet trail from one side to the other. "So fucking deep…right here," he tells me with a slap of his erection above my belly button. "Look at it. Look at the way your cunt wants me to destroy you."

A shudder cuts through me as he guides himself to the apex of my thighs with one hand while the other lifts me a tad more.

God, this is going to hurt.

Destroying seems a kind way of describing what he's going to do to me. And I'm scared, so bloody afraid that there's a screaming voice in my head telling me to stop. I'm screaming at myself. Howling at him.

Stop. Stop.

But I don't, and he can't. Henry's trembling as much as I am. The control he possesses is nowhere to be seen as he rubs the top of his dick through my middle with a bone-rattling growl. Just as my mouth opens, he thrusts into me, and I scream.

The shrill sound pops my ears and curdles my blood. A cold sweat lances through me as my hands claw onto his shoulders with a deathly grip. I've never felt pain like this. A knife twisting and twisting deep inside me. He wasn't lying—I feel him there, tearing me apart from the inside out, an unbearable burn sparking in my belly button. I want to itch and scratch and claw at it until it dissipates. But his body is pressed so hard into me that I can't even breathe to cry as tears rain down my face.

"I warned you," he grunts so low that I can barely make out the words. "Now, you're mine, darling Eve. You're all mine," he continues, the fierce reverence in his words almost like a prayer. And I feel them seep into me like a balm, a soothing consolation of what he took and what I gave.

A stillness falls around us. The air buzzes and the world disappears as he grinds impossibly deeper, and I whimper what's left of my breath into his mouth, opening my eyes onto his. I see it instantly, the recognition that he's my first. The only man that has been inside me like this. He knows, and he looks as pain stricken as I am.

Without a word, he licks over my lips while his hands grasp my arse. Slowly, he walks us to the bed without removing himself from me. I feel every step punch up into my chest. Every new lash of pain sparks a flash of pleasure that heats me through to the marrow of my bones. My toes curl with every circling swipe of his tongue with mine.

It's a fucking rapture that I can't pull away from, even as he kneels on the edge of the bed and lowers us both. Bracing himself over me, Henry nips my lip as he draws out our kiss.

"You're mine now," he repeats, casting his dark stare over my face. There's a softness in his eyes I've never seen. That I never even imagined he possessed. And just like that, my heart breaks itself for him. Everything I ever thought about love shrinks into insignificance with him inside me.

"I'm yours," I breathe over his lips as my hands stroke from his shoulders to his neck, up to his jaw.

Slowly, he eases himself out. Edging in and out, he teases the heat in my core with his relentless, shallow rhythm. And oddly, I'm aching to feel him all the way inside me again. My body is painfully gaping for him. I don't care how much it hurts.

"More," I moan, wrapping my arms around his shoulders and trying to pull him closer, deeper.

"Too good," his garbled, breathless reply blusters into my ear as he pulls all the way out to the head of his dick. A deep hiss rumbles from him as his hands knot in my hair, tugging my face up to his as he rears back and pounds into me.

"Mine," he grunts, and the air leaving my lungs echoes, "Yours."

"This cunt," he says with another deep thrust.

"Yours," my breath mewls as he bites down on my lip and picks up the rhythm of his thrusts.

"These lips."

"Yours." The reply breaks as he hits deeper than before.

Everything is starting to fuzz. My extremities are buzzing. The heat deep in my core is overtaking all my senses. He's all I can feel. His pleasure and his pain. It's all him and only him. And my broken heart is weeping. My aching body is pulsating. My mind is blanking.

I'm his. All his. Only his.

Just the way it's meant to be.

Henry takes, and I give. It doesn't stop. Every rut. Every thrust. Every curse.

His, his, his!

"Mine," he groans as my pussy squeezes around him. My insides twist, and my body shudders.

Everything fades but the heat of the pleasure he's fucking into me. Out of me. It's too much and not enough.

"More," I beg, and he fucks me faster, harder, deeper.

The friction of our bodies echoes with the slapping of our skin, over and again.

"That's it, darling, give it to me. Come," he growls with one deep thrust.

So deep that it chokes my cry as I come undone for him. My body wrings itself with wave after wave of uncontainable pleasure as he continues fucking into me, faster and faster with his incoherent guttural curses as he pulls and pulls at my hair and his groin slaps into mine. I feel him thicken before he pushes off me, and his cum spurts all over me—my pussy, my thighs, and my stomach. Thick, milky ropes pool over my skin and spatter over my tits.

It's only when I open my eyes that I notice he's staring down at me. My head is too fuzzy to read his face, but it's not good.

"You're bleeding." I hear his part-muffled and part-abrasive remark as I try to blink some clarity back to my senses.

It's impossible. My pulse refuses to slow as my vision goes from fuzzy to downright blurry.

"My backpack," I choke past the dread swelling in the back of my throat. "Backpack."

"Don't fucking move," he snaps as I claw at the bedding, trying to drag myself off the bed.

The cold is biting at my skin. The dampness between my legs is turning to ice.

I don't want to die.

"I said don't fucking move," Henry growls as the bed beside me dips. Suddenly, he's cradling me while he brushes my hair from my face. "You should've told me," he barks in a low voice.

"Backpack," I repeat, blinking my eyes as open as I can.

The headache that comes with these bleeds is setting in, and I know that if I don't stop it now, I'm buggered. But it doesn't matter how hard I try to communicate because the words just don't come. I'm thinking and thinking, and it's not translating because I'm scared.

Fear engulfs me. It's worse than death as it numbs me completely. The ice between my legs begins to spread all over. My chest hurts so much. I've never been so cold, and it's never been so dark.

The world is crushing me.

I can't breathe.

There's nothing I can do as Mary's words come back to haunt me. A warning I should've heeded.

The Duke of Gloucester has fucked me dead.

SIXTEEN

Henry

There's a limit after all.

I pull the gauzy scarf off the bedside light, making the room brighter. It's a fire hazard, one I will be pointing out when she wakes up again. Eve still looks pale, and even though her bed is a small double, she's lost in the white bedding.

Replacing the bedside lamp with the dimmed torch on my phone, I swipe away the message from Simon. My head is too much of a fucking mess to deal with anything right now. I can still smell her blood, even though we're both washed and changed. I've never seen anything like it before. *No one's bled for me like that.*

As sick as it is, a murmur of pleasure sparks inside me at the thought as I resist the urge to touch her. To shake her awake and put the fear of my undiluted, uncontrolled rage into her.

"So fucking reckless," I hiss quietly at her, even though I want to shout it in her face until she realises the gravity of what she's done.

The blame isn't on her, I tell myself as I ghost my fingers over the back of her hand. I should've stopped the instant I realised she was a virgin. Eve's just a fucking child. A teenager. A too-ripe forbidden fruit that I plucked from the tree. Now all that's left is a mess.

The right thing would've been to step back and put an end to this madness. Because now, she's more than an itch I can't quite scratch. So much more than a mouthwatering scent I want a curious taste of. Eve's given me something I've never had before, and now I don't just want a taste. I want to feast, all the fucking time until my gluttony threatens to burst my insides.

Whether she wants it or not, she's mine now. Doesn't matter what happens from here on out. She's not just sweet, beautiful Eve. She's my Eve above all else.

"My darling Eve." I took her, and I'm going to keep her.

The loud vibration of my phone causes her to stir before I can stop it. Everything outside of this room can wait. Eve is the only thing that matters right now. After I've put the *Do Not Disturb* on, I pull the cover higher up her chest, watching the steady flicker of her eyes as she sleeps. It takes everything in me not to stroke her face or kiss the upturn of her nose. I've never enjoyed kissing. It's much too personal, a mutual taste of affection that I've never wanted nor given. But I want it with her. All her fucking kisses. Every sliver of her taste.

Today is the first time that I've truly wished my father was here. He would've known what to do. How to fix this disease she has. Fixing people was the thing he was best at. And the one time I need him for it, *he's gone*.

This is the first time I'm feeling his absence deep in my bones. It's choking my insides with a pain that I can hardly bear. Grief blackens my being. And I wish I'd made Chapman's whore suffer. I wish I'd made her scream the heavens down. But it's not over yet—she was just one part of him.

There's more to bleed and destroy.

Twisting the ring on my finger, I take another look around the small bedroom. Everything is neat, clean, and basic. Much like Eve, her home is straightforward. No frills, just the essentials. For a while, I try to force myself to calm down. I close my eyes and attempt to clear my mind, but the deep breathing only makes the smell of her blood stronger. If anything, it makes it harder to stop myself from becoming any more stir-crazy.

him for as long as there is breath in my lungs and my heart beats in my chest.

"I will live with that sight etched into my soul for the rest of eternity. So please, don't ask me to forgive and forget because it's the one thing I can't give you." His hand trails up to cup my face as he leans closer and presses a kiss to my forehead. "I want to give you the world, Eve. I want to give you everything you ask for…" Hot lips trace deep kisses down my nose to my lips. "But I can't give you this forgive-and-forget Christian bullshit," he sighs between my trembling lips with a shake of his head. "I'm not a holy man, Eve."

I don't want him to be anything but himself. The truth is that I fell in love with him for who he is. "I know."

"Then don't ask me to do these good, idealistic things." His thumb strokes over my lip, pulling it lower so he can look in my mouth. "You're still bleeding."

There's an edge of desperate concern in his tone that has me nudging the tip of my nose with his, trying to soothe him. "The doctor said it would take a while for the bleeding of my gums to stop. I'll probably have a period too for the next few months, a heavy one at that. But it'll be fine. I'm okay, Henry."

"Do you remember what I promised about fines and okays coming out of your mouth?" Henry asks with a chortle. His other hand lightly sweeps between the other side of my face and the pillow so that he's cupping my jaw.

"Don't make promises you can't keep, Your Grace," I chuckle back, moulding my hands to his nape.

"For now," he says, licking over my sighs with a longing sigh. "But I intend on making good on my other promise too."

"The one where you defile me?" I kiss his bottom lip as his mouth pulls to a grin.

"Every inch of you." He brings himself flush to me. "My Duchess to be."

My heart stutters at his remark, and I'm incapable of saying anything when he kisses me with his tongue sweeping over mine.

to pacify me.

Pushing myself up slowly so that I'm facing his side instead of being pressed into him, I unravel his arm from around me and hug it to my chest instead. "I didn't know my mum. For all I know, she could've been an awful person."

"I doubt that." A blank expression falls on his face as he peers down at me.

"Either way, I would give anything to have her in my life, and you might not feel that way now because you're angry at her."

"She might as well have put you in here herself." The rage in his voice is unavoidable, even as he tries to dampen it down with the grit of his teeth.

"There's so much blame to go around for so many things. No one forced me to get involved with what your dad or Alastair were doing. I did it because it was a me—"

"Means to an end. Yes, you've told me that many times."

"Because it's true. There are so many ifs and buts and maybes about this. So many outcomes that could've been avoided by different decisions we all made. But I wouldn't have it any other way. In the end, I'm here with you, and to me, that is all that matters."

"You shouldn't be in here," he growls back, his hand awkwardly moulding to the side of my neck as he tries to adjust himself without jostling me too much on the mattress. It's only when he's lying beside me and we're facing each other that I notice the deep sadness in his eyes. It glistens at me with regret and sorrow so strong that it wrenches at my insides. "I will never unsee the sight of you trussed up to this bed with tubes and wires everywhere."

"Henry…" I try to soothe him, but the pain is deep enough that a mere touch won't be enough. I wish I was stronger, better able to comfort him and to show him that I am okay. In a few days, they will allow me to leave this hospital, and I can go back to living my life with a few scars from the tubes they used to suck the blood from my belly. But I will live, and I will be here to love

but he and Henry always seemed close. Maybe closer than Henry and the Prince.

"What about Arthur?" Julian asks while putting his coat on.

"That could work, and this will be his court soon enough, so..." Percival makes note on his iPad. "I'll check with the Prince's secretary later."

"Did you pick up the ruby?" Henry asks Percival when Julian walks out with a small wave at me.

I didn't think he liked me. Julian was always so standoffish and cold. The last time I saw him, I thought he might push me down the stairs at Hush. But something's shifted in the way he looks at me. As though he sees me as one of them instead as one of *the girls*.

"I did," Percival answers Henry, watching him saunter over to my side before he slips into bed beside me. "She's not doing well, Henry. The Princess is—"

"Being punished so that she learns not to meddle where she is not wanted."

"She's lonely," Percival sighs with an air of pity. "Maybe you could allow her to attend the howl with the rest of the family?"

"Absolutely not. I told you before, Percy, I'm not my father. I won't be coerced or manipulated into others' whims. My mother stays at Barnwell until I decide otherwise."

The anger in his voice causes my chest to cave. I never met my mum, and maybe it's why I pity his. But there's a nagging feeling in my gut that says if something happened to her before they make peace, he would be haunted by this. I don't want to be the cause of his unhappiness or give him reason to resent me in the future.

I love him, and I want him to be happy. I want to protect him from himself. Enough so that when Percival leaves, I burrow into Henry's side and tell him, "It doesn't matter what she's done, Henry. She's the only mum you're ever going to have."

"It's not up for discussion," he replies, wrapping his arm tightly around me and turning me into him as though he's trying

before he says, "We should wrap this up. Everything is in place, and I have court first thing in the morning to prepare for."

"Well, Defence Secretary, I wish you luck with your takedown. Prime Minister." Henry stands to address Benedict Gladstone, "Thank you for your support and that of your son. I'm sure this won't be the last time Sinclair Securities will aid the Wolfsden Society."

"I'm sure it won't." Benedict shakes hands with Henry, followed by Julian and Percival. "We all want the same thing, Your Grace. The security of the crown and its future by any means necessary."

"Hear, hear," the defence secretary hoots quietly. "God save the King."

"God save the King," Henry sighs.

He's spent every hour of every day here with me since I opened my eyes. Even though he has the sofa bed, it's not comfortable at all. When I tried to lie beside him a few days ago, it felt like every spring was digging into my body. It was awful, and I don't know how he manages it, but I'm grateful that he hasn't left me.

The prime minister leaves, with the defence secretary following behind him. Neither Henry nor Julian and Percival sit back down as they run through the list of tasks on Percival's iPad.

"Alastair's Howl will be next month together with Ryan's swearing ceremony," Percival says as he hands Henry a thick file. "We need to decide how to go forward with this. The Earl of Rochester is the bearer of the rings and the ceremony master..."

"Find another," Henry replies brusquely.

"There is no other, Henry," Julian retorts. "Tradition is tradition."

"Then break it. Simon will not be coming back, and I will not change my mind on this matter."

I don't know what's happened, but the calm atmosphere from moments ago has turned sour. Yesterday, I overheard Henry and Percival discussing Simon's empty seat. I didn't know him at all,

We are stuck together. Our souls are too well entwined to be split apart. And my heart, it's still beating because of him. For him. It's beating in time with his because it's his too.

His hands envelop one of mine, and the heat of his lips presses to the back of my thumb before he gives it a light nip. And my toes curl and my feet flex, pulling at the muscles of my legs.

"That's it," he chuckles with another, harder nip. "Hold my hand, my love."

My soul beams at his remark. He calls me his love like it's my name. Like this is all I was born to be. My sole purpose in this universe is to be his in the same way that his is to be mine. To love him. To adore him. To be everything he wants and needs.

The headache still thrums deep in my head, a constant pulse that is slowly shrinking away. The curtains are drawn to block out the bright winter sunset as I open my eyes to find Henry sat at the table in the opposite corner of the room with a group of men. They're all talking in hushed whispers that I can only just hear.

"It's all set up," one man says. I don't recognise his voice at all, but when I peer up at him, his face seems familiar. "You'll get the call when the Chapmans go up in flames."

"Make sure every Chapman is in there before it blows," Henry tells him. "You get the glory, Clark, but I want the kills. Get the whore and the traitor on that boat. They can all burn together."

"Done," the man tells him. "The bags are ready to go."

"My contact at the papers is happy to take the story of the East End kingpin's fall in exchange for the headline we embargoed before. It's mostly speculation that adds to the dramatization of the story of an illicit affair turned into a family war. Tragic." Julian stands, turning to grab his briefcase from the chair by the door, when our eyes lock.

A small smile tugs at his lips with a small nod. A silent hello

love again. That I will never see the people I love just one more time. Most of all, I'm terrified of being without him. My duke. My Henry.

"What's happening?" he asks, my panic bleeding into his voice.

"This is normal. It takes a while for the sedative to wear off. In the meantime, it's important she remains calm. Miss Cameron," another voice calls at me. "Eve, you're at St Anne's hospital."

Hot tears burn my eyes, scorching my retinas until all I see are the silhouettes of the blood vessels between the layers of skin, the veil keeping me from my Henry.

"You were very sick, but you are well now. However"—the voice raises as I groan—"you need to stay as still as you can. There was some severe internal bleeding that we have got under control, but you need to relax. You are all right."

"Listen to the doctor, beautiful. Go back to sleep. Rest, my darling," Henry says.

I feel the rough pads of his fingers stroking over my face. Lightly, they stroke over the bridge of my nose and over my cheeks in that admiring way of his. If I can't see his face right now, I can at least imagine it. His deep brown eyes blink at me as he watches me wake up with a smile on his lips. Henry doesn't smile much or often, but he does for me. He smiles for me because it belongs to me. The same way I belong to him.

"Don't cry," he tells me. "Don't be scared, my girl. I'm here, and nothing will hurt you again."

"I'm going to turn the monitor off so you can sleep," the doctor says. "In a few minutes, the nurse will give you some pain relief to help with the sore throat from the breathing tube and the general aches."

"Rest, darling. I'm right here, and I'm not going anywhere. You are not leaving my sight ever again. Do you hear me?"

Yes. I try to get the words to form, but my throat constricts as though it's trying to protect itself. *Yes.*

I'm never leaving him again, and he is never letting me go.

THIRTY-SEVEN
Eve

It's the sun. Warm and bright, it seeps into my bones as my eyes flutter open. My head is sore. My throat. My entire body, actually. The heavy throb makes it difficult to focus on anything but the ache and the taste of blood that lies thickly on my tongue.

Blood.

I can smell it. I can taste it.

"Hey." The soft whisper cracks beside me. His voice is softer than I've ever heard it, maybe a little wet. "Hey, my beautiful darling."

The throbbing pain burns as the words envelop me, the low timbre of his voice making my heart race so fast that it sets off the alarm, so shrill that it causes my ears to ring, and slowly, the realisation sets in. The pain in my stomach churns again, and the tang of blood grows on my tongue.

I'm dying.

I can feel it with every fibre of my being, every muscle that groans as I try to fight the darkness pulling me back into oblivion. My head is screaming, but my mouth is stuck closed, holding in my despair so that I can't beg for help.

I don't want to die.

With my body refusing to fight for me, I have no choice but to lie limply and wait. Wait for the cold to swallow me again. And I'm scared. So afraid that I'll never do any of the things I

when Warren screams, "The boats."

"No!" Mary croaks. Her voice is becoming weaker. "No…"

"Poplar Marina," Richard mutters in a high-pitched keen, and when he falls silent, a shot ricochets around the room, bouncing off the walls as the back of his head blows. Brain and bone spatter and shatter on the wall behind him.

"We have no use for you either now," I tell Mary. "You're scrap. Unwanted. Unneeded. Unsalvageable."

"If she didn't die today," Mary coughs, sputtering blood over her face, "she'll die tomorrow. It's the price."

My hand grips the knife on the instrument table, and without a second thought, I slash the blade over her throat. Big eyes widen with panic and fear, the shadow of death dilating her pupils while I cut deeper, and what's left of her blood pours faster.

"You are the price," I growl, plunging the blade to the hollow of her throat as I tear it down her chest. "You are dying."

No one will ever touch my Eve again. She's mine, and she will stay mine, at my side until I am gone.

fuck bud.

"Give your father up and I'll spare your siblings," I tell her, holding Ryan's phone up to her face so that she can see the photo that Casper sent him of Alfie Chapman and his sister.

The song ends and starts again. It's a trick that we were taught as part of our warfare training, specifically for use in the extraction of intel from persons of interest. It makes time seem like it's going by faster, making it seem like they've been interrogated for longer.

"Someone has to talk. Whether it's you or you"—I gesture between Mary and Warren—"it doesn't matter."

They're both still going to die.

The door to the theatre opens suddenly, and Percival pauses in the doorway. I see the shock in his eyes. The fear of what I'm capable of tugs at his brows as he turns his back on the scene before he says, "The doctor is administering the last of the vitamin K. Eve's stable."

My heart leaps from my chest at the news. It's been almost twenty-four hours since they put her in the induced coma. I'm not losing her now or ever. After this, I'm never letting her out of my sight. I don't care what I have to do, I'm keeping her stuck to me. Forever. My entire being warms at the thought. Eve's everything I need. The only thing I'll ever need or want in my life for the long haul.

"Murphy," I call over my shoulder. "I'm feeling generous."

"How so?" He cocks his brow with a grin.

"Kill him. He has no value, and I'm done wasting my time." I watch closely as Richard follows Ryan's actions.

There's almost a sigh of relief when he puts the dermatome down until Ryan pulls out his gun and makes a show of checking it over. The instant he takes a step back and aims it at Richard's head, he shits himself. His naked body squirms on the chair, pulling at the ties holding him in place.

The click of the safety causes him to freeze, eyes bugging out of his head as Ryan takes his stance. He's about to pull the trigger

here that the second layer has blood vessels and lymphs..." he says as I'm reading the message from Casper.

> We have the boy and the girl.

I didn't want to resort to this. Eve will be upset that I'm about to use the boy she calls her friend to lure his father out. But it's a means to an end. They hurt her to get to me; I'm going to get all of John Chapman's children in one room, and if he doesn't come out of the shadows with his big brother, he won't have any left.

Warren screams when Ryan harvests another strip of skin. Tiny globules of blood build up as the blood vessels are torn, like red beads of sweat bleeding together to run down his chest to his shrivelled cock.

"How long do you think it would take to bleed a grown man dry this way?" Ryan muses, running the dermatome down the other side of Warren's chest.

"He doesn't know anything," Mary pants through another deep drag of the saw through her shin.

She bleeds like a beauty as her flesh peels around her bones. I wonder how loud she'd scream if I sawed right through them a joint at a time.

"Do you love your siblings, Mary?" I ask, putting the saw down and grasping her pale face. She's lost enough blood that she's trembling. Shivers wrack violently through her body, making her bleed more as the puddle drips onto the floor and the music in the background repeats again and again.

I'm not Jesus. I'm not Jesus.

I will not forgive.

Not now. Not ever.

Watching her blood pour from her while her shivers spasm through her body is cathartic. A sliver of justice. Because I know that this is how Eve would've been: cold, scared, and shivering so hard that her body would convulse. She would've been so fucking afraid, and I wasn't there because of this fucking whore and her

her restraints on the surgical table.

There's only one question they have to answer, and I'll put them out of their misery. But until then, I'll keep cutting, and Ryan will keep skinning.

Until I know where Charles Chapman and the rest of his cunts are hiding, there'll be no mercy or humanity from me.

"Do you have something to tell me?" I ask, standing over her bleeding form as I pick up the bone saw and turn it on so that the shrill sound cuts through the music. "I'm bored of the scalpel, Mary. I'm bored of watching your blood drip slowly."

"Go to hell," she spits up at me.

"This is hell, Mary. Mary, Mary…Mary." Holding the saw over the superficial cut along her sternum, I hover down to her belly before I touch the blade lightly to the skin. The sudden spray of blood spatters up into her face and over my hands as I hold it in the same place. The heat from the blade burns the skin and flesh, with the acrid scent filling the air. "Well?"

Tears stream down her temples to her bloody hair as she shakes her head vehemently. "Fuck you," she chokes on her sob.

"I don't fuck whores." I blow out a breath, guiding the saw lower. "But I do cut them. I cut them open—" I press the saw deeper, watching it slice her open like the carcass of a deer. "—I cut them apart…"

The mulching of the blade sawing through her flesh chews through me. It's an ugly sound, but it makes my blood sing. My pulse thrums eagerly in my veins the louder she cries, begging for her father to save her.

"So much skin…" I tell her, bringing the blade away and dragging the flat over her thigh so that it shreds the top layer of skin before I slice through the outside of her leg. "So much flesh. Oh, Mary, Mary…Mary…"

The sound of the dermatome vibrating to life brings on Warren's snivels.

"You seen this, Sloane?" Ryan nudges me with his phone, holding the lit-up screen in my view. "Skin has three layers. Says

ment, and fear cloud her eyes. "You're a dowager, and it's time that your social and living arrangements reflected that."

A hysterical laugh bubbles from her, causing my hands to fist tightly around the gun and the knife in my hands. For years, she's controlled everything and everyone. My father allowed her too much influence, and it's how we've ended up here. I won't make his mistakes.

A scream echoes from the theatre attached to this room. The deep timbre is cracked through with an agonised shrill.

"You've lost your mind," she tells me, grasping Simon's hand tightly in hers. "Is this how you plan on governing this society? Killing and maiming and…and banishing anyone that stands in your way?"

"No, Mother. I will kill the enemy, and I will maim traitors. I will only exile those that are so deeply insignificant that their existence doesn't matter to me. Whether you are dead or alive, you have no use to me."

"Your father would be ashamed."

"My father is dead because of you." The bellow of my voice ricochets around us. I'm so sick and tired of her accusations and manipulations. I just want her out of my sight. I want her gone before my rage demands her blood too. "You are dismissed," I tell her as I face Julian. He's stoically watching everything unfold without so much as a whisper. "Show the Princess and the Earl out."

He nods, ushering them out of the room as I turn to go back inside the theatre, ignoring her fit of anger. The air in here is arctic, and the sound of the music in the background welcomes me again.

"Are they talking yet?" I ask Ryan as he puts the dermatome down and shakes his head. "Not yet. I think it's time to switch things up."

I'm not sure how many layers of skin he has taken from Warren's chest, but he's not bleeding yet. However, when he spritzes the area with ice-cold water, he screams so loud that Mary pulls at

"Take him away," I tell the medical staff on standby. They make quick work of getting Andrew out of my sight before I continue with the rest of this meeting.

"Let this be a warning to you." I look at my mother. A horrified, sickened expression ashens her face. "Whatever happens to Eve happens to you."

"You've lost your senses," she chokes out.

"You put us all at risk, and you"—I turn towards Simon as he watches me with a disgusted scowl—"you will leave, and you will never come back. I never want to see you again. God help you if after today you and I stand on the same ground or share the same air."

The Princess stands in front of the doors, blocking her favourite child from leaving. "I will not allow you to—"

"Move, Your Highness," I order, pulling my gun from the pocket of my hoodie and releasing the safety clip. The sound is low, but she hears it loud enough that she thinks twice about her argument when I aim the Glock at his head. "Move, or his brain will decorate your clothes."

"You can't do this, Henry. There has to be a vote. The King won't allow it!"

"Yes, he will. He already has."

Disbelief scrunches her face. Who knew someone so beautiful and charming could appear so disagreeable. I gesture for Percival to show her the correspondence between me and her cousin, the King of England. I will keep his secret, and he will let me rule this society my way.

"But he's the Earl of Rochester, the rightful owner of the seat…" she tells Percival.

"Yes, Your Highness. The King has allowed him to keep his seat," he tells her, taking the correspondence from her and folding it back into his pocket.

"But he won't sit in it while I'm in command of the Wolves. The same way you will pick one of your country estates to remain at until your bones are ready to be buried." Shock, disappoint-

THIRTY-SIX

Henry

"Do you remember why you're here? Why I kept you with me?"

Andrew looks at me with a confused frown while the others all stand at the side of the room watching. My mother's eyes widen when I flick the knife open and circle him once.

"You're here because you saved my life. I trusted you to keep watch of Eve because you proved yourself faithful to me."

"Henr—" My mother stops when I urge her to shut up with a raise of my finger as I round Andrew again and pause behind him.

"You're no longer my man, but I'm still going to show you mercy." With a deep plunge of the blade to his back, I yank the knife forcefully into the bottom of his spine, ignoring the loud, guttural groans of pain that bellow from him with every tug of my hand. "I'll spare you your pulse and your breaths, but your life is done."

His legs collapse beneath him. A red torrent of blood soaks through his white T-shirt and down his jeans as the blade pulls out of his back when he falls on the ground. I'll allow the doctors to save him, but they won't fix him. He'll never walk again, and every day that he struggles to live life, he will remember that he betrayed me. He helped put Eve in this place. Even when she walks out of here, I will not forgive him. I will not forgive anyone that had a hand in it.

ous shit. You give me a target, and I kill. No questions."

If this is the case, Ryan Murphy is the man I need to count on. Bastard or misfit, it doesn't matter, as long we're on the same page.

Shoot to kill. Kill to live. This isn't about justice for the dead anymore. It's about protecting and surviving. They touched my darling, and now the Coster Kings must die.

"There's no one else on this ward."

"Good. Call everyone here." When he doesn't get going, I bark, "Now, Percival. Everyone. My mother included."

Ryan comes in as Percival is about to leave. Instantly, his stare falls to the bed with a noticeable cringe. "How is she?"

All I can do is shake my head. Everything hurts, and the prospect of replying with words daunts me. I won't verbalise what could happen. I won't give it time to air or breathe.

"What do you want me to do with your girl?" he asks, standing at the foot of the bed with his hands clutching the bedding.

"Put her in there." I nod towards the empty room opposite this one. "I want her and Warren in there."

"What are you doing with them?"

"One way or another, I'm getting the intel I need to put a bullet between Chapman's eyes." I'm going to end this once and for all, and I'm going to make sure that no one ever fucking crosses me again.

"Now I understand why Fred calls you the best of the lot." He grins, but when his gaze lands on Eve again, his face falls with a pained twist of his lips. "Jess needs to be told. Eve would want her here."

She would. I know that, but even now, I don't want to share her with anyone. Not even her family.

"Do you have someone watching over her and George?" More than Jess being here, Eve would want her safe. And I'll do anything she wants to bring her back to me.

"Casper has men watching their place. I told you," he says with an affirmative nod, "I have resources."

"I need your help."

"It's why I'm here. That and to right my father's wrongs." Bracing himself on the foot of the bed, he stares at Eve intently. "Joe was fucking brutal force. I owe it to him to make this right."

"Good, because things are about to get messy, and I don't have time to justify myself to anyone."

Ryan nods. "I'm a soldier, Sloane. I'm not here for the pomp-

The doctor gives me a terse smile before he checks the drip and syringe pump. "The key here is to keep her in the induced coma to avoid any more bleeding until the vitamin K has had a chance to neutralise the Warfarin."

It's only when the doctor leaves with the rest of the staff that I walk around to the other side of the bed. There are fewer cables and tubes, and the dim golden light from the lamp on the back wall lights this side of her face enough that I can see the dried track of blood crumbling around her mouth and jaw.

"Don't be scared, darling," I tell her, recalling the conversation we had a while back where she told me she's afraid of dying. "I'm here, Eve, and I won't let you go. I promise."

The flicker of her eyelids draws me closer. Maybe she can hear me. Maybe she feels me here as I lightly hold her hand, too afraid to cause any more damage with my rough touch.

"Please forgive me," I whisper, leaning over her to press a kiss to her forehead. "Please forgive me for hurting you. I should've protected you better. I should've—"

"Henry." Percival murmurs at the foot of her bed. "This isn't your fault."

My mouth opens to bark at him to leave, but the words ball in the back of my throat. He's wrong—this is my fault. Eve shouldn't be lying here like this, balancing precariously on the verge of life and death. But he's also right; it's not all down to me. There's blame all round, and it's time that the consequences fall at everyone's feet.

"What's in there?" I ask, nodding towards the double doors behind him.

"Emergency theatre," he replies, looking over his shoulder with confusion pinching his face. "Why?"

"And all rooms on this floor are the same?"

"Yes, Your Grace." He nods.

"That room." I point towards the doors leading to the hallway. The wire glass panels look on to another set of doors to another private room. "Empty?"

balling in my throat.

"They're doing everything," he repeats as the lift doors open, and he guides me down another corridor.

The smell of bleach is so strong that it burns my nostrils as we walk through empty glass-partitioned rooms. My feet can't eat at the distance quick enough. I need to get to Eve. I need to see her and hold her.

"Where is she? Where's my girl?" The questions keep rolling off my tongue. Loose words. Endless motions. When all I want is to set my sight on her again. My beautiful darling—the girl who changed my world. Who *is* my world.

"Just…prepare yourself," Percival tells me as we round the corner to a corridor of endless doors.

"Where is she?"

"It looks bad, Henry," he says, turning into me as we reach one of the doors. "She's fighting, though."

The door opens when a nurse steps outside. The pump and release of the machines is deafening, slamming into me with a force that threatens to bring me to my knees. The world is falling and smashing to smithereens beneath me, and there's nothing for me to hold on to as the door opens wide and I see her through all the machines, wires, and tubes.

Fuck.

My body propels itself towards her, even as my mind tells me to turn around. To burn this entire fucking universe to dust along with every man and woman that put here. Along with me.

"Your Grace," one of the doctors addresses me from the other side of the bed. His lips are moving, and the drone of his voice as he explains what's happened and what they're doing to try and fix it is whirring into my ears. But I hear nothing. I see nothing. I feel nothing. Except her and the machines keeping her alive.

I lose her, I've lost everything. The thought doesn't stop battering into me as my fingers stroke over her hand.

"We have faith that if we continue with this treatment and she continues responding to it the way she is, everything will be fine."

been poisoned."

No. That's not possible. "Your brother checked her over."

"He stitched her arm up," he bites at me. "He wasn't to know there was something more."

"I want Richard Warren brought to me." I want to kill the cunt. Cut him limb from limb as he watches me bleed his bitch dry. Or maybe I'll bleed him and gut her. The possibilities are endless.

The possibilities. I choke. The possibility that Eve is dying freezes me to the core. I can't breathe as Ryan races through the city. The streets flash by in a blur of shadows and lights with the garbled roar of my pulse.

I almost lost her, and I only just got her back. "I can't lose her again."

"You won't." Ryan swerves into the underground car park of St. Anne's hospital.

The registration of the car on their system means they cut the usual security checks of the Secret Service hospital. My ears are ringing as I get out of the car, leaving Ryan to deal with the whore in the back.

Percival is waiting at the glass doors. He immediately starts walking me through the long corridor.

"Where is she?" I ask.

"They have her in intensive care. The blood tests have come back with high levels of Warfarin in her system."

"Warfarin?"

"It's an anticoagulant. Too much causes internal bleeding."

The morose expression on his face claws at me. The world around me is tilting. It keeps spinning and spinning, and I'm so fucking dizzy that I can't see straight as he guides me into the lift.

"The doctors believe the Desmopressin slowed down the Warfarin poisoning. With the sedatives, she wouldn't have been able to feel it set in." Percival comes to stand in front of me. "They're doing everything they can to save her, Henry."

I nod, incapable of doing anything else. All the words are

"Here. I took care of our problem."

In the dark, it's impossible to make out her expression, but the thrill in her deep, leisured breaths is audible as she wipes the blade of her knife on her hip before flicking it closed.

"Look at her." Mary spits down at the ground with disgust, nudging the body with her foot. "Cathy Eddowes…the late Duke, your father, liked her. Hours he'd lock himself away with her. He'd fuck her. Bruise her. Cut her. And she thought she ruled the roost."

"What do you want, Mary?" I take another step closer, and she sidesteps over the corpse on the ground. "Are you scared I'm going to gut you like the others?"

A low cackle vibrates her entire body as we continue circling. "Scared? Me? No, Your Grace, but you should be."

"I'm not."

"You should be," she snaps back. Her eyes flicker down to my pocket, where I'm holding the gun. "Go on, shoot me."

There's a trill to her voice that tells me it's the worst thing I could do, but before her words have faded to silence, a shot cracks around us. Mary stumbles forward as the Fiesta reverses into view.

"Get in," Ryan barks. "We have to go *now*!"

"You're too late. She's going to die," Mary laughs. "You're going to watch her bleed."

It's at that precise moment that my heart falls to my feet. The violent twist of my stomach wrenches through me.

Eve.

Panic and rage tornado inside me as I grip Mary's hair harshly and hoist her in the air, holding her face to my face.

"I'm going to watch you die."

"Not before she does." There's a bite of pain to the laughter that follows her words as I smash her head to the roof of the car, again and again until she falls limp, and I throw her in the back.

"We need to get back to the club," I growl at Ryan at the same time as he tells me, "Eve's been taken to hospital. They think she's

dinates on my phone for Catherine's bail address. "When you're banded together like we are on high-risk missions, you're more than just a cadre or a team. You become a family, and if anything or anyone comes at one of us, it comes at all of us."

I nod, trying to ignore the constant whir of worry. That nagging in my chest that Eve isn't right here next to me. Every time she's been out of my sight, I've had this goddamn relentless churning in my gut. Like a premonition that something is coming.

Turning a corner, Ryan pulls over into the back road where Catherine's bail flat is located. It's quiet, the streetlights are off, and everything is a moving shadow. My pulse is throbbing in my throat as I get out of the car.

"Make it quick," Ryan tells me, looking around the street like we're in a war zone.

"It won't take me a minute," I say, closing the car door and heading to the house with the blue door like Percival instructed.

The Brutalist buildings stacked on either side are all dark, as though they've been abandoned. The hammering of my heart picks up, beating faster when the shadow comes up ahead of me. A female form. It takes me a moment too long to recognise it.

"Mary?" *Fuck.*

My head boggles while she pauses beside a large bush. One side of her body seems weighed down and heavy. But in the dark, I can't make out why.

"Your Grace," she coos with a courtesy. "Not who you expected?"

No. I slip my hand into the pocket of my hoodie and grasp my Glock tightly. Slowly, I edge it out of my pocket.

"Richard said you wouldn't see it coming." Her voice trails off with a long breath. "Who knew? He was right."

Fury roars in my chest with every step I take closer. Mary makes no attempt to move. I see it now. "The commissioner and his whore."

"Something like that," she laughs, stepping out from behind the dark bush as she tugs at a large shadow on the ground. A body.

"I'm not pent up." He gives me a knowing look, cocking his brow in challenge. "I'm not pent up, I'm fed up. I want to fix this shit before more people get hurt."

"People or Eve?" he asks, using a blank pass to exit the car park.

"Where'd you get that?"

"I told you, I have resources." He grins. "Answer my question."

Eve. I want to protect Eve. Because if Chapman came for my father and Alastair for one girl, he's not just coming for me after I've taken out his mistress, his sister, and his wife. He's going to come for the people I care about if I don't take him out first.

"Does it matter?" I ask him.

"People in general don't have the added pressure of people we care about." Ryan zooms down the quiet street like we're on a joyride. "Pressure makes mess. We don't have time to be dealing with more mess than you already have on your hands."

"Chapman will come for Eve, and I can't say that he won't go as far as Jess or George."

"I'm not going to let that happen," he says. "I won't let anything happen to Jess or George."

"You're in love with her." It's written all over his face, and the same anger that's coursing through my veins is pounding through his too. I can smell the rage on him and in every one of his heavy breaths.

"No," he scoffs. "We're friends."

"Regardless of what's what, my only choice is to take Chapman out. I'm going to watch him bleed the same way my father did."

"This is why I'm not walking away. Ring or no ring, I'm going to watch that bastard bleed the same way my father bled. We have a saying at the security firm," he says with a stern frown. "Blood for blood. A wound for a wound. A life for a life."

"Sounds good to me."

"You know how it goes," Ryan continues as I check the coor-

my feet.

"Wait," Ryan calls after me as I walk out of the room with Percival following behind. "I'm coming with you."

"No, this isn't a team mission." Continuing down the hallway to my suite, I give Percival orders on what to do next. "I want the address, and I want the car waiting for me in the usual place. No one leaves the club, and no one comes near this room."

Once I'm in the suite, I make quick work of getting changed into my combat trousers, a black T-shirt, and a hoodie. I grab the flick knife from the safe hidden inside the wardrobe and slip it into the pocket of my hoodie, along with my handgun.

While I lace up my boots, I steal the odd glimpse at Eve. She looks peaceful, even though she's still pale. Before I leave, I tuck the sheets around her with a kiss to her forehead. It doesn't matter how much time we have together, I'm always going to be awed by her stunning face and the fact that she's mine.

My beautiful darling. "Nothing will touch you again," I promise as I push through the hidden panel door beside the wardrobe.

I take the steps down to the underground tunnel leading to the other side of the river. The incognito black Fiesta is waiting for me in the underground car park belonging to the Secret Intelligence Service. As I approach the car, Ryan opens the door for me to get in.

"Designated driver," he tells me when I'm about to tell him to get the fuck out. "Jump in, amigo."

Maybe Simon's right—he's not the kind of person we need around our table, even if he brings resources with him.

"Are we standing around, or are we fucking shit up?" he says with a grin, revving the engine of the Ford. "I used to love pushing the shit out of these babies when I first got my licence. The Puma was the one, though. I fucking loved that car."

"I need you to stop talking," I tell him, getting in the passenger seat.

"You need to clear your head and think like a soldier instead of getting pent up like this."

going down even though you buried one of your own today."

"Give him the fucking ring, Simon," Julian bites at him.

"I'm not here for the ring. I've got my own." Ryan flashes his hands at Simon. "I'm here because he's on his own." He nods at me. "While I might still knock his teeth out for bringing Eve into this, there's no way in fuck that I'm walking out of this room until I know she's safe."

"She's one of us," Casper says on loudspeaker. "We protect our own. We don't need a ring to hold our promises accountable."

"So, with that out of the way." Ryan sits back in his chair. "Who am I taking care of? Give me a name, and we'll make them disappear. No questions. No mess. No trail." He levels each of us with a shit-eating grin.

"Warren, Your Grace." Percival hands me the phone.

"Richard," I bark into the phone, making it clear I want him to fill me in on what's happening with Catherine's arrest quickly.

"She posted bail," he tells me.

Blind fury twists my gut. "How the fuck did she afford it?"

"I looked into it. The address checks out as a Coster King property."

The information settles like a lead balloon. I had the bitch right there, in my grasp. I should never have walked away or let the police deal with her. This is why when I want something taken care of, I do it myself with my own hands so that I know when it's done, it's fucking finished.

"The payment came from a Chapman account," the police commissioner says. He pauses for a beat before he adds, "It would appear that you've found your mole."

"You're certain that she is connected to Chapman?"

"Something's off," Ryan states as he types a message into his phone. "If she's working for Chapman, they wouldn't be stupid enough to give themselves away so easily."

"What would you have me do now?" Richard asks.

"Nothing. You've proven you are useless to me," I spit down the line. "I have no further use for you." I end the call and get to

THIRTY-FIVE
Henry

Eve is asleep in the suite down the hall. The sedatives Luke gave her will make sure she rests for the next few hours while I take care of business.

"I'm getting Warren on the phone now," Percival tells me as I finish filling Ryan in on what's happened.

"Well, you fucked up, didn't you, *bro*?" he scoffs at Simon.

After the shit he gave him when he turned up with Luke, I don't know how well these two will get on together, but right now, it's the least of my concerns.

"Give him the ring," I tell Simon as he continues to hold on to it.

"No, there's never been a bastard around this table, and it's not going to start with us." Simon makes a show of pocketing the ring with a sneer.

"I don't need your fucking ring or your poncy-as-fuck club."

"We're not a club," Julian corrects him.

"Whatever makes you happy." Ryan laughs, shaking his head as he looks around the room. "You need me and the reinforcements I bring with me. I don't need you. My life's pretty fucking good where I am right now."

"Why are you here, then?" Simon asks with a smirk.

"Well, you fucked with the wrong bastards, didn't you? Now, you want to sit here and have drinks…pretend nothing's fucking

How I would carry on. I'm watching his thoughts whir a hundred miles a second with the clench of his jaw and his heavy breaths. There's so much anger. So much rage. Pure destruction blazes in his dark eyes.

"Eve," he murmurs.

"Henry," I whisper back.

With a sideward glance, he says, "It's us or them."

"I pick us." I pick him. I pick his life and our love. The rest can be damned.

I'm not good. I'm not righteous. And I will not be miserable without him.

"I wondered what kind of person it would make me to be the woman behind you..."

"Beside me," he says, correcting me swiftly.

"Beside you," I echo. "I wondered if it would make me a killer too...a monster..."

Pausing in front of the gates leading to Hush, he asks, "And? What does it make you?"

"When I'm with you, beside you, Your Grace," I breathe, pressing a kiss to our intertwined hands, "with you, I'm untouchable."

"So you understand what happens now." He drives slowly towards the tree in front of the club. "You understand what I must do."

"Do your worst," I tell him, gripping his hand as tightly while I hug it to my heart. "Be your worst."

If his worst is what will keep him with me, then it's his worst I will love the most, and it's his worst that is the best part of him.

"We have a problem," Percival answers the call instantly. "Elizabeth is dead."

"When?"

"A guard found her outside the gate. Her throat was slit to the spine." The reply turns my stomach over as a shudder rakes through me. I swallow down the bile that bubbles up my throat, only for it to make me retch when Percival says, "Her tongue was gone, like the driver."

"Button?" Henry asks, his hands tightening around the steering wheel in a white-knuckle grip.

"Yes," Percival croaks with an audible swallow. "You should know, she tried to call Simon on the burner phone. The message she left is impossible to understand through her cries. They were chasing her, Henry, like a dog."

There's a long moment where Henry only drives. His eyes are glued to the road ahead as he appears to be deep in thought.

"This needs to end."

"Agreed," Percival says solemnly.

"Eve had a situation with Eddowes," Henry tells him.

"Catherine?"

"Yes. I need Luke Sterling at Hush ASAP to check on Eve, and I want Warren on the phone when I get there. Simon and Julian need to be ready to deal with the Elizabeth situation. I'm done with this war, Percival."

"Yes, Your Grace," Percival replies, reading the hard tone of Henry's voice.

"It's time to wipe the cunts out."

One of his hands rests over mine on my thigh as he puts his foot down through the empty backstreets. My head is hazy, and the wound on my arm is beginning to hurt with the jostle of the car over speed bumps. However, the one thing that keeps my tears at bay is Henry's unrelenting grip on my hand when I flip my palm up to his.

All I can think of is the conversation with Jess earlier today. If anything happened to Henry, I don't know what I would do.

"Henry." I whisper his name as a plea for him to let it go as I grip his wrist with my good hand, and he steps towards her.

He looks over his shoulder with a shake of his head. "No."

My shivers turn to anxious shudders as I watch him stop in front of her. He's silent for a while, and it's not because he's reining himself in. His stiff posture and the tip of his head tell me that he's considering what to do with her. To her.

"Would you like to press charges?" the policeman asks me.

However, before I can answer, Henry does it for me. "Yes, she would. Assault occasioning GBH."

"Grievous bodily harm?" Catherine scoffs. "It won't stick."

"I say it will, or else…" Henry leans over her, bracing himself on the arms of her chair as he whispers something into her ear. Whatever it is shuts her up, instantly wiping the smug sneer off her face. "Don't fucking test me."

"Bastard," she snipes at him as he turns to get back to me. "You and your fucking whore can go to hell along with your devil society."

"Arrest her," he orders the policeman. "I want her locked up."

"Someone needs to shut her up for her own good," Hannah groans as I stand on trembling legs to stop him from doing something that will hurt him.

"I need to get you to a doctor," he tells me, catching me as I trip on my backpack on the floor and stumble over my stupid feet.

"Yes. Yes, please."

"Let's go," he tells me, wrapping his arm around my waist before he leans over and slips the other beneath my knees, lifting me to his chest as Hannah picks up my backpack and follows us to his car on the curb.

"I can walk," I whisper over his jaw with a kiss.

"I don't care."

My arm is throbbing. The comedown of adrenaline has me chilled to the bone. But he still manages to make me chuckle at his over-the-top protectiveness of me. We're driving away when he calls Percival.

throat in the process.

This isn't good. The thought barely registers when he reaches us. Mary falls into her chair while Hannah gives my shoulder a squeeze when Henry crouches in front of me.

He's still in his black suit from the funeral, and he looks tired as he gives me a thorough inspection.

"What happened?" he asks, examining my arm. His eyes flit to the other women before landing on the syringe and then taking in the bloody mess.

"Eve?" His fingers comb through my hair when I look down at my lap, figuring out what to say so that he won't lose his shit as bad.

I can sense his aggravation slowly mounting even though he's trying to rein it in.

"What happened to your arm, darling?" he asks with more edge to his voice.

"Nothing." I try to smile, but the adrenaline is crashing, and I'm trembling all over. "Just an accident with a broken glass."

Henry peels his jacket off and drapes it over my shoulders as my shivers become more pronounced. His scent is still warm as it seeps into me, and I relax into his hold. I can feel everyone staring at us, but right now, I just need him to hold me tighter.

"You're many things, Eve, but you're not a liar." I swear I've said this to him before, but my head is too fuzzy to remember when or why. In truth, I just want him to keep talking because the sound of his voice is all I need to hear right now. His hand cups my face lightly as he says, "Tell me what happened."

Before I can say anything, Mary tells him what happened with Catherine. Now, I feel sorry for her, even if she had it coming.

His eyes flash to mine. Dark rage shrinks his pupils while his nostrils flare with the effort it's taking for him to hold himself together. The tension in his body cords his neck.

"Do not lie to me again." The statement is flat as he stands and spins towards Catherine.

"Let's get you to the hospital. You're going to need stitches," Hannah cuts Mary off, pulling her hairband out of her hair and rolling it up to my elbow while carefully holding the cut on my arm together. "This should help slow the blood down."

"I swear I didn't see it. I'm so sorry," Mary says as the barmaid returns with the smallest kit in her hand and a roll of kitchen towel. "Let's patch you up properly."

The kit is basic, with just a few plasters, some saline, and a roll of bandage. But while Mary flounders around with everything, Hannah pours the liquid over my arm slowly while trying to clean the blood.

"It's not as bad as it looks. Probably don't even need stitches." Hannah is oddly in control of the situation as she uses some of the adhesive tape to pull the small wound together and then wraps the bandage tightly. "Why do you need that?" She nods down at my syringe.

"I'm badly anaemic." It's what I tell anyone that witnesses me having a moment like this, in lieu of making it awkward and having to explain that I have a shitty blood disease that makes me bleed heavily and for a lot longer than most people but it's not contagious.

"Let go of me!" I hear Catherine yell as the man holds her down in a seat, and she kicks and slaps at him. "Hit me again and I'll arrest you for assaulting a police officer."

"Should fucking arrest her anyway," Hannah mutters as the noise in the pub goes back to normal.

People get back to drinking as the barmaid hands me another glass of lemonade. "The sugar will help with the shock."

I doubt it, but I take the drink and have a long sip anyway. It'll help replenish some fluids at the very least. I'm just settling when Hannah lets out a soft sob-like groan.

"Fuck, we're all getting the sack for this." I follow her gaze to the entrance of the pub across the room.

Henry has a thunderous expression on his face as he stalks towards us. My calming pulse kicks up a few gears, drying my

backpack, trying to get my pouch out. I'm not waiting for this to get worse.

"Fuck," Mary and Hannah mutter as Hannah pushes me into a chair and Mary takes my backpack from me.

"I need my pouch," I tell her. "The leather pouch. I need it, please."

Panic always makes this worse, and today is no different. My hammering pulse makes me bleed harder, faster. My vision is blurring as I watch Mary fumble with the buckles of my backpack too.

"She needs an ambulance at the rate she's pissing out blood," Hannah tells Mary when she finally gets my backpack open and rummages through it.

"What pouch?" Mary asks me, still looking through the backpack. "I can't find anything."

"It's right there!" The fear in my voice is sharp. "It's in there!"

Snatching my bag back, I tip it all out on the table until my pouch falls out.

"Everything okay here?" one of the barmaids asks Mary.

"Fine, just need some cloths."

"And a first aid kit," Hannah barks at them. "For fuck's sake, the girl is bleeding out here."

"I'll go find that for you." The barmaid gives Mary a nod.

"Yeah, you do that!" Hannah calls after her, putting pressure on my arm to slow the bleeding as I rip the zip of my pouch open with my teeth. "Fucking useless twat."

"I didn't see it," Mary spits our way.

The medicine won't work instantly, but it'll mean I'm not bleeding for as long as I normally would. The instant I inject it into myself, the panic dies down a tad, enough that I can think clearer.

"How could you not see it? It was right there."

Mary gives me an apologetic glance, "I'm sorry, I panicked. I didn't know you needed something for the bleeding. How was I to know? Like, I—"

"The two of you are fucking stupid if you think that she's one of us." Picking up the amaretto sour, she gives it a long sniff before she drinks it down in a few long gulps. "You just sit on your little throne playing on your fiddle while the rest of us are on our hands and knees."

"If you hate it so much, maybe you should find something else you're good at," I bite back with so much venom that I surprise myself.

Maybe it's nerves or just the frustration of the last couple of weeks, but a laugh bursts from me. I can't be bothered with this crap. There's more to life than trying to be friends with someone that's going to hate me in spite of all my efforts to placate their unfounded dislike of me.

"Little bitch," Cat hisses as I grab my backpack, and she grips my wrist, pulling me across the table. "What did you say?"

Fuck, her nails are digging deep into my skin. It feels like they might pierce through at any moment. Her eyes bore into mine with more spite than I can bear as I try to yank myself free of her hold.

Her grip tightens, and in an effort to ease the strain of her hold on me, I lean closer. My heart is hammering hard and fast. My vision is fraying with my raging temper.

"I said," I growl in her face, "if the dirty chip on your shoulder is so unbearable, you should show yourself out."

I tug myself free suddenly with a pained grit of my teeth. I realise too late how that sounded, and as I look at Mary to apologise, Catherine smashes her empty pint glass across the table, into my arm. Ice cuts through my veins instantly. I know it's bad even before I look at the damage.

Silence cuts through the jukebox playing in the corner as a man pushes up from the table beside us and tackles Catherine. The music echoes through the entire pub: *My, my, my Delilah… Why, why, why, Delilah…*

My breaths snag in my constricting throat as I watch my blood run down my hand while I fight with the buckle on my

THIRTY-FOUR

Eve

"Come on, Eve, it's just one drink," Mary says, putting a similar drink to the amaretto sour Hannah made me at Hush in front of me. "It's not going to hurt."

"She's too good to drink the bottom shelf. Her tastes are a lot more sophisticated." Cat drinks down what's left of her pint before tapping my shoulder with the glass and turning it upside down on the table.

"Don't be mardy," Mary tells her. "We don't want your little green-eyed monster ruining our fun tonight."

"It doesn't matter how you try to paint it. A fucking turd is a fucking turd, Mary," Catherine says with a leering slur.

I did wonder when she was going to start on me tonight. If I had known she was coming, I wouldn't have bothered joining them tonight. Catherine's made it pretty clear she hates me with her constant rude remarks and scowls. I've just about had enough of holding my tongue. We're not at Hush anymore, I don't feel any two ways about giving as good as I get.

"I'm sorry," Mary mouths at me with a grimace as Hannah comes back from the toilet.

"What's going on?" she asks, looking between the three of us. "I thought we were getting along?"

Isn't that the misjudgement of the century? I scoff down at my lemonade.

"Fuck!"

"That's not a good fuck…"

"I have to go, Fred," I tell him as I put my foot down on the pedal.

I don't need directions; I know where I'm going, and I don't care how many speed limits I break as I race back to the crime scene I left behind. George Chapman's pub. His lair.

"Not a fucking drop, Henry," he says down the phone as I hang up.

I don't need his shit. The relentless pounding of my heart is making it hard enough to breathe through the suffocating squeeze of my lungs and the twist of my stomach.

My whole existence is balancing on the sharp precipice of a steep fall, and I'm grappling at it with every vestige of my strength. I just hope I'm not too late to protect my only joy in this world.

head towards her place. She doesn't answer my second call or the third. I begin to question whether I misread her gesture, but I'm certain I haven't. And after another missed call, I start to contemplate all the other reasons she might not be picking up.

This isn't good. The thought keeps turning about my head as I dial the one person I know will be able to locate her without senseless questions.

"You're calling me," Freddie groans, answering his phone. "What's happened?"

"I need a favour." It's a rarity for me to call him for anything, but unlike our cousin the Prince, his talents exceed fucking and drinking.

"Is it going to fuck me over?"

"No."

"What is it?" he asks with a fair enough tone to his voice.

"I need you to locate a mobile for me."

He lightly shushes his grumbling newborn before he asks, "The number?"

Once I've given it to him, he takes a moment to say anything while I try to keep myself calm. "Anything?"

"Give me a fucking minute. I'm working one-handed here." His son gripes again just as a text from him pings on the console screen. "Is she in trouble?" There's an edge of concern to his voice. "If she is, you need to let Casper know."

"I can handle it myself," I snap at him with a loud bark that makes the kid burst out crying. "Shit. Sorry."

"I know, mate, he's a cunt," he coos at the baby before he tells me, "If anything happens to her, I won't protect you. Her brother is a hero around here—he died protecting Casper's wife. And Casper will fuck you up if so much as a drop of her blood is spilt."

"Where is she?" I ask him as I try to pull his message up on my screen without taking my eyes off the road. With all the notifications from Simon and Julian pinging at me, it's impossible to get to the one I need.

"I sent you the ping to a pub. The White Hart?"

curtains are drawn, but the flicker of the TV bleeds through the crack as I walk up the short path to the porch and ring the doorbell. It's almost eight in the evening, but I can hear George announce that I'm at the door before he opens it with an older woman behind him.

"Sir Sloane," he greets me with a goofy smile in his knight pyjamas.

"Sir Cameron," I reply, holding my hand up to him. "Air five?"

He gives me a distanced high five as the woman asks, "Can I help you?"

"He's looking for Eve," George tells her before turning back to me and answering my unaired question. "She's gone home already."

"I see."

"Mummy told her to get a cab, but she's walking." With a huff, he says, "Naughty, Eve."

"Yes, very naughty Eve." I pull my phone from my pocket to check where she might be to be greeted with the endless calls from Simon and Julian. "I'm going to go make sure she gets home safe, okay?"

"Okay." He salutes me as I take a step back.

"I'm sorry to have disturbed you," I tell the older woman looking between us with an amused expression.

"It's all right." She smiles up at me. "She wasn't lying—you are very handsome."

"Nanny!" George groans with a closely followed "Yuck, yuck."

"I'll see you soon, Sir Cameron."

"We fight to the death," he calls after me as I head back to my car, dialling Eve.

"It's a duel," I grab the chopstick that's still in my cup holder and hold it up for him to see.

The excitement in his face makes me chuckle while I wait for Eve to pick up. She doesn't, so I dial again as I get in the car and

I don't look back or acknowledge her as I slam my door shut and open the envelope. The angry rhythm of my pulse trips over itself as I pluck the lock of hair from inside. It's so damn soft that I can't stop myself from stroking over it with my thumb while I wrap the short length around the tip of my finger and hold it to my nose.

Eve's scent fills my lungs, soothing over the unrelenting chaos of the last week. The void her absence has clawed out from my chest pulls itself a little more closed. For the first time in days, I'm not holding my breath in abatement; I'm holding her in, letting her scent warm through my veins a beat at a time. The overwhelming hit of her makes all the wrongs in this world fade into insignificance.

"Henry," my mother calls through the glass, rapping her knuckles on it as if it will make her any more heard.

But there's nothing left to say to each other. She used me and tried to drive a wedge between me and Eve. There's no remorse or contrition for her ill-thought-out plans. And I have no pity nor patience left for her. The time has come to push her aside.

As I rev my engine, she steps back enough that I can drive away with her form disappearing in my rear-view mirror as Simon stands beside her. My phone rings almost at once with Simon's name flashing up on the console screen. I don't know what I'm going to do about him yet. He might still have a part to play in this war, and maybe it will take care of him for me. Perhaps their sins will consume them as they have done my father and Alastair.

Regardless, my only focus right now is making everything right with Eve. She's the only thing that matters right now. I let her go, but it's time I bring my heart back to me.

The sky is black by the time I park outside Jess' place. The

the ring on the small finger of his left hand, beside his oath ring, is in clear view. The initials *KF* are worn but still legible. Kit Fairfax. The day he died was the day that Julian changed; he's never been himself since.

"I do," he says below a whisper, fisting his hand before he presses a reverent kiss to the ring. "More than you will ever know."

I silently pray that's true. I pray that I'm enough to keep Eve safe. To keep her breathing come what may because she's my be-all and end-all. The beginning and the end and everything in between.

The service began with a eulogy from the Sterling heir and ended with a reading by Sterling's successor. It's not the tradition that we normally see, but Sterling wasn't a traditional man. Perhaps it's why he's heading to his grave early.

My phone vibrates as the church is emptying. I'm checking the message when a black envelope pushes into my view.

"This is for you," Jess tells me when I look up. As I try to take the envelope from her, she pinches it tighter in her grip, stepping closer so that her narrowed stare is daggering right up at me. "Hurt Eve again and the next funeral you'll be at will be yours. Do you understand, Your Grace?"

"I have no intention of hurting Eve."

"Your intentions don't matter. If you so much as ding her heart one more time, that man over there"—she points at Ryan as he watches us intently—"will kill you."

"Are you threatening me, Ms. Cameron?" I take a step forward, but she holds her ground.

"No, Your Grace. This is a warning, and you only get one." Jess releases the envelope when I tug it from her grip this time. Turning on her heels, she glances over her shoulder with a top-to-toe glare. "I'll be seeing you around."

I pocket my phone as I head towards my car, with my mother following behind me along with her bodyguard.

"Henry," she calls as I get into the Defender.

"The shame of it," she continues hissing. "What was Alastair thinking? This is no place for—"

"Hush, Mother." I interrupt her venomous snipes. "You're in no place to judge."

"You can't begrudge me forever," she tells me, turning back to the front. "I did what I had to do. Like you should."

I know what I have to do, and she won't like it when she's replaced and retired in one of the country estates. Somewhere she can't stir any more shit or cause problems.

"Careful what you wish for," I say, blowing out a breath as the bagpipes start the coffin's procession into the chapel and everyone rises to their feet.

It's here the intrigue dies with the echoes of "The Flower of Scotland" reverberating around the stone walls. I zone out, keeping my eyes on the ground, while I try not to think too hard about the people I've buried. Every funeral is the same; the hymns change, but the passages stay true to the tradition of the Wolfsden Society.

It's while I sit here, blocking out the present, that the past collides with the future. One segues into the other. If this is the rest of my life, I don't want vipers at my side. There's only one person that should be with me right now, and I think it's time it happened.

I look beside me at Julian as he flicks through the order of service with shaky hands. This isn't easy for him either. Sterling may have been a bastard on many fronts, but he was good to him.

"We'll make it right," I tell him, leaning close.

"It's too late for right," he whispers back, nodding towards Simon on my mother's other side. "And it's not his fault."

"My father…Sterling, they might still be alive if it wasn't for them."

"My father might still be alive, if he wasn't dead," he grits back almost silently. "The reason we're here is because people die. It's a fact that will never change."

"One day, you will hunger for blood like the rest of us."

He turns his face to mine, lifting his hand between us so that

THIRTY-THREE

Henry

Funerals intrigue me. The rumble of animated chatter twists with the sombreness of the event, a collision of celebration and sadness that's unsettling in every way. But never as unsettling as when silence falls suddenly. My first instinct is to look around me for a threat. I wouldn't put it past Chapman to try something today, all the people on his death list in one place. I know where I would hit if I was him. But that's thing about criminals—we respect each other's sorrow. As though there's some unwritten rule of respect. In the end, we're all criminals; some of us simply choose the better side—where monsters rub shoulders with gods, and we call ourselves holy.

Glancing over my shoulder at the open doorway of the chapel, I watch as Sterling's beloved mistress walks down the aisle with her bastard son. I have to double take for a moment.

What is she doing here? The question turns around in my head as Jess locks eyes with me. Her face morphs from morose to angry with a bat of her lashes. The force of her stare is unwavering in its hold as she walks with Sterling's named successor. Behind them, his rightful heir follows with his wife and their son.

"It's a wonder that woman shows herself here," my mother says with a look of repugnance as Grania sits in the front row on he opposite end of the pew with Ryan and Jess beside her and Luke Sterling and his wife between them and Catrin.

that's what matters most."

"Thank you."

"Don't thank me because if he hurts you again, I will get your brother's old nunchucks out, and I'll batter him with them." There's no point in arguing with her because I know she would go at Henry without any hesitation. "All in all, he's not that bad. Anyone that treats George right and makes him smile deserves the benefit of the doubt."

We pause in the open doorway as Ryan gets beaten by George at a Mortal Kombat fight on the PlayStation.

"My mum said she'll come take over at around seven so you can go for your drinks. She'll get George to bed and sort him out. Make sure you get a cab, okay? It's not safe out there," she says as Ryan announces, "Last match, Road Kill." He uses George's gaming name with exaggerated grit.

"I'm not going to drink. The only reason I'm going is because Mary won't stop inviting me out, and it feels weird always saying no."

"It's good that you're getting out and having fun…socialising…making friends."

"Then stop worrying about me," I tell Jess as she watches George and Ryan with a smile.

"That's not going to happen. We're as good as sisters."

Soon after the wrestling match is done, they leave, and while George finishes his game, I read through Henry's notes again and again. Soon enough, I'll know them by heart just as I know that he is the only man for me. He's my beautiful villain with dark hair, a devilish smile, and blood on his hands.

and one of her small elastic bands. Once I've tied it around the end of one of my messy waves, I snip it off and slip it into one of the envelopes he sent.

Henry has always made it obvious that he loves my hair, and I love the feel of him playing with it. Whether he's wrapping it around his fist when we fuck or whether he's combing his fingers through it affectionately. It's the best feeling in the world. One I'm done being without. The same way I'm done being without him.

"We're going to head off now," Jess says, meeting me in the hallway as I'm leaving the bathroom. "Everything okay?" She glances at my backpack, where she knows I keep my medication.

"Yeah, everything is fine."

"You're sure?" I nod in reply to her question, and she asks, "Good love note?"

"Yes," I tell her, holding out the envelope to her. "If you see Henry, could you give him this?"

"There better not be any weird shit in here. No toenail clippings." Jess takes it from me with a suspicious cock of her brow.

"No, just a couple of pubes I plucked with your favourite tweezers."

"You're actually disgusting," she says, pulling a face as she stuffs the envelope into her handbag.

"You started it with the toenail clippings when it's just my used knickers."

"I thought I could smell something fishy."

"Uuugh." A fake gag cuts through my chuckle.

"You're certain you're okay to watch George? I can take him to my mum's on the way."

"No, we're good. I'm going to order us some pizza and maybe rent a film or whatever he wants to watch. Cheer him up a little bit before you get back."

"I'll make sure Henry gets this." Jess lifts her handbag awkwardly as we head towards the lounge. "I know I'm not the nicest about him, but if he makes you happy and looks after you, then

man is letting down his walls for me one note at a time. Maybe it's silly to some, but it's precious to me. He's precious to me.

And the gravity of my love is unyielding.
You push all my buttons and never back down when I push back.

And the magnitude of my love is astronomical.
Your sass knows no bounds.

And the force of my love is unshakeable.
Your kindness reminds me there's hope.

And the tenor of my love is steadfast.
You are the melody to my happiness.

Pulling the new note from its envelope, I'm struggling to contain my tears. At the heart of him, Henry is all that I never knew I wanted or even needed. He's tough and unmoveable, but he's also caring and gentle. For the most part, at least.

With my fingertips tracing Henry's intricate scroll, I read the note slowly, taking in each word with every breath.

And the force of my love is insurmountable.

There's nothing truer. Everything about Henry is forceful, but his love is the strongest of all.

You are the missing piece of my heart.

Henry is everything. He's my everything. These notes, as beautiful as they are, aren't enough. I can't live our love through them any more than I can breathe without my lungs.

Shuffling all the notes together, I throw them into my backpack before I run into Jess' bathroom and grab her hair scissors

way he treats him is beyond awful, and there's no doubt that the rest of his family is like that from all the awful things I've read about them. They deserved to die. They deserved everything they got.

Grabbing a knife from the drawer, I open the envelope before sitting back at the table. Like with every note I receive, I always start at the first.

And the reasons I love you are endless.
You touched my soul and made it yours.

My chest squeezes as tightly now as it did the first time I read the note. It still makes my heart stutter in the same way every note afterwards made it race with excitement and glee.

And the ways that I love you are many.
Your smile makes me feel a lot less lost.

And the measure of my love for you is immeasurable.
Your laugh reminds me there's always more to life.

And the depth of my love is limitless.
Your eyes never lie.

And my love for you is brighter than the sun.
Your lips taste like heaven.

And the rhythm of my love for you will echo through eternity.
Your heart always beats in time with mine.
(We're made for each other)

The words are mesmerising and touching, but it's the sentiment behind them that really gets to me. This proud and severe

groans as the doorbell rings, and she gets up to answer it, leaving me to contemplate our conversation.

She doesn't know it, but I needed to hear all of this. Her frankness and sincerity are why Joe loved her the way he did.

"Where's my favourite kid?" I hear Ryan call from the front door. "And a Darling?"

"That's for Eve," Jess tells him with a quiet laugh as I get up and head their way. My heart is racing in my chest as I walk down the short hallway to the door of the flat. "She's in the kitchen, and George is ignoring everyone because he's annoyed with me today."

Ryan looks a lot like his dad. Icy eyes that have a way of making you feel like he can read your deepest, darkest secrets. Unlike Lord Alastair Sterling, he has a sharp sense of humour that has made everyone in this house laugh through some shitty times.

"This is for you, Darling," he announces with a grin, holding out another rose-and-black envelope. "It was on the doorstep."

"Thanks," I say, taking the flower and note from him and backtracking into the kitchen.

"Nice seeing you too," Ryan calls after me as Jess tells him, "She's got a lot on her mind."

"Yeah, so I've heard." No doubt from Casper. They're still close, and they still work together.

"How're you doing?" I hear Jess ask him with a softness in her voice that has me looking back.

I know they've become close friends, but sometimes I think that there's more to them than they realise. Even though she misses my brother, I wonder if some of the advice she gave me has to do with Ryan too. Jess is still young, and she deserves happiness.

I deserve happiness, and I want to be happy. It had been such a long time since I felt it all the way to my bones. But Henry brought it to life. He made me the happiest I've been in so long.

It would be stupid to let him go because he's not perfect. I'd be insane to condemn him for seeking some kind of justice for his dad, and anyways, I've seen the kind of man Alfie's dad is. The

small glass of lemonade.

"Yes. I guess I need to figure out what I can and can't live with."

A small frown pulls at one side of her mouth as her gaze softens on me. "If you woke up tomorrow and he was gone, could you live with that? Knowing that he feels that way about you." She nods down at my backpack, where the notes from Henry are all stashed. "Could you look in the mirror and not have any regrets?"

"No." My chest tightens with my reply.

"What are you doing loving him through silly notes when he's right there and he can tell you every word to your face? Why?"

"Because. Because it's complicated and…and I'm scared of becoming someone I hate. I'm scared of…of everything."

"Life is complicated, Eve. Look at us—we learnt that lesson a while ago." Perching herself on the table, Jess brushes my hair from my face. "At some point, everyone looks in the mirror and hates themselves. We all do bad shit. We all fuck up. We all do things we regret. There isn't a single, outright good person in this world. For one reason or another, we all have to do ugly shit at some point."

"I know." I grew up in a family where my dad and brother killed people to protect others. It's the context of it. The morality.

"You'll look in the mirror and you'll hate yourself, but you'll turn around, and you'll have him to remind you that shit happens." A light, teary chuckle bubbles from her as she rubs her fingertips where she used to wear her wedding ring. "He'll remind you that it doesn't change who you are. You're always going to be this person. Whether you're a happy or miserable version is up to you. But—" She blows out a long, shaky breath. "—from personal experience, don't choose to be miserable. It sounds a lot more righteous than what it feels."

"You miss him," I say, linking her fingers with mine. "You miss Joe."

"Like an idiot misses the point." Her laugh echoes around us as she dries the tears lining her lash line. "Don't be the idiot," she

"Momentarily forgot you hate funerals? I didn't even know that's what you were doing this afternoon. Whose funeral is it?"

"Ryan's dad's. You remember Ryan, don't you?" She sounds as nervous as I felt when Henry took me to the gala. It's only now that I'm really noticing how on edge she is.

"No, I've totally forgotten the guy that was in and out of here, making sure we were all okay after Joe died. No idea who that guy is."

My attempt at lightening the mood falls flat as she pauses in front of me with a deep huff.

"His dad died suddenly a couple of weeks ago."

"I heard," I tell her, stopping her from fussing with the ends of her short hair. "His dad was a family friend of Henry's."

"Oh. I suppose it makes sense. These people all run in the same circles."

"Henry will probably be there," I whisper, mostly to myself.

"If you stopped playing these ridiculous games, you'd be there with him."

"But you'd be out of a babysitter." My smile earns me another roll of her eyes. "I know you don't get it, Jess, but I need to get my head straight. Falling in love with him wasn't part of my plan."

"And still you fell for him." I nod at her remark. "Because plans are just pretty thoughts; they're not written in stone. Can you imagine life without a change of plan? It's a bit like a book without a plot twist."

"Predictable."

"Yes, and the thing with predictable is that we all think we want it until we have it." Her fingers curl around mine as we walk head into the kitchen instead of the lounge, where George is watching telly. "You don't want predictable for the rest of your any more than I do."

"No, but Henry's life is so different. Their circles are on a completely different parallel to ours."

"But you love him," she says with a shrug, pouring us both a

has the right end of the stick before she beats you with it.

"Doesn't sound like it. He had you playing for him in his suite," she says, zipping up her boots before she starts transferring her purse and other items from one handbag to another. "Was this before or after he started fuc—the two of you became a thing?"

"It's how we became a thing. When you don't know the full context of it all, it sounds bad, but it's not, Jess. He never touched me, not once. At least not until I made it clear that I wanted him to."

Jess nods with a soft, narrow-eyed scowl. "I don't want anyone taking advantage of you. You're young, Eve, and he's…"

"Older. I know." Everyone likes to point it out like it's this big deal. "But no one would care if I was in my thirties and he was in his forties."

"You're not in your thirties, Eve."

"Henry isn't in his forties either."

"God, you're so fucking stubborn," she groans, throwing the packet of wet wipes in her hand at me. "You're just like your brother and your nephew. You always have some kind of retort at the ready."

"You're just annoyed because you know it's true." Turning my back on her, I head for the lounge.

"You're annoying me," she yells down the hallway, poking her head out of her bedroom doorway. "You're telling me it doesn't matter that he's older like you're mature enough to be with him, but you're silly playing games like a child."

Whoa. Where did that come from?

"You just said he was being creepy."

"Because it is fucking weird to be leaving flowers in random places with random love notes and—"

"And what's wrong with you?" I ask, blurting out the question before she finishes her crazy rant.

"I hate funerals," Jess tells me, letting out a long sigh while she meanders towards me. "I don't know why I even volunteered to go to this thing. I just…"

THIRTY-TWO

Eve

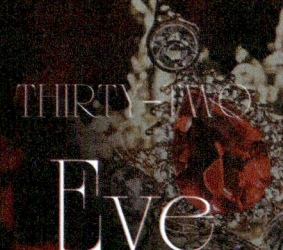

"And you don't think that's creepy?" Jess laughs as I watch her get ready to go out.

"Is it?" My question fades into the silence as she debates what earrings to wear with her cute black dress.

When she settles on a pair of gold hoops, she peers at me in the mirror. "Well, he essentially ghosted you, and now he's stalking you."

"With pretty flowers," I say, barely able to keep my smile from cutting all the way across my face. "And love notes. He leaves me these cards."

When I pull the envelopes from my backpack, she rolls her eyes. "Oh, and you carry them everywhere. Obviously."

"He left the first one on my doorstep, and ever since, there's one everywhere I go. Like at the conservatory and at work. He had the chair from his suite brought into the lounge because that's where I used to sit when I only played for him."

Like he told me, he's giving me space while making it known that he's still there, watching and waiting for me.

"Wait." She pauses in front of me, pulling her knee-high boots on. "You used to play for him?"

"It's complicated." Fuck, of all people to let this slip to, she's the worst. Jess analyses everything with a fine-tooth comb. When she's done with that, she'll pick it all apart to make sure that she

he'll be right there to pick me up and steal me away.

percut that would only make everything worse.

I draw a deep breath into my lungs as I read over the card.

And the reasons I love you are endless...

The black scroll reads on the front of the card, as though it's part of an unfinished conversation. Perhaps that's what we'll always be—an unfinished, unpunctuated ramble of words that never ends. There'll always be more to say and more to feel. I flip the card, and my eyes flit to the red wax seal beneath the writing on it.

The head of the wolf is like an imprint of his ring. A stamp of everything he is. Beautiful and beastly. Majestic and deadly. Somehow, contrary to everything I've ever thought of myself, I'm addicted to him, love and hate interwoven into a poison that has darkened my soul. Still, I love him. I think I'll always love him because beneath everything I know he's capable of and that he has done, I've felt his gentleness and adoration. And maybe it's better to be worshipped by a devil than loved by a god.

My tear-glazed eyes flit to the message about Henry's seal. It's everything I already know. I've known for so long, but seeing it in his writing makes it more than real or true. It makes it a testament. A prophecy fate long wrote about us thousands of lives ago.

You touched my soul and made it yours.

Tears well deep in my chest, suffocating my hot sobs as I try to swallow them down as quickly as they threaten to overwhelm me. It's impossible, and after a moment or two, the dam breaks, and I'm left staring at the blurred card in my hand as the world threatens to cave in on me. If I only loved Henry, it would be easy to walk away. But what we have is so much more, and I know that it doesn't matter how long I fight him, eventually, I'll lose, and

another long drink of water, I focus on the feel of cool liquid down my throat and chest to my belly. My autonomy is returning to me slowly as I fall back on the mattress and trace the intricate plasterwork on the ceiling with my eyes until I can't keep them open anymore, and I doze off with my sadness pulsing all over me.

I made my bed. Now I'm lying in it.

The first rose is waiting for me by my front door when Percival takes me home. The estate is unusually quiet as I pick up the short, odd-shaped vase beside the dinosaur boot scraper George bought for my birthday last year. The bud is a deep burgundy red with just one leaf on the trimmed stem, leaving it long enough to tie a small envelope to it.

Darling is inscribed on the front of the velvet-coated card stock in a gold script that is all too familiar. And I don't know whether my heart is smiling or crying at the sight of it. This strange haze has come over me since the moment I stepped out of the red suite.

Desiderium: that awful hollowness and longing for something that's missing. I feel lost as my feet try to navigate the shaky ground I've found myself on without him.

When I'm in my flat, I put the small vase on the dining table before I make myself a cup of tea and then sit in front of the note. I watch it for a while, wondering what it could say that I don't already know. Henry made it clear that he's not simply going to allow me to walk away.

Like Julian told me the night I signed the contract—I made a deal with the devil. I just never imagined falling for him, loving him despite all his sins. Unable to stare at the envelope anymore, I open it haphazardly with my finger, almost giving myself a pa-

drugged me. Nor had he considered killing me hours beforehand. Not one of those times was I wondering what kind of person I am for loving him in spite of knowing that he's a killer. A murderer. A monster.

"Then prove it," I sob. "Let me go home. Just… Let. Me. Go. Please, Henry."

With a nod, he sits me beside him on the bed before he gets up and strides to the door. His demeanour is a myriad of emotions that wrench at my insides. One look and I feel the full spectrum of love and grief and hate. He makes me feel so much so fiercely, and I don't like it. I wish I could make it stop. I wish I could make it all go away. For once, I wish my veins would bleed dry of this pain.

"Look at me, Eve," he orders brusquely. As always, my body bows to his will, and my stare meets his across the dimly lit room. "I'm not giving you up. This isn't me letting you go." Henry opens the door and stands in the open doorway, watching me intently.

It's impossible to breathe through the merciless squeeze of my chest around my lungs. My vision is hazy from my tears, and my head is throbbing from the sedative he gave me. I'm overwhelmed and exhausted. My wits are at their end.

I am terrified; the longer I look at him like this, the more I love him. The more I love him, the scarier it becomes to think of what I would do to be with him. Who I would become to be his. If behind every great man, there's a great woman, what would it make me to be behind this man? A killer? A monster?

"Listen to me, Eve," Henry barks across the room when I stare down at my hands, wondering what they would look like bloody like his. When I meet his gaze again, he tells me, "I'm not letting you leave me. At least not for good. I'll give you time and space, but I'm always going to be right there, watching over you. Keeping you safe."

"Henry…"

"Percival will see you home." Without another word, he backs out of the room, closing the door as he leaves.

I've never felt so conflicted and so alone as I do now. Taking

self for instantly trying to justify his indifference with knowledge of what I read about his victims and Alfie's family.

"Of course you don't." I press my hands to his chest, hoping that he'll release me this time.

"You can fight me as much as you like, but I'm not letting you go." Henry adjusts his grip on me, threading a hand into my hair while the other claws into my waist.

"I want to go home, Henry."

"I'm not letting you leave me." His forehead lowers to the top of my head so that his lips are at my ear. "I'm your home."

The words are beautiful enough that my traitorous heart melts for him even as it bleeds with the gaping wound he left.

"You could've been…you were, but—"

"Could've, would've, should've," he states, cutting me off as he rolls his forehead over my hair. "I could've done things differently, and if I knew then what I know now, I would've. I should've known better than to push you away, but when you're me, it's hard to trust people."

"When you're me and you've lost everyone you've ever loved, it's hard to open yourself up to anyone." Tears prickle my eyes as I admit, "But I let you in, and I allowed myself to fall in love with you." Cupping his face with my hand, I pull away so that I can look into his eyes. "I loved you, and you left me. Cast me away like I was nothing to you. The saddest part of it is that I still loved you then."

I still love him now, but if he can't trust, then we're going to end up here, like this, again. That's something that I can't do.

"I can't fight you, Henry. I don't have the physical strength to go at it with you and come out on top. But if there's a single part of you that honestly cares for me, you'll let me go."

"No," he says as I release him and try to push myself away again. "I love you."

A deluge of tears breaks free at his words. I've wanted to hear them so much, and I imagined him telling me he loves me so many times. But not once was I incapacitated because he'd

"I'm sorry," he tells me. "The sedative will take a while to wear off completely. You should rest, and then we can talk."

"Talk."

"Yes." Crouching in front of me, Henry scoops me up into his arms and sits on the bed with me in his lap.

"Talk. *Talk*? Don't you think it's too late for that?" I try to push myself away from him, but his hold tightens, and my strength is all gone. "You were going to kill me."

"You threatened me, and you let the Chapman boy touch you. You let another touch what's mine." An arm cradles me tightly to his chest as he reaches for his phone on the bedside table. "I've looked at these photos and tried to understand why. I thought we—I…"

"Alfie is my friend, and his mum is my neighbour. It's not what you thought, but maybe you wouldn't have gone down that rabbit hole if you hadn't killed his aunts." I jostle myself lightly so that I can see his face properly in the light.

Henry's still the most beautiful man I've ever known. Even after he's as good as admitted he was going to kill me, and knowing what I know he's capable of, butterflies flutter in my belly when his stare narrows on my lips with want. My heart still stutters when he drops his phone on the bed and his fingers stroke my face.

Even through my hatred of what he's done and what he's capable of doing, I still love him. The voice in my head still whispers that he would never hurt me. I'm lying to myself and losing all my morals because of him.

"There was no need for him to touch you like that. It wasn't going to bring his aunts back."

My cackle rips through my sore throat. "Maybe it's not about what I did or didn't do," I mutter in between coughs. "It's about the fact that your actions are eating at you."

"I don't regret my actions, Eve," he tells me matter-of-factly, and the stoic expression on his face backs up his words.

I don't know if I'm angry at him for being so cold or at my-

THIRTY-ONE

Eve

"You drugged me," I whisper coarsely. My mouth is so dry that my throat and sinuses hurt. The grogginess isn't letting up fast enough so that I can force my way out of here.

"I had no choice," Henry replies, holding out a bottle of water to me. "It's sealed."

Shaking the water bottle in front of me, he makes a show of opening it slow enough that I can hear the seal break before I snatch it from him and gulp it down greedily.

"Slowly, Eve, or you'll vomit," he tells me, pulling the bottle from my grip when I don't listen. "I don't want you to be sick."

A crackling laugh bursts from me, earning me a frown when I say, "Sick is the least of your concerns right now. You drugged me and…and…" I pause as a lightbulb goes off in my head. "Were you going to kill me? Are you going to kill me?"

Henry doesn't reply for a long moment. Instead, he stares down at his lap in thought. He appears crestfallen and confused, but the clench of his jaw also betrays the anger he's trying to hide.

"At least you're not lying about it," I spit, lifting the heavy covers off me with effort before I stumble off the bed. My legs are jelly as I try to stand, and the strength in my arms gives the more I try to push myself up. "What have you done to me?"

A grave expression falls over his face as he stands and rounds the bed to where I'm sprawled on the floor.

"In light of everything I've told you, she knows nothing, and as for the boy, I believe you owe her the chance to explain."

Perhaps. I stroke my fingers down her legs as she groans awake, and I sit beside her on the bed, waiting for her to open her eyes as I dismiss Percival. I'll deal with him and the rest of them later.

For now, I want to see what is salvageable of me and my darling girl. Eve.

The first woman to catch my eye, to weaken my resolve, to survive me. And when all is said and done, I hope that I'll survive her too.

mans' rivals on the streets, and we struck a deal. They would take care of the problem for us and make it look like a gang attack, and we would help them regain some of the territory they'd lost to Chapman."

My memory takes me back to the meeting in the office. Simon was always that one step ahead of what was happening. Unlike his usual advice, he was pushing for me to let loose on Chapman.

"They brutalised that girl in ways that—" He pauses with a shake of his head, as though he can't bring himself to say what happened to the girl. "We couldn't get to the Republic lover in time. By then, he'd gone to Chapman, and we knew it was only a matter of time before he sent his people for us."

"She used me." The words roll from my tongue, leaving a sour taste that causes me to flinch as I push to my feet and take my phone back from Percival. "My mother used me, and you allowed it to go on and on."

"I made the Duchess a promise while I made sure Eve was looked after like your father would have wanted. I brought her to you because I knew that you'd see in her the same rarity that James saw. Maybe you'd grow to care for her and…" He shrugs like the rest would be nothing but history. A fairy tale.

"I do care for her." More than anyone will ever know.

"She cares for you too."

"My mother doesn't like her."

"She was never going to like the woman who would take her place in both title and affections. It stands to reason that maybe this is why she had Andrew look into Eve. Why she fed him just the right information to make you turn your back on Eve."

"Doesn't change the fact that she knows too much."

"Those threats she made today weren't real. Eve's too loyal for it, and she loves you," he says with a smile tugging at the corner of his mouth.

I stare down at her sleepy form as consciousness twitches her eyelids and limbs. "Doesn't change the fact that she let another touch her."

other thought in the back of my mind, and it angers me beyond any rage I've ever been in.

"Why?" I ask him, wrapping my hand around hers as if its warmth has the power to soothe me even now. "Why don't I know any of this? Why didn't she tell me?"

"There are a few reasons. They're all intertwined, and maybe flawed, but I thought it was the best way to continue after he was killed." Percival pushes up onto his feet and moves to stand over the bed, watching Eve again with tantamount sorrow and affection. "It all goes back to the study he and Alastair were running."

"Is that why they're dead?"

"One of the girls here was studying to be a nurse, and she had a troubled relationship with her family. Morals—the girl had morals, for a time, at least, and Sterling had a soft spot for her."

"He had a soft spot for a lot of them."

"Yes, well, as you can see, it didn't end well." A dry scoff pushes from his lips as Eve stirs for the first time. I check my watch to confirm that it's about right for her to start waking now. "This girl was helping them with the admin side as I helped with the logistics. Her name was Emma Elizabeth Smith when she came to Hush, but before that, she was a Chapman. Her father was George Chapman."

A laugh rips from me. Disbelief and annoyance. I can see where this is going now, and I know my mother's games well enough to know that her innocent, grief-stricken plea for revenge was nothing but a move in her wily games. She and I are not all that dissimilar, but her gumption exceeds what I imagined.

"She became embroiled in a love affair outside of here." He points around the room. "The man was unknown at the time, and I found that he was one of the United Republic's faithfuls. He corrupted her, turned her against us, and she started reporting back to him."

"So, we had her killed before she could provide him with hard proof."

"Yes, your mother asked Simon to approach one of Chap-

in check. There's a medication she takes that the NHS doesn't supply, and he made sure she had it. But he was also trying to help her."

"How?" I ask, turning to look at her.

"He was trying to, Henry. James genuinely thought that if he could work out why her blood lacked the substance, he might figure out a process from removing it in a person that clots too easily and maybe putting it into a person that has trouble clotting. Eventually, the body would train itself to do it on its own, like…" Percival shrugs. He looks baffled by everything he's trying to explain. "I don't know how the science works. I just listened to James and Alastair talk about it."

"He wanted to figure out a way of performing gene therapy." Gene therapy was a hot topic for my father. I used to listen to him preach about it to his dictaphone. For hours, he would sit in his study, reading textbooks and dictating notes for his research papers. All the while, he'd have Fauré on repeat in the background.

"Whatever it is, it's all in the briefcase that's missing," Percival says with a hopeless shrug. "If the wrong people get their hands on it, it will create a scandal unlike any the firm has had. Technically, the study would be branded as unethical because of the deal Eve and your father made. The medicine and the conservatory scholarship. They're all a part of it."

"I see." Sitting on the edge of the bed, I pull a blanket over her. Really, I need to get her out of her damp dress, maybe burn the damn thing whilst I'm at it. "What does my mother have to do with it?"

"She knew about the study, and she would've had Sterling continue, but he didn't care for Eve the way your father did. To him, she was a rare jewel, but to Alastair, she would've been a means to getting what he needed."

That sounds about right. It's why my father was in the business of finding cures and Alastair was in the business of cutting people up. And today, I would've treated her the way he would have. The thought makes me sick to my stomach. But there's an-

one with such a rare blood condition would wind up here in our midst?"

"Not particularly. If anything, I begrudge the fact that she came to me after he died. He would've known how to help her."

"There's hope for you yet," he chuckles lightly with a shake of his head.

The way he's acting is odd, and I don't like that he seems to know a lot more than he's letting on. I've trusted Percival because my father trusted him too. He was his confidant and a true friend. I thought that maybe he would be to me what he was to him once he'd had the chance to mourn his loss. But maybe I was wrong on this front too.

"You have the right information about Eve, your father, and Alastair, but not the context. Nor do you have all the facts, Henry."

Standing, I gesture for him to sit on the chair I vacated. I know I'm grasping onto every straw I can, looking for anything I can to absolve her so I can keep her. But after all of this, I don't know whether she would want me still.

"Enlighten me," I say when he sits and flicks over the information in the email again.

"One in a million," he states, narrowing his gaze on Eve.

"Pardon?"

"Your father used to call her a phenomenon. Less than eight thousand people in this world have her condition, but your father found her. It was like finding a needle in a haystack." Turning my phone towards me, he points out all the dates that Andrew found footage of Eve visiting my father's office at the hospital. "All these dates correlate with blood samples that your father sent off to a lab in Scotland where they were studying the clotting habits to figure out a way of slowing down the King's cancer."

"He used her as a guinea pig." Disgust twists at my insides. It sounds like something my father would do in the name of science.

"No, they had a mutual agreement. He could have as much of her blood as he wanted so long as he helped keep her condition

"It's her," I tell him. "Your mole is her."

A long laugh rumbles from him with a shake of his head. "James would have slapped you by now. Probably thrown you in the fire until you woke up to the smell of your own arse burning."

"My arse is burning, Percival. All our arses are on fucking fire." Twisting his wrist brusquely, I remove his hand from the blade. "The King isn't going to last much longer, Arthur keeps fucking up with the wrong fucking people, and on top of that, we have Gangs of London on our doorstep while the Republicans feed off their chaos."

"And at what point did you conclude that Eve is the one feeding your enemy?"

"*Our* enemy. If I go down, this entire place goes down in blazing glory."

I push him out of the way so that I have a clear view of Eve. Like the first time I saw her, my blood boils with the need to destroy her, and at the same time, every memory we've made together makes me want to venerate her. Because, like this, she's still a goddess. The rise and fall of her chest still remind my lungs to breathe.

"Andrew." I blow out a long breath.

Pulling my phone from my pocket, I hand it to him with the email with all the information Andrew got on her open. There's something unsettling about the nonchalant way he's nodding along while he reads and zooms into the photos.

"Why aren't you surprised?" I ask, flicking the knife closed and pushing it into the damp pocket of my hoodie.

"I've always had a special admiration for your mother. She was always one step ahead of everything. But once in a while, she always takes it too far."

"Why are we talking about my mother?"

"Because she played us good and proper, Henry." He lets out a long, exasperated sigh while he rolls his neck back and forth, pacing alongside the bed while he watches Eve with pity and regret. "Has it ever crossed your mind how odd it is that some-

THIRTY

Henry

It was stupid to think that if she wasn't conscious, it would be easier to kill her. It's not. The last forty-five minutes have dragged by as I've watched her sleep in the bed where I first fucked her. There's something poetic that she should die on the same bed she bled for me.

"Henry, you're not listening to me," Percival says as he steps in front of me, wrapping his hand around the blade in my hand. "You don't want to do this."

"She betrayed me." I glimpse around him to the bed. "And traitors don't get to live."

The words choke me. I can't breathe around them. Can't swallow down the bile that burns up my throat at the thought of killing her. I could've and should've done it out there. But even now, with all the shit that's been brought to me, I know that she deserves better. She deserves more than to die on the cobbles like the others I've killed.

"We both know she would never have whispered a word to a soul."

Percival's too soft—this is why we keep most of the plotting from him. He knows the essentials so that he can keep the right people happy, but aside from that, he's left ignorant. His job is to keep this place running and bring the right whispers to my ears as he did for my father.

I pull my hood over my head, and my eyes prickle as I imagine his gaze on me now. Hope waters his eyes with some of the heartbreak he's inflicted on me. Hope paints an awfully pained image of him, but if he's watching me leave, he can't be hurting half as much as me.

"Don't look back," Percival reminds me as I walk out into the rain, and finally, I can allow my tears to fall.

The constant drum of the rain muffles my suffocating sobs. If anyone could cure me from my fear of thunder and lightning, it is Henry, and he has done it. I wish for the bone-rattling roar and the deathly sparks. I wish so hard that, for once, it comes true. And like every time, I run. Not for cover or for fear. I run from him and this place as if the further I get from it, the less I will hurt.

But it doesn't work, and my desperate breaths jam in my throat, making me dizzy. I have to stop. Stop. Breathe past the gust of wind that hits me, blowing my hood off as a shadow flickers in the light of the streetlamp behind me.

I feel him before I see him.

"Your Grace," I sputter past my pounding pulse when his cold stare bores into mine.

Henry wraps an arm around my waist as his hand lifts to my face. The touch never comes, just a sharp pinch and a chill that shoots to my toes before everything starts to haze, and the only thing I can hear is his warm breath as it ghosts over my face.

"Darling."

Casting a long gaze around me, I take everything in until tears threaten to fall. If it's too late, then I want to take as much of it with me as I can. It's all a part of him. If I can't get one last look at him, then this will have to do.

Percival is quiet as we walk downstairs together. He holds my violin and backpack as I put on my coat that's been left on the reception desk.

"I brought you here because I thought you'd be good for him. James liked you, and I thought that he would've approved, but I've let you both down. I'm sorry for that, Eve. So very sorry."

"It's okay." I swallow down the urge to bark and bite at him. Instead, I plaster a smile on my face as he opens the door.

A creak on the stairs tells me we're not alone. And I feel him. His presence looms behind me in the shadows.

"Need a ride home?" Percival asks me with a flicker of his eyes to the stairs, but when I follow his stare, there's only darkness and a pained pang inside me that wishes and prays for just one more look. A stolen glimpse or even an indifferent glower. Anything.

"No. No," I reply with a shake of my head when I find Percival's glance again. "I'm meeting a friend."

Jess has texted me all evening. She's worried after I left her place in such a hurry. After the night I've had, I don't want to be alone.

As if he knows, Percival gives my shoulder a squeeze with a head-to-toe glance as though this is the last time we will see each other and he's committing me to memory.

"I see." He tugs the front of my coat closed. "Get home safe. Won't you?" When I give him a smile, he adds, "Don't look back."

As soon as he says it, I instantly cast a long look around me. I can't help it. Maybe I am as defiant as Henry constantly liked to tell me. Perhaps it's just that sixth sense that tells me he's watching. If he is, I want him to take a good look at what could've been. At what he could've had.

It's almost two o'clock in the morning, and Hush is silent as I pack my violin away. He didn't come. In spite of all my efforts, Henry didn't come to me. Maybe it's for the best. Perhaps he's saving me from myself. God knows I've been wondering why I'm still here, even after all I know.

Surely love has its limits. Doesn't it?

I take a sip of the cherry-and-lemonade cocktail I asked Hannah to make for me throughout the night. There isn't a single thing I'm not clinging to. It strikes me as odd and unfair how quickly we can make beautiful memories and how much those wonderful moments can hurt you when they're over and you might not get the chance to make any more.

"Miss Cameron." Percival stands in the open doorway in the same suit he was wearing the night I first played at Hush.

That night he told me I was to keep my encounters with Henry's father a secret. He said it was best no one knew that he and Lord Sterling are the reason I am at the conservatory. I traded my blood for a chance to do something I love. Something that I could live without the constant looming shadow of death over me.

"Allow me to walk you out," he tells me with a regretful smile as he looks over his shoulder.

Pulling the order of service from my backpack, I hold it out to him. If I can't get to the mountain and the mountain won't come to me, then maybe it's time for a last-ditch try. Perhaps he'll listen to Percival.

"Tell him I don't care, please." A flicker of surprise crosses his face as he takes the booklet from me. "I know, and I don't care. I still…I still love him."

A tear rolls down my cheek as he throws the booklet into the fire, and I watch it blacken into the hot cinders slowly.

"No, don't tell him that. He doesn't know, and if I don't get to tell him, then—"

"It's late, Eve." Percival stops my babbling with a gentle squeeze to my arm that makes it feel like he's telling me it's too late. I'm too late. It's all done. "Come on."

249

"Shut up!" The vicious order freezes me to the spot as he pushes me through a panel in the wall and tugs me down a secret passage with him. "If you want to keep your head on your neck, you'll forget about all of this. You know nothing, Eve. *Nothing*."

"On the contrary, Percy, I know enough. I've seen enough. If Henry won't talk to me, I'll find someone out there that will."

It's not true. As horrified as I am, I still want to protect him. I love him too much to be the one to hurt him. And I know him. I know that there has to be a reason for all of it. The killing and his distance.

"You stupid girl, you know so little. So very little." Grief and anger paint his face into a twisted glare. "You'll destroy him."

No, I won't. But he doesn't know that, and right now, the only thing I care about is getting to Henry. "It's only fair when he's destroying me." That's the honest-to-God truth.

"I think you should leave now, Miss Cameron." Percival opens the door at the bottom of the dark stairwell and gestures for me to do as he says.

"Does he know that you had me lie to him all this time?" His eyes widen on mine. Shock pulls at his brows while an indignant sneer curls his lips. "What else are you hiding from him?"

Stepping out of the old servants' passage, I snatch the order of service from him and head up the stairs to the lounge, where my violin is already set up. Mary was kind enough to see to that when I walked through the door.

Maybe it's time to up the ante. Tugging at the top of my dress, I pull the first few buttons open until the sleeves slip off my shoulders and my boobs threaten to fall out. There's a lot more of me on show than I'm comfortable with. But needs must.

If I can't get to the mountain, then the mountain must come to me.

TWENTY-NINE
Eve

"**O**pen the door, Henry!" I grit between my clenched teeth as I wrench at the door handle of the red suite, clenching the order of service under my arm tighter so I don't lose it. I'm certain that if it fell on this floor, it would swallow it up.

"His Grace isn't in there." Percival appears behind me. How does he do that? How does he appear out of nowhere all the time? It feels like he teleports around this place, constantly watching everything that's happening, always making sure that everything looks perfect on the surface.

"Where is he, then?"

I just can't catch my breath. The cab ride to my flat and then here was fraught with endless wonderings of why he would kill those women. Not a single one adds up. I know there's more to it, and I know whatever reason he's pushing me away is to do with it.

"I want to talk to him," I tell Percival as he tries to usher me away.

Tonight, he's not getting rid of me so easily, and if Henry doesn't see me, I'll come back tomorrow. Or maybe I'll camp out outside his gates until he has no choice but to face me again.

"Eve, things are a bit tense at the moment and—"

"I know what he did, Percival." I slam the order of service to his chest. "I know he killed her. I know he killed the others too. I saw his file. I saw—"

her regular. He looks different on TV in his official Scotland Yard garbs. Like a respectable family man.

"Three of the victims have been linked to the Coster Kings, an East End criminal organisation rumoured to be involved in drug and sex trafficking." A video of Alfie's dad and another man that looks familiar appears on the screen. They're leaving a church, and behind them, Alfie's holding his sister's hand in the same black attire that they were wearing the other day when I bumped into them.

"At this time, no arrests have been made."

The screen holds for a moment on the images of three women. All around the same age. There's a mean look about their expressions. Cold and haunting.

And I remember that night when I went down to Henry's office. The way he was sitting there, in the dark, staring at the photo on his screen and in his file. All three of these women were in there. I recognise their faces. I…

I made light of it and the way he was so quick to get rid of them. To distract me. And that man—the police commissioner—the one that Mary keeps sweet.

"We keep him extra sweet, and he buries their evils." The words she spoke to me that night we sat at the bar in Hush whisper in my ears again.

"Eve!" Jess clicks her fingers in front of my face. "What's wrong?"

"I have to go," I tell her, standing on my shaky legs and grabbing my backpack from the back of the chair.

"But you haven't finished your tea or had anythin—"

"I know why now. I know…" My stuttering words crack as realisation dawns on me.

It's him. He did it. He killed those women.

His Grace, Henry Sloane, the Duke of Gloucester. My Henry. Is the Ripper.

me their entertainment. I lost count of the times I asked him to let me play in the lounge, and now I have my way, I want to be locked away with him again.

When I finish my make-up, I use Jess' tongs to curl my hair into loose waves before I gather it into a half-updo. I think I've gone too heavy on the eyeliner, but with the voluminous cascade of waves at my crown, it looks good. Better than my blotchy face and tangled tresses.

Quickly, I clean the blood that dripped down my breasts and button up the front of my dress. The sweetheart neckline always flatters my cleavage, and the puffy sleeves make my arms look longer and skinnier. Even though I don't feel good, at least I'll look good enough that every man in that club will look at me. And then we'll see how able Henry is to keep his distance.

"That's better," Jess chuckles as I sit at her kitchen table and take a sip of my tea. "Are you sure you don't want to have dinner with us before you leave?"

"No, I—" *Holy shit!* I stop as the news comes on the telly in the corner, and the face of the woman that was on Henry's screen a couple of weeks ago appears. "Can you turn it up, please?"

"The hunt for the serial killer being dubbed as the Ripper is still on. Police are considering enforcing a curfew in East London, specifically the Spitalfields and Whitechapel area."

My heart is running a hundred miles a second as I finally realise that the woman on the TV is Alfie's aunt. I still have the order of service from her funeral on my dining table. I keep meaning to drop it in to Clara, but my head has been all over the place.

"At this time, the Met are refusing to comment on suspects, however, the police commissioner, Sir Richard Warren, has put out a statement requesting women be extra vigilant and to avoid walking the London streets alone."

"Christ, you look like you've seen a ghost," Jess says as I watch the footage from the commissioner's press conference this afternoon.

My blood chills in my veins at the sight of the man Mary calls

can't silence it because he's slowly breaking my heart piece by piece, again and again. "Like I could've been his everything."

"Eve…sweetie…" Jess gives my knee a squeeze as I get up and start washing my face in the sink.

I'm dressed for work already, and I refuse to show up looking anything less than fine. Even if underneath my pretty dress and make-up, I feel broken. Abandoned.

I haven't seen him in over a week. But on our days, he texts me in the morning. A reminder for me to be at the club. Idiot that I am, I text back and wait for him to reply. He doesn't, though. The three dots appear, and the three dots disappear. Over and again until they stop, and I know that nothing but silence is coming.

When I look up into the mirror, Jess gives me a soft smile as she puts my backpack on the vanity.

"Go on, get yourself sorted. I'll make you a cuppa before you leave." I start fixing myself up again as she picks up the mat on the floor that's spattered with my blood and starts for the door. Pausing, she turns to look at me again. "How is he making you feel now?"

"Lost." The word rolls from my tongue voluntarily. "Alone and broken. Like I might never be able to breathe again." I'm confused. So lonely. Angry. "I don't know what I've done, Jess. Everything was fine…great, and then *poof*."

"Poof?"

"He just flipped."

"Do you think that something happened? Maybe he's trying to protect you."

I watch while she walks away in the mirror reflection. As I go back to doing my make-up, a dry laugh escapes me.

"Protect me?" Staring into my eyes, I try to find something, anything that might give me hope. Or maybe help numb the endless ache and longing for him. "From what?"

None of it makes sense. You can't be all into a person one minute and not give a flying fuck the next. Henry's gone from not wanting any of his privileged members looking at me to making

Jess freezes when I walk out of the bathroom. Her blue eyes soften with pity when I blow my nose again and burst out crying at the sight of the blood. This is my third nosebleed in as many days. Last time I had this many nosebleeds, I had access to stronger drugs.

"Oh, don't cry, sweetie," she coos, placing the ice pack she's holding on the back of my neck. "Crying makes it worse."

"I know. Crying makes everything worse." The sob wracks through me with a hiccup that causes me to choke on the blood running down my throat. "Do you think he loved me even just a little bit?"

Dropping my butt down on the toilet seat, I take over ice pack duty as she clears up the mess I've made of her bathroom. It doesn't escape me that she doesn't reply to my question. She made clear plenty of times that she had her reservations about me being with someone older.

"Jess?"

With a long sigh, she spins from the sink, levelling me with a frown. "Truth or lie?"

"Truth?"

"Okay…" Jess hands me another wad of loo roll before she sits on the edge of the bath. "From the way he looked at you, I'd say yes. But men are strange creatures, Eve. What you see in front of you is only a fraction of what they are beneath all of that."

"I know Henry. I know he's not the sunniest of people, but he's not a liar or someone that treats people more or less than how he feels about them."

"How did he make you feel?" she asks with a sorry shrug.

Tears start trickling down my face again as my lungs threaten to pulverise my heart with their suffocating viselike grip on my insides. "Like—" A sob pushes from my lips. I can't control it. I

to the ceiling before she adds, "And then we end up down here. I tried to warn you, Evie. I did."

"You did?" How did I miss it? Why didn't I listen?

Mary nods. "They're not our friends or our lovers. They're animals," she whispers beside my ear while she fusses with my hair. "It's why they call themselves wolves. They're a pack of dogs, ready to chomp at fresh meat but too spoiled to clean the carcass."

I pull back to see her face. Her words are so vicious that I need to see her face to believe that she spoke them. But there's just sadness there. Her eyes are as weary as my heart.

"We're just disposable toys. Someday we'll all be gone, and new feet will fill our shoes, living the ghost of our words." A sudden smile creeps onto her face as she guides the drink in my hand to my mouth. "Drink up and keep going. It's what we all do here." She glances behind her at Hannah and a few other girls. "Unless you're Cat—then you stomp around like there's a gerbil chewing around your pussy. Fucking miserable bitch. No one fucking likes her."

I watch her walk away before I finish my drink in a few gulps and set myself up. The disappointment and sadness don't disappear as the alcohol warms through me. I thought that maybe it might make me feel better, but it doesn't. It just reminds me that nothing can fill the hole Henry has carved out in my heart.

"What are we playing?" I ask the pianist.

He shrugs. "Whatever you want?"

Taking his sheet music book from the music stand on the piano, I flick through it until I find something that I know and that I can pour myself into. Once I've found it, I let him begin.

Four chords repeated like a mantra, drawing me into a trance where nothing matters. It's just me and my violin and the music sweeping me off the ground. I can pretend I'm anywhere in the world. But the only place I long to be is with him.

of stairs.

"The Duke asked me to inform you that you'll be playing in the lounge tonight." The soft smile he gives me is filled with regret, and that tells me all I need to know.

This is how Henry plans on ending things. He's handing me down to the members of his club. He's casting me out, and I have no idea why.

"Did I do something wrong?" My throat cracks at the sudden swelling of my throat.

All my emotions are running ragged through me. Confusion, disappointment… *I really thought he might love me.* Tears prick the back of my eyes as I follow Percival through to the lounge.

A chair sits by the piano, and as I follow Percival to it, Mary gives me a small wave from where she sits at the bar, waiting for her next lay.

"I'll come and get you when you're done," he tells me with a faint smile. "If you need anything, just ask one of the girls. I know you've met Mary." He nods at her. "It'll all work itself out."

The parting statement isn't the answer I was looking for, but at least now I know that I'm in the bad books. It's just a pity I don't know what I've done. Putting my bag down on the floor beside the piano, I rest my violin case on the chair waiting for me.

Maybe I should leave now. Spare myself the humiliation of his rejection. I'm about to pick my stuff up and go when Mary comes over.

"You look like you're about to bawl," she says, handing me the same drink that Hannah made me last time.

"No, I'm,…I'm fine." It's a lie I try to cover up with a long gulp of the beverage she gave me. I know I shouldn't, but one drink isn't going to be what kills me, and maybe it might settle my nerves and give me some gumption to carry on.

"Don't ever let them see your pain. Not the real one anyway." Her soft hand strokes my face before she fluffs my hair and then uses the back of her finger to dry my lashes.

"We all start up there." My stare follows the flick of her eyes

TWENTY-EIGHT
Eve

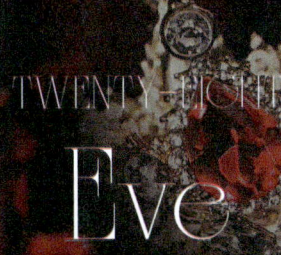

I arrive at Hush as the text instructed me. I get in the car Henry sent, waiting for Andrew to give something other than his impassive stare the entire drive. The dress I'm wearing is the one Henry picked out for the gala he took me to, but I'm wearing my lucky heels that Jess gave me. Every time I've worn them, something good has happened, and from the silent treatment he's given me since he sent me home in his car last night, I know I need something good to happen tonight.

"Eve." Percival comes to greet me with a big smile. He hasn't greeted me at the door since I first came here. "That weather is frightening," he says, continuing to fuss over me as he peels my coat from me and hands it to the butler. "That November chill is coming in fast."

The small talk is only ramping up my anxiety. Is this how Henry's going to break up with me? He'll get his man to do it for him?

"Where is he?" I ask Percival, cutting his small talk short.

A sigh tugs at his shoulders, making him hunch slightly as he tells me, "Something came up last night, and he's been in meetings all day today."

"I see." I start up the stairs with him beside me.

It feels as though all eyes are on me when we reach the landing, and Percival catches my hand before I go up the next flight

Apprehension pinches her tear-tracked face as I hold her there, watching as she struggles to suck in a breath before I take her, one hard shove into her wet heat as I pull her down on me.

"No," she screams past my tight hold on her neck as her heels dig into my calves.

The glorious pain propels me as I pull out and shove myself inside her again. And again. And again. An erratic, frantic rhythm that pulls and twists mercilessly at my unrelenting rage.

I want to kill her. I'm going to kill her. It's all that's left now. She betrayed me, and I will have her blood for it.

"Is this what you wanted?" I spit into her gaping mouth as her fists pound at my sides. "You want to see me unravel? To watch me lose control?"

She chokes out a garbled reply as her legs hitch higher up my thighs. Her feet lock behind my arse as I keep fucking my anger into her, and she sucks it up with her clenching cunt pulling me deeper inside her.

"Little whore." I spit the curse over her lips before I lick the poison inside her, and she drinks it down greedily.

Even now, Eve's so perfect, with tears scorching down her face and sorrow pulling at her brows as she takes what I give her. Anger. Hate. Violence. She takes and takes as I fill her up with the blazing heat of my wrath and the brute power of my judgement, and then I pull away, leaving her wanting and needing. Bereft without the shield of my body from the cold. Empty without me inside her and my cum dripping down her thighs.

Maybe she'll remember this when I slit her throat. Perhaps she'll remember I loved her even when she betrayed me.

"My pretty little whore."

mine as we cut through the throng of guests milling around.

"Henry!" she calls, tripping over her heels as I bound down the stairs with her in my wake. "Henry, please!"

"We're leaving," I bark at her when we reach the darkened archways at the Lancaster House front porch.

"Yes, I can see that," she growls back, snatching her hand from mine as she pulls away, stumbling into a black recess.

There's no light to show us up. There's no one to hear her screams. Everyone is enjoying the music wafting in the air around us. Every soul is busy having a good time, enjoying the party that I brought her to.

"What's happened?" she asks with a trembling voice as I stalk her further into the alcove. "What's wrong, Henry?"

Her back hits the limestone, and I crowd her with my body. Her fear wracks through her as my fury vibrates through me.

"Henry—" I silence her with my hand squeezing her throat as her hands grapple at my chest.

How can something so beautiful cause so much chaos? Even now, my body wants her. I want her even with the sight of her being touched by another imprinted in my head. As much as she fights me, she doesn't stop me from pulling her dress up to her waist.

"Is this for me?" I ask, cupping her hot cunt with a sharp slap of her flesh. "Are you wet for me, Eve?"

Her body trembles as I grip the thin lace underwear between her thighs and wind it around my fist before I yank it from her, relishing the sound of it tearing rip through the air along with her strangled scream.

"No one will hear you," I grit into her ear while I free my cock and her hands fist the tails of my shirt.

The panicked whimpers pushing out of her cause my blood to pound harder, hot with rage, as I watch her eyes fill with tears. All the while, her hands wind tighter in my shirt, pulling me closer as I hitch her up the wall by her throat and line myself up with her cunt.

breath as I watch him flick through his photos like some old slide film. It's all disjointed and jagged, but I can see every action clearly. And my anger roars so loud that I can't hear myself think or talk.

"You're looking for something that's right under your nose. In your bed." The disgust in his voice churns through me. "It's her. It all started with her."

Pocketing his phone, I take a step back from him. The rage keening inside me wants to destroy something. Anything.

How could I be so stupid. So gullible. I glance up towards the bar to find Eve watching us. Her smile dies a quick death when she reads my expression. So perceptive and always in tune.

"Go home," I tell him.

"Bu—"

"Go. Home, Andrew. Get your shit together and meet me at Hush."

He nods, flashing a dark, hateful stare at Eve. Even now, I want to pummel that look off his face.

"There's more. I have more…" He sounds as desperately deranged as I feel.

"Who else knows?" Andrew shakes his head. "No one needs to know."

"But it's—"

"No one. I'll deal with it myself." A dubious frown darkens his eyes as he watches me step back inside the ballroom. "The club. In two hours."

The presence of his phone weighs down my pocket as I stride back to the bar. Dragging in breath after long breath, I attempt to regain my composure. But it's going to take more than the floral-scented air to dampen my fury.

"Is everything okay?" Eve asks as I reach her, one of her hands grasping mine.

How can you hate and love something so fiercely at once?

Tugging her up onto her feet, I throw back my drink and pull her through the ballroom with me. Her hand clutches tightly at

TWENTY-SEVEN

Henry

Andrew looks like shit. His suit is rumpled, and his hair looks like it needs a good wash and a decent cut. Aside from that, he stinks of stale cigarette smoke.

"What are you doing here?" I ask as he tries to hold still in front of me, but his hands, along with the rest of him, are shaking. "And what on earth happened to you?"

"You've put this off long enough," Andrew bites out, holding out his phone to me. "I told you I needed to talk to you, but you sent me on a wild goose chase for a briefcase."

"Have you found it?"

"No, but I found other answers." Thumbing his phone open, he swipes the screen to bring up a photo of Eve leaving her flat.

The first few are just her in her ridiculous cat-eared hoodie, but after a few swipes, she's getting into an electric-blue Corsa. Andrew zooms into the next photo to show me the boy she's with.

"His name is Alfred Chapman." His statement stops me in my tracks as I'm about to tell him to go home and sort himself out. "John Chapman is his dad. George Chapman is his uncle." Andrew swipes to another photo, where Eve is far too close and far too comfortable and altogether far too touched by the boy. He looks her age—young and in love. "That was yesterday. Don't they look cosy?"

The air thickens, making it impossible to take a steadying

lightly. "I'll be right back," he tells me with his stare firmly on mine. "Two minutes."

"All right." My pulse throbs harder with every step he takes away from me, and as I follow him to the side of the ballroom, watching as he greets Andrew and the two of them slip outside the french doors, I know something is wrong.

That dark sense of doom chills through me while the two of them talk, and Henry's gaze flashes to mine every now and then. His displeasure seeps deep into my bones, making them ache to hold him. To make him smile again.

back and wonder if I earned my place.

"Think about it, at least?"

"Sure."

Obviously, he doesn't buy my reply because he spins me to face him again before he takes my mask off and places it on the bar with his.

"Life isn't always about what you do, how you do it, or how amazing you are at what you do. Sometimes it's about who we know and what they see in us." His hands hold my face with his thumbs caressing my cheeks.

Where my hair is up in a low bun, his fingers tunnel into the loose knot at my nape. And my breath catches at the back of my throat when his nails rake over my scalp. The sensation is divine, causing me to sink into him.

"I could listen to you play all day, every day. And I'm not a musical person, but you are that good. You're incredible, and you really should think about this. Consider it wisely."

"Okay." I nod. "I promise I'll think about it."

"Good girl." He winks at me with a soft, sexy smirk.

Fuck, I love it when he calls me that. I don't know what it is, but it makes my insides sing with excitement. I like pleasing him. The thought that I could make him half as happy as he makes me gets me giddy. I love it.

I love him.

More than I can bear.

Beyond the limits of my heart.

Surpassing the constant longing of my soul.

I love him like the tide loves the moon—a necessity, an obsession, a never-ending compulsion that keeps giving and taking.

"Henry," I whisper on a breath. The words are right there, and I've never wanted to part with them for anyone else, not like this. "I—"

The flicker of his gaze over my shoulder gives me pause. Before I can carry on, he stands and sits me on the stool instead.

With a hand cupping my jaw, his thumb strokes over my lips

Henry orders the drink along with his brandy. While we wait for the bartender to finish serving us, I watch the other guests in their costumes. It seems really weird how they all seem to be wearing the same costume in different colours. Like they all coordinated prior to the party. The women are in corseted ball gowns, while the men are in black tuxedos. I've never seen so many glittering jewels in one place.

"I want to talk to you about Hush," Henry says suddenly. "Mainly you working there."

"What about it?"

When he starts to take his mask off, I know this is going to be a serious conversation. "I can't have you working there."

I knew this was coming. The last few weeks, he's found a reason to cut our time short there, and my last pay cheque felt so dirty that I started looking for other options. It's just not right for him to pay me to play for him at the club when we're together.

"I saw you've been looking for a new job, but I thought that you might want to audition for the stand-in programme with the RPO?"

I twist to look at him. "The Royal Philharmonic? But that programme only takes on graduates. I'm not—"

"I know you're still an undergraduate, but once in a while, they make exceptions for the conservatory, and I'd be calling in a favour from the music director." Henry's tentative smile shows that he knows I'm not comfortable with him pulling strings for me.

"That's a nice offer, but I don't want to put you out, and I like getting places by my own merit."

He nods with a soft smile. "It's an audition. If you got the place, it would be solely based on your talent. Besides, Colin is a friend of the family. If anything, he'll be able to offer you great advice and guidance…"

"I don't know, Henry." This is probably one of the best offers anyone has made for my future career. However, I'm scared that if I accept this, I'll forever feel indebted to him. I don't want to look

father-and-daughter dance you're always looking for at these things." With a tug of one of her ringlets, he gives her a big grin. "Happy birthday, Debbie Kerr."

"Thanks...who are you dressed up as?" She looks between us.

"Guests," Henry tells her with a flick to her nose before he guides us towards the bar.

"I'll see you both on the dance floor," Madeline yells after us.

Not likely, I think at the same time as Henry chuckles, "Maybe not."

This new page we've found ourselves on is like kismet. We're finding a normal between us that feels all too good. As we sidle up to the bar, Henry takes my hand, spinning me so that the mermaid tail of my black velvet dress flares around my legs. His hand flattens to my back as he pulls me into him.

With our chests pressed together, he peppers soft kisses to the tip of my nose, where my mask ends. Each peck is a shot of delirious happiness that's impossible to hide.

"Drink?" Henry asks, perching on a bar stool with me between his thighs. Like this, we're about the same height. We're face to face, even as he spins me to face the bartender. "What would you like?"

The whisper tickles along my jaw, causing me to giggle. "I don't know."

"You ever had a Shirley Temple?"

"I've heard of it, but no." I tend to go with a simple Coke or lemonade. It's a lot cheaper than a bunch of fruit juices mixed together.

"If you like ginger ale and cherry, you'll enjoy it."

"Love cherry, but ginger ale...nooooo..." The one time I tried it, it tasted like I was drinking a disinfectant. It burned my mouth, and the aftertaste was gross. Just the thought makes me shudder, something that Henry seems to think is funny.

"I know you drink lemonade, so you can try a kitty cocktail. It's basically cherry juice, lemonade, and maraschino cherries."

There's an unsettling chill in my bones when I walk away that I can't shake no matter what I do. And I know if I try to talk to Henry about it, he'll freak out and have Andrew following me around again. I don't know what I'm going to do just yet, but I'll figure it out later.

"Please, don't leave me?" I beg under my breath when Princess Madeline suggests Henry joins the men to smoke and gossip like old women.

The music is loud enough that she can't hear me, but I think she knows I'm terrified of being left on my own because her arm links with mine, and she whispers in my ear, "Don't worry, there's no vipers at this party."

Something tells me that's not true. It feels like every set of eyes in here is on me. Even with the masks on, it's obvious everyone knows who is who. It's like a sixth sense that comes with money and title.

"Shouldn't you be mingling with your guests?" he laughs at the face she pulls when an older woman greets her with a curtsey. "They'll be calling you a terrible host tomorrow."

"If the champagne keeps flowing, no one will notice." Madeline winks.

Unfortunately for her, everyone notices her in her Victorian ball gown. The lilac ombre silk has the most gorgeous lustre. The gold thread embroidery, along with the pearl-and-crystal detailing, is unlike anything I've ever seen. There isn't a male set of eyes in the ballroom that doesn't stop to admire her.

"Unfortunately, I have no interest in socialising tonight," Henry tells her.

A long huff pushes through her pink lips in a dramatic raspberry. "Or any other night."

"Go. Socialise. Enjoy the party, and make sure you get that

into Alfie's hands.

It's then I look away. Fear shoots from the top of my head to the soles of my feet, chilling me completely.

"No one goes near her, you hear me?"

"Yes."

"You fucking shoot any cunt that looks at her. 'Cause if anything happens to my girl on your watch, I'll be putting a bullet in your head, son."

The venom in his words cuts through my veins. How can any man treat their child like this? To threaten the life of one child over another? It's barbaric and so…awful. My heart breaks for Alfie as he trudges back to the swings, shoving the gun into the top of his trousers as though it's something he handles every day.

"You didn't see any of that," he tells me with a cold, hard edge to his voice that fills me with pity for him. "You didn't hear any of it."

"Alfie—"

"Listen to me, Eve!"

The use of my name is sobering. Alfie always calls me Evie or Cinders because I'm always running to keep up with time. *Like Cinderella running to keep up with the magic*, he told me once.

"You can get into so much trouble if the police catch you with that."

"Better in the nick than in a grave. Don't you think?" That overwhelmed glint in his eyes darkens, and I realise that it's not sadness. It's pressure. "I better get the princess upstairs."

I walk back to our block with him. We're silent for the most part until we reach their landing, and he sends his sister inside to his mum.

"Let me know if you need a ride later, yeah?" He gives me one of his devilish grins as he adds, "Of any kind."

"Alfie—"

"You didn't see. You don't know." Before I can say anything else, he goes inside and closes the door before I can give him his funeral book.

great. It was my dad's sister, and her and Mum hated each other, probably more than Mum hates my dad."

"Oh, well, that's…" I blow out a breath, unsure of what to say to that.

Clara and his dad have had some pretty bad arguments that I've heard through the floor. One time, I thought he was beating her with the way she was screaming and the banging around in her flat. Turns out he trashed the place in a drunken rage.

"Speak of the bastard," Alfie groans as his sister runs to the man striding our way and throws herself at him.

"Alfie," the man calls across the courtyard.

"Stay here, yeah?" Alfie nudges me back to the swing. "Don't watch. Don't say anything. Pretend there's no one here. Just you on that swing."

His dad stops outside the playground. In spite of the sneer on his face, he looks every bit the doting father with all the kisses he peppers to the little girl's head before he puts her down and sends her back inside the playground.

"Why aren't you watching your fucking sister?" he barks at Alfie with a slap to the back of his head.

"Sorry," he replies as the man's ringed fingers wrap around either side of his skull and he touches their foreheads together.

"You're a man, now, Alfie," I hear the man say as I pick up the booklet from the ground and pause. The woman looks familiar and younger in the photograph than the forty-two years it says on the memorial book.

"You hearing me, Alfred?"

My eyes snap up at the echoing sound of a slap that cuts through the man's yell. I can't see Alfie's face properly from here, but I imagine that his eyes are watering from the strike.

"Yes, Dad."

"You need to be looking after your sister, you understand me?"

I watch their foreheads grind together as Alfie's dad reaches into his jacket pocket, pulls out a small handgun, and shoves it

as he pulls back in his. "Look, your face is all red, Cinders."

Releasing my swing, he pushes my back to propel me forward, and when I swing back, he launches himself ahead of me. We're like two pendulums swinging in opposite directions.

"What have you been up to?" I ask him when we cross in the middle.

"Nothing much. It was my birthday last week, so I'm finally legal." The cheeky wink he gives me makes me laugh. "You can pounce on me anytime you like now. You don't have to worry about jail."

"Oh my God, Alfred! Stop!"

"You sound like my mum," he guffaws, pushing my swing as it starts to slow. "Seriously, though. What I lack in age, I make up for in size."

With a waggle of his brows, he jumps off the swing midair and gyrates his hips in an exaggerated thrusting grind when he lands on his feet. While he's clowning around, a small booklet falls from his pocket. He doesn't bother picking it up; instead, he nudges it to the side with his polished shoe and carries on making a show of himself in front of me.

"It's never going to happen."

"Never say never." Alfie catches my swing suddenly, propelling me off it before he catches me. "You're throwing yourself at me already," he rasps into my ear, wrapping his arms around me. "Anything's possible, Cinders…unless you're dead. Then it's really game over."

There's a sad lull to his voice that causes me to stop myself from pulling completely away as I wriggle out of his hold.

"What's with the black suit?" I ask him, staring to the side as I focus on the booklet that fell from his pocket.

"It was my aunt's funeral today." He shrugs in reply as if it's not a big deal, but when I look back up, there is something in his eyes that says he feels some kind of way about it.

"I'm really sorry. Is your mum all right?"

A deep, wry laugh vibrates his chest. "Yeah, my mum is

TWENTY-SIX

Eve

The cab comes to a stop outside my block. I haven't spent that much time at my place in the last month. The evenings I spend at the club. I end up at Henry's place. Then on the days I have a late lecture, he picks me up from the conservatory. Meaning we end up at his place too. If I've spent a couple of nights in my bed over the last six weeks, that's being generous.

"Oi, Cinders!" Alfie calls at me from the kids' playground in the courtyard. "Hey!"

I wave at him, chuckling at his big grin. As always, Alfie is the biggest oddball ray of sunshine. But today, Mr. Colourful is in a black suit while he watches his sister bounce on the seesaw with another kid from the estate. Something seems off as I head over to where he's sitting on the swings.

"Where have you been?" he asks me when I sit on the swing beside his. "Haven't seen you in ages. Mum said you ain't home anymore."

"I've been around. Probably just missed each other with my odd timetable and stuff…"

A smirk cocks one side of his face into a lopsided mask of glee. "And stuff. Is that like a code word for getting laid?"

"It's code word for stuff, like rehearsals and performances and work."

"And bonking," he laughs, grasping the chain for my swing

There's a second of silence where his spoken charm ebbs into the dark night. We don't have time for him to flirt her to the grave. Before she can open her mouth, I spin towards her and slap my gloved hand over her Botox-inflated lips.

"Your life," I grit into her ear with the roar of my rage in my ears as I stick her with the same blade her husband had my father killed with. I nudge it deeper, cranking it between her ribs into her lung. "That's the price."

She's a spirited one. Her legs kick with the flail of her arms, but it only rips her more and more open. Her fight is her undoing as I pull the blade out and thrust it into her again and again, ripping her open.

"Go back inside," I snap at Julian while he watches with his drink.

"Hardly seems fitting that her life should pay for his," he states with a flinch when I stand and yank the blade through her, pulling her up with me when the knife hits her sternum. I use my full force to plough it all the way back down, gutting the writhing body in front of his eyes as I wrap an arm around her chest.

"Leave."

"No." His sharp breaths mix with the wet gurgle of hers as I cut her throat, ear to ear, once, twice, so that her head is barely hanging on by her spine and the scent of her blood is as sweet as petrichor. The scent of rain. The golden blood of immortals.

"Walk away now," I bark at him through gritted teeth as he gulps down his drink. "We're done here."

Julian watches the puddle of blood grow, spreading around me as he steps back and takes in the big picture of it all.

There is no price that will pay for the life of my father. There is no blood that will repay that of his godfather. Those debts will never be paid.

the rain; it makes these things messy. Weaving through the parked cars to the side of the gallery, I cut the cable to the CCTV camera pointing to the back of the building, where the smoking area is situated.

Fairy lights hang over the gazebo structure, casting a soft glow that I take care of quickly. The cover of darkness makes it easier to pounce without a fight. For a moment, the susurration of the rain is all there is above the humdrum of the city. I sit on one of the benches in the middle of the gazebo, my back to the building as the sound of bespoke soles on damp decking comes closer.

"Wait!" The sudden call triggers my pulse. "Hey, you there! I said, wait!"

Measured steps continue up the gazebo steps as the scent of Black Devils cherry tobacco tinges the air. I don't know how the fuck Julian smokes that shit, but tonight, it's come in handy.

"How much?" the woman asks, stomping up the wooden steps.

"More than you're willing to pay," Julian replies, sitting on the opposite side of the bench with his back to mine, leaving space for her to sit between us.

"You don't know what I'm willing to pay," she snaps back. "Name your price and—"

"How about we sit together and negotiate over a real drink instead of the cheap prosecco in there?" The squeak of his old hip flask grinds in my ears. "What price are you willing to pay, Miss…?"

I twist in my seat, taking the knife out at the ready while I position myself on the edge of the round bench, ready to strike.

"Annie," she replies, looking over her shoulder at me.

Julian grabs her attention again, placing his hand on her knee. "Miss Annie…"

"Mrs.," she corrects him quickly, pulling away slightly. "Mrs. Chapman."

"So, Mrs. Annie Chapman, what are you willing to part with?"

nowhere near as sharp to cut me as he intended.

"One of us has to be." The truth lingers bitterly between us. One day he'll realise that we're not here to keep peace or to make this world a wonderful place. The reason we exist is to defend and protect—to rain hell when the world threatens to demolish everything that history has carved out.

"You asked about the wife?" Percival swipes the screen of the iPad to pull up a photo of Chapman's wife leaving a gallery. "On the first Saturday of every month, she attends the private art auction. Tomorrow, there's going to be a Bram Bogart lot that she's been searching for."

"Bogart?"

"Since he died in 2012, his paintings have amassed unbelievable value. One of my contacts at the Tate thinks that within the next decade, his works are going to be as valuable as Kandinsky's."

"How cultured," Julian laughs.

The Seymours own one of the largest baroque collections in the world. Art is in Julian's blood. Perhaps it's time that he got his hands dirty too.

"You're going to go to that auction, and you're going to win that lot with enough of a tussle that Mrs. Chapman will be put out and she'll want a private word." A look of disgust twists his face, and before he argues, I tell him, "Don't worry, you're just the honey trap. I'll do the bloody work."

It's time for Chapman to make another payment for the lives of the Wolves he's taken. Slowly, we'll get to him—the final instalment of his debt.

Softly, softly, catchee monkey.

The light September rain drizzles over the city. I don't like

"It was left on his desk," Percival tells me, sinking into the seat beside mine.

The more I read over the note, the more it niggles at me. "Every life has a price."

"The irony," Julian scoffs at me.

"No, not the irony, Jules. When does a life have a price?" I stare up at him as he glowers down at the note I place on the table along with the two of the buttons. The one I carved, I fist in my hand. "What in this world has a price?"

"Everything," he replies.

"Do you honestly believe that everything has value?" Jules shakes his head. "No. For something to have a price, we have to care for it."

"What's your point?" Julian slaps his hand down on the note. "You're touching what he cares about and he's retaliating?"

"No, Jules. I didn't make the first kill."

"So what? This is a game of who has more to lose? Or who will go further?"

"I don't know yet, but Chapman's right."

"Every life has a price," he mutters down at the photo of Lord Alastair Sterling, his godfather and a Wolf.

"Does his life have a price to you?"

"He was like a father to me. He didn't care who I am or who I love…"

"What are you willing to pay, Jules? Your morality? Maybe your righteousness?"

"When does it end?" he asks while Percival watches on silently.

"When do you think, Percy? When does all of this end?"

With a shake of his head, he sits back in his chair. "It doesn't. Not until either he or us is gone."

"So, Julian, what is it you want me to do now? Sit back and wait for a benevolent miracle? Or maybe until another one of us is dead?"

"You're a bastard," Julian spits. The cutting tone of his voice blazes brighter with every second. "Dick Warren has a certain taste for Mary. Maybe it's time she made herself useful."

"You're enjoying this too much," he laughs dryly.

"I am. It always feels better to do than to talk around in useless circles, debating right and wrong."

"Good, you're both here," Percival says as he comes into the room. "We need to reevaluate ASAP."

The atmosphere changes the instant he puts the iPad in his hand down in front of me.

"He was found this afternoon," Percival states with a solemn sigh.

The sight is all too familiar, causing my chest to fist around my pounding heart. Death is never something easy to look upon. However, there are times when it looks back at you, and it's then that it cuts the deepest. Times like now, where sorrow seems inadequate to plaster over the gaping wound its master leaves behind.

"Jules…" I glance up at him as his fingers zoom into the photo on the screen.

"He's my godfather. Did you know that?" he says blankly.

"Yes."

"Have you told Lady Sterling?" Julian asks Percival. His eyes are red with grief, and an angered flush glows over his entire face. "And…and Grania?"

Julian nods, his eyes narrowing on mine. "Here's your first casualty, Henry. His blood is on your hands."

"I can live with that," I tell him as I focus back on Percival. "I want the commissioner up here, and we need to fill his chair fast."

"Alastair left instructions on who was to take his seat." Percival pulls an envelope from his jacket pocket and hands it to me. "We need to reevaluate."

There's a note inside, along with three pearl buttons. One of which is bloody and carved with a *W*.

EVERY LIFE HAS A PRICE.
WHAT ARE YOU WILLING TO PAY?

compromised. There's an art to being overlooked, and that is by weaving in and out of the shadows.

"Maybe not, but this isn't some black ops mission that we can brush off. There's nothing to fall back on. You're not a ghost anymore."

Once a ghost, always a ghost. People never understand that it doesn't matter whether you're on active duty or not, you're still the person the military trains you to be. In my case: a shadow. A ghost. An invisible killer.

"The way I see it, I'm doing this country a favour."

"By putting everything else at risk. Everything we stand for."

"Justice comes at a price, Jules." Glacial eyes dagger into me. "You should know that."

"I also know that vendettas always end with more casualties than you prepare for."

"That's just war." Finishing my coffee, I go back to the article.

> Police are inquiring into all possibilities, with a source stating that it is very likely that the killer is a highly trained medical professional, with each of the victims having a precise wound to the lung, which is believed to be the cause of death.

"Medical professional," I scoff down at the paper. "Suppose something has come out of all the hunts."

Days spent stalking deer followed by evenings exsanguinating the carcass before we butchered the animal. My father would always take the moment to teach. It was his way of trying to push me into pursuing a career like his instead of the veterinary science I chose. There was enough shadow to live under without adding a career choice to it.

"Henry." Julian braces himself over the table, leaning forward so that our stares are matched. "There's an entire Scotland Yard task force being assembled as we speak to weed you out."

"Yes, and their chief is in and out of our door." I take a sip of my coffee as he watches me intently. The frustration in his eyes

TWENTY-FIVE
Henry

THE RIPPER: EAST END KILLER STRIKES AGAIN.

The headline across the front of the *London Telegraph* glares up at me from the meeting room table at Hush. I wait to feel something other than indifference. But after the first kill, every mission becomes about getting the job done as swiftly as possible. This is no different to all the times I was flown out to the Middle East on a mission to track down and terminate terrorists and war criminals. This just happens to be on our doorstep.

"This isn't good," Julian groans when I sit back in my chair and pour myself another coffee.

"I don't know about that," I tell him, pointing to the paragraph where they attribute my killings to gang-related crime. A war of turfs or perhaps just simply revenge. "This is working out just fine."

Julian stops his pacing to level me with a glower. "They're calling you the Ripper. You're all over the fucking news…"

"It's not the first time."

When I was on missions with my squadron, a lot of the time, we'd make it onto the news. Nobody would know it was squadrons with our headgear covering our faces, but we'd be all over television, newspapers, the internet. Not once were our identities

shrugged it off because no doubt, I would've found a way of changing their mind. However, Eve is not just any woman. She's possibly the most headstrong person I know.

As clearly as I can picture those little girls we might've had, it stands to reason that they wouldn't exist without her. If the choice is between Eve and a future that won't happen without her, then it also stands to reason that she is the only choice.

"You don't have to do anything you don't want to for me."

"But your mum said that you—"

"Forget what she said. She's not part of this equation," I gesture between us. "You and me, Eve, we're the only people that matter here."

"Are we?"

"Yes."

With her narrowed gaze on mine, Eve moulds her hands to my face. The touch is filled with affection. It warms through me, filling all the voids with nothing but certainty that she is the only thing I want. The only thing that matters.

"I won't change my mind," she says.

"I don't expect you to."

"What if you change yours?"

"Don't hold your breath, darling."

"Not even just a little bit?"

The hopeful trill in her voice makes me smile. "Not even a little bit."

"There's nothing wrong with wanting to protect your family." Eve turns to face me. "Nothing wrong at all." A defeated sigh escapes her as she presses a kiss to my shoulder.

"Eve…darling…"

"Do you remember you asked me where my mum was?" Her fingertips trace the scar on my side with a wistful frown.

I don't like where this is going. It feels like impending doom encroaching on us, darkening what promised to be a good day.

"I remember, and you told me I was shit at reading the room."

Pushing between me and the sink, Eve brushes her hands over my chest. Sadness darkens her eyes, drawing her youthful features into a severe, stricken expression.

"She died," Eve whispers, touching her forehead to my chest. "There were complications when I was born, and she bled out."

A sense of relief washes over me while at the same time a sense of overwhelming sympathy and sorrow wrenches deep inside me. This explains why she got so upset.

"I'm so sorry, darling." My arms wrap around her, holding her to me for as long as she'll allow.

"I inherited this stupid disease from her, and I'm scared that I'll end up like her."

Eve pushes away from me as I reassure her that it's not going to happen. "I told you I wouldn't let that happen."

"I can't have children, Henry. I don't want to." The statement hits me square in the chest. A sucker punch that makes it impossible to reply.

Yes, I'm pissed at my mother for bringing the topic up. But she's right—Eve would make beautiful babies with her milky skin and golden hair. It seems sinful to deprive the world of that—mini Eves. Stunning girls with light brown eyes and fiery attitudes to keep us on our toes.

A voice in my head keeps telling me she's nineteen. She has time to change her mind. But the grave, unmoving expression on her face tells me that she's nineteen going on thirty. If any other woman would have told me they don't want children, I would've

them. Oh," she sighs, flitting her stare directly at Eve, "it will be so nice to have children running around again. To have little ones to dote on."

The development in the conversation catches Eve off guard. I see her face fall as Mother keeps babbling on about her future grandchildren. She's doing well to keep her calm. I, on the other hand, am not.

"That's enough," I snap, silencing the child talk permanently.

"I'm sorry." Mother leans across the table to pat our hands. "I got carried away for a moment."

"You did." My growl causes Eve to shudder away.

"I just…I suppose I assumed that you would have discussed your duties to the family. You'll need an heir to carry on the name and to pass the Duchy down to. It's just the way it is." Mother shrugs as Eve stands quietly.

"Please excuse me. I need to use the bathroom." Before I can make sure she's all right, Eve rushes to the bedroom, leaving a trail of panic in her wake that I follow swiftly.

"See yourself out," I tell Her Royal Highness as I slam the bedroom door shut behind me.

The bedroom is empty as I look around for Eve, but a sliver of light shines from beneath the bathroom door. I don't bother knocking when I know she's upset. The only thing I want right now is to comfort her and make sure she knows to ignore my mother's conversation.

Leaning over the bathroom sink, she looks like she's about to vomit. While I want nothing more than to wrap my arms around her, I settle for standing beside her in front of the mirror as she watches her face dry.

"I've asked her to leave," I tell Eve.

"No, you didn't have to. It's not—"

"Yes, I did. I told her to be nice, and she fucked it up." Turning the tap on, I wash my hands as a way of filling the silence. "She's overbearing and forgets herself far too often when it comes to me and the family."

busybody."

"It's okay." Eve nods at me, pressing her face into my hand when I cup her jaw.

"Don't pay her any mind, beautiful. She'll be gone soon enough."

Of course, my mother has other ideas. She drags breakfast out as long as she can, making small talk that I know she believes far beneath her. I think this is why she would rather marry me off to one of the names on her list. She knows them all. There would be no need to make the effort to get acquainted with them.

"You know," she says, taking a sip of her coffee, "I can't remember the last time we had a pot of tea at the table. Ever since his grandfather died, Henry's hated the smell, and we've all had to humour his distaste."

Eve flashes me a sorry glance as she drinks up the tea she's cradling in both of her hands.

"My father-in-law was a mighty tea drinker. He'd have a cup at every opportunity."

"A man after my heart." Eve gives me a warm smile.

"A man after one's own heart, the saying goes, not after one's heart."

Eve's wide stare flashes to mine. "It's all the same," I reassure her.

Mother bleats a short laugh. "James was Henry's idol. There was nowhere he wouldn't follow the old Duke from dawn to dusk. Isn't that right?"

When I nod, Eve's hand finds mine on the table. She's been quiet this morning. I think she's overwhelmed by my mother's surprise visit. Slipping her hand into my palm, she laces her fingers with mine as she edges her chair closer.

"I can see why my son is so…bewitched," Mother muses, taking a sip of her coffee while her eyes study Eve's and my joined hands. A narrow-eyed smile purses her lips before she says, "You'll make beautiful children, no doubt. Henry was precious as a baby. He had big, chubby cheeks and all the rolls to go with

through the cheese and honeycomb, I suck it into my mouth while she glares at me. More for my indignation than my manners.

"Do you think I'm going to apologise for wanting the best for you and this family?"

"No, I believe you need to apologise for being rude about Eve and for assuming you know the kind of person she is without actually knowing her."

"I wasn't rude; I was frank. I said what everybody else will be saying behind your back to your face. Do you know how it looks for a man in his thirties to court a teenager? She's nineteen, Henry. *Nine. Teen.*"

"There's more to Eve than her age. She's kind and intuitive, but more than that, she's lived a lot more than you think. There's an old soul in her. If you gave her the chance—"

"I'm here, aren't I?" she cuts me off with her pissed-off grumble.

"To butter me up."

"Let's start with that." She levels me with one of her austere stares. "Maybe she'll win me over by the end of breakfast."

"Eve's resting and—" I pause as my mother looks around me with a curious cock of her brow. In the reflection of the oven door, I can see Eve standing behind me. She's got a pair of my boxer shorts on and one of my T-shirts knotted at her waist. Before my mother says anything, I mouth, "Be nice."

"You must be Eve." Mother walks around me as I turn to look at my precious girl.

She's flustered, and I can tell that she's uncomfortable in the clothes she's wearing, but at least my mother is good enough to ignore it.

"I thought we could have breakfast since my son didn't introduce me to you last night," she says by way of introducing herself.

"Okay." Eve glances up at me. It doesn't matter how hard she tries to hide her panic; I can feel it rattle in my bones when I guide her to the dining table.

"I'm sorry," I whisper as I pull out a chair for her. "She's a

TWENTY-FOUR
Henry

"What are you doing here?" I spit out the question as my mother pushes past me into my place.

Eve's still asleep after our late night, and I don't want her to have to deal with a disgruntled, pride-hurt princess first thing in the morning.

"Making peace," she replies, lifting the pastry box in her hand as she continues up the stairs to the living area. "It's never good to let things fester."

"It's never good to show up uninvited."

"I don't need an invitation to visit my son," she's quick to retort as I follow her to the kitchen area, with Rufus grunting around my feet. "Last night was ugly."

"I see. You must be here to apologise, then." I watch her open the cupboard doors and pull out drawers as she looks for plates and fusses over my traitorous canine.

Once she's found the crockery, she lays the plates out on the island beside the pastry box. "Peace offering."

"Pastries aren't an apology."

"Not just any pastries." She grins at me. "They're your favourites from that viennoiserie you love. Look." Mother opens the box to show me its contents. "I managed to get the last of them. Fig jam and fresh cheese with honeycomb. *Delicious.*"

"Still not an apology, Mother." Swiping my little finger

"Sleep now, my darling love."

All I can do is smile into the darkness. I love him, and he loves me. My world is complete.

while he nips at my breasts, sucking my flesh into his mouth roughly so that I can feel my blood seep through the layers of my skin. He doesn't stop or give me a moment to gather myself as the heat from his touch pounds through me without mercy or restraint, and I buck and grind and seek him out for more.

"My pretty little whore," he murmurs over my flesh, thrusting deeper with the curl of his finger and his thumb. "My beautiful darling."

His words. His touch. I can't get enough of them. Of him. The fire blazes hotter, shrinking my skin around my screaming bones as my muscles coil, and he fucks me harder. Faster. I'm thrusting and twisting with heavy breaths and a need so great that as he bites down on my breast, it shoots through me, straight to my core, detonating in every cell of my being.

All there is him.

My need of him.

My love for him.

With my body still convulsing, he pushes himself off me, pulling his fingers out brusquely before he flips me onto my front, onto my hands and knees. With my elbows and knees tied, they sink into the bed as I collapse onto my shoulders, burying my face in the sheets as a muffled scream rips through me when he thrusts his cock inside my pussy without warning.

"Fuck," he barks as my orgasm squeezes around him. "That's it, keep coming. I want to feel your cunt milk my cock."

There's a violence in his rutting that slams through me every time his body slaps into mine, over and over with every guttural growl and curse that litters the air as he comes deep inside me, his cum scalding me from the inside out spurt by spurt.

"Good girl," he breathes into my ear as he collapses onto me. "Good girl."

I don't know when or how he unties me. I'm too tired. Too overwhelmed. Too boneless. It doesn't matter when he pulls me onto his chest and he holds me tight, peppering endless kisses over my hair as he bundles the duvet around us.

"Henry, please."

"I want more, darling," he groans with a swipe of his tongue from my crease to my clit. "Every fucking inch, Eve."

The words have barely made it through the fuzz of my orgasm when he licks lower, and the sensation of him there is as wrong as it is amazing.

"My dirty girl," Henry hums into me as one of his hands strokes down my thighs, palming my pussy while his tongue flicks over my hole again and again with the unforgiving grind of hand on my sensitive flesh.

"Oh God…Oh God…Henry. Henry, please." I don't know whether I'm begging or praying. Regardless, my tortured mewls only urge him on as his hand teases lower and lower and his thumb replaces his tongue, rounding my clenching hole with more and more pressure.

"So fucking tight." His growl vibrates through me as I yank uselessly at my restraints, and he spits my arousal over my arsehole.

Warm, wet, and *God*, it's unlike anything I've ever felt when he spreads my juices and his spit, working his finger inside as I buck and squirm, fighting with the tightly knotted stockings.

"The more you fight and strain, the more it'll hurt," Henry purrs, thrusting inside me one knuckle at a time until he's filling me. "You have no choice but to give me what I want." Twisting his finger, he fucks my arse in slow motions, again and again, until I'm so desperate for more that I'm breaking myself to chase after it. "And I want to fuck this tight, little hole until you cry."

"Yes." I shouldn't ask for it. I shouldn't want it. But I do. "Yes, Your Grace."

His grin trails over me from my pussy to my breasts while he continues fucking my arse with his finger. Meanwhile, his thumb rubs through my folds, curling into my pussy as he pulls my nipple into his mouth.

"Henry…Henry." My whimpers morph into breathless moans as he settles over me, fucking me with his finger and his thumb

"Thank you for being so good with George, and I'm sorry he got out of sorts at the end."

"Don't thank me, and definitely don't apologise. When I was his age, I got ratty too at these things. In fact, he did a lot better than I ever did."

His arm wraps around my shoulders as we start for his Defender, parked a couple of roads away. I'm surprised he drove himself tonight; I expected Andrew to do it since it was a formal event.

"He's a good kid," he says fondly.

"I think so too. Even if he is a stickler for his routine."

"I like my routine too," he tells me with a low, drawn chuckle, pinning me to the side of his car as he makes to open my door for me. "I like to take you home, get you naked and in my bed so I can fuck you senseless."

Warm lips press to mine, and I can't even remember to breathe as he kisses me with a deep growl. His large hands anchor at my waist with the lick and swirl of our tongues.

Heaven. This right here is paradise, and I never want it to end.

"Stop. Stop, Stop…stop!" The mangled plea bursts from me as I tug my arms violently.

The bite of the stockings knotted around my elbows and knees only drags out the torture when Henry shoves his tongue into my pussy, and I come again. It doesn't matter how many times I beg; Henry is relentless. He keeps fucking me with his tongue and his fingers. Sucking my soaked flesh into his mouth, he trails his hands over my thighs, pressing them into my chest so that I open wider for him.

I can't take much more of this. My body is ablaze. Every pore is screaming with sensation. That gaping hole he's left me with since the first time he fucked me is aching to be filled by him.

page, however, you're at different stages in your life."

"Jess, please don't."

"If you get hurt and I haven't said my piece, I'll have to live with that. With knowing that your brother is up there pissed off at me for not warning you. You're young, and your life is just starting out. But he's had his fun, and he's lived." With a deep huff, she shakes her head at me. "Don't set yourself up for heartbreak, or worse, regrets."

"I understand, Jess," I say, giving her a hug as her Uber pulls up. "If I give Henry up because he's older than me or because he's lived more than I have, it'll be my biggest regret. I love him," I whisper in her ear as I glimpse at him while he holds the cab for her. "I think he loves me too."

"Of course he does," she coos, pulling back to cup my face between both of her hands. "What's not to love?"

"You're biased."

"I'm also right." With a quick peck to my forehead, she starts for the car with me and George following behind her. "Don't be a stranger. You know where I am if you need anything."

Nodding, I crouch beside George. "Can I have my dress back, please?"

We release it at the same time as he nods at me, and I watch him wait for Jess to get in the car before he follows her. When Henry closes the door, George knocks on the window and flattens his hand to the glass. I do the same, covering his little hand with mine as I blow him a kiss. These sweet moments with him always make me question whether I really don't want to have children of my own.

"Where to, my darling Eve?" Henry asks as we watch them drive away. "My place? Your place?"

"You decide." I shrug.

It's Saturday night; I have no plans for tomorrow other than resting. For the last week, I've struggled with switching off and getting decent sleep. Now that the showcase is done, I'm ready to hibernate for at least the next twenty-four hours.

You said we were going to leave by eleven. We're late."

"George," Jess tries to pacify him. "It's okay if we're a little bit late."

"No. I want to leave now."

"But Geo—"

"No. No. No," he keeps chanting as I get up and crouch in front of him.

"Did you want me to take you for breakfast next weekend?" The distraction tactic seems to work momentarily as Jess gets her coat on and orders their Uber. "We can go to that waffle house you like?"

After a moment of debate, he shakes his head at me. "No. It's time to go home. I want to go home."

His upset is evident in the way his gaze bounces back and forth between me and Jess, avoiding Henry altogether. It's a sign he wants comfort, but he can't get it because everything around him is new and strange.

"Here." I bunch the hem of my dress and hold it out to him. It's a way we can hold hands without actually touching each other, and he doesn't hesitate to take it. "Mummy's calling a cab, and then you're going home, all right?"

With a nod, he clenches my dress tighter with long, steadying breaths. He doesn't let go as Henry settles the bill. Even though I want to argue with him about paying for us all, I let it go this time. It'll only stress George out more than he already is. As the four of us leave, George continues holding on to my dress, always careful that our hands don't accidentally touch.

"I'm so sorry," Jess whispers, mortified, as we wait for their Uber to arrive.

"Don't be silly, it's fine. It's been a long evening for him. The concert, new people, new places, and all the noise. I'm surprised he's handled it so well."

She smiles fleetingly before she tells me, "I know you think I'm nagging, and maybe it sounds that way too, but I just want the best for you. Right now, you might think that you're on the same

TWENTY-THREE
Eve

"Just like that," Henry groans, collapsing back into the chair. His hand slaps onto the table as he goes limp. "I'm beat."

"A match to the death." George laughs loudly while he stabs the chopstick through the last spring roll he was just using in his and Henry's sword fight for it.

I've watched them throughout dinner. George is at his best, and Henry seems to be enjoying their games while Jess and I catch up. It feels like forever since the two of us spent any time together. Although she's putting up a good front, I can tell she's not sure about Henry. She keeps bringing up our age difference like it's the be-all and end-all. I'm finding myself zoning out of her prying questions and focusing on the way Henry interacts with George.

It never occurred to me before that he likes kids or that he wants them. The thought makes me shudder. As if he can sense my discomfort, he glances up at me. There's no hint of the smile he was humouring George with only seconds ago. I've never had someone so attuned to me like he is, and for once, it frustrates me.

"Time to go, Mummy," George announces suddenly.

It's late, and I imagine he's getting anxious about the change in his routine. There was only so long that he was going to be distracted by the faux-sword fighting.

"Now, Mummy," he asserts, getting up and putting his coat on. Pointing down at Henry's phone, he adds, "It's past eleven.

scent warming my lungs, I feel complete. At peace, even. Like I am finally home. "You were right."

"I'm always right."

"Maybe, but you were definitely right about this. You are made for me. No what-ifs, buts, or maybes. You are everything I've ever needed."

"Glad we're finally on the same page." She beams at me.

I feel as though I'm living two lives simultaneously. One where I'm a vindicator or a vigilante and the other where I'm just a man like any other. A lucky son of a bitch in love with the most wonderful woman in the world. While I know that the two will collide at some point, right now, I'm happy living the latter.

red suite."

"You did?"

"Yep, and it worked." Cupping one side of my jaw, she holds me to her when her lips press to my neck in a soft kiss. "Like a lucky charm."

"Are you ready to celebrate?"

Pulling back, Eve presses her hands to my chest. Her big brown eyes darken with a devious glint that causes my heart to run away with itself. Moments like this must be so rare to come by. I can't imagine feeling this same way ever again. A part of me hopes that these pockets of time will only get better, more precious, while another part can't imagine anything feeling better than right now, witnessing her happiness and holding her in my arms.

"What did you have in mind, Your Grace?" The put-on accent makes me chuckle.

"I don't sound like that."

"I guess since you've been slumming it with me, you've lost a few of the prunes stuffed in there," she teases, tapping my lips with her finger.

"I thought it was plums."

"Prunes…plums…same thing." Eve gives me an exaggerated roll of her eyes before she turns and gestures towards her family. "They're waiting to meet you."

"Making someone wait is a bad first impression."

"Only if you're tres poshay, dear." She puts that voice on again, and this time, a laugh rumbles from deep inside me.

"Eve." I tug her back to me, spinning her to face me again. "No matter what happens or who you become, don't ever change, my beautiful darling."

"Never." She shakes her head in reply. "Not one bit."

"Good. You're perfect just like this."

"Henry…"

"You're perfect to me. For me." Curling one of the soft tendrils framing her face around my finger, I breathe her in. With her

When I turn my back on her, she calls after me between gritted teeth. "Henry!"

"I'm walking away now, Mother. This conversation is the past. It's done." *I'm done.*

The red-carpeted corridor seems to stretch endlessly as I walk towards the champagne bar. I have every mind to turn back and make her take it all back. But I'd be wasting my time. It wasn't my father I inherited my pride and arrogance from; it was her. She'll never apologise or back down. Once her mind is made up, Her Highness Princess Margaret, Duchess of Gloucester, is unreasonable and unshakable.

I turn the corner to the bar and pause at the sight of Eve and her sister-in-law. They're in an animated conversation as the boy from the photo circles them. Checking my hands, I make sure that they're clean. Suddenly, the distance shrinks. I want to put my hands all over her shimmering form. My chest squeezes at the sight of her with her mane braided and curled into an elegant updo.

Eve turns to look at me, and a slow, beaming smile tugs at her lips as she walks towards me. No pause. No hesitation. She doesn't wait for me to call her to me. Eve all but jogs to my side. I feel her excitement bubbling through her. It reverberates through me when I take her hand and pull her into me.

How could I not love her when she's the brightest ray of sunshine I've ever seen?

"I felt you watching me." She grins up at me, her hands fumbling at my dinner jacket as if she's as desperate to put hands on me as I am to put my hands on her.

"You were splendid, my darling."

The beaming look on her face becomes impossibly brighter as I press a kiss to the tip of her nose, tracing my fingertips down the deep V of her dress from her nape to the small of her back until she shivers into me.

Rolling onto the tips of her toes, she tucks her face into the crook of my neck. "I imagined it was just you and me back in the

over her. Her face meets mine. "She's a child."

"And still more of a woman than most of the names on your list." Pushing away from her, I start for the door to the box.

"Henry! Do not walk away from me!"

"Do not presume to tell me what to do or who to love because I will cut you out of my life so completely that you will be left with no children to care for you when your title means nothing."

"Will she love you when she knows who you are?"

The question jars me. Eve knows who I am. Maybe not all the ins and outs, but she knows what matters. *Doesn't she?*

"Will she be woman enough to love the killer too? The monster that would dispose of a life without pause or remorse."

"I'm doing it for you because it's what you want."

"I want justice, but you—" A scoff vibrates her body. "—you want blood and the violence."

This is where she has been sheltered from reality. This is what sets us apart and maybe what makes me the monster she accused me of being.

"Do you know, I think Eve may know more of the world than you ever will. You can't have justice without blood or violence."

Her face falls blank. "That girl will ruin you. She will ruin *us…our* good name."

"It's my name now, Your Highness." I am the Duke of Gloucester now. The Sloane name is mine to share with whom I choose.

"Henry…"

"I'm not Simon. You won't dictate my life the way you—"

"Don't you dare bring that up now." She pushes out of her seat with her fists clenched at her sides, standing up to me as though she has the strength to make me submit to her wiles.

"Does it haunt you?"

With a shrug, she sighs. "You can't change the past. Once it's done, it's done."

"Good for you." It seems I'm not the only one without remorse.

"Yes, but a recommendation always helps."

"What do you want, Mother?" We both know she's not here to talk about recommendations or about Eve's talent.

No, the Princess is here to remind me of the list she has with all the eligible ladies she would consider marrying me off to. The one time she showed it to me, I shrugged it off. A part of me knew that one day, I'd have to look at it again and pick the best of the lot. However, back then, I didn't think I'd care for a woman the way I care about Eve.

"I would like you to consult me before you put the family jewels on a…"

"On a?" I level her with a pointed look. This conversation is souring faster and faster with every second she takes to reply. She would've done better by putting her list under my nose again.

"She's a Hush girl, Henry. A…a…"

"Come on, Mother, spit it out." The hiss of my words lingers in the air with an acerbic bite.

With a shake of her head, she sits back in her chair, staring out at the emptying auditorium. My ears are burning with all the things she isn't saying. There's a particular name she has for the girls at Hush, and if she so much as refers to Eve in that way, things will get ugly.

"Do you know what makes a duchess, Henry?" Her face collapses into an imperial glower. "Do you?"

"Marriage in most cases."

"That girl is not duchess material," she bites out.

"That girl is whatever I say she is."

An irate growl vibrates from her before she snipes back, "She's not a duchess, Henry."

Pushing to my feet, I spin to face her, gripping the armrests of her chair as I lean over her. For once, there's a crack in her perfect veneer. Fear blinkers in her blue eyes.

"Eve is *my* duchess." This is the only fact she needs to take from this conversation. It's the only truth that matters.

Mother sits up straight and as tall as she can with me leaning

A proud grin tugs at my lips as I focus back on Eve. The gold beaded dress she's wearing glitters around her, creating a most perfect halo around my angel. I can't tear my gaze from her the entire performance, right until she walks off the stage with the rest of the Royal Conservatory Orchestra.

I find myself still glued to my seat when the lights slowly come back on. Madeline's remark keeps going around in my head.

Am I in love with Eve?

I suppose the affection I have for her is love. I care for her enough that I'll sit with her as she drinks endless cups of tea. The one thing I hate, yet when I'm with her, it doesn't matter. Not the smell or the taste of it on her lips. In fact, I love the way it tastes on her tongue and the way it tinges her breath with extra sweetness when I breathe it into my lungs.

So, yes, I suppose I do love her. So much so that I can't bear to be distanced from her. When we're apart, I find myself distracted by thoughts of her. When we're together, I can't keep my hands off her. The door to the box closes behind, but before I turn, a small hand rests on my shoulder.

The large ruby ring glistens in the diamond halo setting as I peer down at it.

"She's a beautiful girl," Mother states in a clipped tone. "I can see why you're so taken with her."

Here we go. I suck in a breath and bite my tongue, giving her a chance to say what she's got to say before I correct her. This is one of those times where my father would stare off into space and pretend he wasn't listening to her talk me around to doing what she wanted. I wish he was here now to give me one of his useless winks as I endure her diatribe.

"Her talent is impressive, and I'm sure we can recommend her to the music director of the Royal Philharmonic…" Rounding my side, she sits on the chair beside me as her hand slips down my arm to my hand. "Or even the—"

"I'm sure the music directors saw it for themselves tonight." I grip my armrests tighter.

The words scream in my ears, drumming relentlessly in my head while I watch her blood run black in the bleakness of the evening. And I drive the knife into her again and again before I cut her throat from ear to ear. My eyes on her eyes. Her blood on my hands. With another slash across her throat, I drop her quivering body on the ground, watching as her body drains of all life. Just as my father's did.

I can hear him now, whispering in his grave. *"Softly, softly, Henry. Softly, softly, catchee monkey,"* he used to tell me when I was running out of patience with something. Just as I am now. I'm getting tired of waiting for Chapman to come out of his dark hole.

But I'll only be done when his blood runs into the gutters of this city.

The music envelops me, haunting, alluring, and deeply touching. Countless times, I've watched Eve play for me, but this performance is breathtaking. Sitting taller in my seat, I release the tension from my errand and relish the warmth of pride unfurling in my chest as I watch Eve in her element.

"She's very good," Madeline whispers, leaning into me with a nudge of her shoulder.

"Exceptional." A quiet giggle trills from her at my retort. "Don't laugh at me."

"I'm not," she protests, peering up at me at the same time as I glance down at her. "Fine, I'm only laughing because it's cute."

"Cute?"

"The way you're all googly-eyed for her. It's sweet, and I like seeing you in love. It suits you."

"Madeline—"

"Fine, I like seeing you happy. Is that better?" When I smile at her with a soft nod, she settles back into her seat. "She really is incredible, your girl."

TWENTY-TWO

Henry

9:00 p.m.

Eve's performance is at nine thirty; I need to be back by nine. I won't miss it, even if I have to watch from the shadows with my hands bloody and my wits torn.

9:00 p.m.

Taking a deep breath, I stare into wide brown eyes.

"Please." The begging rasps punch into my chest.

I wonder if he had the chance to beg before they killed him. Although I doubt my father would, even given the chance. He was a proud man.

My hand tightens around her throat as I plunge the knife into her side, twisting it deeper while I watch her face contort with pain and awareness that this day was her last.

"No mercy, Polly." The endearment her brothers use for her draws a lonesome heavy tear down one side of her face.

I want her to know who signed her death warrant as her blood chills in her veins. It takes a moment too long for her bloody sputters to wrack her body. I wait for that first drop of blood to run from her lips before I pull the blade from her and thrust it into her pelvis.

"No. No." The guttural coughs spatter on me as I slit her open to the top of her sternum.

No. Fucking. Mercy.

The sated exhaustion is bliss as I lay her on the bed and lie down beside her before I pull her onto my chest. Having Eve this close is heaven. Her warmth. The scent of our sweat and our pleasure mingling together in the air is perfection.

"Henry?" Eve whispers. Her short nails are lightly raking over my chest, swirling and drawing sweet nothings the same way as my fingertips trace over the tattoo on her back. "Did you mean it? Are you really going to keep me?"

"I am."

"Do you think you can change fate? That you can keep me breathing for as long as you want me?"

Bracing her forearms on my chest, she looks down at me, her golden hair shutting out most of the golden glow so that there's nothing but the two of us.

"Yes." I don't hesitate in my reply because even if I can't change fate, I won't stop trying until the day I die.

much life and want. So consuming that I can barely hear her as she moans, "Yes. Yes, Your Grace."

Throbbing around my cock, her cunt coats me in her arousal. So fucking hot. So damn wet. Too bloody good.

"Where do you feel me, Eve?" I ask, driving into her so hard that she yelps while her hands grip my forearm. The sound of my body slapping into hers echoes in the sex-drenched air.

It's all I can smell. Me. Her. My need. Her pleasure. Our desperation.

Taking my hand from her face, she guides it down to her pussy. "I feel you here." Slowly, she drags it up to her belly. "And here. So deep it hurts." Her breaths are but a garbled rasp that I suck into my lungs as I kiss her, and she brings my hand higher to her breasts.

I don't know how much longer I can draw this out. Every one of my muscles is coiled tight and aching. My balls are heavy, and my cock is throbbing with my urgent need to fill her with my cum.

"Everywhere," Eve cries as I pick up my pace, and her hand squeezes around mine, kneading one breast and then the other. "You're everywhere, Henry."

Eve's so fucking sexy like this. Her body straining with every one of her heavy breaths as I pound into her harder and faster. Unable to control my lust for her climax. Loud, raspy pants build to choppy groans as I lower my hand from her breast and circle her clit.

"Oh God...Oh God..." Her cunt tightens around my cock as I drink in her enraptured cries.

The instant I rake my thumbnail over her swollen clit, she shatters. Her shaking body collapses into mine as I fuck myself with her boneless form. Stroke after stroke with every slap of our flesh and fist of her pussy, my dick throbs, and my balls tighten with the unforgiving grip of her body.

"Darling," I grunt into her gaping mouth with my release shooting deep inside her, filling her so good that it drips out of her with every jerk of my cock. Until I'm empty. Spent.

cock while my heart drums wildly.

"So fucking beautiful." The words roll off my tongue as I inhale her sweet scent deep into my lungs and then swipe my tongue through her engorged folds.

Trailing my hands up her thighs, I grip her plump arse hard and mercilessly so that Eve squirms and bucks into my face as I lick over her again. Relentlessly, as I spread her open with my hands, my tongue laves at her clit between nips and sucks.

"Henry." Eve's whimpers get louder, breathier, and frantic as I take one long swipe.

I dip my tongue into her cunt so that I can spread her wetness higher. My hands claw deeper into her flesh as I drag my tongue through her crease. My cock weeps to bury itself inside her, to fuck all her tight holes and defile every inch of her. But my lips yearn to worship her body as I lick over the dandelion at the top of her arse, kissing each flyaway that climbs up her spine.

This need is unlike anything I've ever known. It's infuriating and intoxicating, demanding things from me that I never knew existed inside me.

"Want to know a secret?" I grit into her ear as she rocks back into my cock.

"Yes," Eve hisses as the head of my cock pushes into her. "Yes…"

"I might just keep you, my darling Eve." Edging deeper into her tight pussy, I wrap my arm around her chest and pull her up onto her knees as I stand.

"Yes." The cry pushes out of her as her body falls into mine, impaling her to the hilt. "Oh, God, yes…yes…"

"That's what you want?" Coiling one hand in her hair, I tug her face up to mine as I stroke out of her pussy and shove back inside with one hard, ruthless thrust that has her yelling, "Yes."

I hold her still as she tries to ease my intrusion. Tightening my arm around her, I cup her face as I grind into her. "You want to be my pretty little whore, Eve?"

Her eyes widen on mine. Full of lust. Full of affection. So

tainty clouds her stare as I comb my fingers into her hair and press her lips to the top of my cock, and before I can prepare myself, her velvet tongue swipes over it.

"Wrap your hands around me," I tell her, my voice strained with the sensation of her lips pulsing around my tip in shallow strokes. "Grip. Tight, Eve."

She does as I instruct her, watching me as I thrust between her lips. The feel of her hands clenching the base of my erection is heady. It makes it hard to measure my strokes. In and out, in and out as her tongue laves at my slit with breathy hums.

"Open wider," I growl, shoving my thumbs into either side of her mouth as I fuck deeper, as far as her hands will allow, so that my tip brushes the back of her throat just enough to make her gag lightly around me. "Fuck, that's good, darling."

Wide, overwhelmed eyes pool deeper with tears every time I stroke out and push inside. Each time her hands slip lower down my cock, the urge to shove myself down her throat becomes harder to control as the flat of her tongue caresses my throbbing length. Again and again.

God, she's so perfect like this, tears skittering down her cheeks with the choking hitch of her breaths and intoxicating moans. My muscles tighten, coiling with my need.

"Such a pretty mouth," I grunt, pushing my thumbs deeper as I thrust harder, until her hands push at my groin. Her nails claw at my flesh as she whimpers and cries around my cock. The sound vibrates through me in scorching waves that knot my insides.

Yanking myself from her mouth, I pull her to her feet with my tight grasp on her jaw. "Get on the bed."

I don't give her a chance to do as I say as I wrap my arms around her waist when she turns away from me. Instead, I guide her to the edge of the mattress and lift her onto the bed, tucking her knees beneath her as I crouch behind her.

"So fucking wet," I groan at the sight of her soaked cunt. Her arousal slicks the tops of her thighs.

It's a fucking sight to behold. My blood pounds harder to my

at her feet.

Warm eyes flit up to mine. "I live with death coursing through my veins, but I'm still terrified of dying. I know it will happen one day, but…"

"No, it won't."

A soft, girlish smirk tugs at one side of her lips. The disconsolate expression twists at my insides. She's looking at me as though she knows something I don't. Like a parent humouring their child's optimism.

"It won't, Eve. I'm not going to let that happen. Ever. You'll breathe for as long as I breathe. I'll make sure of it."

Pulling the vest over her head, she gives me a quietly indulgent chuckle as she drops it somewhere beside us. "Your arrogance knows no bounds."

"No limits, remember?" A knot forms in my chest as the words take me back to the conversation we had the night I took her virtue. She is my only limit. I'm discovering that in everything we do together.

"So cocky," Eve whispers, pressing her naked body to mine.

The gentle sway causes my cock to stiffen with the stroke of her belly. So soft, warm, and inviting that I can't keep my hands off her. Moulding my palms to the curve of her back, I hold her flush to me as I flex into her.

"I like it." Her hands slip beneath the top of my boxers, slowly edging them lower between us so that my precum slicks over her skin, lubricating the strokes of her skin over my erection.

"It's sexy." A deep swallow follows her remark.

In the dim glow of the bedside lamp, I watch a deep flush tinge her cheeks as she lowers herself down my body. The torturous brush of her breasts and the friction of her skin on mine make it impossible to control the constant simmering need that pulses in my veins for her, pounding through me.

Half-lidded eyes flit to mine as she crouches in front of me, fisting my underwear in both hands as she licks her lips, and the maddening heat of her breath sheaths my throbbing cock. Uncer-

"Why aren't you in bed?" I ask her, bringing her face to mine and kissing her.

I can feel her lips pull into a gorgeous smile. The same kind of smile that Bette used to have. Except hers eases the tightness in my chest.

"You should be in bed." Pressing the button to send the Mac to sleep, I wait for the screen to go blank as I flip the folder shut and stash it away in the keyboard drawer. "Big day tomorrow."

"Might shit myself." A big, teasing grin cuts across her face when I roll my eyes at her common nervous quip. "I keep having a stupid dream where my strings snap halfway through my performance and—"

"You're going to be perfect, my beautiful darling."

"Henry." She whispers my name like it's the most precious prayer on her lips. "I like it when you call me that."

"You are beautiful."

"Not beautiful. Darling." Trembling fingers comb through my hair. "I like it when you call me *your* darling."

"Well, my darling Eve, I'm going to get you to bed." I push to my feet, lifting her in my arms as she buries her face in my chest.

"Are you going to fuck me?"

"Yes, darling, I'm going to watch you ride my cock until you come with my name on your lips. Just the way I like it."

"Yes, Your Grace." A deep sigh hums from her as I take the steps up from the office and walk through the open-plan living area to the bedroom, with Rufus grunting behind us.

Warm hands knead my neck from my shoulders to my hair. Her touch is the best distraction. It rouses all my senses so that it's the only thing I feel in the heat of the moment when her lips ghost over mine.

When we're in the bedroom, I let her down onto her feet. Eve's so small that I have to lower my face to kiss the top of her head while I inhale the sweet almond scent of her hair.

"Tell me a secret," I whisper into her ear as she pushes the boxers over her hips and kicks them to the side when they pool

at me is how much I miss her. I miss her following me around and getting under my feet. Fuck, I even miss getting into fights because guys couldn't keep their eyes off her.

Dragging in another deep pull, I clutch the photo frame tightly as I lean back in my desk chair and close my eyes. For years, I've tried to recall the last conversation we had. The last time we got into one of our silly fights that ended with her challenging me to a duel I'd have to let her win. I can remember so many things, but not the last time we spoke or the last embrace we shared. It's always her smile that I remember the clearest. That bright and beautiful smile that made it impossible not to smile with her. But beneath all the smiles, there was a darkness none of us ever imagined, and in the end, it took her from us. From me.

The click of Rufus' paws interrupts my reverie as it gets closer until I hear him at the top of the stairs. He'll grumble if he wants me to help him come down here; he won't attempt coming down on his own. While I wait for him to decide, I hear the light shuffle of feet behind me.

"Who's that?" Eve asks, coming down the last of the steps behind me.

"No one." I stow Bette's photo away again, closing the drawer as I sit up and put out the butt of my cigarette.

Wrapping her hands around my shoulders, she touches her lips to my ear. "Then why do you have her photo on your screen?"

Fuck.

"Should I be jealous?" Eve chuckles, twisting herself around me until she falls into my lap. She's wearing one of my vests and a pair of boxer shorts that are loose on her, allowing my hands to trail over her curves and my eyes to feast on her ample tits. "You have a thing for convicts?"

I follow her gaze to the file still open on my desk with a mug shot of Mary Ann Nichols.

Fuck.

This is exactly what shouldn't be happening. Eve can't see this.

disregard for these things is why she burnt your fucking house to the ground."

"Fuck. Henry," Julian warns.

"Do you ever think about that, Simon? Why she did it?"

"Henry!" Julian's bellow reverberates in my eardrums as Simon puts the phone down. "Too far."

Maybe, but I'm so sick and tired of pretending that Simon's still one of us. He's never here when it matters, and he leaves the first chance he gets. The only loyalty and duty he holds is to himself.

"Simon lost everything in that fire."

"I lost my sister." The instant the words leave my lips, I want to swallow them back down. The tightness in my chest is so vicious that I can't breathe to clear my head. A suffocating fog engulfs me.

We don't talk about this. It's one of those things we pretend never happened. That she never existed. The whole tragic affair is buried in the ashes of the Rochester estate.

"Let's get into the website and see what we get from there. Get Elizabeth under John Chapman's nose and leave the sister to me."

"All right," Julian says, letting out a long breath before he adds, "Don't strike out of emotion. Make sure it's the right thing to do."

"Sure," I reply with a shrug before I end the call. I'm agitated, and my head is steaming with the past, the present, and everything that's still to come.

Lighting another cigarette, I open the drawer with Bette's photo stowed inside. Every time I see her face, I can't help but wonder where it went wrong for her. She was always mercurial, hot and cold, but she was sweet too. Almost as precious as Madeline.

The squeeze of my heart becomes unbearable as I trace her smile with my fingertips and search for a warning or a sign in her dark eyes that I missed before. But the only thing that screams

There are bigger issues to worry about than who you're fucking and why he's not here."

"The girl's a distraction," Simon growls. "Can't you see that? We might've been done with this if she wasn't in the picture."

"If it was that simple, there would be no need for any of us. We're never done, Simon. This is what we live for."

"The email you sent, there was a photo of a woman." I go back to the attachments and scroll through until I find the photo in the email before I compare it to the one in the original file he gave me last month. "Mary Ann Nichols."

"Chapman's sister. She owns a chain of beauty clinics across the city. They're all in backstreets with barely any foot traffic, and they're appointment-only. Here, check the website," Julian says just as a message pings in our group chat, and I follow the link he sent through.

"You need a password to book an appointment?" It doesn't make sense.

"Odd, I know. This is why I think we need assistance. If we can get into the back end of the website, we'll be able to pull everything from it."

"Wait." I chuckle at the irony that the legal mastermind is the one suggesting we do something highly illegal. "You want to hack into the website."

"Yes."

"You won't be able to use any of the information we collect to bring the Coster Kings down."

Julian laughs. "There's only one bloody way to get rid of them, and this will help us find their ties."

"We're not running a criminal investigation," Simon says. "I couldn't give two shits what she's selling to whom."

"Of course you don't," I scoff in reply.

"When did you get so judgy?"

"When I killed men and women that traded young, innocent kids for weapons or they raped young girls so that they could sell their babies to fund their religious wars. That's when. Maybe your

After a quick glance through it while he and Simon continue debating what to do with Elizabeth, the only thought that comes to mind on Julian's research is that maybe the United Republic wants to use Chapman for more than his brute force.

"Do you think he's got someone on the force?" I ask, taking one last pull from my smoke before I put it out.

"Potentially. I have some more notes and files to go through. Anyway, that's not the point right now. I got to thinking that maybe Chapman isn't the only one that can lead us to the UR's main man. His brother is his second-in-command. He's part of every dealing the Coster Kings have."

"So we're pimping Lizzie's blowie lips out to his brother instead?" Simon asks.

"You're a pig," Julian groans at him. "But yes, for all intents and purposes."

"Great," Simon scoffs. "Moving on, do we have anything else on the briefcase?"

"No." I've been tracing my father's footsteps from his last few days, but there are one too many gaps that I can't fill without his driver. Since he's gone, it's proving impossible. "But I've got Andrew on it."

"It's taking too long. We're taking too long," Simon states. "They're having enough time to recoup from our blows."

"Maybe, but if we use all our strikes at once, we won't draw Chapman out, and we need him to get to the United Republic."

"There's just too much going on, Henry." Julian's worry is evident in his strained voice. "We need help."

"No."

"Then you need to stop entertaining a baby and—"

"Don't bring Eve into this," I cut Simon off before his whining gains momentum. "I'm here doing everything I need to do to get to the bottom of this shit. What are you doing? Lining your pockets and bitching like a miserable cunt?"

"Give it a fucking rest!" Julian snaps down the line. "We don't have the luxury of being at each other's throats right now.

"What do you have?" I ask Simon, ignoring his and Julian's jibes at me.

"Good news and bad news," he replies. "Chapman isn't interested in Elizabeth."

"She needs to work harder, then."

"She wouldn't have to if you hadn't left that fucking button in his mistress' mouth. That was stupid and careless, and you should know better. Come on, you're the highly trained GI Joe captain, commander, whatever it is they call you now…"

He drones on and on until Julian says, "Chapman knew we'd retaliate. That's not why he's not taking the bait."

"What the fuck do you know about what he's taking or not taking or the whys and hows?" Simon barks at him.

He's on edge. I've known Simon all my life; I know how he works and what gets to him. Whatever's got him fretting can't be good if he's being so bearish.

"He's closing himself off," Julian continues with a bored sigh, as though he's had enough of Simon's tantrum. "When you're under attack, you batten down the hatches, and you protect yourself. He's not letting a stranger close."

"So what's our approach now?"

"Chapman's second-in-command," Julian answers. "I've been digging through old police files and anything I can get my hands on from past investigations."

"Are those relevant to us?" Julian's got a big libel case between a cabinet minister and an ex-advisor that the media are going crazy for. He doesn't need to be focusing on anything else that isn't going to help us.

"I'm not sure, but it's odd that every investigation fizzles out as it starts getting hot. The last time, all evidence had to be dismissed because one of the officers on the investigation didn't catalogue it properly at the scene. It's really basic shit that gets him off every time. I sent you an email with some of the details. Usual password."

Signing on to my Mac, I go to the encrypted email he sent.

growing, spreading."

This conversation is too weighty to be had in this room where twenty-four hours ago, she was bleeding out. Truthfully, the only thing I want right now is to get out of here and take her home with me.

"Still want to get out of here?"

A slow, sad smile spreads across her pretty face. Tear-tracked or not, she's still the most beautiful woman I've ever known. "Yes. Please."

"We can take a walk, maybe get the Clipper from Westminster Pier all the way down to the Tower. It's a short walk from there back to my place, and Rufus will enjoy it."

"Rufus?"

"I told you I have someone to introduce you to. He's old and grumpy, but he's my best mate. We understand each other."

As we're walking out of the room, Eve pauses and turns to me. "I'm glad that you're here," she tells me, rolling onto her tiptoes to press a kiss to my jaw. "I'm glad Andrew saved you."

"Me too."

The buzz of my mobile grows louder on my bedside table. It's dark, and Rufus' snoring echoes from the chaise by the window. Simon's name glares at me as I glance at the phone and sit up in bed. Eve's sound asleep as I get up and pad quietly out of the bedroom.

"Is she with you?" he asks before I greet him.

"It's three in the morning," I groan as I take the stairs down to my office nook. Before I sit at my desk, I open the window to allow the air to circulate when I light my cigarette. "Eve's asleep."

Simon's not happy, and when Julian joins the call, he's not best pleased either. I'm not sure why they're so put out by Eve and me. It's not like I've disappeared or stopped doing my duties.

It's getting worse as he's becoming older."

"The boy in the photo looked happy between you and his mum."

"Jess and I have mastered the art of posing with him. Some creative angles and a selfie stick do the trick." There's so much love in her eyes when she speaks of her nephew that I can't help but smile at the sight, even if she is upset and nervous.

"Don't pick," I tell her, grasping both of her hands in mine. "You'll end up hurting yourself."

"We don't want that." A soft laugh filters past her lips.

"No. No, we don't."

"Jess is trying to get him into this private special-needs school, but it's impossible."

"How so? Why?"

"She can't afford to pay the fees, and the council won't help her because George doesn't score quite enough points on their charts. They think he can cope in mainstream school, but the teachers don't know how to cope with him. It's this vicious circle that never ends."

I'm not sure what's worse—seeing her upset over her brother or angry because of her nephew's situation. In truth, I hate both. And still, I can't keep myself from asking her to tell me more because I love listening to her talk about the people she loves. She doesn't realise how her affection beams from deep inside her soul. How it lights her face and sparkles in her eyes. It's an intoxicating sight, one I cannot get enough of.

"What happened with your brother?"

"Oh," Eve sighs, her eyes flitting to mine through thick midnight lashes. "George screamed, and I think it jarred him. It must have because Joe freaked out and threw him across the room. I don't know how he didn't kill him, but Jess ended up in hospital with a broken rib when she tried to wake him up."

"No soldier comes home from war unscathed." It's the one unavoidable truth about deployment. "We all have scars. Physical, emotional, mental…they're all there like cancer. Festering,

he's waiting for you to put one foot wrong or to look in the wrong direction at the wrong time."

"Then why did you come back? Why did Casper come home unscathed? Meanwhile, my brother is gone, and my dad…"

"Andrew is the reason I made it back. Our squadron was on a ghost mission to take out a war criminal with an American elite team." Eve's eyes widen as I stand and pull her up with me.

I know I shouldn't tell her any of this, but the mission is done.

"When we raided his compound in the middle of the desert, he was fucking one of his wives. I took the open shot on the bastard without seeing her clearly. Turns out she was wearing a suicide vest, and the instant I put a bullet in his brain, she detonated the fucking thing."

"You're here," she whispers, threading her fingers through mine. "You came back."

"Sheer luck in one part and in another because Andrew pulled me out. At that moment, it didn't matter that I was the son of a duke or that my mother is a princess. When shit hits the fan, we're all the same. Me, Casper, your brother, Andrew…we're just people looking out for each other while we take the enemy out."

"I hate it. I hate being on my own and that George is never going to know how great Joe was before he went to war. Every time he came back, there was more of him missing. The last time he came back, he had awful night terrors." She pauses with a pitying look on her face that sets me on edge.

I know all about the nightmares. There are times I wake up and I can still hear the bullets whistling past me or the screams of women and children that were caught in the crossfire. It's all so vivid that it doesn't matter how much I try to bring myself back to the present; I'm stuck there, reliving every fucking second like it's a penance for my sins.

"One night, he was sleepwalking, and George found him. He's autistic. Doesn't like being touched at all." Eve inhales deeply as she picks at the pearlescent polish on her nails. "Not his mum, not me, no one. And if you touch him, George freaks out.

door on the wardrobe, watching as she faces the door and her hand hovers over the doorknob.

Unease fists my lungs with every second that ticks by and she doesn't make a choice. I'm teetering on a knife edge while she refuses to decide.

"Eve!"

Turning swiftly on her heels, she falls back into the door. Tear-glazed eyes flit to mine in the mirror. "I can't."

"You can't."

"I can't leave. I don't want to leave, but I don't want to be here either. This place…I…"

"Okay." I breathe out a sigh of relief as I push to my feet. "Where do you want to be?"

Eve shrugs as though she's lost all sense of herself. It bothers me that her encounter with the Gladstones has caused her this much distress. Crouching in front of her, I grasp her hand and pull her onto her knees so that we're closer.

"How do you know them?" I could've asked the question during our meeting, but it would overstep the boundary into something personal. Making business personal is never a wise thing. "How does Casper Gladstone know you?"

The tears glazing her eyes swell until they have no choice but to rain down her pretty face when she sucks in a trembling breath.

"Did he hurt you?"

"He lied to me. Casper promised he'd always bring Joe home, but—" She shakes her head with a long, body-wrenching sob. "He lied."

"I see."

"No. No, you don't, because men like you and Casper Gladstone always come back. There's always someone there to take the bullet for you."

"Look at me and listen carefully," I tell her, combing her hair from her face and catching the tears dangling on her lashes so that she can see me clearly. "In war, every man is the same. Bloodlines and titles don't matter when you're staring death in the face and

her as she comes away from the door. "Why? Because you're better than me? Your title and your family somehow make you superior. Is that it?"

"What's gotten into you?" We were having a pleasant enough evening. At least, I thought we were, but as always, it becomes twisted or fucked in some way. I don't know how else to appease the grudge she has against who I am and the world I was born into.

"I don't want to be here anymore," she states, turning for the door.

That's her go-to defence mechanism: lash out and then run away. I don't run, though. I've always liked facing things head-on.

"Walk out of this room and you won't like what happens."

Spinning to face me, she levels me with an indignant glare. "Stop threatening me!"

"It's not a threat." I keep my voice level despite the anger roiling inside me.

I thought tonight was a good night. I thought we'd turned a corner. It appears I was wrong.

"It's a fact. I won't run after you. Whatever this is, is over. My eyes will never look at you again, and my hands will never touch you. You walk away and we're done."

"Maybe it's for the best," she whispers down at her feet with a crack to her voice that causes a lump to form in my throat.

I don't want her to go. Whatever we have between us isn't ready to be done. I'm not ready for it to be done. I don't think I'll ever be.

"If that's what you truly want, Eve, walk out."

Walking to the bed, I sit on the edge like I've done so many nights. I stare at the spot where she normally sits. The thought of watching her leave is bleak, and I know that listening to her walk away will be just as unpleasant. But it's her choice to make, and I won't force it either way.

"You know where the door is."

"Yes," she bites back, "and I know how to use it."

"What are you waiting for, then?" I glance at the mirrored

TWENTY-ONE
Eve

"Why do you insist on disobeying me at every fucking chance?" The door slams as my question grates from my mouth. Before the echoes of it fade, I cage Eve to the back of the door with my arms.

"Disobey you," she scoffs back at me with a frown. "Disobey you like I'm beneath you."

"What?"

"Pardon, Your Grace." There's no humour in her endearment or affection. Eve's glaring at me like I'm the one that's being stubborn and difficult. "Isn't that the right way to talk?"

"Now's not the time for your sass or petulance," I snap back, and she's quick to retort, "What about your unreasonable reactions and volatile behaviour?"

The clench of her jaw tightens as she grinds her teeth in frustration. When she pushes me away, I take a step back. This isn't one of our usual verbal sparring matches where she barks and I bite. Something's wrong. I can see it in her eyes, and I felt it before she left me earlier.

"I told you not to go in there," I remind her, taking another step back so that she can move away from the door. "You get here and you come straight up to my suite. Those are your instructions."

"One rule for me and another for you." A wry laugh escapes

Forcing myself not to look back, I glance at the group further down the bar. One of the men has his eyes firmly set on Mary. The ferocious glint in his stare causes me to shudder. There's something devious about him. Like they share a secret.

"Who's that?" I ask Mary.

"Sir Richard Warren, the police commissioner and my cue to get off my arse and get on my back or on my knees. We keep him extra sweet, and he buries their evils." Her gaze falls to my neck again. "They give with one hand and take with the other. Using pretty things to disguise ugly deeds." Sad eyes flit back to mine, reminding me of the reason I ended up here in the first place. Grief and anger, and it's reflected in her eyes. "Don't fall for it. He doesn't love you. They don't know how to love anything other than power and wealth…and the Crown."

A small smile ghosts over her bright, painted lips as she unties her robe again and flounces it open to show her body.

"Well, if you're going to drink it," she says, picking up the drink Hannah made me, "I will. Courage and lubrication in one. Chin, chin."

My chuckle dies a quick, suffocated death when I glance at the doorway. Henry's scowl stabs me in the chest. His anger suffocates me. The print of his hand on my throat pulses as though he commands it to strangle me for doing what he has told me not to. And like he really does own me, my feet meander to him. Eating the distance between us until I'm standing in front of him.

"I'm sorry." The apology leaves my lips as he grasps my hand and takes me away without a single word.

"What is it?"

"Every time he comes to you, wet your lips and pretend you're somewhere else. If you think too hard about where you are and what you are, eventually you'll become whatever they make of you." Mary takes a sip of the drink Hannah sets in front of us. "Bottoms up, chick."

The warm scent of nutty almonds makes my mouth water, but I can't bring myself to drink any of it. Instead, I hold the glass to my lips and dip my lip along the rim with an exaggerated swallow so that it looks like I've taken a sip too.

"You should come out for drinks with us," Hannah suggests. "It's good to have friends in here."

"The majority of us look out for each other," Mary adds, watching me carefully when I put the drink in my hand down. "And you're one of us, even if the Duke keeps you locked up."

"He doesn't." The words snap right out of me before I can stop them.

"Little whispers go around, Eve." Mary side-glances at Hannah before she continues. "Whispers are that they called a doctor for you." With a curious cock of her brow, she studies me carefully. "What did he do to you? Where did he hurt you?"

The twist of my stomach sends a sudden frisson of panic through me. If Henry doesn't want anyone looking in his room, I'm certain he doesn't want anyone knowing what goes on in it. Neither do I.

"Hen—" I pause, correcting myself. "The Duke didn't do anything to me. He didn't hurt me."

Disbelieving eyes narrow on the necklace around my throat. "Of course he didn't."

An awkward silence instils itself before she finally smiles again, and Hannah goes back to manning the bar when a group of men walk in. I know I should leave now, but Mary's still finishing her drink. Then there's the uncomfortable scene playing out behind me that's like a car crash. I can't seem to keep myself from peering at it over my shoulder.

through mine, and she tugs me along with her into the bar room.

I've never been in here. The walls are half panelled in deep mahogany and half pasted with a deep midnight blue and gold embroidered silk. The man that was playing with me at the dinner is sat behind a grand piano, playing away even though no one is really listening.

"What's your poison, then, my lovely?" Mary asks when we sit at a couple of stools at the dark marble counter.

"I-I don't have a poison," I tell her, looking over my shoulder.

A tall man walks in with a girl crawling behind him. Her red robe trails on the wooden floor. When he sits in one of the large long-back chairs by the fire, she kneels in front of him with her hands on her knees and her face lowered. She sits at his feet while he leisurely lights his cigar and then sits back with a tug of the girl's body chain so that her face meets his crotch.

"I don't drink." My remark is an abashed bluster.

"That's where you're going wrong. How do you think any of us get through this?" Mary gestures around us. "Go on, pick something. Anything. If you're going to start, it might as well be with the best."

The bartender comes to a stop in front of us when Mary waves her down. "What do you want?" she asks her with a haughty quirk of her brow. They're friends.

"What do you have for a novice?"

"Amaretto is good. A bit sweet with a lovely cherry-and-almond kick. A bit like this place." Leaning over the bar, she whispers, "Fruity and heavy on the nuts."

Mary laughs at her friend's dirty joke. "What's the popular one you make?"

"Ah, the leaky snatch."

"Stop it, Hannah." Mary pushes her friend away. "Just make the bloody drink."

"Okay, amaretto sour coming up."

While Hannah makes the drink, Mary settles in beside me. "Do you want to know a secret?"

Casper doesn't reply or push back as he stares between Henry and me. Nothing has changed. He never said much when Joe was spiralling into chaos, and he hasn't said anything since.

"Henry," another man calls from the shadow of the corridor. "Your Grace, we're not here to quarrel." The prime minister steps forward, coming to his son's rescue as always. It's the reason Casper's alive and my brother isn't. His life wasn't as important after he'd served his purpose. This is why I hate them. All of them. Rich, powerful bastards.

Turning to face me, Henry gives me a top-to-toe glance. His hands are balled at his sides, and the lines of his face are sharpened with indignation. It's as though he's checking that everything is in its rightful place—that I'm not ruffled—before he relaxes slightly.

A barely there smile softens his expression. "This won't take long." I acknowledge his statement with a nod. "I'll come get you when I'm done." Another nod. "Go on."

When he reaches for my hand, I pull back. I'm an idiot. Henry's the reason I'm here. The reason I keep coming back. The reason I'm turning around and taking each step up to the red suite, even though my whole being wants to be anywhere but here, surrounded by riches and grandeur. I'm betraying Joe, myself...all for him.

Henry was right; he takes, and I give. I keep giving even when I hate him, and to the point I hate myself.

"Don't you look glum?" Mary calls ahead of me as I reach the top step. "It's a shame you look like you've been stung in the arse when you're all dressed up pretty."

The grin on her face is so wide it reaches her eyes. She's gleeful, and there's something about the way she carries herself that exudes confidence. Nothing seems to faze or get to her. I wish I was like her—able to keep my cards close to my chest.

"Oh Lord," she sighs. "What's he done, then?"

"Hi," I chuckle at her brassy demeanour.

"Hello to you too, little Eve." Mary meanders over, pulling her robe closed so that she's not starkers when her arm threads

hand held tightly in his, our fingers woven together.

"There's someone I want you to meet later," he tells me, giving my hand a light squeeze.

"Eve?" a deep, familiar voice calls from behind me.

When I turn, I'm greeted with a confused stare. "Casper."

"What are you doing here?" he asks, ignoring Henry completely as he steps closer. The lion tattoo on his neck reminds me of Joe. He had an identical one on his bicep. It's been a while since I've felt this dark cloud of grief over me. The guilt of how things ended is a sucker punch I'm not ready for.

Why's he here? Casper's married. He has kids and...*and so do most of the men in this place.*

"Eve's with me," Henry answers on my behalf, tugging me into his side before he wraps his arm around my shoulders and whispers into my hair, "Are you okay?"

No. I haven't seen Casper since Joe's funeral. He promised me he'd bring my brother back. He never did.

Nodding, I muster a smile. "I'll wait for you upstairs."

Concern is etched into the drawn lines of Henry's face. I don't know what he thinks, but I'll explain later. Once I've had a moment to process the jumble of feelings whirring inside me. Affection, grief, anger, disappointment, and fear all shake into a cocktail that's headier than any drink I've ever had.

"I'm fine, Your Grace," I whisper, trying to forcefully tug a smile onto my lips with a light caress to his jaw.

The false smile is for him, but the touch is for me. I need to feel him. To focus on him—feel, scent, warmth—to pull myself from the storm brewing inside me.

"Eve—" A large hand grasps my wrist suddenly as I take the first step up. "—wait."

"Let go." The choked yell rips from me in a torrent of breath that pushes from my lungs.

"Now, Gladstone," Henry orders with a brusque push of Casper's chest and a tug of my wrist from his grasp. "Touch her again and you won't walk back out of here."

"Madeline? Why?"

"You told me that you don't know how to do gentle, but when you look at her, it's all you are. And I—" I pause as I look up to find him watching me intently.

"How do you think I look at you?" he asks, his voice quiet, soft. When I shrug, he answers his own question for me. "When I look at you, you're the only thing I see. In that moment, you are the only thing that exists for me. A reprieve from this world."

Emotion swells in my throat, rendering me speechless to the ardour of his words and the vehemence in his unwavering stare. My poor heart doesn't know what to do with itself. It aches as it threatens to burst with all the affection pulsing in my chest.

"And God help anyone that stands in my way, darling. I'll burn them to the fucking ground. I'd create chaos to find your peace."

"Your Grace." I choke out the title that's become my endearment of him. The emotion is almost too much to contain as it prickles up my throat and stings the back of my eyes. "Henry…"

"Are you jealous now?" he murmurs over my lips, nudging the tip of his nose with mine. When I shake my head, incapable of answering without blubbering, he crushes a quick, hot kiss to my lips. "Good."

Pulling me back tightly into his side, Henry combs his fingers through my hair with one hand while the other reaches across us and holds my face tucked into his chest. The rest of the ride is peacefully silent. The thick air crackles with all the things he said and all the things I can only feel because they seem too crazy to speak out loud.

"My meeting won't take too long," he tells me as we arrive at Hush, and he helps me out of the car. "Wait for me in the suite."

"Okay." I nod, even though the last thing I want is to let him go, but whatever this meeting is about has him tense the second we walk through the club doors.

Tonight isn't as busy as yesterday. There's an air of unnatural stillness as Henry walks me to the bottom of the stairs with my

earlier, via the private VIP entrance. A car is already waiting for us when we reach outside. The weather is just about to turn. I can feel the rain in the air and smell the sweetness of its impending arrival.

"So, how was that?" Henry asks when we're in the car.

"Not all that bad," I reply, resting my head on his shoulder as he grasps my thigh—where his hand has been most of the evening. "I didn't shit myself, so that's a plus."

A low guffaw rumbles through his chest. "Madeline likes you."

"She's nice."

"She's one of my favourite people in the world," he says with a chaste kiss to the top of my head and a sigh that's too wistful not to be sad. When I peer up at him, a frown furrows his brow with a deep V creasing his forehead. The grave expression makes him appear older. His dark, hooded eyes look haunted. "If I had a sister, I'd want her to be like Maddie."

"Yes, I can see that."

We fall into a temporary silence where we bundle together. His arm wraps around my shoulder, holding me tightly into his side while I trace the hard muscle on the outside of his thigh with my fingertips. It's rock hard and so strong. He could be as impenetrable as he is unshakeable. Like a fortress in a storm, we might just withstand anything.

"Henry," I whisper into the streetlight-strobed air.

"Eve."

"I'm not a jealous person."

"I know."

"But for a minute, I was jealous of her."

Sitting straight, he peers down at me down the length of his straight nose, directly into my eyes. "Her? Who?"

Perhaps this was a stupid thing to bring up. It certainly feels like a ridiculous admission to make. However, I'm already in for a penny...

"Your cousin."

"You're welcome to stay with the fun people."

"Thank you, Your Highness, but too much of a good thing is bad for you."

Which is just as well that Henry is bad and dirty through and through because I can't get enough of him.

"Stay out of trouble," Henry tells his cousin before he has a chance to reply to my remark.

"Bring Eve to my birthday party." Madeline levels him with a no-arguments furrow to her brows. "It's a small soiree. Friends and family."

"Oh yes, you'd look fetching in matching costumes," Prince Arthur laughs. "Maybe you could go as the Phantom and what's her name?"

"Christine," Julian chuckles.

"What the fuck are you—"

"I'm not much of a singer," I cut Henry off before the undertone of their joke dawns on him. He clearly has issues with age, and the last thing I want is for their joke to cost me more precious moments with him.

"I'm sure with the right conductor, you could hit the high notes," Arthur retorts with a leering laugh.

"Ignore him." Madeline gives me an unexpected hug. I'm frozen to the spot as she pulls away and goes on to give Henry one too.

She's not what I expected at all when Henry introduced us at the beginning of the evening. Madeline has the same austere demeanour as her brother and cousin, but once she warms up to you, she's really *normal*. Maybe more normal than me and so personable that you can't help but like her.

"You don't have to dress up," she tells Henry before we leave, and as we're walking out, she catches my eye with another beaming smile. "Make sure he brings you."

Somehow, I'm not sure that's a good idea. Madeline may be nice, but I don't think I'm quite ready to meet any more family or friends. Henry walks me out the same way Andrew walked me in

know himself. Not one bit. Especially with the way he looks at her. His affection for her is overwhelmingly palpable, something that strikes an odd chord with me as I look between them. The jealousy of his care for her comes from nowhere, but I can't bring myself to feel bad for it. If anything, I want to steal all of that affection he holds for his cousin to myself.

"I'm not a bloody baby," Madeline huffs with a defiant roll of her eyes at him. "I'm twenty-three in thirty-four days."

She's four years older than me, and he calls her a baby.

"Stop being agist," I remind Henry quietly, stealing his attention back to me when Princess Madeline focuses on Julian. He's so morose that glancing at him from across the table feels like an intrusion.

Moulding his hand to my face, Henry leans closer, guiding me the rest of the way until his lips meet my ear. "I believe that in our earlier discussion, we ascertained that I am most certainly not agist. In the slightest." He punctuates the last statement with a rough stroke of his other hand up my thigh.

When he pulls back, his stare locks on mine, so dark that the whole world comes alive in their depths. I'm bewitched by the magic in his eyes. Lurid. Volatile. So fucking beautiful that I can't catch my breath. My chest squeezes so tight that my heart threatens to explode with the overwhelming emotion pulsing through it.

I don't know what he is, but what I know is that Henry Sloane isn't the sun, the moon, or the stars. He's everything. And there's nothing I can do to contain the way I feel about him as it sparks and flames through every nook and cranny of my existence.

"It's time, darling," he says, stroking over the bejewelled choker around my throat with his thumb.

"Time?"

A molten grin pulls at one side of his lips. "To go, Eve."

"Do you have to?" Madeline asks with an over-the-top whine as Henry stands and offers me his hand.

"Yes, do you have to?" The Prince echoes her words in more of a grumble. Blue eyes narrow on mine with a cocky grin.

Lights, camera, action, and everything in between. I'm sandwiched between the Princess Royal, Madeline Dorchester, and Henry. It feels odd sitting with all these people that have known each other from childhood, yet here I am, holding a constant smile because I'm a stranger. Even in expensive clothes and glittering jewels, I'm nothing like them.

"Henry said you like music," the Princess says, leaning into the space between us so that she doesn't have to raise her voice over the cacophony of the chatter around us. "My uncle used to like music too."

Returning her smile, I nod. It's hard to think straight when Henry's hand is on my thigh. My pulse refuses to settle, and when he squeezes my flesh, it's impossible not to squirm on my chair.

"Someone somewhere once said that music is the food of the soul," I say after a beat. It takes more effort than it should to keep my voice level.

"Yes, the language of feeling and passion," she sighs with a dreamy sway. "I've never been one for words and reason." With an affectionate grin, she adds, "I leave that to the buttoned-up types."

"It's a luxury only the baby can afford," Henry retorts, giving her a mock glare across me.

If he believes that gentleness isn't in his capacity, he doesn't

teardrop rubies and surrounding diamonds look relucent against her creamy skin, hiding the marks I left.

"Not too tight?" I ask, tracing the vintage, heirloom choker with my thumbs from the clasp to the front.

"No."

"Good." Turning her to face me, I can't resist the urge to bracket both of the Vs of my hands around the necklace. "Now you look perfect."

"A perfectly nervous wreck." The remark is a bluster of sweet breath that I suck into my lungs greedily.

"No," I correct her, hardly able to muster the words properly with the way my chest is squeezing my lungs and my stomach is twisting at the sight of her.

There are really no words to express how she looks or what she is. In fact, that says it all. There is nothing, nor has there ever been anything like her. Eve is the set precedent. Whether she knows it or not, she's a goddess. A fucking saint with the smile of a sinner and the lure of a devil. Eve's everything I never knew I needed and everything I've ever wanted.

"You look perfectly beautiful, my darling Eve."

clubs go. Or I imagine they go?"

My phone vibrates in the pocket of my suit trousers with a loud accompanying trill. "That will be our car waiting for us. Do you have your pouch?"

"Yes, it's squeezed into the ridiculously tiny bag your stylist said would go with the shoes."

My stare chases hers down to her feet. The light from inside hits the crystals dotted on the skin-coloured mesh just so, making her feet appear like they're glittering.

"I have something for you." I pause as we get inside and turn her to face the glass pane.

With the day fading outside, her reflection ghosts back at us while I reach into the inside pocket of my jacket and pull out the diamond necklace I had Percival send over with the stylist.

Dark eyes bug wide. "Holy fuck," Eve blurts, watching as the heavy piece of jewellery hangs from my grasp on the clasp. "I can't. No. Nope. That's…I can't. If something happened to—"

"It's insured, and there's going to be a lot of security around you."

"Me? Why me?"

"Because you're with me, and I'm with the next King of England."

"Of course." She lets out a deep breath before inhaling deeply again.

"You're doing your babbling thing again."

"It's that or I shit myself. Given you've only really fucked me once, I don't think that's the done thing, right?"

There's no way I can resist the urge to kiss her when she's this adorable with her odd potty mouth and flustering nerves.

"The necklace will be safe around your neck, and you will be fine next to me. I promise," I add the latter as she continues craning her neck back onto my chest after our kiss. "It belonged to my great-great-grandmother on my father's side."

"It's very pretty," Eve murmurs as I stand her straight and put the necklace on her. It sits perfectly around her throat. The large

She shakes her head. "Not really." The reply surprises me. With her love of music, I thought dancing would be her thing too. Sounds silly now that I think about it, but it made sense before.

"Neither do I," I tell her, grasping her left hand with my right one in front of her waist and spinning her again to face me. Swaying her from side to side, I give her a breakdown of tonight. "The car will stop, and Andrew will be waiting to take you inside the hotel through the staff entrance at the back. The offer is still there for you to come with me."

"I'm okay. Thank you," she whispers, holding tighter to my arm with her other hand. The heat of her touch seeps through the cotton of my shirt and my skin as I continue swaying us in slow circles around the balcony overlooking the garden and the river.

"Don't thank me. I'll be making it worth my while later."

"Can I ask you something?" she ventures, looking up at me. Her teeth gnaw at her deep-red-painted lips. "Do you get anxious before these events?"

"No."

"Not even a bit nervous?" The grimace of discomfort on her face makes my chest tighten. "Not even just a teeny tiny bit?"

"No, I get grumpy. I don't like these farcical things, but as you like to say about me and Hush, it's a means to an end."

"You're always grumpy, Your Grace," she laughs softly. After a quiet second, she adds, "I was wrong about that…or you, mainly. You're not a means to an end. At least not anymore."

"Once I've walked through with Arthur, I'll join you at the table. Julian will be there already."

"He doesn't like me very much."

"Julian isn't himself, and things are fraught at the club right now," I say casually. It takes a moment for me to realise that I'm on the verge of saying too much. Of divulging information no one outside of the Society is to know.

"How so?" Eve asks, rolling onto her tiptoes to wrap her arms around my shoulders as I anchor my hands on her waist. "It always looks like it's running smoothly as far as…*those types* of

gues, I take full advantage of her open mouth and kiss her until she's breathless and pliant in my hold.

I meant what I told her. I'll never ask. Everything is what it has always been—what I want it to be. When I want it to be. How I want it to be.

There's something incredibly taking about a woman when she's dressed up and you can tell she feels good about herself. In truth, I can't say that she looks more beautiful than ever because Eve always looks stunning. Even when she's soaked through in one of her dinosaur or cat-eared hoodies. However, tonight she's breathtaking, in every form of the word.

"The dress looks good on you," I tell her, putting out the cigarette I was smoking before I meet her at the balcony threshold. "It looks really fucking good."

Too good to make it outside the front door without taking advantage of the way the black, heart-shaped bodice strains over her tits, emphasising her tucked waist.

A bashful smile greets me when my eyes rove up to her face. "I draw the line at cannibalism," she chuckles, smoothing her hands over the top of the full tulle skirt before she brushes her loosely wavy hair over her shoulders.

Grasping one of her hands, I spin her on the spot. Once the whole way round, and a second time so that her back is to me and I can whisper into her ear. "Sweet darling, I'm going to eat your cunt until you've died at least a few deaths when we're back later."

A nervous, sputtering laugh bubbles from her. When she tries to turn around and face me, I hold her still. Taking a quiet moment, I inhale her sweet scent deep into my lungs as she leans back into me.

"Do you like dancing, Eve?"

plump arse in both hands.

"No, darling." I squeeze her supple flesh. "I'm an all-body man. There isn't a part of you I'm not going to defile." An audible swallow swells down her throat with another breathy squirm. "No holds barred. I'm going to do things to you that you've never imagined."

"Okay." The choked whisper causes me to chuckle.

"You belong to me, Eve. This isn't me asking for permission. I'll never ask. I'll take and take, and you'll have no choice but to give."

Lust-glazed eyes flutter with every one of her tremulous breaths as she whispers, "Henry…"

"You'll want me to stop. More than that, you'll beg me to stop, but I won't. I'll torture and torment every inch of you until you hate me…until you hate *you*."

I sit on the edge of the bed, with her between my thighs, taking in the way her brandy-coloured eyes course over my shoulders while I kneed her arse.

"Look at me. I want to see your eyes." Slowly, they flutter up to mine. Her timid stare burns bright as my hands trail over her curves to her waist. "Do you still trust me?"

Slowly, Eve edges closer. Her small hands go to my shoulders, tracing to the top of my arms. "Yes, Henry, I still trust you." The reply is barely a whisper—a soft susurration that shocks my heart into overdrive.

The gallop of my pulse burns in my veins as I shift her to straddle my thighs. As much as I want to fuck her, I want to hold her more. I've never just held a woman. Not like this. A part of me knows that I shouldn't be doing it, but I don't care. I want what I want, and everything else can be damned. Consequences are a worry for tomorrow, not today, and most certainly not right now.

"Tonight," I start again after she got us sidetracked, "I'm taking you out."

"But you have an event."

"You're coming with me," I state plainly, and before she ar-

my beloved bulldog doesn't have much time left. He can barely walk around this place without running out of breath. I can't leave him on his own for long, and when I have to, Percival likes to take him home with him.

"It's okay, I'll bring him back from the club later."

"All right, well, I'll see you later."

"Thank you, Percival," I say before ending the call and giving Eve my full attention. "Tonight," I start, but she doesn't give me a chance to finish when she asks, "What happened to your side?"

"My cousin." With a shrug, I hook my finger over the top of the bath sheet and tug her closer. "We got carried away with a jousting tournament?"

"Jousting?" The sound of her laughter makes me smile. My pulse quickens at the sweet trill, making it impossible for me not to snicker along. I could live off that sound for the rest of my life. "I know you're a bit along on the age spectrum, but jousting seems old for you. Even for you," Eve teases with a crinkle of her nose that makes it impossible not to nip at the dainty tip.

"Are you calling me old?"

"Well, you called me a child." The excited rhythm of my heart stutters at her words. "If I'm a child, what does that make you, Your Grace?"

Swallowing down every argument I could give her, I admit the only truth. "Wrong. It makes me wrong, Eve."

"Because you're fucking me?"

"No, because you're legal," I tease her, "and you have great tits and a fucking incredible cunt."

A lovely blush spreads across her cheeks with a hitched breath that tenses her entire form while I step backwards, closer to the four-poster bed her eyes keep bugging out at. I intend on making exceptional use of each poster one of these days—when she's recovered from last night and ready for the full measure of my desires.

"So you're a boobs man," she rasps, blowing out a shaky breath when I slip my hands beneath the towel and grasp her

bedroom.

This place has always been refuge, more so when I returned from Afghanistan with my head too fucked to be around people. I've never brought a woman here. This is too personal to let people in. Even my mother. But Eve...Eve is the exception to every fucking rule.

Trust isn't something I give easily, but her sincerity makes it difficult not to lose it to her piece by piece. With every endearing smile and sultry laugh—even her incorrigible stubbornness and sharp tongue have a way of disarming me. That knowledge does nothing to quash the feeling constantly pulsing in my chest—the constant need to have her close. To know every move she makes. To witness every smile she graces this world with.

"Yes," I answer Percival's question just as the bathroom door opens and Eve steps out, wrapped in a bath sheet and her hair a wet, sopping mess that I want to twist into a thick rope and use it to collar her throat as I fuck her. Hard. Really fucking hard so that neither one of us knows where we end and the other begins. "Make the arrangements."

"Yes, Your Grace," he chuckles down the phone with a soft note of affection.

He likes Eve. He's always liked her. Maybe it's why he was so adamant that she play at my father's memorial howl and then on protecting her from me.

"Sort everything out like we discussed earlier. You remember everything, yes?" I ask, drinking in the soft, bashful smile on her lips while her eyes flutter over me, pausing on the scar on my side with a scowl.

"Options."

"Yes, and the rest."

"I have it all under control and will send someone over shortly. Do you want me to bring Rufus back tonight, or should I take him home again?"

My faithful friend. Rufus used to be the only love in my life. We've never gone to sleep upset with each other. At six years old,

won't fall for it or some pretty girl that the country likes because her father died in office."

"What do you suggest?" I ask, replacing Rufus' water and topping up his kibble.

"We get rid of *all* distractions and focus on what's important." I already know he's pissed about me missing the breakfast meeting this morning. Truth is that I don't care how he feels about Eve—she's my girl. While I understand his feelings on relationships are tainted by his experience, he chose to make the mistake that led to who he is now. There's no way he's deflecting that shit onto me.

"Is that what you're doing every time you swan off to Manhattan?" I ask coolly.

Before he answers, Percival cuts the conversation. "Six minutes."

"Laura's not all bad. Besides, she knows the importance of keeping people happy. More than that, she's good at it, even when they don't pity her." As Simon's about to argue, Julian adds, "She has connections that benefit us."

"Great, another business trade-off." Simon's tone is strained. "We all know how well those work out."

"Who's the pessimist now?" Julian snickers as Simon's line goes down. "Whether it ends well or not, Benedict is right. Arthur's weakness is women—"

"Commitment," I correct.

"Same thing. As long as we can keep him interested in Laura long enough, this is a great plan."

In my eyes, I don't care whether he's interested or not. He'll use her to woo the public, and what he does behind closed doors doesn't matter. It's all about appearances, and that's the only thing Arthur needs to worry about right now—the public's perception of him.

"I'll see you at the gala," Julian says before he hangs up, leaving me and Percival alone.

"Are you sure about tonight?" he asks as I head back into the

NINETEEN

Henry

This phone call is dragging while Eve steeps in the bath and I make another coffee. I want her again. My body is so acutely aware of her presence that it refuses to relax. The taut gnawing of desire sparks over my skin. There's never been a woman I've longed for as much as I yearn for Eve, with every echelon of my being. It's something entirely new, a feeling that encompasses everything I am or will ever be.

"You're not serious, are you?" Simon laughs. "Do you honestly think that this will end well for either of them?"

"That's what I'm meeting with Gladstone about tonight. I need to make sure the girl is fitting. Everything I've seen of her says so."

"Her father was an ally," Percival adds.

"Please, the only reason you're even considering her is because she's the country's pity doll," Simon groans at the same time as a cabin announcement sounds behind him. "My jet's landing at Teterboro in ten."

"When are you back?"

"Fuck, I don't know, Henry. When I'm done here."

"You need to be here." Julian blows out an exasperated breath. "It's all falling to shit."

"Does it ever get exhausting being the eternal pessimist?" Simon retorts. "I don't know about this distraction plan. Arthur

"Henry." My tremulous cries fill the air, echoing around me.

"That's it, darling, give me everything," he growls, fucking my pussy with long strokes that draw out the never-ending avalanche of sensation and overwhelming relief.

"Good girl." Henry palms my pussy, collecting all my juices before he braces himself over me.

One hand roughly combs through the roots of my hair while the one wet with my orgasm fists his dick between us.

"Good fucking girl," he repeats, fucking his hand harder and faster with guttural grunts and raw groans that I drink up greedily with the scent of my pleasure ripe on his lips.

"Fuck!" The strangled curse booms into my lungs.

I'm choking on the sound of his orgasm as he quakes above me and his cum spurts over my belly and my breasts, hot and sticky.

"Fuck," he growls low and breathlessly, collapsing on top of me.

For a long moment, we don't move. I relish the thrum of his heart over mine as I trace the beads of sweat on his back and hold him as tight as I can. I don't know what's better, the dirty sex or this. The aftermath. Where we're both too spent to move, too breathless to talk. We can just be and revel in the stillness of the world.

stares meet, I want to throw myself at him. I want to be held by him. To be loved in ways that no one has or could ever love me. Not like him. I want his intensity to own me. To never let me go.

I want to be the only star in his sky. The only moon the light of his affection shines on. And it doesn't matter how much it hurts. I'll take this unending torture every day if it means I'm the centre of his obsession.

"So fucking wet for me." Dropping my underwear from his face, he sucks his glistening fingers into his mouth. "You taste as sweet as you smell," he rasps, palming my pussy with his other hand while he sucks his fingers again.

"So good," he rumbles with a hard slap to my clit.

"Fuck!"

"Not yet, darling," he chuckles darkly with another swat to my soaked flesh before he pushes two fingers inside me. "I'm going to give you what you deserve, Eve."

Curling his fingers inside me, he pushes deeper. I can't stop the frissons of pleasure from bowing my body and writhing over his hand and face as he licks my clit, working his tongue in endless circles and unforgiving lashes that cause me to moan and buck.

I'm chasing everything he gives me—every stroke of his fingers and every rake of his teeth. Edging his fingers out of my pussy, he shallows in and out, short thrusts that have my body tensing, my pussy squeezing tighter, clenching and clenching until his fingers feel too big. Too much to bear.

"Come for me, beautiful girl," he coaxes into my throbbing flesh in between soft nips to my thighs.

"Oh, God," I mewl into the air as I claw at my thighs for some kind of reprieve as my insides twist savagely, sending endless shocks of pleasure to my core.

The frenetic rhythm of my heart pulses through my hands, pounding harder and faster to my toes as they curl with every lick of ecstasy. I'm shaking and shuddering, and I can do nothing but feel the heat of my orgasm ripping through me with his name on my lips. Moan after moan cuts through my lungs.

me what I want, and I want you wet for me. So fucking wet I can drink you up."

"Fuck." I choke out the curse with a gasp as my body does exactly what he asked for. My pussy is throbbing, squeezing as the heat of my arousal soaks through my underwear. I've never been this wet in my life. This needy. This fucking senseless.

Releasing my chin, he cups my breasts with both of his hands. With a pinch of my nipples between the V of his thumb and forefinger, Henry smiles down at me.

"You're mine now. I get to do what I want to this body. My body," he growls with a slap to my breast. "My body to torment. My body to tease." Henry licks his lips as his eyes trail down to my pussy. "Mine to fuck…"

He slowly manoeuvres me onto my back before tugging the dress over my curves until it waterfalls down my legs, leaving me only in my underwear.

"To please," he states with a smirk, lowering himself between my legs until all I can see is the top of his head between my thighs. "My body to worship." He blows a hot breath over my soaked knickers.

"Oh God," I moan when his hands grip my hips and drag me right to the edge of the table.

His lips are flush to my pussy, his nose nudging my clit as he inhales deeply.

"Mmm," he hums as his tongue flattens over the dark lace, and he licks all the way up to my clit, sucking it into his mouth along with my underwear.

Nothing's ever felt so good. My blood pounds through my veins as I clutch at the edge of the table, and he continues toying with my sensitive nub. Uncontrollable shivers roll through me as Henry tugs my knickers over my hips and down my legs.

"Look at you," he groans, running his fingers through my slit as he peers up at me with my knickers pressed to his nose. His eyes are closed as he inhales deeply with another pleasured hum.

I can't bring myself to be embarrassed because the instant our

pulls with deep sucks. My pussy is clenching tighter as my insides twist harder.

"Please," I beg him to give me something other than this torturous foreplay. Every time I think he might just make me come, he pauses to watch me suffer.

It's mean. Sadistic. So fucking frustrating that I want to scratch and claw at him. And I would if I wasn't tied up in my dress. The more I beg, the more he teases me, taunting me with his wicked mouth until my pleasure is the most unbearable pain I've ever felt.

"Henry," I sob, trying to drop my legs from his hips, but he just thrusts closer, opening me so wide that my groin screams for mercy even as my pussy weeps at the heavenly friction of his erection behind his buttoned fly. Every bump feels like a blessing as he rolls his hips, and I feel everything.

Glorious, glorious friction. I writhe beneath him, getting as much reprieve as I can from the agony of my unsated, highly strung need.

"You're at my mercy now, darling." He grins, pushing himself off me so that I'm left completely open to the cool air as it assaults me, snapping viciously at my hot skin.

"I'm not done yet," he purrs when I breathe a sigh of relief.

"I can't...I can't..." I can't take any more. I'm aching in places I didn't know I could ache in. My lungs are burning so fiercely that breathing is torture, and yet, I'm gulping down the leathery-scented air like I might never draw another breath again. The tears rolling down my temples are hot blades cutting deep into my skin. "I can't...please. *Please.*"

Henry takes a step back and makes a show of slowly undressing himself. The sight is breathtaking, more so than I ever imagined it to be. I'm so lost. Every one of my senses is exhausted and overstimulated. I can't feel myself anymore. I can only feel him as he comes back to me.

"You can, Eve," he says, gripping my chin. "You have no choice but to take everything I give you. No choice but to give

time starting lower with a torturous nip of my collarbone. And this time, I can't contain the blistering ache.

"Fuck." The soft curse tumbles from my lips as my hands claw at the painted metal surface of the table.

A low laugh rumbles from him. It's raw and with a taunting edge that tells me he's enjoying torturing me with every languid stroke of his tongue over my skin. The more I squirm, the tighter he bands his hands around my wrists, slowly shifting them behind me until I'm braced on my hands and my body bows. It completely arches to his so that when he pulls back, releasing my wrists, he can tug the top of my dress down my arms, leaving me completely restrained and incapable of moving without falling back.

Henry smiles down at my breasts as they threaten to spill from the cream lace cups. The see-through fabric leaves nothing to the imagination. He can see how terribly hard my nipples are for him. He can see how swollen and heavy I am. And he likes it. Henry likes that I'm trussed up by my own lust, so needy that I can't move, let alone think.

Caressing my thighs with his fingertips, he slowly edges my dress up until my underwear is on show. With a step closer, he hitches my knees over his hips without warning.

"Henry," I whimper at the rake of nails on the underside of my thighs as he leans over me and bites my lip.

There's no way I can stop him as he bites and laves at me from my mouth to my throat, and slowly, he curls to brace over me so that he can continue the torturous trail down to my chest. A low groan vibrates from him when he finds my nipple, and I gasp so deep that the air chokes me.

I'm gagging on my own breath, and he's laughing at my despair. I can't control the fissures of pain that crackle through me as he rolls my nipple between his lips, pulling at the turgid nub over the lace.

Jesus, Mary, and Joseph.

Jesus, Mary, and Joseph, I chant in my head as he moves from one nipple to the other. Over and over, he licks, bites, and

EIGHTEEN

Eve

The heavy wooden door slams shut behind us as Henry sits me on the entry table. My legs spread open the instant he nudges my knees apart, and his hands encapsulate my face roughly before he descends on me again. I don't have time to take in my surroundings as he nips the tip of my nose and rains hungry kisses over my cheeks and forehead.

Deep, wild breaths fan over my skin while his hands trail down my jaw and deft fingers unbutton the high neck of my dress. I'm not shy—I've never been shy—and it's not going to start now. Dropping my hands to his belt, I unbuckle it quickly before he changes his mind.

"Jesus, Eve," he hisses, grasping my wrists to stop me from unbuttoning his jeans. "Slow down, for fuck's sake."

Slow down? Glancing down at my chest, I note the open collar of my dress with a hitch of my brow.

"I wanted to do this." A lopsided grin tugs at one side of his face as he leans forward, lowering himself while his hands cuff my wrists at my sides. With a deep inhale, he bends, burying his face in my neck.

Fuck! My pussy clenches hard at the first swipe of his tongue over my jugular. The hot trail burns deep into my bloodstream as he blows over it, kicking my heart into overdrive. Just when the sensation eases, he repeats the teasing swipe all over again, this

with all his strength. "My fucking plague," he echoes ferociously into my ear before sucking the tender flesh below my ear into his mouth with a deep groan.

I don't care if it's a good or a bad thing, so long as I'm his. Plague, nuisance, nightmare…I'll be whatever he wants me to be. Anything to own every one of his kisses like this.

them around his sides, I bunch his top in my grasp, lifting the hem at the back so I can feel his smooth skin. I really like *this* Henry. Rumpled and out of his comfort zone. He looks so boyish with his thick hair all messy, but his overgrown stubble is there to remind me that he's all man.

The only man that's been inside me. As sore as I am from last night, I'm aching to feel him touch me with his calloused hands, desperate for him to take me again.

"You're a nightmare," he groans, lowering to press his lips to my forehead.

"I am?" I sigh into his neck.

"My darling," Henry grumbles lightly, trailing his lips down the bridge of my nose. When they reach my lips, he combs his fingers through my hair with a gentle tug, then tilts my face completely to the heavens, and he shadows it with his unmoving stare.

My heart can't take it. The ridiculously handsome sight of his face nor the need reflecting back at me from his dark depths. It's so much more than the one thing we share in common. It's a feeling that flows between us, a desire for something just ours, outside of this world.

"You're a nuisance," he says, licking over my bottom lip before his tongue dips into my mouth, stroking over my tongue with the bitter taste of coffee and tobacco.

God, it's so fucking good. My stomach twists around the butterflies fluttering wildly inside me as Henry kisses me deeper. My hands flatten to his strong back with my nails clawing into the hard muscles to relieve some of the need scorching me from the inside. The heat of his hand roving down my spine causes me to shiver deeper into him at the same time as his other hand coils tighter in my hair.

"You're a plague," he growls, licking out of my mouth and up to my ear as his arms wrap around me in such a way that he's twisted around with a hand kneading my arse and the other fisted in my hair.

We're an upright tangle of limbs that he's holding together

self. If ever there was a cantankerous soul, his is it. But it makes me wonder how much of it is him as opposed to the military man that's seen and done some seriously rough shit. Joe went from happy-go-lucky joker to a shut-off stranger. My brother didn't really exist anymore when he returned home. My heart squeezes with grief, a sadness I haven't felt in a while. But as I continue watching Henry, a spark of hope flickers inside me. He exists. In fact, he doesn't just exist; he walks this world like he is existence itself.

"Where are we?" I ask when he opens the door, trying not to sound like I'm not angry or even just a little bit upset over the way he's reacting.

"I need to get showered and dressed," he replies, looking down himself with a grimace. "There are a few calls I have to make before tonight's gala."

"This is your place? You live in a warehouse? Here?" I glance through the driver's window, down the path that appears to lead to a wraparound garden overlooking the river. Obviously, this place isn't a shithole, but it's not where I imagined him living. "Thought you'd live in a palace or something."

"Come on," Henry coaxes me out of the car with a low chuckle, giving me his hand so I can jump down. He makes no move to direct me anywhere other than into him. Stroking his hands over my exposed shoulders, he tucks me into his chest in a surprising hug. "I don't want every interaction we have to turn into a fight."

The earnest remark tugs at my heart. When I glance up at him, he's got a torn expression on his face as if he doesn't know where to go from here. I've never seen this side to Henry—awkward and unsure aren't something that I would usually associate with him.

"The remedy to that is quite simple, Your Grace," I murmur over his jaw while holding on to his waist so I can roll right onto the tips of my toes. "We should do a lot less talking."

A smile tugs at the corners of his mouth as he tries to remain serious in spite of my big grin and wandering hands. Stroking

my time, aren't you."

The sound of his statement doesn't sit well with me. Me being on his time implies that he's paying me to spend time with him, and everything that happens during that period is all paid for. It doesn't matter how much I like him; I'm not that girl.

"Henry—"

"Don't start an argument, Eve. We know it doesn't end well," he warns, levelling me with his dark gaze as we stop at a red light.

"It's not an argument if we talk like civilised people."

"I'm not paying you to fuck me," he states, as if he can hear my thoughts. "There's your conversation, and now it's over."

"Conversation requires more than one person giving orders and getting their way."

"That's compromise," he scoffs, taking off as soon as the lights flash amber. "If that's what you want, I'm not the man for it."

Breathing out a heavy sigh, I bite all my arguments back. Instead, I settle for suggesting a remedy to the situation.

"When Percival offered me the job, he said I'd be playing at the club."

Henry gives me another cocked-brow side glance. "Which you are."

"I'm playing in your suite. For you."

"My suite is in the club, isn't it?"

"Yes, but I thought I'd be playing in a less private setting… like maybe the bar or—"

"I don't want you near the members," he snaps suddenly, his hand slapping hard enough on the steering wheel that I flinch. Letting out a measured breath, he pauses in front of tall wooden gates as they open slowly for him. "They have enough to admire, Eve."

"Henry…"

"I won't have it." The statement is final as he drives into a parking spot ahead of the gates beside a large yellow brick warehouse and gets out with a hard slam of his car door.

I watch him round the front of the vehicle, grumbling to him-

keep you really fucking close."

"Yes." A giggle bursts from me when the soft nibbles morph into light licks and the occasional suck. "Yes, you would."

I really hope he keeps so close that I'll never be rid of him ever again.

Henry's staring at me intently as I drink my tea. He's quiet, pensive, more so than he usually is. But even in slept-in clothes, he looks handsome. A whole of a lot more put together than some of the guys in the trendy coffee shop he's brought me to.

"Do you have plans tonight?" he asks me, taking a sip of white coffee.

"It's a Saturday, so I'm at the club?" That's where I am every Saturday evening. With him.

"Yes." Henry nods, and a small grin tugs at the corner of his mouth as he grabs my tea from me, tugging me up as he stands and puts my tea back down on the table with a scowl at the cup. "It works out well."

"What works out well?" I bluster as he walks me out of the coffee shop and straight to his car.

The smell of waxed leather envelops me again, along with a hint of tobacco and his cologne. It's so perfect and warm that when he opens his door and the cold air rushes in, I'm desperate for him to close it again. Being in his SUV is like being in a concentrated Henry bubble.

"I have a function this evening," he tells me as he starts the car and drives off without telling me where we're going. "But I'm leaving early. I have a meeting at the club, and then we can have the rest of the evening together. We can have dinner together again."

"Is that an order or a request?"

He gives me the side eye. "What does it matter? You're on

think about how he would feel about it. I didn't think about much other than what I wanted. "I should've told you."

"But you're right," he says, tipping my face back to his as he straightens. "I would've stopped."

"Why?"

"Because," he breathes out, wiping his thumbs across the bottom of my eyes. "Because you're delicate, Eve…you're fragile. And a man like me—" He swallows hard. "—a man like me isn't gentle. I'm not built for delicate things."

"That's not true."

"It is," he asserts, tunnelling his fingers into my hair to stop me from shaking my head as I protest, "You're being gentle right now."

I hate this. Whatever *this* is feels like he's letting me down slowly. Trying to gently break my heart instead of just smashing it in one blow. I can't bear it. The world is screaming around me as I watch him ponder the best way to obliterate me. This is worse than waiting under cover for the storm to hit. You can feel it in the air, smell it all around you. You know it's coming, but you're still waiting and anticipating. On and on and on. Then it hits.

"Eve." Henry blows out a breath, and his hands fall to my waist, holding me still. "You see gentleness on the outside, but on the inside, I'm a grenade ready to blow. You can't contain me. No one can."

"Maybe I don't want to." Dark eyes narrow on mine as I rake my fingertips over his stubble. God, I love the scratch of the thick hairs on my skin with the heat of his body seeping into me. "I mean…"

"You mean?" he asks with a lick of his lips when I pinch his chin and lean closer.

"What if I'm made for you?" Rising onto my knees, I nudge the tip of my nose over his. "What if I'm your pin, Your Grace?"

"I'd have to keep you," he replies with a nip to my lip. His arms wrap around me tighter than ever. So tight that I can't move when he softly bites a trail over my jaw to my ear. "I'd have to

I'm not ready for Henry to pull away from me yet. I know that he will eventually, so for now, I'm going to hold on to him any way I can.

When Henry rolls onto his back, I turn in to face him with a yawn. He stiffens as I blink my eyes open, but before he closes himself off, I smile. "Good morning, Your Grace."

"Eve," he replies with a curl of his arm, rolling me onto his chest. His heart is hammering hard and fast. I can feel it beat its unrelenting rhythm into my ear as one hand squeezes my hip and the other presses the side of my face deeper into his chest. "How do you feel?"

"Okay." I resist the urge to chuckle at his grumble at my reply. "I'm good."

"You still look tired." Cupping my jaw lightly, his thumb strokes over my cheek when I tip my head back to look at him.

The pounding of his heart has barely slowed when he sits up, manoeuvring me onto his lap so that I'm straddling him. Both of his hands grasp my face lightly. I've never known him to be this gentle in our entire time together.

"Last night," he starts, causing my heart to drop deep into my stomach.

This is it. I can see the regret in his eyes as he thumbs my hair from my face and sucks in a steadying breath. My hands flatten on his chest as I try to get my last feel of him. There's no going back to normal after last night. We can't go back or undo any of it. The only way to move forward is by walking away.

I open my mouth to tell him to get it over and done with. I'm not bleeding anymore. There's no reason for him to hang around anymore. Before I can say anything, he lowers his face to mine.

"I'm sorry," Henry whispers with a light kiss to the tip of my nose. "I didn't mean to hurt you like this…" Stroking his thumbs down my face, he trails them over my lips to my chin, following the curve of my throat as he tips my face back and peppers light kisses down to the marks he left on my neck.

"I'm sorry too." My actions were reckless and selfish. I didn't

SEVENTEEN

Eve

"**D**on't fucking move!"

The yell startles me from my sleep. With my head still heavy from my episode last night, it's hard to get my eyes to focus past the golden haze screened by the curtains.

"Don't." Henry's arms tighten around me when I try to sit up. "You'll set off the trigger."

It takes a moment for me to process what's happening, but I freeze the instant it hits. Night terrors. Joe had them all the time when he came back from deployment. His were so bad that he would sleepwalk through the house, hiding behind furniture like he was in a war zone, ready to shoot out.

Taking a deep breath, I try to relax. It's not the easiest thing to do when everything in me tells me to protect myself from him. Slowly, he's settling, but his hold on me doesn't ease for a long while. All I can do is wait and breathe, try to stay calm even though I know he's bigger and stronger than me. I've felt his unforgiving force.

Eventually, Henry's arms relax around me. His tense body sinks into the mattress before he wakes up. My back is to him, but I sense his confusion as he gets his bearings. Slowly, it fades to alarm. Disregarding everything I learnt about PTSD with Joe, I steady my breathing, making it deeper as I close my eyes and pretend to be asleep.

arms and take her back to bed.

"Will you stay with me?"

"I'm not going anywhere, darling." There are a million and one things running through my head, making it hard to form a single coherent thought. But if there's one thing that prevails over the rest, it's that I don't want to let her out of my sight.

I don't care that the bed doesn't look big enough for the two of us. Toeing off my boots, I lie back against the headboard and pull Eve onto me so that she's lying over me.

"Rest now," I tell her as I pull the duvet over her shivering form.

It's one in the morning as I turn off the light on my phone, and even though my head is pounding with a million and one different things I need to be doing right now, I can't bring myself to leave. Even if I'm uncomfortable and out of place, there's no other place I need to be but here.

my soul for eternity if I don't want to mark her all over, cover every inch of skin so that there isn't a single part of her that isn't mine.

"I would've never been able to resist you." The confession pushes from my lips as her hands flatten to my chest. "My sweet, darling Eve, in the end, I would've had you regardless. I would've had you even if you didn't want me to."

"So I'm right," she says. "We would always end up right here, Your Grace."

A soft, teasing smile pulls at her lips, one that I can't resist tasting as I nudge the tip of my nose over hers and skim my tongue across her plump pout. She's too sweet and too supple. Before I can stop myself, I lick into her mouth, tugging her closer as she moans, twisting her grasp on my top.

What's wrong with me? How can I still want her so desperately that my body is fighting my head as it reminds me of how we ended up here. I'm not right for Eve. I'm not the kind of lover she needs.

Sucking her lip into my mouth for one last taste of her, I pull away slowly, releasing her mouth only when it's impossible to keep kissing her without hurting her again.

"Henry," she sobs quietly, holding on tighter when I attempt to step away. "I've done my research. I've read about it, asked the right people questions…"

"Tonight—"

"Was always going to be like this for me. At least you didn't think you were going to catch something from me."

"Now's not the time to joke." A few hours ago, she looked like death. From the panic in her eyes, I'm fairly certain she thought that might be a possibility. "These matters are never for joking."

"These matters?" she laughs, shaking her head at me while her hands palm over my chest. "You know, if we're going to be whatever we are, we're going to have to work on getting some of those plums out of your mouth."

"Why don't you focus on sleep first?" I pick her up in my

written in the fabric of my existence.

In other words, I'm completely fucked. I give her a smile.

"You touched me," she whispers, sighing when I nod. "And I-I just wondered what it would feel like everywhere. Here," Her fingers trail over the length of her neck, down to her chest. "And here. All over."

A long, needy breath escapes her as I tug her closer with my hands still holding her jaw. The gold threads of her hair are a tangled disarray as I comb my fingers through them, tipping her head back when I coil them at her nape. The rosy tint on her cheeks spreads lightly to her ears and down her throat to her chest.

What a marvellous sight she is as I step flush to her, leaning down so I can breathe in her shallow breaths.

"I wanted you inside me," she murmurs with a wet flutter of her lashes. "I wondered how it would be. Imagined what you would feel like. But it just wasn't enough because I had to know. The rest"—she shrugs—"doesn't matter."

"You're still bleeding."

"I'm fine. It doesn't matter now."

"It doesn't matter?" I scoff. That anger that had been quietly rumbling in the background roars to the surface. "It fucking does matter."

"It's fine," she whimpers at the sudden twist of my fingers in her hair. Each strand threatens to slice through my skin and flesh the more I tighten my grip. "I'm okay. It's okay."

"No." The dry rasp of my voice causes her eyes to widen. "It's not fine, Eve. It's not okay. And if you don't stop saying it, so help me God, I'll spank those fucking words out of your vocabulary for good."

There's a long, suffocated hitch to her breath as she licks over her lips. My threat blazes back at me in her eyes as she squirms deeper into me. The blush on her cheeks deepens. I know she's imagining the scenario I just painted for her from the lust glazing her eyes. When I stroke over the marks I left on her neck with the back of my fingers, she mewls as if she wants more. God damn

"Eve." I say her name as though it's all the answer she needs to her question. It's the most accurate reply I can give her. I'm still here because of her.

"I'm fine now," she bites back, slapping my hand away when I try to tuck her hair off her face. "And anyway, it wasn't your fault."

"Not entirely. You should've told me."

"Shoulda, woulda, coulda…" Eve shakes her head as though it's a trivial point, and with a shrug, she turns to walk away.

"Don't." Clasping her hand in mine, I tug her to face me again, making sure my hold is secure enough that she can't run away from me. Surprisingly, all the anger that's been simmering for the last few hours doesn't boil over. My feelings aside, I am curious about her actions. "Why didn't you tell me?"

The first hint of colour flushes the apples of her cheeks. A relief that I wasn't aware I needed warms through me. Although she's still pallid, that pinch of colour, along with the bashfulness in her eyes, is enough to ease the vise around my chest.

Eve's reply is a deep sigh with a shrug, and I still, lightly grasping her shoulders. Again, I'm met with the marks I left on her neck. Before I can brace myself, my gut wrenches.

I warned her. I told her I would destroy her. And I almost did.

"This isn't an answer," I tell her when she shrugs again. "Why would you be so reckless, Eve? How could you not—"

"You would've stopped," she finally grumbles.

"I should have."

"But I didn't want you to." The timid statement echoes in the outside stillness that follows it.

That honeyed gaze I've grown so deeply desirous of flutters over my chest as my hands smooth over her collarbone to hold her face. The earth-pounding gallop of my heart makes it impossible to hear anything other than the hunger I can't sate for her. Eve will never understand or perhaps even know how deep my fondness for her goes. It's too natural to my skin and bones. It's etched into my flesh and the markings of my DNA. A soul-deep obsession

did before. The image of her bleeding for me—*because of me*—is as beautiful as it is sickening. Eve is my beautiful sickness. So wrong and so right.

"My dad died on a recon mission to Afghanistan a few years later, and I ended up living with Joe and his family. Jess was pregnant with George at the time, and Joe was being deployed. It worked out in an odd way." She continues fussing over the photos. "This is Jess." She points out the dark-haired woman in one of the pictures. Eve smiles over her shoulder, adding, "And this is George. He's my favourite person in the entire world."

The kid may be cute, but I don't like that he's her favourite person. Following her gaze to the large photo at the back of the cluster, I take in the small blonde woman in the image. It's dark and a little grainy—an old picture— but I can make out her arms wrapped around her pregnant belly.

"Where's your mother?" I ask, watching her face morph into a morose expression. It seems as though she's contemplating whether to answer or maybe how. When she doesn't reply, I pick up the photo to examine it for myself.

The woman is as stunning as Eve. Paler and very slight in comparison. If I thought Eve was delicate before, I'd say this woman is positively frail.

"You're not all that great at reading the room, are you?" Snatching the photo from me, she wipes it clean again before putting it back down.

"Have I pushed your button?" The question rolls from my tongue when she scowls up at me. I found her limit just as she found mine, and she doesn't like it. She doesn't like that I know her better than she wants me to.

"Why are you still here?" Eve snaps back, crossing her hands over her chest.

When will she realise that nothing can protect her from me? Not her violin or her trembling arms. Certainly not me or her. In the end, she won't survive me. No one does. One way or another, I break them beyond repair.

I wander over to her chest of drawers, pausing in front of the cluster of photo frames. There's a few of her and a dark-haired woman with a boy. He has her blonde hair and dark eyes, but aside from that, he looks like one of the men she's posing with in another photo. A young Eve is smiling broadly while the men are both in ceremonial uniform, but the older of the two is wearing army colours while the younger is wearing Marine colours. I wonder if I ever met him, maybe even served with him.

"You're still here," Eve whispers from behind me.

She sounds tired, and when I turn to look at her, she still looks awfully pale in the black attire the maid at Hush brought up for her. I'm not sure how she manages to get on her feet with how frail she still looks. The black leggings make her legs appear thinner than ever, and the black long-sleeved top brings out the stark pallidness in her face.

"Get back into bed and rest."

Giving me a faint smile, she comes to stand in front of me. I can sense her nervous energy as she focuses on the photo in my hand.

"That was taken when Joe graduated from Lympstone," she whispers, stroking over the photo. "It was the last photo the three of us took together. After that, Joe was moved to Stonehouse, and Dad and I stayed on at the Woolwich Garrison."

"Just you and your father?"

"Yep." She blows out a breath, taking the photo from me and wiping it with her sleeve before putting it back down.

A quiet laugh stirs in my chest as she adjusts it just so, right back where it was before I picked it up. The nervousness that emanated from her earlier morphs into sadness, piquing my curiosity. I should've asked more questions before. Maybe I wouldn't have hurt her the way I did today.

All the times I thought about it before, my insides flamed to life. The need to feel her to the extreme was overwhelming then. It still is now, and it's why I should put as much space between us as possible. But I can't, and I won't. I want her more now than I

Our bodies are so close that I can feel the dips and grooves of his chest when I breathe him, and he drinks my hums.

We're a loose tangle of limbs when his phone rings on the overbed table. It vibrates closer as we come up from our cuddle. The levity that was on his face before falls to a stern frown. This is the call.

"Sloane," Henry answers curtly. There's a beat of silence before he ends the call, and his eyes meet mine again. "It's done."

"Alfie? Clara?"

"They're safe. Casper's put them up in a cottage in Cornwall for now. I told you I wouldn't hurt the boy or his mother." He levels me with a straight face. "Unless he touches you again."

"He's my friend," I tell him with a soft laugh as he lies down beside me again.

"I don't care. No one gets to touch you but me," he asserts, wrapping an arm lightly around my waist.

He's ridiculous, but at the same time, no one has made me feel more cherished or loved. Henry may not be perfect in the grand scheme of things, but he is perfect for me.

"I love you." The whisper rumbles from deep inside me. "I love you so much."

"Never more than I love you, darling," he replies, peppering ardent kisses over my face.

If I ever did die like this—in his arms and with his lips worshipping me—it would be the best way to go. But while we're breathing, I'm not leaving his side ever again. No matter what happens. This man is my perfect villain. My beautiful killer. My once-in-a-lifetime miracle. He's everything I never knew I wanted and all I'll ever need.

EPILOGUE
Eve
ONE MONTH LATER

The howls are deafening as Henry leads me out of the ballroom at Lancaster House. The lights are dimmed to a gold glimmer, and there are candles dotted on every surface as we leisurely take the stairs down one at a time.

"Last time we were here, I was a bastard," Henry says, lifting me off the bottom step and carrying me through the long corridor towards the back of the house.

"You're always a bastard, but I guess you're my bastard, so…" I shrug, looking around the large room he takes me into.

The most beautiful, almost black roses, calla lilies, and gold-dusted ivy arrangements are scattered on multiple surfaces, with black feathers and rich berries draping from them. The fires at each end of the room are flickering with the warmest glow that makes the place feel cosy.

"I am yours, Eve," Henry tells me as we meander over to the large glass doors that make up the back wall of the room. "I'm always going to be yours, no matter what happens."

The stutter of my heart causes me to choke on the quiet laugh that vibrates up my throat. The last month has been special. We've gone to bed together every night and woken up to each other every morning. He's the first and last thing I see, and I don't want it to be any other way.

Henry opens one of the double doors and guides me out to the porch overlooking the topiary maze set into the sunken garden. A trail of lampposts s the way to the centre, where a statue of two lovers peeks above the shrub walls.

"I never got to give you this," he tells me, pulling a familiar black envelope from inside his dinner jacket. "I debated giving it to you the first night I took you back home, but it just seemed too soon after everything that happened."

"It's never too soon, Your Grace." I smile, trying to lighten the sudden heaviness that enshrouds our escapade from Alastair's Howl and Ryan's swearing in.

"Perhaps not, but…" He sucks in a deep breath as we take the steps down to the maze. The music from the party upstairs echoes into the night as we follow the crowned lampposts. "I thought I lost you that night."

"You didn't." The thrum of my heart picks up as he tears the envelope open for me with his finger and hands it to me. "I'm still here."

"No, I didn't, but I could have." He guides me through a hidden gap in the maze wall that leads us to the statue in the middle. "Sit with me?" he asks, sitting down on the stone bench as his eyes rove over my star-embellished dress.

When I sit beside him, turned into him, his hand brushes lightly along my jaw. A gentle caress with a rough touch. It amazes me how the two can coexist and be something so incredible that I miss it the instant his hands clutch over his thighs.

"It occurred to me while I sat beside you, waiting for you to come back to me, that if I did lose you—" He pauses, shaking his head at the possibility. It's then I notice the way his fingers are clawed into the back of his hands. "If I did lose you, Eve, I would never have a duchess of my own. There'll never be anyone else for me. You're it."

Tears flood my eyes at the sincerity in his. The warmth of his body slowly seeps into mine as I lean closer into his side.

"Oh God, don't make cry." A sob cracks my voice as I fan myself with the envelope in my hand. "I'll look a mess when we go back in."

"We're not going back in there tonight."

"We're not?"

"No, I'm going to take you home, Eve, and I'm going to love you." The deep gravel of his voice causes goosebumps to prickle all over me. As though his promise is a physical caress, I shiver as it seeps deep into me.

It's been a long time since we were intimate. As much as I've wanted to, he's been so careful and protective of me that sometimes I feel like his glass doll.

Henry's eyes flit down to the envelope in my hand while he releases the rose from his lapel. I take the silent moment to read the card with trembling hands and more emotion filling my chest than I can contain.

And of all the reasons I love you,
there's only one that truly matters.

I flip the card over with butterflies fluttering wildly in my stomach. My tears are no longer controllable as I thumb over the red wolf seal.

I have given myself to you. Every part of me belongs to you.
As the clouds belong to the sky.
As the moon belongs to the sun.
As thunder belongs to lightning.
I am yours.

When my eyes flick up to find him, Henry is crouched in front of me, the rose that was on his lapel twirling between his finger and his thumb.

"And you're mine," he murmurs, handing me the rose.

A thin black bow is tied around it, and when I look closer, my heart stops. This is it—he's broken me completely. All my life, I've never belonged to anyone. More than that, I've never wanted to be someone's as much as I want to be his everything. All that I am wants to be all that he needs.

My finger strokes over the ruby ring tied to the stem of the rose as his hands rest on my thighs and he sinks to his knees.

"I will never unlove you or not need you. You will always be my heart and my soul. My universe and my existence. And nothing would make me happier than if you are my duchess."

Holy crap.

I'm lost for words as I try to compute anything half as eloquent to say back. But really, I don't think it exists.

"I love you." It's all I manage to hiccup past my overwhelmed tears. "I love you so much."

"Never more than I love you. Than I will always love you, cherish you, and worship you." Henry smiles as he tugs the bow on the stem loose and the ring falls into his waiting palm. The red, oval ruby glitters in between two diamonds when he holds it up and grasps my left hand lightly in his other. "What do you say, darling?"

"Yes," I sob through my happy laughter. "Always yes."

The ring slips onto my finger before I can wrap my arms around his shoulders. As he tugs me down to straddle his thighs, his mouth crushes to mine in a burning kiss. Everything fades. The world disappears.

It's just me and my duke.

My savage duke.

My perfect villain.

ALEXANDRA SILVA

READ CASPER'S AND FREDDIE'S STORIES IN THE VIRTUES & LIES SERIES:

BURN
(Leo & Cassie)

SCORCH
(Christopher & Arabella)

BLAZE
(Casper & Fleur)

SMOKE
(Freddie & Georgina #1)

FLAME
(Freddie & Georgina #2)

ALSO BY Alexandra Silva

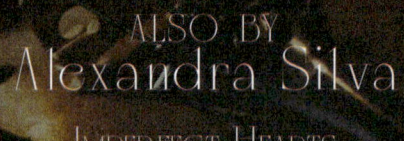

IMPERFECT HEARTS
Contemporary British Romance

No One But You
A Second Chance, Blended Families Romance

For You (Beautifully Broken 1)
A Best Friend's Brother Romance

Someone Like You (Beautifully Broken 2)
A Friends to Lovers, Single Mum Romance

Fighting Fate
A MMA, Accidental Pregnancy Romance

STANDALONES

The Liar
A Forbidden Office Romance

One Weekend in Budapest
A fling to forever Romance

Careless Whispers
A F1, Small Town Romance

SWEET VINE ROMANCE
Co-writes with Sophie Blue

Love to Jingle You
A Snowed In Romance

Love to Hate You
A Hate to Love Romance

Need to Have You
A Workplace, Single Dad Romance